THE

SECRET

SUN

THE SECRET SUN

A Novel of Japan

FRED HIATT

A Cornelia & Michael Bessie Book

PANTHEON BOOKS · NEW YORK

Library of Congress Cataloging-in-Publication Data

Hiatt, Fred.
    The secret sun / Fred Hiatt.
    p. cm.
    A Cornelia & Michael Bessie book.
    ISBN 0-679-41306-5
    I. Title.
PS3558.I2177D3   1992
813'.54—dc20   91-50890

Book design by Debbie Glasserman
Manufactured in the United States of America
First Edition

To my parents

CONTENTS

HISTORY

PART I

*P*iper stepped out of his well-worn office building into the foul steamy air of Tokyo's rainy season and breathed deep the distinctive aroma of mildew and bus exhaust, raw sewage and frying sesame oil. Across the busy street the cherry-tree leaves hung heavy and dark with moisture. An assortment of low-lying concrete buildings behind the line of stunted trees blended into the mist and smog. Built during and just after the U.S. Occupation for American troops, the compound now housed Japan's Self-Defense Agency, Tokyo's Pentagon. From his fifth-floor office window, Piper often watched the troops playing volleyball and softball in their exercise yard.

Piper glanced up to the office window now to see whether Kyoko might be watching him leave, just as he often followed her from above as she disappeared into the swirling crowd. But the window blankly reflected the clouds. He lowered his head and squeezed onto the congested sidewalk, turning right for the three-block walk to the subway. Past the twenty-four-hour noodle shop, where he sometimes slurped down a bowl of greasy beef and ramen after filing a late-night story. Past the vacant lot where wreckers not long ago had demolished a trendy discotheque after its central chandelier had crashed, fatally pinning a young Japanese woman to the dance floor and injuring an American investment banker. Stumbling across the ambulances on his way home late that night, Piper had felt obliged to hang around to make sure the banker wasn't from the *Advertiser*'s circulation area. Why the owners had now decided to destroy a building they had erected only six months before, at great cost to Piper's peace and quiet, he didn't know, but he imagined the mishap proved that evil spirits had occupied the disco. A host of superstitions, largely hidden from foreigners, governed Japan's daily life. The Japanese had gotten where they were through technology, science and rational thinking, but they hedged their bets by calling in a Shinto priest to bless every factory opening and new semiconductor design. And why not, Piper thought. It seemed to work well enough.

On the crowded and narrow sidewalk, he slowed to keep from bowling over the bent-over grandmothers in their everyday kimono out to buy the morning tofu. A bicyclist, balancing a swaying tray of box lunches in one hand and frantically ringing his bell with the other, nearly ran Piper down as he tried to maneuver through the crowd. As so often when he found himself trapped amid Tokyo's dense throngs, Piper had to restrain himself from taking a poke, this time at the white-uniformed delivery boy who cycled obliviously past. Fridays were especially crowded, for some reason, and Fridays were especially sour for Piper, since it was on Friday evenings that Kyoko slipped into the office washroom, changed into her tight black sweater and tight black miniskirt, and disappeared for her secretive weekends away from their newspaper bureau, and from him.

On this Friday morning in July he was more dyspeptic than usual, thanks to the message from the home office. The telex, in smudged block letters on cheap yellow paper, had been the first thing Piper had seen as he entered their narrow boxcar of an office. Kyoko, efficient as always and well aware of Piper's habits, had made sure of that, laying the message gingerly atop the mound of newspapers, junk mail, stock market reports, invitations, clippings and press releases that overgrew his desk, a scratched gunmetal job squatting against the far wall next to the bureau's only window.

He had slumped onto the couch without reading it, sighing, "What do they want now?" His sense of foreboding depended on no special clairvoyance; messages from home invariably brought bad news.

"Good morning to you, too," Kyoko had said.

"Sorry," Piper bowed slightly. She looked more beautiful than ever, he had thought; Kyoko always seemed to glow brighter on Fridays. "Have I ever told you that we're too good for this rag?"

"You've mentioned it, yes," Kyoko said. "The *New York Times* has a story datelined Tokyo claiming Toyota's car exports to the U.S.

are going to drop next year, and they would like us to match it by today."

"Of course they're going to drop," Piper said. "Because Toyota's building more cars in America. Didn't we report that months ago?"

Kyoko shrugged. "Yes, but now it's in the *Times,* and with everything that's going on, you know any car story is going to be news." She paused. "And they had one more request—there's another anniversary coming up."

Piper just closed his eyes. His mid-sized newspaper had opened this Tokyo bureau almost three years before, after his publisher, a polo-playing third-generation newspaper tycoon, had been told by one of his friends in the local chamber of commerce that the Pacific Century was dawning, and that any publisher who wanted to hold his head up at the annual publishers' convention—not to mention chair a panel or two on international coverage in the post–Cold War era—would need at least one Asian bureau as ante. Piper's editor, who had climbed the corporate ladder by finding wisdom in whatever the publisher proposed, went along, although he privately held no doubt that the funds could have been better spent covering the University football team. No one at the paper had a clear idea of what Piper should be doing, beyond serving as guide, porter and drinking buddy to every editor who came through Tokyo on "fact-finding" missions sponsored and paid for by Japan's Foreign Ministry propaganda bureau. As a result, his editors mostly asked him for stories which they had read the previous day in the *New York Times.* If Piper sent along something which had not yet appeared in the *Times,* his own editors were inclined to disbelieve it; but if a story showed up in the *Times* first, they wanted to know why he had failed to see it coming.

The publisher, on the other hand, didn't really care what Piper wrote, as long as every hometown politician, businessman and socialite who visited Tokyo, and every hometown company that scored a success in the Japanese market, received some press. Even firms that didn't score in Japan could persuade the publisher that they deserved a write-up, and the publisher's whim would filter down through the ranks, hardening into an order and finally clattering into the Tokyo office in the form of another dreaded yellow telex. Piper's favorite had been the entrepreneur who planned to get rich by developing a Japanese taste for catfish sushi. He had beaten a retreat, whiskers drooping, even before Piper finished writing about him, but the *Advertiser* ran the piece anyway. Nothing like a good local angle.

And then there was deputy managing editor Ace Barnett, a former Marine turned sportswriter who had fought at Iwo Jima and who hounded Piper to mark any anniversary hearkening back to Japan's defeat.

"What is it this time?" Piper asked.

"Can't you guess?" Kyoko said. "It's almost August again."

"A-bomb time." Piper sighed again. "We did Hiroshima two years ago, we did Nagasaki last year. We've done the survivors and the victims, the guys who dropped the bomb and the kids who saw their airplane. We've done the pros, the cons, the anguish, the memories. What else do they want? Maybe this year we could do maimed pets."

"Why don't we do a story on Japan's bomb this time?" Kyoko said.

A bad joke, Piper had thought. Japan, victimized by the only two atomic weapons ever dropped in combat, prided itself on its "nuclear allergy," on having become a superpower without atomic weapons. One diplomat had told Piper that Japan would build a bomb only if Korea built one first.

But Kyoko had not been joking. "I'm not sure, but I seem to remember hearing that during the war the Japanese government tried to come up with its own 'secret weapon,' its own bomb," she said. "I guess they never got too far, but still . . ."

Piper had been retrieving press releases from the floor, crumpling them and shooting them vaguely toward the wastebasket in the corner, managing mostly to litter the floor with balled-up Foreign Ministry proclamations of aid projects dispensed to various third-world countries—Zambia, Malaysia, Tennessee. The announcements rolled into the office over the fax machine like flotsam onto a beach.

But as Kyoko spoke, Piper stopped shooting baskets and sat up. "It could be a good story, if you're right," he said. Japanese texts on World War 2 tended to focus on the victims of Hiroshima and Nagasaki, casting the Americans as monsters and jumping quickly over minor incidents like Pearl Harbor. If Japan had been trying to get the bomb too, it would shine a different light on their moral innocence, he thought. "And some of the war criminals who worked on it should still be alive. You think we can track them down?"

"I don't know," Kyoko said. "It might be possible."

So here he was, descending into the grimy but efficient subway on his way to the press club, where he could begin checking out the story. The staircase was barely wide enough for two unending streams of passengers shouldering past each other, and with each step down, the air grew warmer. No escalators, no air-conditioning; some goddam economic superpower, Piper thought sourly. When he first came to Japan, the shabbiness of daily life had astonished him. After some time, surprise had given way to smug satisfaction. They might be taking over, he would think after filing yet another story on the latest Japanese technological triumph or corporate conquest, but at least we have backyards, uncrowded beaches, supermarkets worthy of the name. Let them keep their trade surplus if it comes with two-hour commutes in sweltering cattle cars, with fifteen-hour workdays, with pitiful playgrounds of asphalt and cement.

But with a little more time, Piper began to suspect that even these uncooled subways and scruffy apartment blocks were part of some grand strategy. Those chubby Americans in their air-conditioned Buicks, in their leather recliners in spacious family rooms, on their tennis courts so numerous they didn't have to play four to a side—are we blessed, or are we suckers? Piper began to wonder. What do these people know that they aren't telling us? Or is it just that they're unhappy unless they're suffering and sacrificing?

A train approached, exactly according to the schedule posted on the wall, and Piper stepped aboard, started toward a vacant seat, then stopped. The train was even hotter than the station, and he decided to stand under one of the ceiling fans that stirred the hot thick air. Despite the heat, many of Piper's fellow passengers still wore their jackets and neckties. Piper had given up on both his first summer in Japan, contenting himself with chinos and open-necked white shirts.

He rode the train one stop too far, to give himself a chance to walk and clear his head; last night had been a late one with Marianne, the *Boston Globe* reporter. He was in the Ginza, perhaps the world's most elegant shopping district, but as he trudged up the unventilated stairs of the subway station, he passed an old lady in an apron, stooping to scrape bits of paper and gum off the stairs, crack by crack. Some superpower, he thought again.

On the corner aboveground, a dozen workers on their lunch break had ducked off the crowded sidewalk to stare up at a constellation of lights glowing red and orange on a stock market board. As usual, everything was up in morning trading, but the bystanders looked glum as ever, and Piper felt a rush of fondness for them. They really are the Eeyores of the world, he thought.

Piper strolled past the elegant little dress stores, established by wealthy businessmen as farewell presents to aging mistresses, now supplanted. Past the discreet art galleries whose owners would comb Europe and America, on commission, to bring back just the right Van Gogh to the world's newest collectors, like the Japanese zillionaire who needed a few Picassos to decorate his race track. Occasionally he passed a bedraggled, beaten-down couple of American tourists in crushproof traveling raincoats, clutching each other as they disbelievingly converted yen price tags to dollars in their minds, looking for something, anything, they could afford to bring home as a souvenir or present for the kids, and often taking refuge finally in the familiar surroundings of Burger King or Kentucky Fried. This was a neighborhood that hid its real jewels in basements and penthouses, in members' clubs and tiny bars that the uninitiated could never find, let alone afford.

Still, walking here never failed to invigorate Piper, even in the rainy *tsuyu* season. He had developed a strange, possessive affection for the narrow tree-lined streets, for the thousands of tiny bars and restaurants and coffee shops, for the bookstores packed with browsers, for the crowds, always so polite, so worried, so intent. It was a fondness that surprised him, for he was an unlikely foreign correspondent, and an even less likely Japan hand, and not only in his informal dress.

He had grown up in a midsized Carolina city, the son of a banker who had hoped that Piper would succeed him in the family business. Those hopes dimmed when Piper dropped out of college to bum around the world, first in the merchant marine, and then, when he couldn't face another night washing dishes aboard his tramp steamer, as more or less of a hippie. A few photographs from those days showed him with long curly hair and loose baggy pants, painfully thin and unimaginably relaxed. He had followed the hippie trail from Bali to Kathmandu, down to Hikkaduwa and back up to Kashmir, traveling sometimes alone, sometimes in the company of Indian mystics, French addicts, Australian surfers, German nudists, or Danish ethnologists. It was a strangely intimate world of travelers within the world's most populous continent, a world where paths crossed and recrossed and sojourners swapped and shared what little they had—stories, books, papaya (the seeds were reputed to ward off hepatitis), marijuana. The sixties survived on the trail, and fear of AIDS was yet to be, so for Piper there had been plenty of women, and enough drugs that he would never feel tempted again. But there had been something beyond that, too, something jarring and exalting. The sheer range of differences in the world, the startling possibilities so beyond the imaginings of his tame American upbringing, had exhilarated and freed him, and he had resolved never to be chained to his own expectations again.

A multinational force of intestinal parasites finally had reduced his already spare frame so much, however, that, with his money belt equally thinned, he had returned home. He accidentally found himself a job on the *Daily Advertiser*—circulation 350,000 daily, 500,000 Sunday—whose motto was: "The truth, the whole truth and nothing but the truth." Somewhat to his surprise, Piper discovered that he was an excellent reporter and, although that quality seemed largely irrelevant to his advance at the paper, his one-year lark had stretched to five and then ten. He was in danger of being vested in the corporate retirement plan, and he shuddered to think he might one day join the company's Twenty-Year Club (members of which were awarded a small bronze bust of the publisher's grandfather). But he loved his work, something he never would have admitted at the regular evening drink-and-bitch sessions at Charlie's tavern. He loved puncturing the arrogant and exposing the corrupt. He loved the adrenaline rush of daily deadlines. He loved spinning a good yarn into a newspaper article, taking a messy, complicated swath of real life and sifting the essential from the irrelevant. He loved seeing his byline on the front page.

The summons to Asia came as Piper hustled into the newsroom

one afternoon to bang out twenty inches on the murder case he was covering, one of the juicier of the year. As he slid behind his word processor, notebook in one hand and pint of milk in the other, fat Gravitz, the obit man, who had been at the paper longer than anyone, said, "Mad Dog's looking for you." Piper glanced across the wide newsroom and through the glass wall to see Huddleston, the managing editor, in his usual pose, seated behind an entirely bare desk, holding a coffee mug and staring vacantly above his employees' heads.

Inside the office Huddleston said, "Jack! Take a load off your feet." This had to be bad news, Piper thought. No one ever called him Jack, and Huddleston usually didn't call him anything.

When Huddleston explained what he had in mind, Piper at first thought he was kidding, and then assured his boss that he was precisely the wrong man for the job. Piper couldn't speak Japanese, knew little about Japan and less about economics. But he was an expert economist compared to his grasp of technology. And he didn't much like fish.

"Perfect! Just what we're looking for—a fresh eye, a new approach," the editor responded. "We don't want you to write those same, tired, gray trade stories we can read in the *New York Times*! We want color! Bring the place alive for our Ordinary Reader! And besides," Huddleston added at a lower volume, "this one comes direct from The Man Upstairs." He pointed heavenward. "This is your chance to really earn some points!"

Piper swiveled his chair and looked out across the newsroom, an eerily silent beehive through the glass wall, and suddenly couldn't think of any reasons to say no. So two weeks later, Piper had found himself surrounded by returning Japanese businessmen in the economy-class section of an All Nippon Airways jetliner. That he had survived the next three years was entirely thanks to Kyoko.

He had hired her shortly after his arrival, and she had guided him safely through the minefields of Japanese etiquette. Together they had picked their way among the infuriatingly inefficient, anal-compulsive bureaucracies of Japanese banks and realtors and ward offices, with Kyoko keeping Piper from exploding along the way. When landlords balked at renting to a *gaijin*, a foreigner, because he might stink the place up with butter and meat, might plop his wet towels on the straw tatami, might poke a boot through the paper screens, Kyoko reassured them. When Tokyo bureaucrats demanded Piper's fingerprints for his alien registration card, Kyoko soothed him.

Like most foreign correspondents in Tokyo, he relied on his Japanese assistant to read the newspapers for him, make appointments, find telephone numbers, watch the news. But their relationship went much further. They had eaten together, watched sumo together, spent more hours together than he ever had with any girlfriend. On work trips to the hinterland, they had slept side by side in freezing Japanese inns, each modestly under separate covers on the floor. They had even bathed together in scalding country hot springs, he trying to avert his eyes from the handkerchief-sized washcloths that she held to only symbolically cover her breasts bobbing just beneath the water's surface. When, after the bath, he had tied his robe incorrectly, as only a corpse would be dressed, Kyoko had gently but firmly retied it. And, back in their room, as he sat on the floor at a low table with his long legs poking out absurdly from the always-too-short yukata, she had taught him the etiquette of sake, her slender arm gracefully emerging from her flowing sleeve to fill his cup, her long fingers holding her own cup up whenever he poured for her.

Soon, he was dreaming of Kyoko, of her long, soft, white neck, her deep-throated, slightly accented English, of how she sipped her tea with the same unself-conscious self-assurance that seemed to govern every aspect of her life. He woke most mornings with Kyoko still on his mind. Her beauty was not that of classic Japanese delicacy; her eyes were rounder, her nose more Semitic, her lips a bit fuller, and she was relatively tall, with wide shoulders, full breasts, a narrow waist, and the walk and poise of an athlete. And she was different in other ways, too. Most Japanese women, Piper had found, no matter how beautiful, did not achieve that calm centeredness, that easy self-assurance which to Piper spelled sex appeal, until they had ruined their lives by marrying Japanese men. There was something oddly sexless about them as teenagers and young working girls, and not only because of the constricting brassieres that seemed to be nationally mandated. To be attractive to Japanese men, it seemed they had to behave like arrested twelve-year-olds, covering their mouths when they giggled, blushing at every opportunity, wearing their hair in pigtails and Minnie Mouse hair ribbons, flattering their boyfriends and rewarding the immaturity and selfishness inculcated by the pampering the boys had received at home.

Such flattery had never appealed to Piper. As soon as women showed interest in him, as soon as he detected the first sign of nervous flirtatiousness—a sidelong glance at his reaction, a slightly exaggerated interest in his opinion, a deliberate staring into his eyes—he would fall right out of love.

Of course, if returned affection was a turnoff, Piper had to admit that, after three years, he seemed to have little to fear from Kyoko. She appeared to enjoy his company at work, but he had never met her family, never seen her apartment, never had a purely social occasion with her of any kind. From the start her one condition of employment had been no weekend duty, and Piper had no idea to where she disappeared each Friday night, try as he might to track her into the crowd from his fifth-floor perch. He would invite himself along each week, and each week she would just laugh and say, "See you Monday." Only once had she given him a straight answer. "You don't even try to speak my language," she had said. "How can I take you seriously?" From then he began studying Japanese, without letting her know, and only his abiding hope, no matter how foolish, that she would come around kept him secretly slogging through his flash cards of Chinese-derived ideographs night after night in his one-bedroom flat, washed by the blue light of inane Japanese television programs he still couldn't understand, until, more often than not, he dozed off in his chair, flash cards fluttering from his lap.

Some Friday and Saturday nights he would wander the clubs and back alleys of Roppongi, where explosions of neon lit the streets more brightly than during Tokyo's gray days. He would look for Kyoko among the thousands of other women in tight black skirts, some in giggling groups, some on the arms of baby-faced American investment bankers with more money than they knew how to spend and an attractiveness to some Japanese women that was beyond Piper's understanding (and beyond the understanding of many competing Japanese males as well). But he never found Kyoko nor, for that matter, anyone who came close.

Piper was not accustomed to unrequited love, and he refused to give up hope. He was reasonably good-looking, though by no means startlingly handsome, with soft, curly brown hair and a tall, loose-limbed frame that could coil into surprising athleticism, softened only a bit by three years in overcrowded Tokyo, where his chief exercise seemed to consist of watching the volleyball games from their office window. His laugh was sudden and infectious, and he was a good listener. Kyoko, though, seemed to demand something more. He was still trying to discover exactly what that might be.

By now it was past noon. Piper crossed one of the world's busiest intersections with a flood of other pedestrians, walked underneath the elevated railroad tracks, past a lottery ticket seller, a palm reader, a fashionable Italian restaurant. For a moment he dreamed of just walking on and on—forgetting Toyota, forgetting the anniversary, forgetting all the ignorant demands from his ethnocentric editors back home. But he wasn't ready to chuck it all. He needed the job, he needed his days with Kyoko, and, though he didn't like to admit it even to himself, he needed his dream of someday bagging the Big Story, the one that would bring him fame and prizes and a job with the *New York Times*. A decades-old tale about Japan's bomb wouldn't be that big story, that was for sure, especially when the two countries seemed headed for an all-too-contemporary clash. But who knows, he thought; it might prove moderately interesting.

At the least, he thought, there would be some irony. After all, he had written about Japan's nuclear virginity at length. If it turned out they had tried to build the bomb, too, that would change everything. Piper wondered how the world would be different if Japan had built the bomb first. Maybe we'd be making better cars, he thought. He began to frame leads in his mind: "If the Japanese generals had had their way, the world might be commemorating the horror of Seattle today instead of marking the anniversary of the inferno of Hiroshima." A little weak. Well, a few facts might help.

Reluctantly, then, he stepped into the lobby of a stubby twenty-floor office tower and rode the elevator to the Foreign Correspondents Club at the top, in search of a few facts.

2

*T*he wood-paneled dining room was noisy with scraping silverware and loud lunchtime conversation. The club served western-style food of notoriously average quality, but the room enjoyed a rare view over the emperor's palace at Tokyo's center, and luminaries of the Japanese advertising and media worlds considered it a prestigious spot to bring clients and show an international flair. Some foreign correspondents, too, fairly lived in the club, more consumed by its internal politics than by the affairs of the country they were supposedly reporting on. Genteel on the surface, the club was a hotbed of ageless vendettas between print reporters and television reporters, between Third World reporters and First World reporters, between Japan defenders and Japan bashers and between relative newcomers like Piper and lifers who had made careers out of Japan and who drifted from the employ of one newsletter or specialized magazine to another, all the while declaiming on the nature of the Japanese from their roost here on the twentieth floor.

Piper turned away from the dining room and past the wall of photographs of former club presidents obsequiously welcoming heads of state and generals and foreign ministers. Ducking into the one-room library, he began working his way through the World War 2 books.

He knew from research on past anniversaries that the volumes tended to bunch up at the war's beginning and end, at what each country saw as its day of infamy—Pearl Harbor and Hiroshima. Japanese historians especially tended to focus on their victimization, gliding over Japan's empire-building, the repression of Korea, the massacres in China—what the Japanese called "incidents"—and the mistreatment of prisoners-of-war. In almost every index Piper found references to the American bomb—under "Fat Man," and "Manhattan Project," and "Oppenheimer"—but nothing about a Japanese effort. The German bomb, yes; intelligence about that had spurred the Americans into their crash program. And Japan's chemical weapons and even biological weapons, also yes; plenty had been written about the infamous experiments on prisoners. But no Japanese A-bomb. Piper was beginning to doubt Kyoko's story when suddenly, in one volume, he found a few snippets of confirmation.

He felt that familiar flush of discovery, the early stirrings of a good story of still unlimited potential, when he read that, as early as April, 1940, a young lieutenant general in the Imperial Army had ordered an aide to investigate the military possibilities of nuclear fission. The aide reported that, with Japan's empire stretching far into Southeast Asia, obtaining uranium would be no problem. So in 1941, at the behest of Tojo himself, the Imperial Army Air Force ordered an urbane and respected physicist named Yoshio Nishina to build a bomb. With that, Piper read, Japan's Manhattan Project was born.

Nishina, the Oppenheimer of Japan, had studied in Denmark before the war. He knew the great European physicists of his day and he kept up with their work. He also, Piper calculated quickly, would be a hundred years old by now. Not much hope there, Piper thought. But at his small Tokyo laboratory, the Riken, a handful of Japan's best young scientists had worked for Nishina and, apparently, almost worshiped him, calling him "the Old Man" and "the Professor," bespeaking a fondness rare in Japan's formal academe. At least some of those acolytes, Piper thought, must still be around.

A hundred pages on, Piper found a few more paragraphs. A separate and competing Imperial Navy committee had met near Shiba Park in Tokyo, near the spot where the Japanese after the war would build a replica of the Eiffel Tower, only a few feet taller, for boasting rights. The experts on that panel had concluded that neither Japan nor America could possibly build a bomb within the coming ten years. Maybe for the next war, the navy boys said; meanwhile, concentrate on this new-fangled thing called radar. Well, they weren't the first military experts to guess wrong, Piper thought, and even in America there had been more doubters than believers. Wishful thinking had pervaded Tokyo—some would say from the moment the emperor agreed to bomb Pearl Harbor—and this was no exception.

But Nishina and his young devotees, ignoring the Navy experts, had kept plugging away, against all odds, Piper read with growing absorption. As Tokyo's war machine crumbled and its empire receded before the bloody American advance, as Japan's industry sputtered and its buses began running on charcoal because the oil was gone, as children learned to live on a scoop of rice and one pickled plum per day, the Riken team kept working on that single secret weapon that could turn it all around, that could vindicate the godly emperor and bring the mighty American juggernaut to a bewildered stop. The Manhattan Project faced almost insuperable odds, but Nishina had to grapple with problems the American team couldn't imagine. He had to scrounge for every part, for every chemical, for every yen. He had to contend with blockhead generals who suggested, since uranium was now in short supply, that he make do with TNT instead. But he and his deputy, a younger physicist named Okamoto, did make progress. And—

"Ah, hitting the history books again? That's a hell of a place to find your news."

Piper wheeled around. There, looking over his shoulder, was Clive Christopher, the silk-suited bureau chief of the *New York Times*. In search of clues to what his competition might write, Christopher regularly stalked the club library, eyeing the books and clips which others were reading. Piper slammed shut his book.

"Hey, Clive," Piper said. Christopher, who called all his colleagues by their last names, hated to be called by his first. He was known among his colleagues not only for his silk suits, which he wore even to riots in Seoul or Islamabad, but also for the endless historical lectures he delivered in the guise of questions at news conferences, liberally salted with references to his own past scoops, and always finishing with Christopher triumphantly scanning the assembled reporters, rather than the questionee, as if waiting for applause. He was also remembered among other correspondents for his political predictions that had proved false, his financial analyses that were false even before he wrote them, and his sociological features that skimmed over the surface of Japanese society as lightly as a sparrow on ice skates.

His setbacks and errata never slowed Christopher down, nor did they seem to disturb his editors in New York, for Christopher had talent where it really counted for a foreign correspondent: arranging his publisher's trips. From the Mercedes limo waiting at Narita Airport to the newsless interviews with fawning ex-premiers to the faultless dinners at Tokyo's priciest French restaurants, Christopher could orchestrate an ego-stroking visit like few other correspondents, always ensuring that his publisher could fancy himself on the cutting edge of news-gathering while preserving his comforts down to the last manicurist. So no matter what Christopher filed, or didn't file, his job was secure.

But if Christopher's editors took no notice of his mistakes, Piper was less forgiving. He could—and at the bar of the Foreign Correspondents Club, at the slightest provocation, would—recite the entire catalog, complete with dates, page numbers and, in particularly egregious cases, the actual leads of offending stories. Christopher, of course, was the source of most of the stories that Piper had to follow, including, no doubt, this latest article on Toyota.

"Hear you had another big scoop on the auto trade," Piper said now. "Congratulations."

"Ah," Christopher smiled. "I hope you didn't hear from the home office again on my account." He pulled a pipe from his jacket side pocket and began filling it. "You think Congress will really go ahead with this business?"

Like everyone in Tokyo, Christopher was talking about what the Japanese press had dubbed the "X-bill" (which in Japanese ended up as *ekusu biru*) or simply "Black X." It was a proposal to expropriate Japanese factories in the United States and turn them over to American firms that had allegedly been harmed—or had their market share "expropriated"—by rapacious Japanese business and trading practices. Its supporters back home, whose numbers were growing fast, saw it as a clean and satisfying solution, finally, to years of frustrating trade deficits, bankrupted U.S. firms and snowballing Japanese takeovers. Many Americans, who had taken to demonstrating outside the Japanese embassy, smashing Japanese cars and sometimes smashing Asians whom they took to be Japanese, saw it as a last bulwark against an economic invasion they couldn't control. But in Japan, despite American promises to keep the seizures in proportion to actual harm suffered by U.S. businesses, the X-bill was being viewed as a threat to the very way of life the Japanese had worked so hard to build since the war. It was confirming the Japanese in their perpetual belief that the world was out to get them, especially since Europe was now wondering whether to follow the U.S. lead. And it was provoking something close to panic throughout Tokyo.

As usual, without waiting for Piper's reply, Christopher offered his own evaluation. "Those people in Washington are so blind, so irresponsible," he clucked. "It would mean all-out war, doesn't anyone there understand that?" He pulled on his pipe and shook his head in disgust. "I can tell you, it was all anyone was talking about at the DCM's last night."

"Oh?" Piper said. What a jerk, he thought. "What was the occasion?"

"Oh, just a little welcoming party for the new economic counselor," Christopher said. "But some interesting pols were there. Hata, you know, the new agriculture vice minister, and poor Iwai. Not much news, but I picked up a tidbit or two."

When he landed in Tokyo, Piper had never heard of a deputy chief of mission. He might just as well still not have for all the access he had. The number-two man at the U.S. embassy had invited him only once to his official residence, a small and elegant Art Deco masterpiece complete with miniature pool and garden, just behind the Soviet embassy. Since the DCM on that occasion seemed not to know who Piper was, he assumed the invitation had found its way into his box at the club through a clerical error, one unlikely to be repeated. The party itself, in honor of an American jeweler who was that season's hope to right the trade deficit, had featured a remarkable spread, with thicker slices of rare beef than Piper had seen before or since anywhere in the country. He had hovered near the buffet through most of the evening, as Japanese maids in gray uniforms and white aprons, with the air of fallen aristocrats, filled and refilled the platters; his behavior might have something to do with his not having been invited again, he had to admit. Those were the days when, early in his tour, still shell-shocked by prices that made him feel like an impoverished colonial in a great world capital, he would parlay as many invitations as possible into free meals. Twice each year, the big multinationals—the Toshibas, the Nissans, the Nomuras—would invite the foreign press corps and assorted hangers-on to fabulous buffets at the Imperial Hotel or the Palace Hotel. These were ostensibly news-gathering events, but most of the reporters tended to talk only to each other, while company minions, wearing dark suits and nervous smiles, hovered on the edges of the banquet rooms. Piper usually stationed himself near the smoked salmon, though as time went on, he gravitated more toward the sushi bar. But then, after some time, he had lost interest. He had learned how to eat dinner in Tokyo for less than a week's salary, and he found himself more and more craving rice and being put off by the sight of big slabs of meat. And when Kyoko would ask the next morning what he had picked up at the reception, he would have to shake his head: nothing but a pile of name cards of faceless corporate drones he would never call. So one day he just stopped going.

But the embassy was different. Piper would have liked to cultivate some sources there, but most of the diplomats, like the higher-ranking officials at Japan's Foreign Ministry, had no time for a hack like him. Part of it was snobbery, pure and simple, but it was also pragmatic, Piper knew. The *Times* and the *Washington Post* could influence the debate in Washington, and so the embassy folks were eager to steer the *Times* and the *Post*. If that meant flattering a few reporters, maybe feeding them roast beef or letting them play tennis on the embassy courts, it was worth the price, even if they were reporters. Every morning the State Department cabled the embassy with copies of every Japan-related article in the major dailies, but the diplomats never saw what Piper wrote. Piper had only one real friend in the embassy, a slightly oddball character in the arms sales division—they called it the Office of Munitions Cooperation, or some such, but it was really just the gun merchants—who didn't trust the Japanese government and so wasn't trusted by his colleagues in the embassy. Homer McGee, like Piper, was single, and they sometimes went drinking together in one or more of the smoky, noisy, hole-in-the-wall bars that McGee seemed to know in every Tokyo neighborhood, ending the evening at a karaoke bar, where

McGee would astonish the tipsy, red-faced Japanese customers by singing sad songs about the rain in Nagasaki more mournfully even than they.

McGee had been living with Japan, one way or another, much of his life, and he loved the ugly, unpredictable jumble of Tokyo, and he helped Piper appreciate it, too. He had a few friends and many acquaintances among the military and political establishment, but most of his Japanese friends were on the fringes, sixties radicals who had chosen not to climb onto Japan's corporate ladders when the demonstrations ended. They were poet-musicians, or bartender-farmers, or journalists at obscure, antiestablishment weeklies; they were the tiny counterculture that often seemed not even to exist in Japan, since the establishment media acted as though it did not exist. And, while most of them were no longer terribly political, they shared a vague distrust of the establishment, of the Tokyo University graduates who had once been their classmates and who had gone on to rule Japan, and their distrust grew stronger as Japan grew stronger in the world. McGee shared their misgivings, especially about Japan's military might and its ability to restrain itself from repeating past follies. Within the U.S. embassy, which saw its job as preserving the U.S.-Japanese alliance, encouraging Japan to rearm and hold-ing off the rising anti-Japan sentiment back home, his views weren't appreciated. And since he expressed himself openly and sometimes without great tact, McGee himself often wasn't appreciated either. He mockingly referred to his boss as Knight-san, since Jim Knight fancied himself a great connoisseur of tea ceremonies, haiku and sumo and therefore a true student of Japan. But everyone knew that McGee understood the place better than most, and so he was toler-ated. And unlike Piper, he was always at his desk on time in the morning, no matter how thorough their previous night's exploration of Tokyo nightlife. Piper, on the other hand, would sometimes drag himself into work by noon, only to find yet another yellow telex berating him from atop his desk, with Kyoko on the phone, already trying to repair the damage.

In any case, Piper didn't know what secrets the DCM might be sharing with Christopher, or what "tidbits" he might have gleaned at the official soiree. But judging from Christopher's copy, Piper thought, again unkindly, the *Times* reporter was more interested in guarding any secrets he learned than in printing them.

"Well, good to see you," Piper said. "I've got to run." Just once, he thought, it would be nice to have Christopher have to follow his story, instead of the other way around. This might not be the one, but there was no point in hanging around and giving Christopher the satisfaction of knowing what angle Piper was pursuing.

"By the way, what did you think of my profile of the finance minister?"

"Magnificent," Piper said. "I bet he loved it, too. Keep blazing a trail for the rest of us." Christopher smiled, oblivious to what most reporters would have considered an insult, and Piper slipped his book back on its shelf and headed for the elevator.

3

"*T*oyota says the *Times* story is all wrong," Kyoko said as Piper stepped back into their office, perspiring after his short walk from the subway.

"I don't know which is likelier, Christopher getting it wrong in the first place or Toyota lying about it now," Piper grumbled. "Let's just forget it."

"What about the telex?" Kyoko pointed to the yellow message that still lay atop Piper's desk.

"They can take wires. Probably already have, in fact, just to make me look bad. 'The *New York Times* reported today . . .' Or else they've already forgotten about it, and we'd spend the next two days killing ourselves to check it out and then they'd spike it anyway." Piper strode the length of the office in five steps, picked up the telex for the first time, crumpled it and tossed it into the corner. "There. My first executive decision of the day."

"You seem in a better mood."

"I started checking out your idea," Piper said. "How's this for a lead? 'If Yoshio Nishina had had his way, the world today would be commemorating the savaging of Sacramento rather than the holocaust of Hiroshima.' "

"Needs work," Kyoko said. "And you know they always edit out your—what is it called?"

"Alliteration," Piper said. "But one of these days I'll slip it through. Anyway, I didn't have much time to work on it. I'd only gotten to 1943 when the Dean of the Far East Press Corps came snooping behind me. You'd think he'd have better things to do. Like visit his tailor."

"He was probably only being friendly," said Kyoko, who had an irritating way of looking for the best in everyone. "Anyway, I did a little research, too, just in case you couldn't make it past 1943." She offered him one of her fleeting smiles that disappeared so quickly he could never decide whether it was sweet or mocking.

"Ah, typical Japanese efficiency," Piper said. "Let's hear your lead, then." Actually, writing in English was the one thing Kyoko could not do well, and the only reason he needed to show up at the office at all, he sometimes thought. She had spent two years watching "Sesame Street" and taking tap dance lessons as a schoolgirl in New Jersey, while her father pursued a business venture that apparently didn't pan out, and another two years as a student at the University of Maryland. As a result, her spoken English was misleadingly colloquial; Piper had come to realize that she sounded more bicultural than she was. Beyond that, Piper knew surprisingly little about her, given the depth of his interest and the time they spent in each other's company. He knew that her father was now dead and that her ancestors had been Koreans, brought forcibly to Japan for their pottery-making skills after one of Japan's earliest imperialist adventures. That had been in the sixteenth century, when Hideyoshi tried to conquer the Korean peninsula. For centuries after, her ancestors worked and lived in a special village in the southern island of Kyushu, making pottery, isolated from the Japanese but protected by the shogun. It was Kyoko's great-grandparents who adopted Japanese names and citizenship and began edging into the mainstream. In this century Japan had repeated Hideyoshi's crime on a grander scale, importing hundreds of thousands of Koreans to work its mines and arms plants before and during the war. The descendants of those forced laborers remained, even after three generations in Japan, a population apart, with Korean names, Japanese language, and citizenship in no country.

As far as Piper could tell, Kyoko seemed not to identify with this downtrodden Korean minority, though she also did not seem ashamed, or eager to hide her Korean past, as did many "converted" Koreans "passing" as Japanese. The only vestige of ethnicity that Piper had detected in her was a fondness for spicy Korean kimchee, which some Japanese shunned as typical of vulgar, garlic-eating Koreans. But Piper believed that her status as both outsider and insider helped make her a natural reporter. In appearance, she was Japanese, of course, but she was a Japanese whom other Japanese would reject as foreign if they knew her history. That, along perhaps with some deeply imprinted ancestral memory of imperial injustice, had imbued her with a skepticism, an ability to stand outside herself and her culture. She had majored in English at a junior college, the best her mother could afford, designed to render Japanese girls marriageable. But instead of marrying after graduation, she had, to her mother's horror, managed to win a place at the University of Maryland in College Park. When she returned, like most young female graduates, she found work as a tea pourer in a big Tokyo office, running errands, gossiping, hiding out in the ladies' room, tidying up after the men who did the real work. It was a job of indignity, in which the young women exacted revenge for all manner of slights in the most impotent of ways, spitting in the teacups of a particularly hated boss or failing to completely rinse the soap from the teapot.

She came to despise the job, but it was only through a fluke that she had applied to Piper. A boyfriend of one of her girlfriends, a young advertising executive, had taken both women for cocktails at the Foreign Correspondents Club, where Kyoko had chanced to see Piper's notice and, on a slightly tipsy whim, had jotted down his phone number. The next day, entirely sober, she nonetheless called, and at their interview Piper saw immediately that she was smart, and special. She met his gaze squarely, without blushing or tittering, and admitted frankly what she did and did not know. Besides, Japanese with more conventional qualifications were unlikely to be satisfied with the low salary, cramped office and lack of prestige the *Advertiser* could offer. So he hired her, and after she caught on to the rules of the game, she became, as they both knew but never discussed, even more underpaid than he. Her only shortcoming, besides her writing skills, was that she refused to marry him or, failing that, accompany him some evening for a drink.

Of course, she seemed in no hurry to marry anyone. Her Korean heritage, as well as her being the daughter of a widow, would surely have handicapped her in the game of *omiai*, of arranged marriage, if she had cared to play that game. She didn't care to, though—again to the exasperation of her mother, Kyoko had once told Piper. She was already twenty-six, the *kurisumasu-keki* age, as some Japanese men would say—as worthless as a Christmas cake still on the shelf December 26. But if that worried her, she never let on. Certainly, she never seemed dispirited setting out on her Friday evening jaunts.

"Well, don't keep me in suspense, stuck in 1943," Piper said. "Did Nishina build his bomb?"

"I'm afraid there's no surprise ending like that," Kyoko said. "I'm not clear how close he got, but probably not very. In any case, one day in 1945—on a Friday the thirteenth in April, in fact—the Americans bombed his laboratory. Just by chance, as part of the general firebombing of Tokyo."

"And that was it? The end of the Tokyo Project?"

"Well, pretty much," she said. "After the Americans dropped the first bomb, on Hiroshima, and everyone was trying to figure out what kind of weapon from hell had flattened the city and turned the rain black, the army flew Nishina over the ruins to get his opinion. Supposedly, he knew as soon as he looked that the Yankees had done the impossible and beaten him to the bomb. Whether, at that moment, he was sorry to have come in second, or ashamed to have ever tried, is something I really wonder."

"I take it we can't ask him."

"No. He died in 1951."

"In prison? Did we try him as a war criminal?"

"Well, that's a funny thing," Kyoko said. "As far as I could find out, the Americans never really asked him what he'd been up to, and Nishina never told them. The Occupation army may have suspected, because they collected all five—how do you say it—" Kyoko, who hated to mispronounce any English word, paused to write out "cyclotron" and show Piper, who read it aloud. "Yes—the Americans collected them all, smashed them to bits and dumped them at sea. And that was the end of atomic weapons research in Japan. Some American scientists criticized their own army for doing such a crude and antiscience thing, and not much more was ever said about it."

"And so Japan passes itself off as an innocent victim of our monstrous criminal behavior, when you would have done the same to us, if you could," Piper said.

"Well, maybe," Kyoko said. "We don't know that for sure. It does seem to change the moral balance a bit, though. Which I guess is why nobody ever talks about it."

"And to think of all the crap we've regurgitated in every anniversary piece until now. Little paper lanterns floating down Hiroshima's river to symbolize the lost innocent souls, and little innocent girls folding chains of paper cranes to plead for peace in the world, and all the rest."

"Well, I don't think it was all wrong," Kyoko said. "Innocent souls were lost, thousands of them." Kyoko almost never responded to Piper's jabs at Japan, serious or otherwise, but now she said, "The point is, Japan has changed. People don't want military power anymore, and they don't want nuclear weapons, and that makes Japan pretty unusual in today's world, no matter what else you think about us."

Piper was silent for a moment, sprawled across the couch and fiddling with a pencil. Then he said, "So how did you find all this out?"

"Well, one of Nishina's deputies, named Yamada, wrote his memoirs. I found them in the Diet library—they hadn't been checked out in years."

"And I suppose this Yamada is dead, too," Piper said.

"Yes, as a matter of fact," Kyoko said. "But when the memoirs were written, at least, another of Nishina's deputies, a guy named Okamoto, was a professor at Tokyo University. I haven't had a chance to check whether he still is. I thought you might want me to work on the car story."

"Will you forget about that damn Christopher hype job?" Piper said. "Let's go find Okamoto. My reporter's intuition tells me he's alive and waiting for someone to ask him his life story."

4

*T*he subway was more crowded now. It was too early for the *salarimen* to be going home, but the OLs, the office-lady tea pourers to whose ranks Kyoko had once belonged, had exchanged their dainty blue uniforms for stylish blacks and grays—nothing too bright or distinctive here—and were off, in groups of three or four, to spend their money—playing tennis at 8,000-yen-per-hour indoor courts, where they would spend more time flirting at the juice bar than working up a sweat; or nibbling pasta and sipping Cinzano at chrome-and-black-marble Italian restaurants; or shopping in trendy boutiques. Others, traveling singly, were on their way home, to help prepare dinner for brothers and fathers who would arrive later. Many of these dozed, a few read small paperbacks covered in brown wrappers. It was considered rude for women to read newspapers in public, although a few men were unabashedly folding and unfolding their splashy sports tabloids, which mingled baseball photographs with shots of topless women in various poses of feigned pain and agony.

Piper's shirt stuck to his back and he was painfully conscious, again, of being the gaijin—bigger, clumsier, sweatier than everyone around him. Kyoko, in her white silk blouse buttoned to the throat, seemed not to notice the heat or the humidity that had steamed up the train windows. Piper had never seen her sweat.

Still, he could tell she was unhappy about this errand. Kyoko could be as intrepid as anyone, but there were times she felt Piper just didn't know how to behave. She had never complained when Piper walked beside her eating an ice-cream cone or downing a skewer of grilled chicken from a street vendor, but she had nonetheless communicated her discomfort. Piper had come to realize that no

Japanese would eat while strolling, and that Kyoko was feeling an embarrassment that was almost physically painful, and he had stopped. As they grew to know each other better, she hesitated less before correcting him. There were a thousand ways a foreigner could unknowingly insult a Japanese, and Piper sometimes felt he had tried most of them. He had never been so gauche as to stomp across the tatami in his shoes or to slip into a Japanese bath without first washing and rinsing. But he had, upon meeting someone new, committed the unpardonable offense of handing his name card—always an essential element of social relationships in Japan, since it allowed new acquaintances to immediately fix each other's places in the universal hierarchy of life—with the letters upside down. He had entered someone's office before removing his outer coat. He had stuck his chopsticks into his rice bowl and left them there, a particularly egregious sin since it called to Japanese minds their common funeral practice of using chopsticks to remove the larger pieces of bone after the incineration of a loved one. In each case, Kyoko had explained his offense.

Paying a call on a university professor without an appointment, and especially a professor at the University of Tokyo, Japan's most prestigious—that was almost as cloddish as strolling through the Ginza while chugging a beer. But Piper had tried the Japanese way of arranging interviews. He had sent his polite letters of introduction, citing some mutual acquaintance, and he had sat through the requisite two or three social calls before being so forward as to ask a question that might conceivably produce information useful for a newspaper article. Inefficient at best, the system often broke down entirely in Piper's case, since in those universal mental hierarchies, the *Advertiser* ranked low or not at all. And a professor at Tokyo University, which ranked number one, would almost certainly have no time for someone like Piper—a foreigner, with no personal connection, and no prestige. Presuming that Okamoto was still alive, Piper thought, better to drop in and surprise him. As painful as that might be for Kyoko, he had found that many Japanese were simply too cordial, or too astonished at his boorishness, to actually kick him out.

They squeezed out of the train at Hongo-sanchome, climbed the stairs and walked in silence along a narrow alley of cheap noodle shops and other student hangouts. Across a busy intersection, two blocks down a wide, grimy avenue lined with small stores peddling CDs and computer software, and thus to Akamon—the great red wooden gate, through which thirty years earlier frenzied student radicals had snake-danced, throwing rocks and breathing tear gas through white cloth masks while chanting anti-American slogans. Those theatrical days were ancient history for today's disengaged students, but on each side of the gate a few banners, torn bed sheets adorned with giant Chinese ideographs brushed in red paint, still hung desultorily in the smog, vestiges of that energized time.

Inside the walls the campus was quiet, an oasis amid the clutter and traffic of Tokyo, but a surprisingly shabby one. Here, at Japan's most prestigious campus, there was mud where grass should grow, and the few solitary students walking briskly only heightened a feeling of isolation. Kyoko asked one for directions to the physics building, but he shrugged and walked on. Finally, they found a map affixed to a signboard.

The university's physicists turned out to be housed in an especially unkempt yellow-brick building marooned in the midst of a construction zone. Inside, on an old hand-painted sign board, Kyoko found the Chinese characters for hill—Oka—and base—moto. "Looks like he's still here," she said without enthusiasm. "Now what?"

"Let's go," Piper said. Reluctantly, Kyoko led the way up a dimly lit stairway and along an even dimmer corridor to room 312.

"He's chairman," she whispered, reading the characters etched into the smoked glass of his office door, and hesitating again.

"And has been since the Tokugawa era, by the looks of the place," Piper said. Kyoko, not finding Piper's jauntiness contagious, stared at him more glumly than ever, with her you're-about-to-stomp-across-the-tatami-in-your-hiking-boots look.

"Look, he'll probably be delighted to talk to us," Piper whispered. "The bomb project was the highlight of an otherwise dull career, and no one has ever asked him to reminisce about those glory days."

"What if you're wrong?" Kyoko said.

"What's the worst that can happen?" Piper said. "He could refuse to talk to us. Painful for your Japanese ego, trained since infancy to avoid conflict and embarrassment at any cost, but probably not fatal. Just bow and be demure, and blame everything on me."

"That won't be difficult," she said icily, and then knocked and, barely pausing, entered the office, calling out, "Please forgive us for creating such a nuisance." This was the standard Japanese expression meaning "May I come in," but Kyoko in this case seemed to deliver it with more than standard emotion.

They stepped into a kind of darkened anteroom, barely big enough for the two of them, bounded by an overstuffed bookshelf that stretched to the ceiling. Sidling gingerly around it, they entered the small office proper. Piles of yellowing journals and manuscripts and teetering mountains of books had entwined themselves throughout the room, nearly obscuring a few pieces of furniture that might have been salvaged from Goodwill. At a small wooden desk, jotting with a pencil on a lined pad, sat a diminutive man with a shock of pure white hair dwarfing a wrinkled, kindly face with hooded eyes. Okamoto continued working for a long moment and then looked up without expression. When he said nothing, Kyoko bowed and began speaking in those high-pitched, submissive tones with which Japanese ladies are expected to cloak their words but which Kyoko only assumed when flustered.

Bowing slightly whenever he heard his name mentioned, Piper paid scant attention as Kyoko introduced them and their mission. He was thinking about her voice, which in English had an unusually deep timbre that he found one of her most thrilling qualities. He was always amazed how it could disappear when she spoke Japanese, and he found himself wondering whether she made love differently in English than in Japanese, too. As she went on now—too long, Piper thought, betraying a nervousness that would put Okamoto at an advantage—the professor watched her intently, never glancing at Piper, even when she mentioned his name. But when she finished, bowing and apologizing once more for their intrusion, Okamoto turned his head slightly toward Piper and said, in only slightly accented English, "Will you take something to drink?"

"Please. Anything cold," Piper said. Okamoto picked up a black rotary telephone that wouldn't have been out of place in an antique shop and grunted into it, then finally motioned the two reporters to an imitation-leather banquette against the window. Piper barely squeezed his knees behind a coffee table piled with more journals and books, in English, German, and Japanese.

Okamoto resumed speaking in Japanese to Kyoko. She had set a notebook on her lap, assuming the pose of disinterested interpreter. Dusty venetian blinds on a window behind the couch screened the sun but not the heat, and Piper began to feel drowsy. He scanned the titles of the books and manuscripts around him; those in English were no more understandable than those in Japanese. Okamoto, his hands neatly folded on his desk, fell quiet, and Kyoko, after scribbling a few seconds more, turned to Piper.

"He says he never heard of a Japanese bomb," she said. "He said he is curious what gave us such an idea."

Piper looked at Okamoto, who watched him without expression. "Tell him about the book you found," Piper said, wondering why the professor was insisting on going through the charade of translation. Kyoko spoke again, Okamoto answered impassively, Kyoko relayed his words. As he spoke the second time, an old, bent woman in slippers and dark kimono shuffled in, struggling with a clattering tray of three glasses of orangeade.

"He says that, unfortunately, the memoir we found should have been catalogued in the fiction department. He says that Mr. Yamada was no better at autobiography than he was at science, and he was no scientist. He says that is why Mr. Yamada left the university to write fiction."

The vitriol was so out of keeping with Okamoto's soft tones and mild expression that Piper, taken aback, said nothing for a moment. The old woman set a glass and napkin on a pile of books in front of him and one in front of Kyoko. As she moved to Okamoto's desk, and before Piper could speak, Okamoto turned to Piper and said in English: "Mr. Yamada was a sad case, unhappy about many things. I hope you have not wasted too much of your precious journalist's time chasing his stories. You must have many more important matters to attend to—or perhaps our news here in Japan is too dull to satisfy American readers."

"That's truer than you could know," Piper said. "But let me make sure I understand. You're saying there was no effort to build an A-bomb during the war?"

Okamoto smiled almost imperceptibly. "How much physics do you know?"

"I gave up when they told me light traveled both in waves and in particles," Piper said. "It always seemed to me that only one or the other could be true."

"Well, I won't try to persuade you," Okamoto said. "Let me try to answer your question without delving into the theory of relativity. Like everyone in the 1930s, we closely followed the work of Bohr, of Fermi, of Einstein. Some of my teachers worked with some of them. This should come as no surprise. We were scientists, like them. We chased after the same secrets of nature. It was an exciting time." Okamoto paused, and took his first sip of orange drink. Piper already had drained his glass. "But that is not the same as building an atomic bomb, I'm sure even a layman can understand."

Kyoko was feverishly taking notes, without looking up, as though she might be called upon to translate from English to English. Piper glanced at her, and then said, "So the army and navy—they graciously funded you, in the middle of a war, just so you could indulge your scientific curiosity? They gave you money to refine Bohr's theorems while the Japanese empire was falling apart, while they were making spears out of wood?"

"Ah, the cynical reporter," Okamoto said. "I think that is the proper term, yes?" He took another sip and smiled. "I have heard of the species but never encountered it before. I admire the intelligence reflected in your very perceptive question. Indeed, we did take money from the Imperial Army, and we told them we were engaged in weapons research. The navy admirals were not stupid enough to think that we could build an atomic bomb with no materials and in quarters that were"—his hands unfolded to gesture vaguely around him, and then clasped again—"considerably less majestic than these. But some of the generals were true—may I say in English—stupidheads? I recall one who asked why, since we could not obtain uranium, we didn't simply use TNT. We had a good laugh over that."

Okamoto eyed Piper as if waiting to see whether this oversized Yankee would ask the same stupid question: "Well, golly, Professor, why not use TNT?" Instead, Piper said, "So it was all a game? An early case of grantsmanship, is that what you're saying?"

Okamoto's eyes narrowed and seemed to harden for a moment. "If it was a game, it was a very serious one, Mr. Piper," he said.

"Professor Nishina and I had dozens of fine young men working in our laboratory. If they had not been with us, they would have been fighting and probably dying in what every intelligent person knew was a hopeless cause. Did we lie? No. We were, by some definition, working on a bomb. Did we deceive the army? Yes. There was never any chance that we could build a bomb, nor did we think there was, nor did we want to. Frankly, I believe it is your scientists who should have been tried as war criminals for turning the atom into a tool of mass destruction." Piper's back was sticking to the leatherette, and he leaned forward uncomfortably as Okamoto stopped and sipped. "You know, I was in Hiroshima with Professor Nishina two days after the bombing," the professor added. "Believe me, it is something I have lived with ever since."

He paused again, and seemed to be looking at Kyoko without actually seeing her. After a moment he resumed. "But that is neither here nor there, as you might say. Yes, we did deceive the army, and I hope you will not judge us too harshly for that," he said. "We felt we had a duty to protect as many young lives as we could, and to safeguard as many young minds, so some would remain to rebuild Japanese science out of the rubble that we knew would be the end result of our foolish war."

Okamoto seemed to have finished, surprised at how long he had spoken. There was no sound in the room except the scratching of Kyoko's pen as she rushed to catch up. Then Okamoto, leaning back and speaking in a softer voice, said, "You know, when your B-29s, your so-called Superfortresses, destroyed our laboratory, we were lucky that no one was inside, and no one died in the fire. But at the same time we were not so lucky, because we could no longer protect many of our students. The game, as you called it, was up. One, who felt shame for not having fought while his friends and classmates were dying, volunteered for the special attack squadrons—what you call kamikazes. He was in training and only one week away from sacrificing himself when the war ended. He went on to become one of our best men in the field. I attended his retirement party only a few months ago. But not all of our students were so lucky."

Okamoto looked at his watch, and Piper said, "Well, we shouldn't take any more of your time." He stood, knocking a few journals off the low table in front of him, and knocked over a few more as he bent to retrieve the first.

"I'm sorry to disappoint you with such a dull tale," Okamoto said, watching without comment and without rising as Piper tried to rebuild the piles. "But surely your newspaper is not interested in such ancient history in any case?"

"It's always hard to say what will interest my paper," Piper said. "But you're probably right."

"Especially when we seem to be on the verge of a crisis that should more than keep you busy, I should think," the professor added. "By the way, Mr. . . ."

"Piper."

"Yes. Mr. Piper. As an eminent journalist, what is your view of this move to seize our factories?" Like Christopher, Okamoto was referring to the expropriations bill, the X-bill, Black X.

"Well," Piper hesitated. "I'm just a reporter, you know. I'm not supposed to have opinions." A veil of contempt slid over the professor's face in reaction to this evasion. "What is your opinion?"

"Oh, well, I'm no politician, just an old academic, so like yours my opinions are of little consequence," Okamoto said. "But I can tell you this—I haven't seen people this angry since Roosevelt shut off our oil." He was referring to the U.S. action which most Japanese believed had forced them into World War 2.

"You see this as an act of war, then?" Piper laughed. Okamoto did not laugh. After a moment Piper said, "Well, thanks again." Kyoko tucked her pad away and bowed, and they let themselves out of the office.

They walked in silence, Kyoko a half-step behind, as far as the first landing of the gloomy stairwell, and then Kyoko said softly, "Well, what do you think?"

"It was a good story while it lasted," Piper said. "Looks like we better make reservations to fly to Hiroshima again. Or maybe we could just send last year's story. I doubt anyone would remember."

"So you believe him?"

"You don't?" Piper asked. Kyoko had stopped on the second floor to fasten her briefcase, and Piper stopped to wait for her. Still speaking in near-whispers, he added, "The guy must be nearly eighty—why would he lie now about something that happened so long ago?"

Kyoko started down the stairs again without answering. At the next landing a tiny figure almost leapt out of the gloom, nearly knocking her over and eliciting a quick scream.

"Shhh!" It was the bent-over woman who had served the drinks. She clutched Kyoko's sleeve, bowing and apologizing and whispering urgently and bowing some more, all the while darting glances up and down the stairs. Piper followed her frantic looks to see whom she might be fleeing, but there was no one, and no sound. The building seemed nearly abandoned. Kyoko whispered a response, and the old woman whispered and gestured and bowed some more, and then headed for the second floor, scuffling to keep her slippers on. Kyoko whispered after her another question, but the old woman disappeared into the dim reaches of the corridor above them.

"What the hell was that?" Piper said, startling himself and Kyoko with his voice.

Kyoko shook her head. "Outside," she said.

It had rained briefly, and wet leaves steamed on the pavement. Kyoko and Piper walked side by side until they found themselves descending toward a small murky pond, celebrated in Japanese literature and a focal point of nostalgia for Tokyo University alumni. A dirt path followed the water's edge.

"She said she heard what the professor said about Yamada, and she wanted us to know that Yamada was a good man. She does not believe he would ever have told lies. She does not want us to think ill of him."

"Why would she care what we think?"

"I don't know. But she also told me that his wife is still alive, living not far from here, in the same house they shared together, and that if we want the real story, we should talk to her."

"Can you find it?"

"I think so," Kyoko said. "Anyway, from her directions, we can get close."

Before trying, Piper and Kyoko stopped for a bowl of noodles across the street from the campus. Piper ordered cold soba with tempura, omori—extra large. Kyoko ordered plain cold soba and, as she waited, read over her notes of their interview with Okamoto. When the flat wooden boxes heaped with light green noodles and darker flakes of seaweed arrived, she slid the pad back into her case, tore the wrapper off a pair of disposable chopsticks and, without further conversation, began to eat.

5

*D*usk was falling as they slid the restaurant door open along its track and ducked out beneath the blue cloth *noren* hanging over it. The cicadas had resumed their tone-deaf screeching, and Piper wondered again how so many insects could find homes in this leafless megalopolis. Their blackboard-scraping music, remarkably, was a favorite subject of Japanese poetry and nostalgia. Other beloved insects, like lightning bugs and butterflies, had been thoroughly routed during the nation's heedless, pell-mell rush to industrialization, and existed only in poetry, and perhaps in a few insect zoos. At the busiest corner of the Ginza, Piper had once seen hundreds of Japanese office workers line up during their lunch hour to enter a darkened trailer in which a few caged lightning bugs were on display. But the cicadas—they had survived, and prospered. In fact, it sometimes seemed that Tokyo already had spawned the animal life that would emerge elsewhere only after a nuclear holocaust. Cockroaches, crows, beetles: they were the dominant species in this new world.

There was something poignant, Piper thought now, in the way Japanese found redeeming cuteness in the least attractive creatures of the earth, composing haiku to honor animals that could honestly be classified only as vermin. Even before these craggy, unblessed volcanic islands had been encased in cement and blanketed by smog, people had found poetry in cockroaches and cuteness in squirrels. Kyoko once actually persuaded Piper to visit a squirrel zoo in Gifu, after they had toured a semiconductor factory nearby, and she had insisted on the full experience, feeding the rodents from her palm and being photographed with one riding on her shoulder. Piper had tried to persuade her, in return, to visit Gifu's "soapland," one of

Japan's most famous red-light districts, but she had refused. The zoo did nothing to change Piper's opinion of squirrels as beady-eyed rats with bushy tails. But, then, maybe there are rat haiku, too, he thought.

"The unhurried rat / sniffs the moonlit breezes as / my tears fall softly," Piper said aloud, composing as he walked. "Perfect. Seventeen syllables on the first try. What do you think?" Kyoko just looked at him. "It's haiku, couldn't you tell?" Piper said. "Maybe I'll submit it for the emperor's contest this year, in the foreign rat category."

"I think His Majesty is more drawn to fish," she said.

"True," said Piper. Many Japanese were. Old men fished in the shadow of elevated expressways, crouching on concrete walls and dropping their lines into scum-covered pools stocked by municipal authorities. Carp, another Japanese fetish, animated every ornamental garden with flashes of orange and silver. At a distance they at least were pretty, but up close, when they crashed to the surface of a decorative pond and with great sucking noises opened and shut their revoltingly large mouths to beg for crackers, they were no more appealing than squirrels, Piper thought. And then there were the beetles—furtive, twitching hard-backed insects with overgrown right claws that boys in Piper's neighborhood kept as pets, sometimes walking them on dental-floss leashes and matching them against neighboring beetles in bonsai-sized cockfights. In Tokyo, where whole families, and not poor ones, shared bedrooms the size of American walk-in closets, beetle-raising probably made more sense than kite-flying or soccer, Piper had to admit. Yet he had trouble understanding the appeal.

The king of the Japanese jungle was the crow—huge, threatening, cawing monsters that thrived and multiplied in downtown Tokyo, squeezing out any birds more winsome or melodic. Piper often had run-ins with them during his early-morning jogs, when the greasy black scavengers would be squatting on roads and sidewalks, tearing through last night's garbage outside clubs and restaurants. Even for oncoming cars, they would give way sullenly, reluctantly; when Piper approached, they would just flap a malodorous wing and turn their back, hunching over to protect their fish heads and chicken bones from him.

Yes, it was a postholocaust world, Piper thought. And yet the

Japanese fancied themselves nature lovers, and their islands the most beautiful in the world. The vastness and variety of America's wilderness, the grandeur of the Grand Tetons or the beauty of Yosemite, might impress and awe Japanese visitors, but, Piper thought, they also returned a bit repulsed, like North Americans confronting the teeming Amazon jungle and finding it frighteningly fecund. Nature beyond Japan was too disorderly, in bad taste, beyond the ability of humans to comprehend and compress into seventeen syllables.

With Kyoko leading the way, they entered a neighborhood of tumbledown, haphazard wooden houses that seemed to have escaped the American bombing and, for that matter, the Great Kanto Earthquake of 1923, too. Inside each a television glowed, while occasional streetlights outside seemed only to accentuate the darkness. Now and then, they passed a middle-aged man on his way to the public bath, rubber thongs flapping, a T-shirt covering his round stomach, a towel flung over his shoulder and a soap dish in one hand. A teenager still in her high-school sailor-girl uniform walked a yapping little dog. The street jogged and jagged, and grew narrower. A mother on a bicycle, her toddler nodding off in a tiny seat behind the handlebars, rang her bell and nearly lost control as she tried to pedal past without brushing them. From the cramped houses life seemed to spill into the alley—tiny potted trees and vegetables, pint-sized hand-cranked washing machines huddled under corrugated tin or green-plastic overhangs.

Kyoko knocked on the door of a corner house, motioning Piper to wait. It was a local real estate dealer, always an excellent source of gossip, where Kyoko would try to refine and extend her directions. Piper stood outside, watching moths dance around a lone streetlamp shining silver in the misty night. A distant rooster crowed out of place and time. Piper thoughts drifted back to the bent-over tea pourer in the physics building. What had she heard of their conversation with Okamoto, and why did she care? An old friend of the widow Yamada, perhaps. But what shadows were chasing her in that gloomy stairwell? Or was she just nervous to be in the company of a gaijin? For some Japanese, especially older ones, just the sight of a gaijin could induce panic; they would hold up their arms in front of their face in the shape of an X, as if to ward off blows, or as if in some peculiar Japanese adaptation of signing the cross to ward off the devil. It had infuriated Piper at first; now it merely amused him. The tea pourer might have been fifty or seventy-five or even older, it was impossible to say. And Okamoto—what kind of life had he led? He looked as though he might have been sitting at that very desk since the war ended, amiably jotting calculations on his little pad as journals piled up around him. But his English was good, very good.

Of course, none of this had anything to do with producing a decent newspaper story, Piper knew. This chase wasn't going to win him his Pulitzer, or his job on the *Times*. It probably wouldn't lead anywhere, in fact, and he probably shouldn't be wasting his time, or Kyoko's. But as he leaned comfortably against a wall, waiting for Kyoko, listening to the quiet sounds of the night in this working-class neighborhood of Tokyo, he thought, well, anyway, it beats working. It certainly beats writing auto trade stories for page D17.

"Sorry," Kyoko said, ducking back out of the realtor's entryway. "She knows quite a few Yamadas, it turns out, and she wanted to tell me about each. There's the priest, who recently married a woman half his age, and there's another Yamada up the street whose son is quite a hero on the high-school baseball team. But it sounds like the one we're looking for is just around the corner—left at the tofuya-san, if we have the right one."

"What shall we tell her about why we've come?" Piper asked as they resumed walking.

"Why not the truth?"

"Unorthodox, but there's always a first time, I suppose," Piper said. "But maybe we shouldn't mention the A-bomb at all. Maybe we should just say we're doing a series of profiles of great scientific minds of the century, and we want to include her husband. Maybe—"

"John—why don't we just be honest, and see what happens?" Kyoko said.

"Okay," Piper said doubtfully. They reached the well-lit tofu shop, where a white-uniformed apprentice was still hosing down silver trays and cement floor, and turned into a yet narrower alley, no more than a little path. Piper wondered if they'd ever find their way out.

"Although," Kyoko said after a moment, "it might be best not to mention how we found her."

"Why not? I figure the tea server as her best friend and defender."

Kyoko didn't answer. She had stopped in front of a small wooden home again, and was peering around the doorframe for some identification. "I think this is it," she said, and knocked.

The Yamada house was one of the most dilapidated of the neighborhood, a heap of corners and right angles that seemed to be slipping slowly into each other, or into the ground. But Mrs. Yamada herself proved to be upright and vigorous and handsome in her gray kimono and gray hair. After only the briefest introduction she welcomed them into her best tatami room, into which Piper could barely fold himself, and then disappeared. Piper and Kyoko sat on their cushions, listening to a good bit of clattering and at least two cats in some other part of the house, and then were surprised when Mrs. Yamada appeared through a different door, carrying a clanking old electric fan and then, a minute later, a pot of fresh green tea. Only after she had poured them each a cup and set a tray of rice crackers on the low table before them did she settle into a kneeling position to listen to Kyoko. She sat motionless, totally calm, and when her turn came, she spoke in quiet, measured tones.

In the end, though, she couldn't tell them all that much. She insisted that everything in her husband's journal must be true. She said that he had just begun writing the second volume of his memoirs when he died, and that he always said the world would not ignore volume two as it had his first. She refused to be drawn into a discussion about Okamoto, though she did not hide her distaste. "Everything changed after the professor passed on," she said, talking about Nishina's death. "Okamoto had meant nothing to Nishina, but he soon took over. Wait—I can show you."

Rising effortlessly from her knees, she disappeared into the creaking back rooms again, and Piper took the opportunity to stretch and jiggle his aching legs. He was definitely the wrong size for this country, he thought again. When she returned, it was with a black-and-white photograph in a polished silver frame. "This is the professor," she said, pointing to a man in a starched collar and dark hat. "And these were the boys he called the 'five fingers of my right hand'—my husband, here, and the four other graduate students who helped him most during the war." She passed the frame to Kyoko, who studied it a moment and then passed it on to Piper. The picture seemed to have been taken in a field somewhere, in front of a long, low farmhouse. The six scientists all stared straight ahead, unsmiling, although Yamada looked as though he was trying not to laugh. In the shadows of the picture, a young woman in kimono was walking out of the old farmhouse, looking startled to have stepped into a photo session. A cherry tree to the side was in bloom.

Mrs. Yamada slid the picture out of its frame and showed Kyoko the names and hometowns of all five "fingers" neatly printed on the back. There was an inscription, too, from Nishina, which Kyoko translated for Piper: "You should be proud of how hard you tried, and happy that we failed. With deep appreciation." But when Kyoko asked where the others were now, Mrs. Yamada threw up her hands. "Everyone scattered after the war," she said. "Even before the war, really, when the laboratory burned. I suppose the professor kept in touch with all of them, but after he was gone—I just don't know."

She agreed to lend the photograph to Kyoko. "I do not like hearing that Okamoto is saying such things about my husband," she said, looking up to a formal portrait of Yamada tipping forward slightly above the door. "It was a long time ago, and I don't suppose anyone cares, but my husband always said it would be better if the truth were known. After he lost his job, he spent all his time writing, and when his book seemed to disappear without a trace—that took ten years out of him, I thought. He began on his next book right away, but his spirit was weak."

She kneeled, motionless and impassive again, while Kyoko translated all this for Piper. "Ask her how her husband died," Piper said. The translation took some time, as Kyoko lengthened and softened his question, but the widow seemed untroubled as she answered.

"They called it a hiking accident," she said, again speaking through Kyoko. "They never found him, actually, but they found his things, and at the edge of a cliff some footsteps and other signs that he had slipped off the edge. I must say, I never believed them, though."

"What do you mean?" Piper asked.

"I don't think it was an accident," she answered. "He had sent me a letter not long before, asking for my forgiveness. He did not actually say he would take his own life, but to me it seemed clear." She shrugged a bit, and dabbed her forehead with a handkerchief, which she then stowed back in her kimono sleeve. "He was not proud of his life, I believe. Still, what did it matter what they called it?" She looked at Kyoko, and then at Piper. "I'm sorry," she said. "These matters must be of no interest to you young people at all." She smiled and rose, and bowed them to the door. As they stepped back into the darkness, another cat slipped through their legs and into the house.

Once or twice on the walk back Piper put his hand on Kyoko's back, as if to steer her away from a bonsai plant or milk bottle. She neither shook it off nor leaned into it, but seemed not to notice at all, and when they reached the brighter streets, he moved away. On the muggy subway ride home his fingers still recalled her suppleness, and he closed his eyes, imagining her long torso. Back in the office, Piper remembered that it was Friday night and suggested a jazz club around the corner. She declined with a fleeting smile, and slipped into the bathroom to change.

From their fifth-floor window, Piper watched her emerge from the front door below and disappear into the crowd. Then he lay on the couch with the office lights off, only the computer glowing green and Roppongi's neon seeping through the window in shifting patterns of red and blue and yellow. Finally, he rose and called McGee, finding him still at his office.

"The love of your life stand you up again?" he asked cheerfully.

"You can't be stood up by someone who never says yes," said Piper.

"Meet me at the Hachiko statue in Shibuya in forty-five minutes," McGee said. "I'll help you forget all about her."

6

*H*achiko was a classic Japanese hero: loyal, long-suffering and a noble loser. Unlike most such heroes, however, Hachiko was a dog, not a samurai. He had met his owner at the bus station after work each night and, after his owner died, Hachiko continued to faithfully meet what had been his owner's bus, every night, for another ten years. For this display of perseverance over brainpower, Hachiko was revered throughout Japan. His body was stuffed and preserved in the National Science Museum. Recently, a full-length movie biography had been released, but had lost out at the box office to Stallone and Schwarzenegger. Maybe Japanese are more into winners these days, Piper thought as he waited in a light drizzle.

The statue itself was a modest landmark, in a small plaza beside one of the busiest train stations in the world. So many people passed through the gates here that ticket punchers were said to wear out their metal punches every three or four days. It was typical of Japan, Piper thought churlishly, that everyone nonetheless picked the same landmark when meeting friends at Shibuya, so that the dog was continually surrounded by a confused, swirling mass. Piper's attitudes toward Japan tended to be at their sourest on Friday nights, after Kyoko had disappeared into the pulsing Roppongi night.

Still, he had no trouble spotting McGee and his scraggly beard when he appeared as promised out of the station. Piper was pleased to see that their friend Sato from the foreign ministry had come along, and he was less pleased to see that Theo Zarsky had somehow managed to tag along as well. No doubt Sato's good-heartedness was at fault, Piper thought; Tsuyoshi believed everyone was redeemable, and he couldn't say no to anybody.

Zarsky was a magazine editor from New York who had spent

three months in Tokyo and then written a book telling the world everything that was wrong with Japan and the Japanese. Most of what he knew he had learned by picking the brains of Piper and other foreign correspondents over chummy lunches at the club. Afterward, when they all were feeling they'd been had, they had traded notes about his methods. He had telephoned each of them, it seemed, one by one, and told each of them how much he admired their work and their understanding of Japan. In some cases he had even dropped delicate little hints about how he hoped someday they might come to work at his (high-paying) weekly. Then he humbly asked whether they might have time—he knew how busy they must be, considering how often they filed; they really were leading the pack!—but maybe they could spare just a few minutes for a quick lunch, to help bring him up to speed. Of course, he would pick up the tab. Piper hadn't yet met the reporter who could resist a one-two punch of flattery plus a free meal.

So later, when they found their insights and anecdotes, only slightly altered, studding Zarsky's book—proving his deep knowledge of the country—most of them felt more sheepish than angry. But seeing the book float atop the best-seller list week after week didn't make the swindle any easier to take. Zarsky had timed his diatribe just right, both feeding and taking strength from the growing anti-Japan hysteria; Americans were eager to hear that the Japanese, though they might build better cars and own a rapidly growing chunk of America, were monsters—and not only monsters, but unhappy monsters, repressed, robotic monsters who led inferior lives, probably had low sex drives and secretly wished that they could be Americans, too. Every visitor from Piper's hometown now arrived with Zarsky's book in his carry-on bag, bubbling with insights and observations that in some cases Piper knew only too well. It was almost enough to turn Piper into a defender of Japan. Not that Zarsky was wrong, exactly, but he had patted one leg of the elephant and thought he'd felt the whole beast. What was most infuriating, of course, was that Piper had taken plenty of the same cheap shots himself.

So tonight, as he saw Zarsky approaching, he resolved to keep himself in check. What could he say, what could any of them say, without sounding jealous? (Which, needless to say, they all were.) By now Zarsky was a star of the Japan-bashing set, vigorously pushing the expropriations bill. Piper greeted him with a friendly handshake.

"Good to see you too, John!" Zarsky said. "You've been filing some great stuff lately!" This was a lie, of course. More to the point, Piper thought, there was no way Zarsky would even know if he had written a decent article lately. But that never stopped him from dishing out the compliments. Nor, Piper remembered with some discomfort, had it stopped Piper from believing the compliments when Zarsky first blew into town. This time he just said thanks, and fell in as McGee led the way to his latest discovery, a noisy red-lantern joint that proved not quite up to his usual standards. They drank sake for a time, then switched to beer.

Piper sat quietly at a corner of their low table, eavesdropping on a quartet of Japanese businessmen to sharpen his Japanese while Zarsky held forth. Only once did Piper tune back in and allow his bile to bubble to the surface, when he heard Zarsky modestly admit that, in the past, when he had visited Japan only one week at a time, he had overlooked whole layers of subtle complexities in this ancient society that revealed themselves to him only during his extended, three-month stay.

"Anyone who reads the book can see in a minute that you'd been here a full three months," Piper said, nodding agreeably, but the sarcasm sailed right past Zarsky. Only Sato smiled. The rest of the evening they all listened quietly to Zarsky's aphorisms—the Japanese were this way, the Japanese are that way—which he had honed into twenty-second sound bites during his weeks on the book-tour circuit, chatting with talk-show hosts who hadn't read his book.

Sato seemed to sink deeper into his beer as the night wore on. He was a Foreign Ministry section chief, a friend of McGee, and one of the few bureaucrats whom Piper liked and who related to Piper as a person, not as the representative of a lesser but not entirely negligible U.S. newspaper. It wasn't surprising that he and McGee were friends. Like McGee in the American embassy, Sato was smart but a bit out of place in his ministry. He wore his suits rumpled and ash-flecked, despite the best efforts of a doting wife, and his hair longish and tousled. He was never obsequious to his superiors, nor to the politicians whom most bureaucrats flattered and fussed over in person and disparaged behind their backs. And while most bureaucrats would talk to the press only on background or off the record, loath to risk offending anyone by attaching their names to a point of view, Sato would talk to anyone, on the record or off. Sometimes he even went home for dinner. He was one of the few bureaucrats Piper knew who had married for love. Most young diplomats hooked up with women who could advance their careers: daughters of vice ministers or politicians or wealthy businessmen, elegant ladies who could host parties without embarrassment abroad, where wives could not, as in Japan, hide out of sight in the kitchen, and who could pay for the Italian suits and mountain homes that a government salary could never provide. Piper knew one twenty-nine-year-old deputy section chief whose boss had told him, in June, that he should be married before his next overseas posting the following January. The deputy booked a wedding hall for December 29 and then began the omiai process, the arranged meetings. After three dates he found a wife. Her family was in auto parts.

Sato, on the other hand, had met his wife at a violin recital, when through some box office error they had been assigned to the same seat. He found a seat nearby, they began talking at intermission and never went back in. She brought no money to the marriage; he didn't care. And in some ways, he was equally artless as a diplomat. He believed, almost naively, in the substance of Japan's postwar foreign policy, its role as a peaceful, nonmilitary, nonnuclear trading nation and junior partner to America. Whereas for others in the government that was simply a strategy to advance Japan's interests in a hostile world, and one that worked well, for Sato it was a religion. And so while most diplomats viewed Zarsky as just another public relations nuisance to be handled, albeit a particularly distasteful one, Sato took his book almost as a personal assault. At one point, when Zarsky launched into his explanation of why Japan was not truly a democracy, Sato started to rise to the bait. But then he subsided back into his beer; like Piper, he seemed to have decided not to bother tonight.

The party broke up relatively early, while the subways were still running. Rain had slicked the streets again and many revelers, seeing that, put up their umbrellas as they exited their bars, although no rain was falling now. The foursome stood at the station entrance for a few minutes, while men in suits streamed past and Zarsky delivered his final homily on the psychic deficiencies that caused Japanese men to drink to excess. Then they headed for their separate subway lines. Piper took a few steps into the crowded underground passageway, and then changed his mind, opting for a walk in the fresh air, or what passed for fresh air here. Before he had taken ten steps, though, he felt a hand at his elbow. It was Sato.

"You're not tired, John?" Japanese almost never used first names when talking to each other, and Sato seemed to delight in the custom with his American friends.

"Not really," Piper said. "You?"

Sato shook his head. "Too depressed by that conversation to be tired," he said.

"I was heading for Yoyogi Park," Piper said. "Care to join me?" They walked for a time without speaking, listening to the swish of tires on wet pavement. Sato was one of the few Japanese with whom Piper could honestly relax, he reflected as they walked. There were plenty of Japanese whom he liked, of course, and found interesting, and pleasant, and even funny. But with most of them, he had to be always on guard. An intricate, unspoken web of rules and obligations governed every facet of human relations in Japan, and any infraction, no matter how well-intentioned, could prove fatal to a friendship. If you failed to give a gift on certain occasions, you were rude, but if the gift was too expensive, you might be even ruder. If you tendered an invitation, you were expected to ignore the first two rejections and press at least three times, or your original invitation would be taken as insincere. But if you pressed too hard, you unforgiveably made it impossible for your friend to say no. Only a Japanese, Piper often thought, could consistently find that shadowy no-man's-land between insincere and too hearty, and only a Japanese could distinguish a polite rejection from a heartfelt one. If you missed some subtle signal, or unwittingly failed to dispatch an equally subtle response, a friend might be mortally insulted. And what was most frightening was that you would never learn what you had done wrong; indeed, only a further series of subtle coded messages—a barely perceptible chill, a slightly too-formal greeting— would alert you that any wrong had been done at all. It was an exhausting and, for a gaijin, unwinnable game. But with Sato, as with Kyoko, Piper could relax. If something was on their minds, they said so.

What was on Sato's mind now was Zarsky. "John, do you think we're really as bad as he says?" he asked. There was something touching in the plaintiveness of the question. Why even take the guy seriously, Piper thought. But what he answered was, "Anybody who talks about 'the Japanese' more than ten times in every paragraph has to be full of shit. You know that as well as I do, Tsuyoshi." Piper shrugged. "But he's the best-selling author, not me."

"Yes," Sato said. "That is a problem." They waited for a light to change at a deserted intersection. The Japanese never jaywalk, Piper thought; there's a stereotype you can bank on.

Across the street Sato spoke again. "You know, sometimes I feel I spend half my life telling the world why we're not as terrible as they think we are, and the other half telling the Japanese how we have to change to be less terrible than we are. Stop eating whale meat. Stop catching dolphins in your tuna nets. Stop killing elephants for your ivory jewelry. Stop reading *Little Black Sambo* to your children. Take in more refugees, buy more American cars, give more foreign aid, build up your army." He stopped for a moment as a green bus, well lit inside and nearly empty, roared past, its tires raising an oily spray. "The other day my wife said it would have been better if we had never let in your Black Ships at all, if we had just kept our country closed to foreigners forever. Sure, we would be poorer, but we could do things our way, no matter how strange that way might seem to the rest of the world. Now, everything we do that's Japanese, some foreigner finds fault with." Sato, a constant smoker, was breathless, so Piper slowed his steps. "I believe in internationalization as much as anyone, you know that, John, but I understood what Akiko was saying. I like my life here, after all. I don't mind so much commuting on a crowded subway car, I like my little rabbit hutch, I like going out drinking at night with my friends. Why is that so awful?"

"Nobody cared how you lived until they began thinking you were going to take over the world," Piper answered. "It's very cute that you all do calisthenics and shout out company slogans in unison every morning before work. But if my kid is going to end up having to work for Toyota and do calisthenics, too, then it's not so cute. It's insidious, and downright un-American."

"Yes, I understand that very well," Sato said.

The street here was untraveled, although they could hear traffic rumbling along an overhead expressway that filled the narrow band of sky. When they had nearly reached the park, Sato said, "John, are you still not tired? If you don't mind being out a bit later, there's something I'd like to show you." Piper nodded, and a minute later they were in a taxi, with Sato instructing the white-gloved driver at some length.

When he leaned back, Piper said, "How did you do that?"

"Do what?" Sato asked.

"Get a taxi after midnight," Piper said. "They never stop for me, especially on a Friday."

"Ah, that's because you're a gaijin, and they assume you don't live in some faraway suburb," Sato said. "This time of night is their big chance to find a drunken salariman who's missed his train and needs a 20,000-yen cab ride home. It's not racism, believe me," Sato laughed. "But I guess it looks that way. Just another reason for Zarsky to hate us, right?"

"Yeah, that'll be in volume two."

They drove through narrow back streets that turned and turned on themselves again until Piper was utterly disoriented. Finally, they stopped on a one-lane road, crowded with houses and small apartment blocks, in front of a temple gate. Sato paid the hefty cab fare and the driver opened the automatic back door. After the air conditioning of the taxi, the night was pleasantly warm.

Inside, graves jammed a pocket cemetery, each marked by what looked like a giant popsicle stick adorned with Chinese characters. Piper followed Sato behind the modest temple building, treading carefully on a dimly lit path. The flagstones were set too close to walk on each and too far apart to hit every other one, leading Piper to reflect once again that he just wasn't sized right for this country. Behind the temple a small garden had been planted around a tiny fish pond. Off to the side, hundreds of tiny stone Buddhas watched unblinkingly, many of them dressed in red smocks and white caps, some carrying children's pinwheels in their tiny stone hands.

"Do you know what they are?" Sato asked. Piper shook his head.

There was something unsettling about their blank stone eyes in the darkness. "They are for fetuses that were aborted. That one there"—he pointed to an undecorated one—"is for my son." Piper didn't answer, and after a moment they sat on a wooden bench near the pond, which was really no bigger than two children's wading pools crossed by a stone bridge. The night was very still.

"It happened right after Akiko and I married," Sato said. "He would have been born less than nine months after, by the way, but that's not the reason we did it. We had no place to live at the time, I was always traveling, and we thought—I thought—it would be better to wait a year. Abortion is no big deal here, you know, or at least that's what we tell ourselves." He fell silent for a moment, and then continued. "Akiko didn't argue, but she insisted on having a service here for the child. At the time I thought it was silly. Now, of course, we have a beautiful daughter, and Akiko never talks about this. But for some reason, I like to come here from time to time."

One of the plastic red pinwheels flapped softly in a puff of wind. Piper wondered why Sato had brought him along, and felt flattered. He wouldn't do this with a Japanese friend, he thought. They sat without speaking for some time. The rumble of traffic was so distant it might have been a powerful engine hidden deep in the earth.

"I didn't bring you here to tell you about myself, though," Sato said with an apologetic smile. "I thought you might be interested, sociologically. You know, sometimes I look at all these little statues, and I think we really do have a disease of the spirit. We all have cars, we all have refrigerators and televisions and VCRs, and soon now we'll all have heated toilet seats and perfume-scented central air conditioning to help us work more efficiently. But the richer we get, the more it seems we've lost something."

"Now you sound like Mishima," Piper said. "The old samurai spirit, the divine emperor, and all that."

"No, that's not what I mean," Sato said. "But I wonder if, in the old days, people didn't have a better sense of purpose. I mean, we live in tiny cubicles surrounded by cement, we spend all our hours working, or getting to work, or sleeping so that we can work again, or drinking to relax from the pressure of working and commuting. And for what? We used to believe there were gods in every tree, every rock, every stream. Now we never even see such things. Young people today—they dress alike, act alike—and what do they believe in? Madonna, Marlboros, Kentucky bourbon. There's nothing spiritual in Japanese life—and nothing Japanese in our spiritual life. And so people have these abortions just like taking cough drops. And why? Is it because people don't want more children? No. They can't afford to have more children. Not that they don't have the money, they have plenty of money. But they don't have the time, the space, the leeway."

Piper thought of the Tokyo park where on warm summer nights the ground was dotted with couples covertly making love, each pretending to be alone and unwatched, because they had nowhere else to go.

"You're just ahead of the rest of the world, that's all," Piper said. "More crowded, more polluted, more bulldozed and paved-over, more crows and cicadas. We'll all catch up eventually. And when we do, we won't make it work half as well as you do, that's the depressing part. At least you make it work, without crime, with civility and a minimum of complaining."

"Maybe so," Sato sighed. "But maybe if we complained more, things would be different." He stood up. "We'd better get going, or my wife will do more than complain."

Piper stood with him. "Anyway, I thought you were happy with your rabbit-hutch life," he said, as they retraced their steps toward the temple gate.

Sato smiled. "I am, I am. Don't pay attention to my rantings here." They reached the street and walked to the nearest corner, where Sato somehow managed to find an empty taxi. Before Piper could protest, Sato pushed him in and waved him off. Piper looked back to see him standing alone on the wet pavement and then, just before he disappeared from sight, turning back toward the temple gate.

7

*L*ater the next morning, Piper awoke full of admiration for the Japanese men whom Zarsky had so disparaged the previous night. It was true, Piper had to admit, that many Japanese office workers seemed to drink excessively on weeknights, and at least one vomiter on a late-night subway ride was to be expected. Yet everyone managed to show up punctually the next morning, and show up with tie squarely knotted, hair neatly in place and stomach in good enough order to tackle, with noisy enthusiasm, the morning rice and raw egg and seaweed and soup accompanied, in cosmopolitan Tokyo, by green salad with Russian dressing and black coffee.

Whereas Piper could barely roll off his futon. His memories of the expedition to Sato's temple were warm but hazy. His memories of the earlier part of the evening were clearer and less warm. After lying on the floor for some time, staring at the peeling paint of his bedroom ceiling, he decided that only a scalding Japanese bath could soak out the alcohol and poisons of suppressed professional jealousies from the previous night.

Piper bicycled to his local public bath, took off his shoes in the foyer and stowed them in one of the tiny open cubbies. Then he entered the steamy bath chamber, a shadowy but spotlessly clean hideaway. Four rows of knee-high faucets and mirrors extended through most of the room, with a black-tiled bath at the rear under a faded mural of Mount Fuji. Piper handed his coins to the old woman who sat on a kind of throne atop the plasterboard that divided the women's section from the men's. From her perch she could see into both, and in addition to taking money and selling disposable razors and cheap washcloths, she functioned as a kind of human satellite, bouncing messages or gossip from one side to the other. Unlike a satellite, however, she provided her own exegesis and embellishment to all the neighborhood news. As always, she seemed delighted to see Piper. She never failed to comment on his colorful boxer shorts and on the curly hair on his chest, and possibly on more personal aspects of his physique as well; his relationship with his proper young Japanese teacher hadn't permitted him to explore the vocabulary he would need to know for sure.

He set a low three-legged stool in front of a spigot, scoured himself from crown to sole, rinsed and then eased into the steaming pool inch by inch. Some days his tall and comparatively hairy body seemed to chase everyone out of the bath; some Japanese assumed that any white man must be practically shedding the AIDS virus. But today, as often happened, the old regulars slid toward him along the tiled bench to strike up a conversation. These days he could understand as much as half of what they said, and for the rest, he knew to nod and suck in his breath and cluck in dismay at what he hoped were appropriate times. He hated to think what he might have unknowingly lent support to, but so far no one seemed to have been permanently offended by anything he had said or had not said. Today the subject seemed to be the high cost of Tokyo land, the tiny million-dollar apartments of the neighborhood, so all Piper had to do was cluck sympathetically. Though, in truth, a number of these geezers had undoubtedly become millionaires themselves.

An hour later, with a final bow to the old money collector on her throne, he left, shaved and dressed, cleansed and happy. He bicycled downtown, toward the palace, feeling good about himself and his language skills, optimistic that Kyoko would come around sooner or later, well-disposed toward all the Japanese he passed. Boisterous high-school boys in their Prussian-style uniforms were heading home from Saturday classes, office workers were smoking and chatting as they headed back to work, a bit more relaxed than on a weekday. The rainy season seemed to be ending, although the weathermen had not declared it officially over, and the day was warm and dry. In the soft sunshine, trade wars and conflict melted into absurdity, and blank-eyed child-statues and furtive gropings in the dark seemed just as unreal. If only those snarling, anti-Japanese mobs in Detroit and Washington and Brussels could see all these pleasant people, these people who couldn't possibly be plotting world domination

. . . At the palace young couples held hands as they strolled around the moat, and children threw bread and popcorn to the swans and ducks. As he bicycled around the moat to the other side of the palace, Piper came across older couples posing beside a statue of postwar prime minister Shigeru Yoshida, who had traveled to San Francisco in 1951 to lead a defeated Japan back into the company of accepted nations.

Near the statue Piper laid his bike down in the grass and then followed suit a few yards away, closing his eyes with his face toward the sun. What a country, he thought; in Central Park, the bike would be gone by now. As he dozed and woke and dozed some more, Mrs. Yamada swam back into his thoughts, straight-backed and correct in that little house that probably had not changed, except to creak gradually closer to the ground, since Yamada died. And there was Okamoto, urbane, pleasant, close-faced in his office that also seemed untouched, the columns of dust twirling slowly in the few shafts of sunlight that penetrated, yellowing the journals. Which of them was telling the truth? Of course, they might both be; Mrs. Yamada naturally believed in her husband, but he hadn't necessarily told her the truth.

And to be honest, for the purposes of the story, it didn't really matter who was being truthful. Okamoto had admitted that they had, ostensibly at least, been working on a bomb. Piper could lead with that, then quote Okamoto protesting that they hadn't really intended to build one, and his quote would only strengthen the story: a denial that proved the case. The story might not be honest, but it wouldn't be wrong: nothing to sue over there, Piper thought. In fact, they'd be better off doing no more reporting, from that point of view; another denial, another physicist supporting Okamoto, would only weaken the story. And yet, and yet. What about the tea pourer, why did she care so much? And did Mrs. Yamada really seem like the wife of an aggrieved crackpot? No one at the home office would care, but Piper himself was curious. For some reason, the answer mattered.

Later that afternoon he pedaled lazily through town to Gab Inn, a kind of club for the lowest stratum of expatriates. Here, for a thousand yen or so, a Japanese could get a cup of coffee and an hour's conversation with a native English speaker, and so here

tended to gather young native English speakers with no better way
to earn their next bowl of rice. This was a world of young foreigners
happy to just get by while they learned Japanese, or played jazz in
a tiny nightclub, or penned a novel or practiced some obscure
martial art. They supported themselves by talking at Gab Inn, and
by modeling, especially if they were blond, or hawking Indian jewelry or Indonesian batik, or playing guitar on street corners. They
taught English, and some of the young women worked the hostess
bars, spending nights in low-cut dresses smoking and smiling and
being pawed over by Japanese businessmen. They lived three or four
to a tiny room, and every six months they took the ferry to Pusan,
Korea, to renew their tourist visas. As Americans or Europeans, they
knew they could always find something, something better than the
construction and dishwashing jobs which the Japanese increasingly
were leaving to Pakistanis and Filipinos, better than the brothel
slavery into which many Filipinas were sold. But even so, they didn't
do much more than scrape by.

Piper was older than most of them, and more prosperous, but he
felt more comfortable in this shabby second-floor coffee shop, with
its plastic chess sets and coverless paperbacks, than in the American
Club of Japan. That, of course, was the home of the upper tier of
expatriates, whose companies could pay their $10,000 annual mem-
bership and who therefore could still pretend that America was a
conquering power in Japan. These middle-aged executives and
young stockbrokers, most of whom spoke no Japanese, often lived
better here than they would at home. Their apartment buildings,
slathered in marble and thick carpeting, were out of the reach of any
natives but the most successful gangsters, and their club reminded
Piper of nothing so much as the country club of his childhood,
except, of course, without the trees and grass. He had spent most of
his summer afternoons at that country club, first as a caddy, later as
a lifeguard, and he had no desire to relive the experience now,
listening to teenagers from the American School in Japan bully the
Japanese help as they signed their parents' membership numbers to
cheeseburger chits. And the single young men, the investment bankers and stockbrokers who had flocked to Tokyo to sell off bits and
pieces of America to the Japanese—they were even harder to take.
Many of them barely out of business school, they weekended in Bali,

had suits made in Hong Kong, dated Japanese girls whom they usually treated like dirt. And in between, they worked long hours, as they liked to let you know, trying to wed cash-rich Japanese to failing American companies, failing American universities, failing American country clubs, to American stocks and bonds and skyscrapers. Of course, the *Advertiser* hadn't offered to buy Piper a membership at the American Club, so a superior attitude came in handy.

Piper played two games of chess, ate two bowls of vanilla ice cream, traded some English conversation for some Japanese with an earnest young computer programmer, and swapped stories of the Asian trail with some recently arrived New Zealanders, without mentioning how dated his own tales were. Before nightfall, he bicycled home to study Japanese. On Sunday he jogged, and read, and watched sumo, and thought about the Tokyo Project some more. By Monday he was looking forward to work as he hadn't in weeks, and he actually reached the office before Kyoko.

He was sorting the mail and piling the Japanese-language newspapers on Kyoko's desk when she arrived, ravishingly, a few minutes after nine, astonished to find him there so early, and so chipper.

"I have something to show you," she said, pulling Yamada's book, and the photograph, from her bag.

"I thought you never went near work on weekends," Piper said.

"Things have been a little slow lately," Kyoko answered. "Besides, I couldn't get these people out of my mind. Anyway, look. I didn't notice this the first time around."

She opened the book to its cover page and showed Piper how the words "Volume One," printed in small letters at the bottom, had been crossed out with two thick black lines. "And look at this." At the back of the book was a grainy black-and-white photograph showing Yamada with a young woman, the same woman in the same kimono as in the photograph that Mrs. Yamada had lent them.

"You think it's Mrs. Yamada?" Piper said. He couldn't imagine the gray-haired widow as a young woman, but she must have been quite pretty.

"Oh, come on," Kyoko said with a touch of disgust. "I know we all look alike to you, but even you should be able to see . . . It doesn't look anything like Mrs. Yamada."

"So who is it?"

"She doesn't look familiar to you?" Kyoko seemed disappointed. "Well, I'm not sure, but I bet it's our tea pourer. In any case, it's strange he would choose that photo for his book, don't you think? And not him with the professor, or someone like that?"

"I suppose," Piper said. He handed the book back to Kyoko and sat on the couch. "So where do we go from here? We have Okamoto, alive, saying they didn't really try to build the bomb. We have Yamada, dead, saying they did. We have Mrs. Yamada standing by her man, and we have the Americans smashing the Jap cyclotrons and dumping them into the sea, which suggests that at least somebody believed Yamada's version. And we have two weeks before the anniversary. Two weeks before we have to file this story that they're not going to want anyhow."

Kyoko had been staring at Mrs. Yamada's photograph as he talked. "Well," she said, as if it was the most obvious thing in the world, "we need to find the other fingers of Nishina's hand, right?" She slid the old photo out of its frame and read from the back. "Tetsuo Inoki, from Osaka. Shigeo Okamoto, Tokyo. That's our professor. Shigehara Hashimoto, Tataki village, Gumma prefecture. Bun—I guess you'd read this character as Bun—Kawamura, from Kuji in Iwate prefecture. And our Yamada, also from Tokyo."

"Given Japanese longevity, two out of the other three should be alive, if the odds are with us," Piper said. "And all you have to do, as faithful Japanese gal Friday, is track them down."

"Thank you."

"They were all working for the military during the war, right? Don't you think the *boecho*"—he gestured across the street to the Japanese Pentagon—"must keep records on all these guys? There must be a veterans' organization, right?"

Kyoko looked dubious, but said she would inquire. Piper planned to spend the day reporting a piece on Japan's economy that he hoped would keep the desk off his back the rest of the week. There was a lunch for foreign correspondents with Sumitomo's chief economist, and a tea at the Bank of Japan with the deputy who handled international affairs. With any luck, Piper could throw those together with a few clips he'd been saving from the *Japan Economic Journal* and send home thirty inches that night.

When he returned to the office after the tea, he had enough for an economy story. Analysts say this, though they worry that. The economy seems strong, though on the other hand it might be weaker than it looks. Nothing too different from what the *Times* or the *Economist* or Zarsky's *Business Chronicle*, for that matter, had already said. His editors should be happy.

Kyoko had had less luck.

"We have to file our request in writing, and they search their records, and in a month or two they may or may not tell us what we need to know," she reported.

"Did you explain to them what a daily newspaper was?" Piper asked. He took a deep breath and walked to the window. The stubbornness of the Japanese bureaucracy never failed to infuriate him. Kyoko, on the other hand, fought the stubbornness when it made sense, but gave up calmly when there was no hope. Her ability not to waste her anger sometimes irritated Piper, irrationally, as much as the original inanity.

After a minute he said, "So what now?" They could call Okamoto, of course, but he might well get to the others first, if any were alive, and advise them not to talk or tell them what to say. They could call from university to university, but there were hundreds of possibilities, and the men could well have become company researchers, or left physics altogether. They could try calling their hometowns, but a phone call across such a distance in space and time would probably elicit more suspicion than information, even if they found the right place.

"So let's just go," Piper said. "Gumma first, since it's closest." He was always happy to leave Tokyo and travel into *inaka*, into the countryside, especially when he could put it on his expense account. People in the hinterlands were friendlier, and more curious, and more honest about themselves than many of the polished "internationalists" he met in Tokyo. And Kyoko was fearless on these journeys, accosting strangers and charming them into long talks; finding the hidden local restaurant that used only the freshest local fish and seaweed; proposing hikes through the mountains to distant ancient temples that tourists never saw.

"And for Osaka—"

"We could ask your yakuza friend for help," Piper finished her sentence.

"He's not yakuza," Kyoko said. "But yes." Kyoko knew from long ago a private detective in Osaka. He looked and dressed like a gangster, a yakuza, but he made an honest living checking out family backgrounds of prospective marriage partners. One side always wanted the same answers about the other: was there any record of insanity? Any hidden financial problems? Any pollution by *buraku-min*, or untouchable, blood? Were there Korean ancestors? The detective, like Kyoko, was himself Korean, but he accepted that question along with the others as a normal part of life. Still, he was bored much of the time, and he liked Kyoko (at the least, Piper thought) and happily helped her from time to time with more exotic investigations. He could certainly track down Inoki's family register and find out if Inoki was still alive, while Kyoko and Piper took the train to Gumma.

Kyoko pulled her maps and train schedule out of a drawer and found Tataki in Gumma prefecture. "It's tiny," she said. "It might not even really exist anymore." But she agreed it was their best shot, and they arranged to meet at the Ueno train station the next morning. Kyoko got on the phone with her Osaka friend, and Piper settled in front of his computer to spin his dull tale on the Japanese economy. He would send it along with a brief message about their travel plans. By the time his editors organized themselves enough to wire back a telex ordering him not to go, he and Kyoko would be on the train, and out of reach.

MYSTERY

PART II

8

*P*iper reached the station and ordered a bowl of udon at a stand-up noodle counter, from where he could watch the commuters spilling past. There was nothing more awesomely Japanese than Tokyo's railroad hubs at rush hour. From offstage left, where the trains disgorged, a seemingly impossible, unending swirl of people swept into view, cutting and weaving across the station, well-dressed, unsmiling, purposeful and polite, moving briskly but not frenetically until they disappeared stage right, toward the subway lines. One still photo would capture thousands, and every ten seconds they were replaced by an entirely different cast of thousands, the men with sober umbrellas and briefcases, the women carrying faux Louis Vuitton bags, no one cramming in a last-minute Danish, no one dropping styrofoam cups or cigarette packs, hurrying from trains that were always on time to subways that were always reliable so they could all catch just the right elevator at work. And millions more were dancing to the same choreography at Shinjuku and Ikebukuro, Tokyo Station and Shimbashi. There was something exhilarating in the scene, if you didn't have to take part in it, and something oddly moving as well: all these people trying so hard, struggling so uncomplainingly, so well-meaning, so earnest, so accepting of life's limits.

Piper paid for his breakfast and stepped out into the commuter ballet. The secret to survival, especially when moving against the crowd, was to keep your eyes on the ground, picking your spots like a halfback and never, ever hesitating. If you hesitated, or if you looked someone in the eye, you threw the whole thing off. Unlike in America, the choreography depended on no personal contact, no unspoken challenges, no aggressive claims of right-of-way nor any polite holding back. The absence of such signals helped explain why Americans found Japanese crowds so rude and sullen, and why Japanese found American streets so threatening.

Kyoko was waiting, as agreed, by the ticket puncher farthest to the right. Even from a distance Piper thought he could sense the island of calm dignity she carved out of the swirling crowd. She had dressed for the country, a sober, inexpensive skirt, a cotton sweater, flat shoes: a dutiful niece taking off from her city job to visit a sick aunt in the village. She smiled when she spotted him, holding up his ticket, and they passed through the gate.

Kiosks lined the station; for returning travelers who had forgotten to buy the always-required gifts, the stores sold typical foods of every province of Japan, along with chocolate-covered macadamia nuts for those who wanted to pretend they'd been to Hawaii. Kyoko stopped for a gift box of candied fruit, so they would have something in hand in Tataki, in case there was anyone to hand it to. Then they descended two plunging escalators to the bullet-train tracks far below ground.

Once aboard, they easily found two pairs of seats in the un-reserved no-smoking section and turned one to face the other, so they could kick off their shoes and put up their feet. The southbound bullet trains hurtling toward Kyoto and Osaka and the industrial heartland would all be full at this hour, but Piper and Kyoko were heading north, to what the Japanese liked to think of as their rough, undeveloped outback, and it was uncrowded, especially in the non-smoking section. In the smoking car in front of them, travelers had begun popping open beers, lighting up cigarettes and passing around dried squid even before the train doors shut.

The train glided out of the station. Kyoko dozed. Piper watched her chest rising and falling, the soft hair on her lower arms, the lovely curve of her calves. He thought of proposing marriage right now. "A union of two great cultures," he would say. "From the Japanese side, intelligence, perseverance, probity, civility. From my side, long legs. What do you say?" Not quite persuasive enough. Besides, he didn't want to be guilty of *seku-hara*, as the Japanese called sexual harassment, on the job.

As the train climbed out of its tunnel into the jumble of some of Tokyo's oldest neighborhoods, Piper wrested his gaze away from

Kyoko. From inside the air-conditioned train, the sunshine outside seemed deceptively pleasant, but already a thick smog was descending on Tokyo Bay. For a while they ran parallel to an elevated expressway in the distance, where miles and miles of clogged truck traffic seemed frozen, silhouetted in the morning sun. After Yanaka Cemetery there were no trees, no green; just grimy factories and apartment blocks draped with drying laundry and bedding out to air, cheap love hotels and business hotels, garish pachinko parlors and forbidding Dickensian schools enclosing cement-paved schoolyards, all squeezed in at crazy angles. Then more apartment blocks, more narrow shopping streets with cheap plastic decorations, more billboards and factories and three-story bicycle parking lots. Occasionally they crossed a river, its water grayish-brown, its banks walled with concrete and flanked by narrow strips of dirt and grass which on Sundays would serve as picnic grounds, golf driving ranges and baseball fields.

This was a bullet train, Japan's fastest, but close to an hour passed before they entered some hills and began to see rice paddy, lush green by now, and vegetable patches and vineyards. Even here, Piper noticed, there was no sense of extra space, no leeway at the margins. Houses bunched together, and rice fields lapped right to each back door. There were no yards for whiffle ball, no empty fields where kids could chuck a Frisbee. Only the dusty courtyards of the concrete schools, their tattered volleyball nets hanging like limp flags.

As always, the rituals of the smooth-flowing bullet train lulled Piper into a half-sleep. A soothing voice on the loudspeaker thanked the passengers from the bottom of its heart, apologized for any inconvenience they may have felt for any reason and informed them of a wealth of connecting possibilities at the next station. A young woman in uniform pushed a cart into their car, apologized for the disturbance and then slowly pushed up the aisle, calling her edible wares in a soft singsong before turning, at the head of the car, to bow apologetically and pull her cart out of sight. And meanwhile the compressed green-and-brown scenery slid past, a moving picture outside the sealed gliding tube of a train.

Five minutes before their station Kyoko opened her eyes and stretched. It was one of her many magical talents, never to under-sleep nor oversleep nor have any concern about doing either. The soothing voice announced the approach of Ichinoseki, and Kyoko brushed out her hair. "There's a train to Hiraizumi in ten minutes," she said. Then she added, "It should be cooler up here."

Transferring to the local from the bullet train was like transferring into another country, into the country that Japan used to be. The bullet train pulled away on its elevated platform, high above them, and then a kind of sunny premodern stillness filled their nearly empty car with its open windows and wooden floor and benches. A couple of older women, hugging bundles tied up in blue-and-white scarves, sat across from them. The engineer chatted lazily on the platform with a sweeper. Behind the stationmaster's tiny brick house, in a kind of island between tracks, a skinny rooster pecked in the dust. A conductor ambled through, glanced at their tickets, and sat at the front of the train. The doors shut, opened again, and then shut once more, and the train lurched forward, putt-putted along for five minutes, and pulled onto a siding to let a local express go past. It was a few minutes past ten in the morning.

Half an hour later they pulled into the grand old capital of Hiraizumi, once a rival to Kyoto in splendor and importance. Here, eight centuries before, Japan's most fabled hero, Yoshitsune, met his requisite tragic end. He was a younger half-brother of Yoritomo, one of Japan's greatest warriors and a general who helped unify the country into the shogunate that lasted for most of this millennium. But it was Yoshitsune, a flawed warrior forced to rip out his own intestines at the age of thirty, who became the stuff of Japanese legend. Yoshitsune was loyal to his older brother, since every tragic hero must be loyal, but Yoritomo was jealous and suspicious, and forced him to flee Kyoto, leaving behind his beloved Shizuka, Japan's most beautiful woman and talented dancer. Disguised as a monk begging temple funds, Yoshitsune and a few retainers wandered Japan for months, eluding a massive manhunt staged by an increasingly obsessed Yoritomo.

Eventually, Yoshitsune took refuge here, in Hiraizumi, where the independent lord promised protection but then, of coursse, betrayed him. As a huge army attacked, Yoshitsune's small band fought bravely to give him time to honorably end his life. One especially loyal servant nobly killed Yoshitsune's wife and son as Yoshitsune watched, bleeding and immobile, and then set fire to all of them inside their house. The treacherous Hiraizumi lord managed to drag from the fire Yoshitsune's head, which he pickled in rice wine and dispatched to Yoritomo in a black lacquer box. The gift was not enough to save the Hiraizumi lord, soon conquered by Yoritomo. But Yoshitsune went on to become the most popular character of Japanese drama and legend. Piper had gone so far as to sit through an entire Noh play on the subject, and he remembered still what he thought of as Yoshitsune's, and Japan's, emblematic remark: "This is indeed a sorry world, where nothing happens as one hopes."

In front of the one-room train station there was, as usual, nothing to bespeak such past glories. Piper by now was used to such disappointments. Before every trip he dreamed of finding the Japan of old woodblock prints, of neat wooden farmhouses and graceful old temples, but that Japan no longer existed if, indeed, it ever had. Here, as Kyoko pulled out her map and approached a taxi driver lounging in his car, Piper eyed the sleepy country town that Hiraizumi had become. The station faced a semicircular drive guarded by a couple of dilapidated wooden buildings, and a couple of functional cement ones: a convenience store, a burger joint, a realtor's office. Two scrawny dogs barked in a weedy field off to one side. Piper tried to imagine Yoshitsune lifting his sword out of the way to slide into a plastic booth at the hamburger eatery, there to dash off a quick poem to his loved one in Kyoto.

Kyoko returned from her consultations and reported that one of the buses idling a block away would bring them close to Tataki. It was an old country bus, with a lighted display above the windshield like a bingo board, showing the fare due at each stop. The vinyl seats had been patched and repatched. The bus swung onto the two-lane national highway and then turned left, toward the mountains, the engine complaining and whining all the way up.

"Whatever happened to Yoshitsune's girlfriend?" Piper asked Kyoko as they bounced and swayed on their bus seat.

"Shizuka Gozen?" Kyoko said. "She was betrayed by Yoshitsune's soldiers and handed over to Yoritomo, who saw that she was pregnant. He was so afraid of Yoshitsune that he ordered the baby killed if it was a boy, which of course it was. They smashed the baby on the rocks near Kamakura. Then—or maybe before that, I can't remember—Yoritomo made Shizuka dance for him. She dedicated her dance to Yoshitsune and then went back to Kyoto, cut off her hair and became a nun."

"Very cheerful," Piper said. "Then what happened?"

"That was all," Kyoko said. "She died the next year, at the age of twenty, or so the story goes."

"You know better?"

"Well, you know," Kyoko said. "If she'd gone back and gotten on with her life, organized a dance company, maybe found another boyfriend—they couldn't let that into the legend, right? So who knows?"

The fare board lighted up on 220 yen. Kyoko lurched forward, gripping each seatback on the way, checked with the driver and motioned to Piper that the next stop was theirs.

They dismounted at a primitive shelter, the bus disappeared over the next ridge, and they were wrapped in silence. Pine forests lined the road; there wasn't a house or farm in sight. A hawk circled far overhead, and a crow broke the silence with a hoarse cawing from atop a tall cedar. The sun shone less fiercely than in the plain below, and the sky was bluer than it ever got in Tokyo.

Kyoko pointed to a narrow footpath leading uphill into the woods. "That should be the way," she said uncertainly. "Apparently, a road comes in from the other side, across the mountains, but it's a two-hour drive from the nearest train station. This is only supposed to be a five-minute walk."

They plunged into the woods, and into a sweet piney smell that Piper had almost forgotten. He silently apologized for having slandered Japan as being beyond nature. The ground here was soft with pine needles, and the air was cool. Here, doubled over, eyes to the ground, farm women might search for the treasured matsutake mushrooms that grew only in the shadow of the rare red pine, and that were worth more than their weight in gold. Here, in the hungry wartime years, while Yamada and his friends built their cyclotrons, scavengers might have combed the woods for more prosaic sustenance, for bamboo shoots and edible roots and bark.

After a thirty-minute climb they suddenly found themselves in a clearing behind a farmhouse. The house, fifty feet farther uphill, seemed to front on a blacktopped country lane meandering alongside a stream. They could see five or six other houses, all in the old wooden style, along the road before it curved out of sight; two of them even had thatched roofs. Every house had its television aerial, and electric lines followed the road. Otherwise it would have been difficult to date the scene.

Balancing on a narrow grassy ridge dividing two tiny plots of cabbages, spinach and cucumbers, they reached the road. At first, they thought they were alone; then Piper noticed, squatting by the stream, a tiny woman, the small brown circle of her face nearly hidden by a broad straw hat and a scarf tied under her chin. She had been washing radishes in a bucket; now she watched, without expression, this strange apparition emerging from the woods. Piper wondered if any white person had ever been here before, a frequent conceit that in this case might have more truth than usual.

Kyoko asked the woman where they might get some information and she pointed, still wordlessly, up the road. As they rounded the curve, they saw another dozen or so houses scattered along the narrow ravine. In front of one was a telephone; this was the Tataki general store and reception center, selling dusty cans of drink and plastic bags of salty snacks. Kyoko slid open a door and talked briefly to a woman who stayed kneeling on the tatami floor of the room behind the shop. A baby slept on her back, wrapped tightly in cloth. When Kyoko mentioned Hashimoto's name, the woman was quiet for a moment and then pointed back down the hill. Kyoko thanked her, put two hundred-yen coins on the counter and took two warm cans of orange drink from a cabinet. Then they stepped outside again.

"What'd you find out?" Piper asked, peeling the foil top off a can.

"She said the Hashimoto house is last on the right."

"So he lives? He exists? He's here? I can't believe it! What would a nuclear physicist be doing here?" Piper gestured with his juice can. "Of course, it's attractive and all. The air is clean, but—"

"I don't know if he's here or not," Kyoko interrupted. "She just said 'the Hashimoto house.' It could be his grandchildren for all we know."

They walked slowly down the hill, reluctant to reach the house too quickly. The old woman, still on her haunches washing radishes, kept them in her sights as they passed, her head slowly swiveling.

The road continued to curve, and the radish woman was out of sight before they saw the Hashimoto house.

It was the only modern house in the village, a blocky, stucco home with a bright-blue-tiled roof behind a whitewashed wall. The garden was built around a small carp pond and three craggy rocks, which Piper knew must have been expensive. "The Hashimotos seem to have found a better cash crop than the rest of the village," Piper said.

As they approached the front door, a gray-haired woman, as blocky and substantial as her house, appeared from the side garden. Kyoko introduced herself and said, "Hashimoto-san?" The honorific could apply to women as well as men. The woman nodded, and Kyoko explained that they were looking for Shigehara Hashimoto.

The woman let out an explosive, hoarse laugh. "Please! Come in!" she barked, and led the way inside, exchanging her wooden geta for furry house slippers. Kyoko and Piper stepped out of their shoes and followed, Piper whispering, "I don't think she's a granddaughter."

In the living room the woman laughed again and pointed to a photograph inside a little shrine in the corner: a handsome young man in uniform, in a black frame, with a black ribbon running diagonally across.

"She says, if we want to meet Shige-kun, that's as close as we can get," Kyoko translated. "She says, we're a few decades too late."

"He died in the war?" Piper asked.

"Just as the war was ending," the woman answered, through Kyoko. "He gave his life in a very secret project, of great importance to His Highness and to our people. Here! You can see for yourselves!"

She pulled an envelope from a footlocker, handed it to Kyoko and bustled off to the back of the house. Kyoko and Piper sank into the western-style couch. Except for the shrine and a couple of small chests, there was nothing Japanese about the room, with its overstuffed furniture, china figurines, mirrors and crystal bowls.

Kyoko slid the letter, almost crumbling with age, out of its envelope.

"It looks pretty standard," she said quietly as she scanned it. "But it does say he gave his life for a secret project of utmost importance, and the emperor will always be grateful."

"Yeah, but look at the date," Piper whispered back. "October 16,

Showa 20." Showa 20, the twentieth year of Hirohito's reign, would have been 1945. "Two months after the war ended. How can that be?"

"Well, a lot of boys died near the end, and I'm sure things were confused in the ministries. Some letters probably just got sent out late."

"But then how did he die? The laboratory burned down six months earlier."

Their hostess returned, carrying a tray with three cups of tea and a dish of sticky rice-paste sweets. She set it on a table and settled into an armchair across from them, looking delighted to have company. Smiling across the table at them, she was so large that her original small-mouthed face seemed grafted onto a second, wider one, with extra chins and neck folds. Kyoko handed her back the envelope and said she must have been proud of young Shige-kun, and the woman beamed and said something, and Kyoko commented on how hand-some he was, and she beamed again and said something more. Her northern dialect was too thick for Piper to pick out more than a word here and there. Then Piper said, "Ask her what the secret project was," and when Kyoko translated, the woman flushed with anger.

"What do you think secret means, anyway?" she said. "How would I know? And why are you asking all these questions? Who are you?"

Indeed, up until that moment, she had shown no curiosity about why a gangling white man and a slender Japanese city girl would have hiked to this remote village to inquire after someone who had died two generations before. Now she looked as though she wanted to throw them out of the house, and Piper didn't doubt she could do it. He spoke hurriedly to Kyoko.

"Tell her we work for an important American newspaper, and our editors think that for too long Americans have only known about American war heroes, but that enough time has passed that our readers would be interested in hearing about some of Japan's heroes, too. And so we wondered if she'd tell us a little about her husband."

Kyoko shot him a look but translated dutifully, and the woman's face softened gradually until, as Kyoko finished, she burst out laugh-ing again. "What's so funny?" Piper asked, smiling and nodding at the woman as she continued to chuckle.

The woman, her suspicions apparently forgotten, began chattering away, with Kyoko just managing to interject an occasional, "Ah, is that so? Ah, I see." When Kyoko tried to break in to translate, the woman ploughed ahead, glaring at Piper as if sufficient volume and intensity could overcome his congenital inability to understand due to the unfortunate accident of his foreign birth.

Finally, Kyoko jumped in and insisted that she would have to translate for Piper. The woman sighed and leaned back, watching Kyoko's lips intently as she spoke. "She's not his wife, but his sister," Kyoko said. "That's why she laughed. She was twenty, and her brother only twenty-five, when he died, but already he was a brilliant scientist. Everyone said so. No one knew how it happened, because her parents were ordinary farmers, and she herself is nothing special in the brain department. But her brother stood out from the time he was a little kid. One time, when he was ten—"

"Can you summarize this part, and maybe expand on it during our hike back down?" Piper said.

"Okay. Well, he married during the war, a couple of years before he died, and his wife came to live here. Beautiful girl. But after the war she moved away, to Niigata. Said she didn't want to be a farm widow all her life. His parents had counted on having her around to help with the farmwork. But she didn't have kids, and in those days everything was turned upside down, and one day she just left. The parents were furious. But you have to give her credit: every month she sent money from his war pension, and it must have been most of what she got. The sister says she knows that, because the wife died a year ago, and now the pension comes directly to her, and it's not much more than the wife used to send. That's how she built this house, she said."

"Can you try again, with your trademark tact, on what he was actually working on?"

The two women chatted for some time, this time without any apparent emotion, before Kyoko translated again. "She says she doesn't know, and never asked, and she doesn't think the wife knew, either. It had something to do with science, though, and it was very secret. He would never talk about his work during his visits home. And after his wife left, she never came back and she never wrote, which the sister thought was a little strange. Just sent the money, month after month, decade after decade."

"When did they last see him?" Again, Kyoko translated, listened, translated.

"He visited in May. He loved these mountains in the spring, and he even helped his parents get the seedlings ready for transplanting. He told his family then how lucky they were not to be in Tokyo, how city people were traveling to the country and selling precious heirlooms, priceless gold-threaded kimonos and jewels, for a few handfuls of rice. He said the war would be over soon and he would be coming home. That was the last time they saw him."

"I don't suppose she knows any of his colleagues, where they might have ended up?"

The sister shook her head, no. "She says if she had, she would have married one. Her brother always promised he would find her a husband."

They rose to leave. "Tell her she's still very beautiful, it's not too late." The woman cackled and pushed herself out of her chair. "Please come again," she said.

Piper and Kyoko walked through the gate, a kitsch version of a Shinto portal, and headed back up the road.

"Drat," said Kyoko. "I forgot to give her the fruit. Now I've got to lug it back down this mountain."

"That's okay, she didn't need it," Piper said. "And maybe it's an omen. Maybe we'll find a live one at our next stop."

The sun had sunk behind the hills that shadowed Tataki, and they moved quickly toward the forest path.

9

*L*ittle more than a fading fishing port clinging to the rocky eastern coast, Kuji seemed a metropolis after the village of Tataki. They arrived after noon the next day, by a circuitous route that was nonetheless the fastest: back from Hiraizumi on the local train, then farther up the spine of the island on the express, and finally back down the coast on another oft-stopping local.

The night had fallen short, as usual, of Piper's fantasies. Tripping down the forest path behind a pensive Kyoko, Piper had imagined that they might find a quiet country inn where they could soak their tired muscles in the local waters—effective, his guidebook promised, against bilious conditions, neuralgia and menstrual ache—and drink some local sake. And then, who knew? Perhaps this would be the night when Kyoko, deep in the night, would slide open the papered door of his room, slip underneath his warm quilt, unwrap her thin yukata and turn the warmth of her body toward him, her soft black hair in the darkness caressing his chest, her long smooth legs against his. . . .

But when they reached the bus shelter, Kyoko had formulated a different plan. They would briefly visit Chuson-ji, the temple that was all that remained of the once-great capital of Hiraizumi. And then they would return as far as Ichinoseki and, before proceeding northward, find one of those cheap western-style business hotels ubiquitous and identical throughout Japan, where the entire room would be premanufactured from a single piece of molded plastic, inserted into a faceless block of a building and equipped with every essential for the traveling Japanese salesman: a cube of a bathtub into which Piper could never fold himself, a narrow single bed over which his feet would flop, an electric water heater for green tea, a cellophane-wrapped toothbrush with a tiny tube of foully sweet apricot toothpaste and a twelve-inch television set for viewing pornographic movies.

"I can't sleep on the floor tonight," she said, as if to dismiss his unspoken proposal to find a romantic inn. "I need a bed. I need civilization."

Piper sighed. He knew better by now than to try to enlist Kyoko in an adventure for which she had no enthusiasm. "Japanese youth is going soft," he said. "Too many burgers and comfortable chairs."

"You sound like my mother," she said. "She says I can't even kneel the right way."

And yet Chuson-ji was more magical than he could have dreamed. They arrived too late: the temple grounds were closed. But a bright moon shone, and they sidestepped the gate to hike up a long, sweeping footpath lined by towering cryptomeria trees. This was the Moon-Viewing Slope, and indeed the moon seemed to follow them as their feet crunched on the pebbled path, their shadows preceding them up the hill and sometimes up the ancient trunks. They passed hoary outer temple buildings, a shuttered tea shop, the old wooden home of some monks. From inside one thatched-roof temple they could hear a monk chanting. Two others, with shaved heads and long robes and wooden sandals, glided by without a glance; it was as if Kyoko and Piper had been transported back, invisible, into the past.

The jewel of the temple grounds was closed to them. The Konjiki-do Hall, entirely covered in gold, so ornate it had inspired jealousy in Kyoto centuries before, had been moved inside a fireproof building, open to tourists and pilgrims only during daylight hours. So they walked on, and found themselves finally in front of a simple outdoor stage, built of wood and roofed with thatch. A backdrop of a faded pine, painted decades or centuries before, seemed to come to life and twist toward them in the moonlight.

They hoisted themselves onto the stage and dangled their legs over, the faded pine behind them lit by the ghostly spotlight of the moon. The silvery leaves of a bamboo thicket shimmered in the mild summer breeze where an audience once might have sat. A small animal darted through the underbrush and still, very far off, the monk chanted and struck his bell.

"Yoshitsune might have hidden right here, not knowing who was coming, not knowing whom to trust," Piper said softly. "I wonder why he didn't just keep going, farther north, away from all of them, into the wilderness."

"This must have seemed like a huge, wild country in those days," Kyoko said. "He wandered for months in his monk's disguise, and his brother's soldiers never found him."

"Until he made the mistake of coming here."

"Well, it wasn't a mistake at first," she said. "The lord of Hiraizumi, who had helped raise him, did protect him. But the lord was old, and when he died, it was the son who lost courage and gave in to Yoritomo." She pulled her legs beneath her to sit cross-legged on the stage. "You know the story of the faithful retainer who was so loyal that he beat his master Yoshitsune?"

"Sounds very Japanese," Piper said. "Tell me." In fact, Piper knew the famous story well enough, but was happy to keep Kyoko's deep velvety voice washing over him along with the moonlight.

"They were running from his evil brother, and they were exhausted, when they came to another barrier set up by Yoritomo's soldiers," Kyoko said. "This one was manned by the smartest and toughest soldier yet, Lord Togashi. To fool the guards, Yoshitsune pretended to be a servant, and his servant, Benkei, pretended to be the monk. They had almost made it through, when one of the guards noticed that the servant looked very much like Yoshitsune. At that moment Benkei started beating Yoshitsune for being too slow, figuring that the guards would never believe a servant would dare hit a real samurai, even in disguise."

"And it worked."

"Well, in a way," Kyoko said. "Lord Togashi understood what was going on, but he was so moved by Benkei's loyalty, and by the agony it must have caused him, that he let them through."

"The agony of beating up his master, you mean?" Piper said.

"Right," she said. "You can imagine how painful that must have been. At least I can." She smiled at him.

"I'm sure," Piper said. "And cutting off my head after I disemboweled myself? Would you do that for me?"

"Of course. And burn up your family, too. I like you a lot."

"That's the thing about other cultures," Piper said. "You just have to learn to read those little signposts."

They fell silent. The monk had stopped chanting, at least for now, and all they heard was the whispery rustling of bamboo leaves. "Have you ever been in love?" Piper had never dared ask before.

Kyoko cocked her head, looked at her fingers. "I thought I was once," she said slowly. "At Maryland. But it turned out he didn't think so, and afterward I wondered whether I could have been." She looked at Piper. "Do you think all Americans, at some deep level, are prejudiced?"

"Why?"

"He once said he would always see me as an Oriental," Kyoko said. "Not that it was a minus, but just that he was always aware of it. It was during one of those late-night conversations in someone's dorm room when people say many foolish things. But still, I never forgot it."

"To me you're simply you," Piper said. "One of a kind."

"Thank you," she said quietly. After a moment she added, "But that wasn't the question."

"Well, do you think all Japanese are racist?"

"In some way, yes, I suppose so," Kyoko said. They were quiet again. A lone cloud raced past the moon. The monk resumed.

"What a life that must be," Piper said. "Who do you think that guy really is?"

"Oh, maybe the second son of a doctor from Nagoya, and his older brother inherited the father's hospital, and he didn't know what to do with himself," Kyoko said. "Or maybe he had a tragic love affair, and decided to forsake the material world."

"Or maybe he had a little art gallery in Manhattan, and sold it to come east and find his soul, and his parents are still wondering when he's going to give all this up and come home," Piper said.

"And will he?"

"Well, after a couple of winters here, I would guess you'd really start to miss a good deli."

"Ah."

Piper sensed he'd said something wrong again. But when an owl screeched nearby, they both started and found themselves holding each other. For a moment, they stayed that way, until what had felt natural began turning to embarrassment. Kyoko slid off the stage, and Piper noticed that for the first time in months he felt chilly. He pushed up with his arms and vaulted off the stage, too.

"I hope we don't get arrested on the way out of here," Kyoko said.

"Or kidnapped and have our heads shaved," Piper said. "I've heard there's a real monk shortage these days."

Kyoko took his arm as they walked back down the path. "I think you'd look very distinguished," she said. His whole body tingled at her touch, and her sweet smell mixed with the fragrance of the pines, and he let himself float away again on his dreams.

But the rest of the night had been less magical. Piper had folded himself into his little plastic tub and brushed his teeth with the foul apricot toothpaste. He had studied the cigarette burns in his room's thin carpeting and bought a can of Sapporo beer from a vending machine in the corridor. On his tiny television he had watched pudgy, small-breasted Japanese women with stringy hair being hurt in various ways. Then, disgusted with himself, he had slept poorly, worrying about rising early enough to pay for his room before Kyoko came downstairs and saw the movie charge on his bill.

And so here they were in Kuji, and he was tired, and they couldn't find Kawamura. They had tried the police, the telephone office and the local courthouse, and had just finished quizzing, out of desperation, a few taxi drivers lounging outside the station.

"I don't know how else to look," Kyoko said. They were taking a break in a Dunkin' Donuts. Gourmet civilization had penetrated even to Kuji, Piper thought.

"Maybe we should head down the coast, do a travel piece and go home," Piper said. "We can't get away with spending money on this much longer." South of Kuji were some rocky headlands and piney islands much revered by Japanese tourists, although Piper was sure that, as usual, they wouldn't compare to Maine or California on a bad day. At Matsushima was one of Japan's Three Famous Views. Almost every location in Japan boasted one of Japan's Three Most Beautiful Gardens, or Three Most Shapely Rocks, or Three Most Famous Locations at Which Basho Wrote Poems, and tour groups of elderly Japanese, once told how a particular sight fitted into the pantheon, were always suitably impressed, no matter how many smokestacks or piles of trash or concrete pilings seemed to Piper to compromise the Beautiful View. The real purpose of tourism, after all, was the drinking and bathing, and more drinking, and no one was going to spoil things by failing to gasp and cluck at whatever wonders had to be endured along the way. Piper, needless to say, accepted and perpetuated the domestic propaganda whenever he filed for his travel section, because his editors would certainly not publish, let alone pay expenses for, a piece that, for example, compared the Japanese coastline unfavorably to an industrial development zone in Newport News. On those rare occasions when he allowed himself to entertain an ethical qualm for urging his readers to visit such places, he would reassure himself that none of his readers could afford to come anyway, and that if they could, they should have had the sense to visit Tahiti instead. And that if they didn't have the sense, they probably deserved to be visiting Japan's Third Oldest Carp. Still, he lived in fear of confronting some hometown pensioner who had drawn down his retirement nest egg to visit Japan's Three Best Wooden Shelves on the recommendation of the *Sunday Advertiser* travel section, and was now prepared to pay for the advice with a shotgun.

"Still, I can't stop thinking that there may be a better story here than we know," Piper added.

"Like what?" Kyoko said dubiously. Piper spent much of his time concocting conspiracy theories involving Japan's corrupt politics and its designs for world domination, and Kyoko knew by now not to take them seriously. Besides, today she seemed tired, too.

"Well, look," Piper said. "Why would they not have told what's-her-name in Tataki how her brother died?"

"Like she said, because he was working on a secret project," Kyoko answered.

"Okay, he was working on a secret project, but how did he die? If he was killed in a bombing raid, why not say he was killed in a bombing raid while working on a secret project?" Piper said. "And as far as we know, the project ended when the lab was bombed in April. She didn't hear he was dead until October. Did he volunteer or get drafted for duty in the spring, like Okamoto implied? And if he did, and he died in Okinawa, or as a kamikaze, or at sea near the end of the war, why is that so secret?"

"Okay, what's your theory?"

"Well, maybe he really did die in the secret project," Piper said. "There was some kind of accident, and the government wanted to hush it up, and they've hushed it up ever since. Like in Nevada, or the Bikini atoll, where all those sheep and soldiers were exposed to radioactivity, and nobody knew for decades. That would be a pretty big story." Piper finished his coffee. "Maybe not Pulitzer material, but anyway something Christopher couldn't ignore."

"Maybe," Kyoko said. "But maybe there wasn't any secret at all. Maybe the government told his wife how he died, and she just never bothered to tell the sister, she was in such a hurry to clear out of that village. Or maybe he died of dysentery, and the government didn't want to admit that his unit existed, or that they hadn't had enough food."

"You are such a killjoy," Piper sighed. "You know, a good journalist has to have some imagination. Anyway, let's give it one more day."

And the next day they picked up a scent at the local high school. The school had been rebuilt after the war, but an old science teacher took them down to the basement, where were recorded, in beautiful calligraphy on pages half as tall as Piper, the names of all graduates who had enlisted or been drafted during the war. They found Kawamura's name without much trouble, and took a taxi to the address listed in the big book. Or tried to; when they reached the right block, they found the address itself no longer existed, having given way to a drab four-story office building of employment agencies, computer schools and cluttered head offices of little fishing companies. But in the block behind the new building, after meeting with a few blank stares, they found a grandmother who remembered the Kawamuras. They had owned a little grocery, she said, and when it had been knocked down, they invested the proceeds in another little grocery on the far side of the harbor. A strange couple, she added. The day they moved, as far as anyone knew, was the first time he'd been out of the house in years. Though certainly the wife was pleasant enough, who knew what kind of a life she'd led? The woman was still talking as Kyoko backed away, thanking and bowing.

Kyoko and Piper slid back into their waiting taxi and drove

through narrow streets and across narrower bridges, around the harbor. Here the streets seemed poorer and the houses tackier, painted in pastel colors that had faded and cracked and peeled in the cold sea wind like some cruel parody of a Mediterranean fishing village. Rusting fishing boats, dredging platforms and wide flat barges cluttered the harbor. Stopping several times to ask directions, the taxi driver finally pulled into a particularly barren lane and braked across from a corner store. A metal Coca-Cola sign, battered and washed out, hung over the door, and an old wooden bench stood in front. The windows were so dusty they might have been made of smoked glass. Kyoko again asked the driver to wait.

Inside, the little store was dimly lit but cleaner and better-stocked than Piper had imagined. A refrigerator case held plastic packages of udon noodles, cucumber pickles, slices of processed cheese, rolled crab sushi. There was a rack of thick comic books, a shelf of dried seaweed, big tins of cooking oil. A calendar on the wall with a girl in a bathing suit was three years out of date.

No one responded to Kyoko's polite, "Excuse me." Behind the tattered brown curtain that screened the store from the living quarter, a television voice chattered, and someone rustled about. Piper picked up one of the comic books, which fell open to a drawing of a large-breasted woman, naked but for a chain around her waist, manacled to a dungeon wall. Several leering gangsters smeared honey between her legs and then turned loose some kind of giant reptile with a prodigious tongue. The woman writhed in what seemed a combination of agony and intense pleasure. Piper was wondering why the Japan Society in New York never exhibited this sort of culture, instead of ethereal calligraphy and ivory carvings, when he heard the curtain being pushed aside, and he quickly closed the comic book. A bony elderly woman in a dark kimono nodded to Kyoko and then gave out a startled "Ah!" when she spotted Piper. While she stood, mouth agape, at the curtain, Piper noticed with surprise that the room behind her was at the same level as the store, and floored in linoleum, not tatami. Then he saw that behind the woman was a white-haired man in a wheelchair, facing away from the door, with a blanket across his legs and a newspaper on the blanket.

The woman recovered quickly, bowed slightly to Piper and walked behind the counter.

"Actually," Kyoko said in Japanese that Piper could understand, "we're not looking for groceries. We are looking for Dr. Bun Kawamura."

This time the woman's double take was nothing like her brief surprise upon seeing a tall foreigner in her store. Piper thought he could literally see the blood drain from her thin face. She looked at Kyoko, then looked toward the curtain, then looked back at Piper.

"How do you know Bun Kawamura?" she asked in a hoarse whisper.

Kyoko explained their search, their interest in the atomic bomb project, their desire to find some of the talented young scientists who had helped Nishina. The woman seemed only to half-listen. "Bun Kawamura was my brother-in-law," she replied. "But he died"— literally, "became no more," the Japanese equivalent of "passed away"—"in the war."

Piper cursed under his breath. When Kyoko translated what he had already understood, he said, "I just can't believe it. Why can't any of these damn physicists stay alive?" Sensing his anger, the woman took on the look of a hunted rabbit, as if Piper were about to confirm her worst fears about uncontrollable, unpredictable gai-jin. "Ask how he died," he muttered.

Kyoko translated the question for the woman, who had been looking from one to the other as they spoke in English, watching their mouths with concern but no apparent comprehension. Now she looked like a rabbit about to have a coronary, and for a long moment she didn't answer at all.

"Well, he died in the war, right at the end of the war," she said finally. "It was a long time ago. He was a very young man. Nobody has come here for him in a long time. How did you find us? Our store used to be on the other side of town, but a man offered us good money, he kept coming and pestering us until we finally said yes, although really I had no desire to move. You have me a bit flustered, I'm sorry—"

Suddenly, the curtain yanked open. The man in the wheelchair silenced the storekeeper with a glare and said, also in Japanese, "The man you are asking about was my brother. Please forgive my stupid wife's foolishness." He nodded toward the old woman. "My brother died in a bombing attack, when his laboratory burned down."

While Kyoko translated, the storekeeper bowed hurriedly and slipped past the wheelchair, disappearing again into the back room. The man paid no notice. He had a great white head, bushy white eybrows, fiercely intelligent eyes and big, strong, veined hands that now pushed his wheelchair a few yards into the store.

"When was that?" Piper asked. The man also watched their mouths as they spoke English. Kyoko translated and the man said, "In April of the war's final year. Showa 20."

"I thought no one died in that fire," Piper said, more to Kyoko than as a question. But she said, "I thought so too," and spoke in Japanese. This time the man answered at greater length, but Piper could understand. Unlike the old farm woman in Tataki, he seemed to speak standard Japanese.

"He said maybe we know more than he does, he can only tell us what he was told after the war," Kyoko translated. "He was at sea when his brother died, and took a fragment of an American bomb in his spine, which is why you see him like this, he said. So he said you should please forgive him if the details are wrong."

"I just can't believe it," Piper said again, more exasperated than doubting. "We've wasted the whole goddam week. And something about it just doesn't feel right." He absent-mindedly reopened the comic book while Kyoko and the man in the wheelchair waited awkwardly. A sensitive-looking hero with round, Caucasian eyes and dark hair had crashed through a window of the dungeon to rescue the chained big-breasted woman, and was doing battle with the reptile while she watched. It wasn't clear whom she was rooting for.

"Why is it so important to you how my brother died?" the man in the wheelchair asked softly.

"Explain our theory," Piper said.

"*Our* theory?" said Kyoko.

"Okay, my theory," Piper said. "Maybe he knows how to find his brother's colleagues."

Kyoko told the man that they were beginning to wonder whether the government had covered something up. They had been to see a professor who had worked on the same team, and he had told them that no one died in the fire, yet the government told Kawamura that his brother perished there, Kyoko said. Then, another member of the team, she explained, a man named Hashimoto, had died, but his sister didn't know how, and she wasn't notified until two months after the war ended.

The man listened with half-closed eyes, his big hands resting in his lap. When Kyoko finished, he made no comment. After a moment Piper pressed further. "Look, tell him that maybe he could find the truth now, if he pushed. It's been decades. If the guy's own brother asked how he died, maybe they'd tell him now." Kyoko translated, and the man appeared to consider what she had said. He started to talk, then stopped, closed his eyes, and was quiet again.

Then suddenly he was wheeling himself along the narrow shop aisle, and braking with a jerk, the chair just grazing Piper's legs. Up close, he looked stronger than Piper had imagined, and he spoke with startling intensity, staring up into Piper's eyes and continuing to stare as Kyoko translated, so that Piper couldn't shift his gaze away.

"He says he doesn't believe in troubling the dead," Kyoko said. "He says he had two brothers. One of them came back, one didn't, and he himself came back half a man. He says he doesn't blame your country, and he doesn't blame his own. That's just how things happen. He says you can only get people hurt by stirring up old trouble. And he asked whether you'd like to buy anything today."

Piper looked at the man, started to reply, then stopped. He slid the comic back onto the rack and said to Kyoko, "No, I don't think I need anything today. Let's go." To the man, he said in English, "Sorry to have bothered you." From his perch of metal and rubber the man watched them leave.

Outside, a few seagulls wheeled overhead. The taxi driver was leaning against his car, having a smoke and chatting with a young man in a business suit. A large tanker of some kind was sliding across the little slice of harbor they could see at the bottom of the street.

Piper and Kyoko crossed to their cab, where both men tossed their cigarettes onto the ground. The younger man sauntered off and the driver slid behind the wheel. He had left the engine idling, and the car was still cool inside.

"Where to?" he asked Kyoko, eyeing her in the rearview mirror.

"The station," Piper said glumly. "And on to Tokyo." As the driver put the car in gear, Piper thought for an instant that he saw a face floating high in the dusty window of the store. But when he lowered the cab window and looked again, there was nothing behind that murky glass.

"Now what do you think?" Piper said. "One dies after the war, the other in a bombing that didn't kill anybody. And the brother practically throws us out when we suggest he might want to find the truth. Tell me that's not suspicious."

"Okay, it's not suspicious," Kyoko said. "At least there are logical explanations, including the one he gave you, which I know it would be against your principles to believe." They both winced as the taxi pulled into the lane of oncoming traffic to get around a bus. "Anyway, what if you're right, and they died mysteriously. How do you propose to find out about it?"

"I don't know," Piper said. "Let's head back. I'm sure you'll think of something on the train."

Piper leaned back against the taxi's lacy antimacassar. Through his mind drifted wheelchairs, peasant women with double chins, rough-tongued reptiles, samurai families going up in flames. And no physicists. Damn! Three days on the road, and nothing to show. He'd have to come up with a pretty creative explanation to satisfy the bookkeepers back home about this one.

10

*P*iper took his first breath of Tokyo night air, so hot and dirty that it singed his throat, and felt he had never been away. He had taken the subway around from Ueno Station, all its windows open to allow the hot tunnel wind to rush through, a pool of vomit at the feet of one sleeping drunk. A heavy-set girl in black fishnet stockings had sat next to Piper and promptly dozed off. Her head would sink slowly toward his shoulder, her slightly oily hair coiling on his shirt, until her cheek grazed him and she would jerk upward, only to begin her neck-wrenching descent again. As he sat on that noisy subway car, surrounded by tired commuters avoiding each other's eyes, he thought of the *Time* magazine bureau chief, with his car and driver, and of Christopher, who took taxis everywhere and liked to drop little jokes about his ignorance of the Tokyo subway system. Ah, but would Piper trade his sense of the real Tokyo in exchange for that kind of luxury? In a *second,* he thought, as the sleeping girl's hair began to brush his shoulder again. Piper abruptly stood, and the girl opened her eyes in alarm, straightened, and then dozed off again.

So it was when he emerged from his subway station at Yotsuya-sanchome that he gulped his first breath of acrid Tokyo air. By now the only vehicles on the street were taxis, hundreds of them, their meters shining red and green as they lined up in front of hostess bars and clubs waiting for one last, long ride to the sub-urbs. Piper carried his bag down a quieter street to his building and up two flights to his flat, flung open the window to exchange stale air for staler and then peered into his waist-high refrigerator: some bread, a jar of peanut butter, a container of sour-smelling milk. He shut the refrigerator and punched rewind on his tele-phone-answering machine. Marianne from the *Globe* had called to ask whether he was filing anything from the Foreign Ministry briefing, and if so, what; that must have been Tuesday. His Japanese teacher wondered why he missed class Wednesday; he'd forgotten to tell her he would be away. There was nothing from the home office. That was reassuring, but not sufficient; they only resorted to the telephone in desperate emergencies.

And in fact, at the office the next morning a sheaf of yellow telexes lay ominously atop the mound of his desk. One look at Kyoko was enough to tell him that none contained news of a raise. This time, without asking, he leafed through them. The first, from the foreign editor, instructed him not to take the trip north. The second inquired about the status of the requested piece on auto trade. The third wanted to know how he was coming on the A-bomb anniversary piece. The fourth, from the business editor, thanked him for the outlooker on the Japanese economy, and asked whether he would mind "filling in a few holes," which, as Piper scanned the message, seemed to entail gathering enough new statistics and quotes to fill an almanac. Then a curt message inquired why he hadn't responded to the earlier messages, and the features desk asked him to file eight or ten inches on pet burials in Japan and Korea for a roundup on animal funeral practices around the world. Piper actually had once visited a temple in western Tokyo, where thousands of little cubbyholes lined a circular crypt, each containing the ashes of a cat or dog and, leaning against the tiny urns, flowers or snapshots of the pets in sunnier days.

But Piper was in no mood to be filing features on pet cemeteries. He had once filed a story about a dog-meat restaurant in Seoul where a patron, looking for the men's room, had opened the wrong door, inadvertently freeing a prospective entrée, who proceeded to take a bite out of the customer instead of the other way around. The patron had then filed suit. Piper had been quite pleased with himself to have found an antidote to the hoary adage that man bites dog is news, but dog bites man isn't. His editors, though, deemed the article in poor taste, as it were, and spiked it.

Now he looked through the telexes once more, growing more and more despondent. One by one, he crumpled them into small yellow balls and tossed them, over his shoulder, into the corner, missing the wastebasket each time.

"Shouldn't you save those questions from Financial?" Kyoko said.

"The hell with Financial," Piper said. "Have I told you before that we're too good for these people?"

"Yes," Kyoko said.

"But now you believe me, right?"

"What are you going to tell them about this trip? We're out about eighty thousand yen," she said.

"How about this," Piper said. "We'll get married, quit this rag and go run a weekly paper in a small town in Alaska. And I'll swallow the eighty thousand."

"I don't like cold weather," Kyoko said.

"I'm flexible," Piper said. "How about Guam?"

"And what about this trade story?" Kyoko went on. "The Toyota people sent us a fax while we were gone."

"I'll bet," Piper said. "Look, this nuclear thing could be our biggest story ever. First, that they were working on a bomb at all—that's going to surprise people. And now this cover-up—how did these people die? When we figure that out, none of this other stuff"—he pointed toward the yellow balls scattered around the wastebasket—"will mean anything."

"So what do you want to do?"

"Let's call your gangster in Osaka and see what he found out, and then we'll send a message home explaining what we're onto," Piper said. "If we use nice, simple language, maybe they'll understand."

"He's not a gangster. And, he called already," Kyoko said. "Right after I got in this morning."

"And?"

"He said he finally tracked Inoki down yesterday. He died in the war."

"Of course," Piper said. "How?"

"Well, Shunichi didn't find out," Kyoko said. "He thought we wanted to talk to the man, and if he wasn't around, we wouldn't care about anything else. After I explained, he said he'd try to go back and get more."

"In the meantime I think Sato is our best bet," Piper said. "What? What's that look for?"

"Well, if there really was a cover-up, don't you think the Foreign

Ministry would do everything they can to keep it quiet?" Kyoko said. "If there was a cover-up."

"Sato isn't the Foreign Ministry," Piper said. "He's different. He really believes in this peace-and-harmony jazz, and he doesn't lie. Whether he would actually want the truth out, I don't know. But it's worth a try. If we can make him curious, that's half the battle." To himself, Piper too wondered whether Sato could be trusted. Even if he was honest, he was a bureaucrat, and he was Japanese. Would even he break ranks? But Piper had a simple reason for trusting Sato: he didn't know where else to turn. Having headed the Foreign Ministry bureau in charge of U.S.-Japan defense relations, Sato had good contacts in the Japanese Self-Defense Agency and could inquire, if he chose, through unofficial channels.

Piper decided it would be best to visit in person; he would stop by his office casually, as he often did, after the Friday briefing for foreign reporters at the ministry. In the meantime, while Kyoko sorted through a mountain of mail and newspapers that had arrived while they were gone, he spent the morning making calls on Japan's economy and the auto trade. He chatted with someone at the trade ministry, with a Toyota public affairs man, with a couple of auto analysts at brokerage firms, and then quickly typed up sixteen inches that roughly replicated Christopher's story. The humiliation of chasing Christopher yet again stung less than usual; Piper was already savoring that front-page *New York Times* story that would have to credit the *Advertiser* after his A-bomb piece came out.

With the article he included a message describing their progress thus far. "The cream of Japan's young generation of physicists seems to have been mysteriously wiped out near the end of the war," he wrote. Hyping a story was essential to getting on the front page, but hyping the story description ahead of time was even more essential; otherwise, when the actual story hit their desks, the editors would boot the piece to the financial section without glancing any further than the Tokyo dateline.

"How they died, we are still investigating," Piper continued. "But they were all tied in some way to a secret and mysterious Japanese effort to build an atomic bomb first, and force America to its knees.

More soon." That ought to get someone's attention, he thought, feeling pleased with his efforts.

On the subway to Kasumigaseki, home to most government ministries, Piper tried to tote up the number of subway rides he had not yet submitted for expense reimbursement. They cost about a dollar apiece, and he couldn't afford to let them go, but he never remembered to keep track. His first expense account had been rejected because he hadn't submitted receipts for all the subway rides. Since you had to hand in your ticket before returning to street level, this had been something of a setback. But Piper soon realized that any scrap of paper with Japanese writing and a number at the bottom could serve as a receipt, and he began collecting dry-cleaning bills, advertisements for palmists, labels from condom packages. For some reason, he never actually cheated the company; he made sure the total of receipts about matched his expenses. And his creativity was only called upon because he was saving the company money, he reasoned; Christopher, who took taxis and ate in fine restaurants, certainly never had trouble collecting genuine receipts. If the *Times* even bothered to ask, Piper thought. But Piper wasn't sure Accounting would be impressed by the morality of his position if they ever hired someone who could puzzle out the Chinese characters of the documents in his expense account file.

He resurfaced on a street shaded by cherry trees, their leaves hanging low in the humidity, and turned into the Foreign Ministry parking lot. A guard watched sullenly. Piper had noticed that even the outside guard seemed able to tell who was important enough to merit a salute, and who could be safely snubbed. Inside, he flashed his ID and rode to the third floor.

In the briefing room, the proceedings had just begun; several East European reporters were already napping. The briefer was a high-level bureaucrat who had studied in Cologne and spoke English with a heavy Teutonic accent. In the best of circumstances he would not have been a scintillating speaker, and the Foreign Ministry did not provide the best of circumstances. Despite being, by some measures, the richest country on earth, Japan seemed to take pride in outfitting itself with the shoddiest, dingiest, most overcrowded government offices this side of Calcutta. Working sixteen hours a day wasn't enough punishment; to satisfy their sense of devotion and suffering,

Japanese functionaries had to work sixteen hours a day in the most unpleasant conditions. Gunmetal desks were crammed by the dozen into rooms with walls of peeling paint, and if the rooms had windows, they hadn't been washed since the war. The briefing room, as a concession to the surly press, was equipped with an air conditioner, but the machine was such an antique that it took up most of one wall and operated with the noise efficiency of a propeller plane, so that it had to be turned off as soon as the briefing began or the Teuton became utterly unintelligible. On days when a television network brought its cameras and bright lights in an almost certainly fruitless quest for news, the room quickly heated to sauna levels.

Perhaps as a result, facts were not the essential currency of these twice-a-week briefings. These were, in any case, forums for the second-stringers, the journalists from countries and newspapers that didn't rank at the top of that rigid hierarchy that every Japanese carried inside his head. The *New York Times*, after all, could pick up the phone and talk to somebody important anytime, and so Christopher rarely turned out for this circus. But if the *Advertiser,* or the Mideast News Service, or Tass, wanted a quote, they had to come here. And so the sessions often turned into bizarre sparring matches during which the Teutonic briefer, speaking with painful slowness, did everything he could to avoid making news, while a bureau chief from Pakistan, say, asked a dozen questions in a vain effort to elicit something new on Japanese-Pakistani relations. To make the punishment more humiliating, the Teuton often began the sessions by reading aloud, and slowly, four or five press releases the reporters had received and discarded days before, on a new humanitarian grant to Panama, a new Japanese-funded hydroelectric project in Bangladesh, on the foreign minister's mealy-mouthed response to the latest world crisis, in which the minister wished for negotiation, hoped to avoid bloodshed and assiduously managed not to offend either side.

Piper slipped through a door at the back and slid behind one of the schoolboy desks next to Marianne. Sometimes he came to these sessions for sport, to goad the Teuton with questions implying a certain gutlessness or selfishness on the part of Japanese foreign policy. "What does it say about your country that you've accepted fewer Vietnamese boat people than any other developed nation, including many that are smaller and less wealthy than Japan?" Piper would say. The Teuton would flip frantically through his briefing book for the boat-people page and then deliver a long, tortured defense of Japan's refugee policy. At which point Piper would nod and say thank you, knowing that any number of rabidly anti-Japanese reporters from France and Italy could be counted on to continue the battle, challenging the Teuton's defense with red-faced moral indignation, and in accents the Teuton found even more difficult to decipher, thus heightening the potential for wounded feelings and dangerous misunderstanding.

But today Piper wanted a quote to pad out his Japanese economy piece. If the Teuton would comment on the strength of Japan's economy, Piper could attribute it to a high Japanese official, without mentioning the briefing, and his desk would think he'd bagged a big interview. So he asked his question politely, and the Teuton, warily, as if waiting for the question to explode, answered as expected. Quote in hand, Piper slumped back in his seat as a wire-service reporter returned, as someone did each week these days, to the X-bill.

Marianne slipped him a note. "Very respectful question—what got into you?" Piper wrote back, "I've decided I'm never going to win a Pulitzer, so I'm shooting for a Grand Cordon of the Chrysanthemum." Marianne wrote back, *"Gambatte!"*—Japan's favorite word: try hard, don't give up, persevere.

Piper had gone out with Marianne Healy a few times when they were both new in Japan. They had slept together a few times, with such lack of passion that, without discussion, they had simply stopped. Then they became good friends, who could commiserate together, swapping horror stories about ignorant editors and the slights they shared in Tokyo as correspondents for second-tier newspapers in a city obsessed by first-tier. Now, they agreed by note to have dinner together the following night. Then she leaned over and whispered, "I can't take this anymore. See you." The Teuton, for the hundredth time and as insincerely as the first, was expressing his faith that Congress would not act unwisely.

After the briefing, Piper gossiped with a few other reporters and then slipped away from the group to Sato's office. In the cluttered room where Sato and his staff functioned, all together in one open space in the Japanese tradition, the chief was asleep, feet on his desk, head back, mouth open. Piper sat at an empty desk and waited as Sato's underlings, who adored their boss, tiptoed about and lunged for the phone at the first ring. This wasn't the first time Piper had found Sato in such a position. During times of intense negotiations with Washington—what seemed like crises to Japan, barely noticed quarrels to the United States—Sato would work around the clock, subsisting on fifteen-minute catnaps and black coffee, briefing the prime minister or the foreign minister, then rushing off to confer with counterparts in other ministries, trying to prod them toward compromise. In the increasingly frequent confrontations, the rest of the government viewed the Foreign Ministry as weaseling accommodationists, but Sato maintained the respect of other ministries, perhaps because they too sensed his sincerity, a quality, Piper thought, as prized in Japan as it was rare. Though probably no rarer here than in any government. In any case, it was his sincerity that often got Sato in trouble with his superiors, who knew they couldn't do without him and resented him for exactly that reason. To have one person stick out as Sato did, even for his usefulness, upset the Japanese system, and it was even more upsetting that Sato didn't pretend to be any less smart than he was. Piper always felt they would cut Sato down to size someday.

After about ten minutes, just as Piper felt himself sliding into a snooze, Sato sat up and swung his legs off his desk. An aide whispered to him and Sato looked over to Piper and welcomed him with a big smile. "Hi, John!"

"Thanks for the other night, Tsuyoshi," Piper said.

"Oh, please," Sato said. "I'm sorry for wasting your time." They both knew, however, that it was Sato's time that was truly at a premium, and the bureaucrat looked a bit pained when Piper asked if he could spare a few minutes. "It's a bad time, John," he said. "You know the telecommunications talks start up again tomorrow."

These days, as relations deteriorated, each round of supposedly crucial trade talks followed the next, almost without a break. The Americans would bluster, congressmen with campaign contributions at stake would threaten, editorialists would warn of the dark storm clouds of war. And then, at the last moment—at least until recently—there would be an agreement, presented as a victory for the

American side but really not changing much. The Americans would forget about the whole affair, moving on to the next battle, and the Japanese would go back to beating the pants off American industry.

Of all the players in the drama, Sato alone seemed not to have a cynical view. He viewed each negotiation as a powder keg, the one that could ignite a trade war, or worse, and he never believed agreement was preordained. And maybe without Sato the outcomes would have been different; Piper couldn't say. Certainly, both sides seemed to have exhausted their post–World War 2 goodwill. Each agreement came with more name-calling, more vitriol, more bitterness. And if the X-bill became law, all bets were off.

But today Piper really wanted to talk to Sato, and he didn't care about the telecommunications talks, which he had never understood anyway. "It's important," he said.

"Okay," Sato sighed. "Let's get a cup of coffee."

In the ministry's dreary coffee shop, they ordered iced coffees as Piper explained what he was up to, and the help he needed. When he finished, Sato shook his head and gave Piper a long look.

"John, John, John," he said finally. "Why are you doing this? You know it can only make things worse."

"It's not my job to worry about making things worse or better, you know that," Piper said. "My job is to write about how things are."

"Oh, please, I know all that," Sato said. "But what does this have to do with 'how things are'? Something that happened so long ago! Things are bad enough—if Congress goes ahead with this latest scheme, I honestly don't know what will happen. So why dredge up some obscure wartime project now? Maybe it's true, maybe Japan did try to build an atomic bomb. So what? We did not build it, in fact. And you dropped the bomb on us, not the other way around! Twice! And ever since, we've sworn we would never allow nuclear weapons on our soil. We've borne witness to the horrors of nuclear war, and we've stayed true to our pledge. So which is more important?"

"I'm not saying this is more important, Tsuyoshi," Piper said. "I'm just saying it's an interesting piece of history that people don't know about."

"Fine, fine. If relations were normal right now, maybe people would take it that way," Sato said. "But these days, if you write

about a Japanese bomb, people won't treat it as some curious historical footnote. They will forget about our peace constitution, and they
will take it as one more sign of our sneaky, aggressive nature. Why
should you want to cause that kind of damage?"

"I don't think it would necessarily cause damage at all," Piper
said. "It would show how Japan has changed, how far it's come—I
think it could make you look really good. Not that I'm writing it for
that reason."

"Please, John," Sato said. "You once told me you used that line
with the mothers of murderers, to get them to talk about their sons.
So don't try it on me."

Piper laughed. "I never should have told you," he said. "Look,
maybe you're right. But what about this cover-up? How come none
of their relatives know how these young scientists died? If they
covered up some kind of nuclear accident, wouldn't you admit that
was a legitimate story?"

"I cannot believe it's true, John," Sato said. "Think about it. By
the end of the war we couldn't build planes, we couldn't build trucks,
we couldn't even build guns. We were equipping children with
wooden sticks! How could there have been a nuclear accident?"

"Well, then, how do you explain these guys disappearing?" Piper
said. "One dies in a bombing that we know didn't kill anybody.
Another doesn't get reported until two months after the war, and his
sister has no idea how he died. You don't think that's strange?"

"Everything was strange in those days, John," Sato said. "You
and I can't imagine it, looking at Japan today. Orphaned children
wandered the streets hacking with tuberculosis. People slept on
rubble where their houses had been, and dug through the wreckage
to find a photograph, or a spoon or two. When the emperor tried to
surrender, there was nearly a civil war right here in Tokyo. You
know all that. So why is it so strange if a notification of death letter
went out in October?"

"So you won't help?"

Sato sighed. "What do you want me to do, John?"

"Just check the records at the defense agency about these three
guys, how they died, and when," Piper said. "That's all—nothing
classified."

Sato smiled. "We don't have 'Classified,' you know that," he said.

"We are a peaceful nation." He called for another coffee. "Look, I'll tell you what. I'll find out about your three physicists, on one condition."

Piper nodded. "I know I'll regret this. What condition?"

"If there was some kind of cover-up, as you say, you do whatever you feel you have to do," Sato said. "But if these young men died like everyone else, blown up or sunk or shot in the war, and all you have is this ancient, forgotten, halfhearted bomb project, you'll forget the whole thing."

"How do you know it was halfhearted?" Piper said. "But okay. If there's no cover-up, no story. I'll go to Hiroshima and do another damn piece of bullshit antinuclear propaganda."

"Why is it bullshit?" Sato looked hurt. "We are the first great power in history not to back up our economic might with military muscle. Don't you think that's remarkable? Why don't you write about that?"

"Don't get started, Tsuyoshi," Piper said. "I don't want to get blamed for the next trade war, so you better go prepare for the telecommunications talks." He gave Sato the names and hometowns of the three physicists plus, for good measure, Yamada and Kawamura's wounded brother, whom they had met in the grocery. "How soon do you think you can check?"

"I'll do it as quickly as I can," Sato said.

Piper picked up the bill, and they headed for the cash register at the door. As he left the building, he thought: Kyoko won't believe this. He had always told her that no self-respecting reporter would ever make a deal with an official for information, and now he had given away the store. But Sato had that effect on him, always convincing him while they were together. Only later would Piper begin remembering the other side.

In any case, Piper thought, we'll find out how these guys died.

Outside, the heat was abating, and Piper decided to walk back to the office. The parking lot was full of cars with diplomatic license tags, supplicants of one sort or another to the great power Japan had become. Piper saluted the surly guard, left the compound and headed uphill, past a right-winger's sound truck draped with the rising sun and playing scratchy recordings of martial music from the days of the Great Pacific War.

Beyond the ministries, Piper passed a luxury hotel, a Volvo dealer, the Soviet tourist office, deserted as always, a Swiss fondu restaurant, a pottery store. Another Friday evening, and Roppongi was beginning to come alive. Piper's thoughts turned to Kyoko.

Back at the office he recounted his conversation with Sato, as she listened without comment. "Aren't you going to needle me?" Piper said.

"Needle?"

"Give me a hard time," Piper explained. "For compromising our ethics."

"No," Kyoko said. "Maybe Sato's right. Like Okamoto said, who's going to care about this ancient history, anyway?"

"Thanks," Piper said. "Now I feel as though I caved in to Sato and Okamoto, too."

He settled down at his computer to "fill in a few holes" for the business editor. After a few minutes Kyoko wished him a good weekend and left. It wasn't until she was out the door that Piper realized she hadn't ducked into the bathroom for her usual Friday night transformation. He rushed to the window for a glimpse, wondering whether he could spy anything from five floors up—the direction she chose, the attitude of her walk, whom, God forbid, she might be meeting—that might give some clue to the change in routine, some clue from which he could take heart. But before he could spin his usual chain reaction of unrealistic hopes and fantasies, the telephone rang. It was Zarsky.

"John, it was great to see you the other night," Zarsky said. "Just listening to you is an education. You really have a handle on this place!"

Piper didn't bother to reply. What the hell could Zarsky want now, he thought. It had been exactly a week since their drinking session. He couldn't possibly want to go out again, could he? Piper began formulating excuses in his mind.

"Listen, John, I was just wondering, have you ever taken money from the Japanese?"

"What do you mean?" Piper asked.

"I mean, would you ever take money for trips, or what have you, from the Foreign Ministry, or any of its foundations, that kind of thing?" Zarsky asked.

It was an odd question, Piper thought, since if anyone could be accused of improper behavior, it was Zarsky himself. He had financed his initial research, such as it was, with a grant from some Japanese-U.S. friendship association or other, one of many financed directly or indirectly by the Japanese government in its desperate hunt for friends in America. Ironically, when Zarsky's book came out, the chief complaint of many Japanese was not that he had bashed them, but that he had taken their money and hadn't stayed bought.

"Of course not," Piper said. "God knows my paper isn't overpaying me, but I haven't stooped that low yet. Why?"

"Oh," Zarsky said. "I was just checking. Working up a little piece on Japan's attempts to win friends and influence people back home, you know. I'm sure it's nothing you haven't already done, and better."

"Well, sorry I can't help you," Piper said.

"No, no, you've been a big help," Zarsky said. "Listen, we have to get together again sometime. Real soon, okay?"

"Absolutely," Piper said. "Give me a call."

He hung up and wondered again what Zarsky might be up to, and why he might be picking on Piper. But he couldn't come up with anything plausible, so he shook it off and turned back to his computer screen. "Japan's steel industry, written off only a few years ago as a certain victim of Korean competition, last year grew by—" Damn, where did that statistic go? Piper halfheartedly leafed through a stack of papers on the floor, and then leaned back with a sigh. He would be here all night, he could tell already, and there wasn't much to look forward to tomorrow. The A-bomb story seemed to be slipping through his fingers, the home office was going to be royally pissed off, and he wasn't really looking forward to another platonic Saturday night gripe session with Marianne. Yes, he thought, another weekend without Kyoko.

He turned back to the Japanese steel industry.

11

*H*e woke Saturday morning to the sound of Kyoko's voice, as he had so often in his dreams. This time, as he roused himself from a groggy, thick-headed sleep, he realized it wasn't a dream, though it wasn't exactly real, either. He had fallen asleep on the office couch, and someone had phoned, triggering her recorded message, in English and then Japanese, on the answering machine. Piper must have slept through the rings.

He propped himself up on the couch while the message played, making no move to grab the phone. Probably Zarsky again, he thought. On the floor, near the shoes he had kicked off sometime during the night, lay an empty milk carton and the bowl that had held his dinner, delivered by the local noodle store. A few noodles and what Piper thought of as congealed MSG had crusted on the blue-and-white china. As Kyoko shifted into Japanese, her voice rising a notch, Piper pushed himself to a sitting position and looked at his watch. Nearly noon. Well, he hadn't finished rewriting and sending the economic piece until nearly three and then, just as he was dropping off, the telex machine had begun to rattle. Piper hadn't checked the message, but he had kept himself awake imagining the bad news it might contain.

The machine beeped, and after a pause Piper heard a voice say, "Hello, John? This is Sato at the Foreign Ministry. I just wanted to—"

Piper lunged for the phone. "Tsuyoshi? It's me. Sorry. I was just walking into the office."

"Oh, I'm glad I caught you," Sato said. It would never occur to him that anyone might take Saturday off. "I checked into that matter we were discussing, and I wondered if you might want to get together sometime to talk about it."

"Sure. When?" Piper asked. Sato sounded odd, he thought. He wasn't usually so circumspect, or proper, on the telephone.

"Well, do you have any time today? Next week will be hellish for me," Sato said.

"Great! I'll come by your office."

"No, no," Sato said. "Why don't we . . . hold on." The phone was beeping. He must be at a booth, and his ten yen had run out. Piper waited while Sato dropped another coin into the machine.

"That message of yours uses up too much time," Sato grumbled. "Listen, you know Hibiya Park?"

Of course Piper knew Hibiya Park. It was at the heart of downtown, framed by the Imperial Hotel, the Health Ministry, the Nippon Press Center and the palace moat. Asking if he knew it was a bit like inquiring whether he could use chopsticks, or marveling that he liked sushi.

"Of course, of course you do," Sato said. "Well, you know the little pond on the Kasumigaseki side, with the crane fountain in the middle? There's a little arbor on the far side of the pond, with a bench. Let's meet there, okay?"

"Sure," Piper said. This was odder and odder. Sato usually didn't have time for lunch, let alone a stroll in the park. "I can be there in half an hour. Did you find something?"

"See you in half an hour," Sato said, and hung up.

Piper pulled off his shirt and walked into the WC to splash water on his face and under his arms and to brush his teeth, all the while puzzling over Sato's call. He must have found something, or why meet? But he was reluctant to be seen telling Piper about it. That alone was remarkable; Piper had never known Sato to be nervous about anything. But if he was nervous, the meeting place made sense. A busy salariman could cross Hibiya Park a thousand times, taking the main paths through the formal rose garden, and never see the pond, tucked away in a tiny grove of red maples and oaks and firs. On the other hand, Hibiya Park was so public, so central and so close to the Foreign Ministry that no one would think twice if they happened to see Sato there.

So! Piper thought. There had been an accident! And a cover-up!

I knew it! He reached for the phone to call Kyoko, breaking the cardinal rule by telephoning on a weekend, but he checked himself. Better hear Sato out and then call, he thought. He slipped into a clean shirt which, with unusual foresight, he had brought to the office, along with the jacket and tie which he kept hanging by the front door for formal-wear emergencies. He stepped into the hall and was about to lock the door when he remembered the telex that had rattled him awake during the night. He considered reentering to check it, and then decided, the hell with it, why ruin a fine morning. It was already nearly midnight Friday at home. If they wanted something for Saturday, he was too late, and if they wanted something for Sunday, he had plenty of time. He'd read the telex later.

The subway was uncrowded but Piper was too excited to sit. He rode to Hibiya Station and emerged a few minutes early at the park's eastern entrance, which gave onto a huge round fountain. The day was steamy, and Piper paused in the fine spray before taking a seat on a shady bench. Nearby, an old man fed peanuts to pigeons. Younger men and women scurried past clutching paper bags laden with packages in department-store gift-wrapping. It was the summer gift-giving season, when tenants gave to landlords, parents gave to their children's teachers, politicians gave to reporters, and special pleaders of all kinds gave to the bureaucrats who populated the faceless stone buildings around Hibiya Park. It was a custom, repeated in December, which all Japanese loathed but none could shake, entwining them as it did in a trail of obligations and debts descending from generation to generation. The gifts were expected to be expensive but mundane, as unwelcomed by the recipients as they were begrudged by the givers. Laundry soap, vegetable oil, sake, smoked ham: anything that could be consumed and forgotten. Giving something more lasting would be rude, since its very persistence would serve as an unpleasant reminder of the recipient's debt. Of course, Piper knew, at the higher levels of government in this very neighborhood, politicians had expanded the definition of consumables to include cash, and a ten-thousand-yen note tucked neatly into a box of socks was not an atypical gift.

Still too excited to sit, Piper rose and walked over to a kiosk to buy a soft ice cream cone for breakfast. Behind the fountain, he saw, the local ward office had set up its earthquake trailer, a movable stage that could be made to shake and roll. One wooden table was nailed to the floor, as if for a stage set of an impoverished theater company, and a sign above the truck reminded residents what to do during a quake: turn off the gas, grab a flashlight, stand in a threshold, don't panic. A gaggle of squealing schoolchildren rode the trailer, clinging to the table legs and laughing delightedly as an unsmiling fireman turned the dial to higher and higher levels of agitation. Hundreds more children waited in line for a turn. Tokyo may have been decimated by a quake when their grandparents were young, and it may have been due for even greater devastation any day, but for these children the earthquake trailer was more free amusement ride than cautionary experience, no matter how grim-faced the fireman. After it stopped shaking, most of the children jumped off and scooted to the back of the line to wait for another turn.

Piper, on the other hand, had ridden out enough moderate quakes to last him a lifetime and saw nothing amusing in the experts' prediction that Tokyo was due for another major grinding of tectonic plates. Hundreds rocked these islands every year, most too weak to be felt, but many of them disturbingly palpable. When they would hit in the middle of the night, Piper would bolt, naked, to his apartment threshold, as instructed, and then stand there feeling foolish, wondering whether to run back for his pyjamas, or make a dash to shut off the gas, or stand fast until either the quake ended or the building collapsed in rubble, bringing his naked body down with it. Once one of his neighbors, a pleasant middle-aged woman, had come to her own doorway and been more terrified, certainly, by Piper's hairy nakedness than by the quake itself. (The next morning they exchanged their usual pleasantries as though the encounter had never taken place.) The horizontal slipping and sliding of the quakes was not all that frightening, but the uncertainty over when it would stop, whether it would, once more, subside after thirty seconds, or whether this time it would gain steam and heave Tokyo into the sea—this was unsettling. Tokyo politicians liked to boast that their city was now engineered to withstand a big quake, unlike in 1923, when everything burned to the ground and corpses choked the Sumida River, and Piper's neighbors seemed to put a touching faith in their civil defense rituals. They all kept gallon jugs of water in the closet, and once a year donned yellow hardhats and marched, wielding flashlights, to a nearby cemetery that served—too appropriately, Piper thought, but none of them seem troubled—as their earthquake gathering zone.

Piper sucked the last of the vanilla cream from the cardboardlike cone, threw the remains into a wire-mesh trash basket and set off toward the pond. Entering the quiet of the small wood, he felt cooler, and distant from the muffled sounds of the city. The pond's fountain, a bronzed bird with thin upstretched neck, spurted a meager stream upward that tumbled over and splashed into the brown water with a constant murmur. On the far side of the pond a father and daughter stood on a flat, round stone at water's edge and fed popcorn to the greedy carp, which slapped and butted each other as they jockeyed for position. On the near side, Piper saw as he rounded a curve, Sato was already sitting on a bench under the primitive wooden arbor with his back to the dirt path. Smoke from his cigarette curled into the pine branches above him, where a flock of sparrows flitted about.

"Sorry to have kept you waiting," Piper said.

"Not at all, I just got here," Sato said. Sato had served, early in his career, in Saudi Arabia, and he spoke English with a kind of rumbling Semitic accent that foreign women seemed to find attractive. Marianne had once told Piper that Sato was the single Japanese man whom she could imagine sleeping with.

Now Piper and Sato shook hands and Piper sat, noting that Sato looked more tired and rumpled than ever. His wavy black hair spilled over his shirt collar in back, and his tie was tucked into his shirt between two buttons. He looks nervous, Piper thought, he's found something. Piper tried to look nonchalant.

"I'm afraid I don't have much that will help you," Sato began. "There does in fact seem to be something strange about the cases you mentioned, but I can't tell you much more than that."

Piper's heart skipped a beat. I knew it, he thought. I knew it. But he listened without comment. His reporter's notebook was shoved into his back pocket, as usual, but for now he would leave it there. Sato seemed skittish enough already. Better not to scare him off by taking notes.

"I thought it would make sense to check things out on a Saturday," Sato began again, after a pause. That figured, too, Piper thought. Saturday was a work day, so no one would be surprised to find Sato in the defense agency; but in fact fewer people would be about, and so he was less likely to have to explain why he was poking around. Piper knew from personal experience that most of the Self-Defense Agency seemed to spend Saturday out on the dirt-covered exercise yard, playing softball and volleyball.

"So this morning I checked the records of the names you gave me," Sato continued. "And—well, quite frankly, I've never seen anything like it. There's a big red X on each file, and an instruction to begin paying death benefits to the survivors. But there's no mention of how each one died. It's irregular, I have to say."

"Do the files say when they died?"

"Well, that's odd, too," Sato said. "There's no exact date given for any of them. But the notations seem to have been made sometime in September 1945, just after the war ended."

Piper tried to make sense of that, and failed. "What do you make of it?" he asked.

"I don't know, I really don't know," Sato said. "I can't believe it's anything as sinister as you seem to be thinking, but I can't really explain it, either. I don't know what else to say."

Piper said nothing for a moment. He wondered whether Sato was telling him everything he had found. He tried to push him a bit further.

"Well, what if there was some kind of accident in the atomic program?" he asked. "A leak of radioactivity, or some dangerous explosion. A bunch of scientists were exposed, and the government wanted to hush it up," Piper suggested. "Maybe because some civilians were exposed, too, and they didn't want to admit it. Or maybe because the Americans were coming, and the Japanese didn't want to call attention to their own atomic bomb program, because they figured the whole team would be hauled up on war-crime charges. It doesn't have to be sinister, you know. They might just have been trying to protect as many of their own as they could."

"It's possible," Sato said, "but not likely. I don't think the atomic program was advanced enough to even get to the accident stage. And besides, I don't think anyone was organized enough at that point to be planning so far ahead."

"I don't know about that," Piper said. "You know, even before the war ended, a secret group was planning the rebuilding of Japan's industrial might. Of course, they had to disguise what they were doing, because it was treason to say Japan would lose the war, and they had to bicycle through rubble to their meetings. But they already were thinking about how to salvage victory from defeat. I've talked to one of those guys. Some people were thinking ahead, believe me."

"Maybe so," Sato said despondently. He fished another cigarette from his shirt pocket and lit it. "Maybe so."

"Well, what other explanation could there be, Tsuyoshi?" Piper pressed.

"I don't know, I told you already, I don't know," Sato said. "But I would be careful about jumping to conclusions. I still think there must be a straightforward explanation."

"Which is why you wanted to meet in the park," Piper said.

"Look, it's strange, I admit it's strange, I already told you it's strange." He sounded angry, but Piper knew the anger wasn't directed at him.

They sat in silence for a few minutes. The daughter across the pond shook the last kernels of popcorn from her paper bag into the pond as the carp swarmed and sucked swinishly.

"I'm worried about what's going on in Washington, John," Sato said abruptly. "If they go ahead with this expropriation, no matter what their legal fig leaf, there won't be any restraining the right wing here."

"But what can it do?"

"That's just it—we don't have a military, and we need your market, so what can we do?" Sato said. "Which is why your Congress can push us around and make excuses for your own failure to compete." Piper had never heard him so bitter. "But the nationalists will say that if we had a bigger army, maybe even a nuclear deterrent, we couldn't be pushed around this way. It could get ugly, and dangerous."

"It's in your job description to worry," Piper said, trying to joke Sato out of his mood. "You've been saying this for years."

Sato didn't smile. "This time is different," he said. "I'm hearing strange rumblings from the right, spilling over to people who have always defended our alliance with America until now."

Japan's right was a murky and shifting alliance of militarists, gangsters, industrialists and conservative barons of the ruling party. Some operated openly, some less so; some were former war criminals, some were young recruits to the cause. Sato usually dismissed foreigners' talk about rightist conspiracies, so Piper was shocked to hear him now.

"What kind of rumblings?"

"I don't know, I can't make sense of what I'm hearing," Sato answered. "But I know it's not good."

He lapsed back into silence. Piper's thoughts returned to the dusty files in the boecho basement. "By the way," he said, speaking slowly as he puzzled over what Sato had reported. "When you said that every file had this red *X*, you weren't including Yamada and Kawamura's brother, were you?"

Sato stuck his burning cigarette between his lips and, squinting to ward off the smoke, reached into his shirt pocket for a scrap of paper, folded over many times into a small rectangle, on which he had scribbled notes in various directions with a fountain pen. "Kawamura's brother, no," he said after turning the paper this way and that and deciphering his notes. "But Yamada, yes."

"Yamada, yes what?" Piper said excitedly.

"Yamada the same as Kawamura, Inoki, Hashimoto," Sato said. "The same red *X*, death benefits beginning in September, no cause of death given."

"But that's impossible," Piper said. "Yamada didn't die until 1955 or so. His own widow told us. And we have a book he wrote after the war."

"As far as his file is concerned, he was dead in 1945," Sato said. "Maybe he and his wife somehow conspired to defraud the government, not that there was much to give in death benefits. But I suppose it happened."

Mrs. Yamada wasn't the type, Piper thought. But he didn't argue. "And Kawamura's brother lost the use of his legs in a naval attack, right?"

"Right," Sato said, squinting again at his notes. "When the *Yamato* went down in April 1945. And he didn't die until eight years ago."

"He didn't what?"

"Die. Until eight years ago."

"Well, that's damned odd, too," Piper said. "Because I talked to him last week."

Sato looked at Piper, looked wearily at his notes, looked up at Piper again. "Where?"

"At his store in Kuji," Piper said.

"I don't know what to tell you," Sato answered. "It could be a clerical error."

"Look, Tsuyoshi, there is something strange going on here, and I can tell you think so, too, even if maybe you don't want to admit it to yourself," Piper said. "If you were in my shoes, what would you do next? How can I find out what this is all about?"

"John, maybe there's something strange going on, maybe not," Sato said. "I told you I don't think you should let your imagination carry you away." He dropped his cigarette and ground it into the dirt with his toe. "In any event, I'm afraid I've helped you all I can," Sato said. "You know, if it was my own ministry, I could do more. But as it is—"

"I understand," Piper said quickly. "I appreciate what you've done already. I just wish I knew where to turn next."

Sato said nothing but, absentmindedly, as if he were already thinking of his next meeting, lit a match and held it to his folded-up note. He held it by one corner until it had mostly turned to black, and then dropped it. "I better go," he said. "These telecommunications talks are looking worse and worse. You know, John, the Japanese side already has made many concessions that the American press and Congress are not giving us credit for. Why do you not write a story on that?"

"Let me think about it, Tsuyoshi," Piper said. "First I need to go home and shower."

Sato rose with a sigh and shook Piper's hand. "We're heading for big trouble, John," he said wearily. "I know you are a very fair reporter, but I wish you would do something to help out, instead of digging up all this ancient history." He took a few steps down the dirt path, then turned back once more.

"One other thing," Sato said in a quiet voice. "Each of the

files I looked at, except the brother's, was marked 'Top Secret.' "

"Is that unusual?"

"For a personnel file?" Sato said. "I never heard of such a thing before. Under Japanese law, 'Top Secret' isn't even supposed to exist."

12

*T*he next morning he woke in a panicky sweat, this time on his own futon, dreaming again of Kyoko. Waking to the dream had reminded him of waking yesterday to her voice, which instantly called the telex to his sleep-clouded mind. The telex! He sat bolt upright on the floor. All stirred up after his meeting with Sato, he had come home to shower and telephone McGee, who said he'd never heard of a Tokyo Project but who promised to poke around and get back to Piper. In his excitement Piper had completely forgotten the message from home. If they had wanted something for Sunday, he'd be in serious trouble now.

Not so long ago he might not have cared. The job had started as a lark, and at home, working in his one-newspaper town, it was hard to take the profession seriously. But here, competing against reporters from all over the world, he had developed a respect for the job, an understanding of what it took to be good and fair and honest, and a new contempt for the lazy and the toadying. And with that had come a new kind of ambition. He wanted to be good, and he wanted everyone to know it. And despite all his grumbling, he liked Tokyo, he felt at home abroad. All his life he'd felt like an outsider; in Japan he didn't have to apologize for that feeling. He shuddered at the prospect of returning home, living again among the malls and expressways of America, among all those English speakers, within shouting distance of his bosses.

And, of course, there was the story of the moment, if he could ever figure it out. And there was Kyoko. If he lost his job, he would lose his days with her. So he had to keep them at least minimally happy back home, and he knew he had been skating on thin ice lately. Taking that trip north without permission, ignoring the auto trade story, even cold-shouldering pet funerals might hurt. You never knew what they were thinking, or when a complaint from the features editor, usually as ignored by her bosses as by her reporters, might fall on receptive ears. If they'd asked for something for Sunday, and he hadn't even replied, it wouldn't be good.

He turned off the rackety little electric fan that stood on the floor, pointed at his pillow. Then he stepped into his cube of a bathtub, sprayed himself with the handshower, and quickly shaved. It was late morning already, after another late night. Piper was on the verge of swearing off all of his bad habits: beer-drinking, meat-eating, pulling all-nighters at the office, smoking cigarettes when he went out drinking with his Japanese friends, all of whom smoked. Of course, he had been on that verge for some time. He would wake in the morning, full of self-loathing, after breaking one or more of his pledges, pour himself a glass of milk and swear that things would be different from now on. But in the emptiness of the long weekends, as day gave way to night, he would shrug off his healthy intentions.

Last night neither he nor Marianne had been in the mood for their usual gripe sessions, and Piper hadn't known whether he could keep himself from talking about the atomic bomb, so he had proposed a movie instead of dinner. But after the film, Marianne hadn't been ready to go home alone, and they had ended up in a Cambodian restaurant on the far side of town. And by the time they had finished there, and had a couple of beers in a joint nearby, and catalogued Christopher's most recent outrages, and vented their spleens again about Zarsky, and bemoaned the dearth of attractive single men in Tokyo, and discussed, at length, whether Japanese and Americans sounded different at orgasm—by then Piper had missed the last train and had had to hike halfway across Tokyo for a taxi. And despite Sato's assurance that the drivers weren't discriminating against him, but were only cruising for one last long ride to the suburbs, Piper had launched into one of his anti-Japan tirades, lunging at empty taxis as they swerved around him, cursing their drivers as racists and wondering how Tokyo could hope to be a cosmopolitan capital of the world when its trains shut down so early. By the time he reached home and his blood pressure eased to a simmer, it had been late again.

He poured himself a glass of milk, pulled on shorts and a T-shirt, socks and sneakers. Japanese men never wore shorts in Tokyo, and women only with stockings and high heels. During his first summer Piper had allowed himself to be intimidated into wearing jeans even on the hottest days. But it was too hot. He didn't care anymore what people thought, except when it came to not embarrassing Kyoko, and he wouldn't be seeing her today. Never on Sunday.

He decided to bicycle to work. Hellish six days a week, Tokyo's streets were delightfully empty now, and he reached his building in less than half an hour. He entered through the basement door that was kept unlocked on Sundays and, leaning his bike against a wall there, took the service elevator upstairs. The office was hot and stuffy; the building managers wouldn't pay for air-conditioning on a Sunday. Not quite ready to face the telex, Piper gazed out the window; all quiet in the defense agency. He checked the answering machine; several calls from a pay phone, but no messages, just the beep of the phone, the clink of a coin and the click of someone hanging up. Finally he bent over the telex machine.

PROPIPER EXPUCCIO URGENT, the message began. Vinnie Puccio was a a decent young guy, an assistant editor on the foreign and national desk who tried to look out for Piper. He had no power within the newsroom, though; he was basically a copy editor, and he could only transmit messages and, sometimes, alert Piper to significant office gossip.

SORRY TO SPOIL YOUR WEEKEND BUT THE BIG ENCHILADA ASKED TO ONPASS FOLLOWING MESSAGE. TELL PIPER QUOTE WE ARE NOT PAYING FOR HIS FANCY TOKYO PAD, HIGHFALUTIN FOREIGN CORRESPONDENT LIFESTYLE AND THAT ORIENTAL HONEY OF A GAL FRIDAY SO THAT HE CAN GET A PHD IN ANCIENT JAPANESE HISTORY UNQUOTE. TELL HIM ALSO QUOTE WE ALREADY SAID NO GO ON HIS STORY IDEA AND WE DON'T LIKE TO SAY THINGS TWICE UNQUOTE. ALSO TELL HIM QUOTE WE HAVE AN OPENING COVERING SCHOOLS IN WINFIELD COUNTY HE MIGHT BE QUALIFIED FOR ALTHOUGH HE SHOULDN'T COUNT ON IT AND HE SHOULD TAKE THIS AS A LAST WARNING TO CLEAN UP HIS ACT AND GET HIS ASS IN GEAR UNQUOTE. JOHN JUST SO YOU CAN PICTURE THE SCENE HE WASN'T SMILING. HAVE A NICE DAY VINNIE.

Piper read through the message five or six times and then slid it into a desk drawer. This might be one to frame, he thought, better not crumple this one. He slumped onto the couch and closed his eyes. Well, maybe he wouldn't be getting that bronze bust after all. Usually, after getting slapped down by the desk, he'd spend an hour or two composing brilliant, defiant responses which he knew he'd never send. This time he didn't feel brilliant or defiant, only deflated. His meeting with Sato yesterday had left him exhilarated, vindicated, convinced he was tracking something so big and mysterious it scared even the most unscarable Japanese, a story that would shock the world and make his career. Now, as he lay on the couch, with the heat pressing down, he thought, big deal. What did he really have? A mystery, yes, but a mystery so old it was covered in cobwebs. So Yamada had died and come back to life. So Kawamura's death had been covered up. Why should anybody care? And even if anyone did, where else could Piper turn for information? If he was at a dead end with his best source, there wasn't much hope. The desk was right—it was time to chuck the whole thing, and maybe the job, too. He couldn't any longer bring himself to churn out the crap they wanted, and they didn't seem to want anything he did want to write. He could telex his resignation right now, before they could fire him. By morning he could be in Osaka, catching a freighter to Hong Kong. Eventually he'd steam round to India. He could live in Cochin or Madras for a long time on the little money he'd saved. Maybe Kyoko would come along, too. He pictured the two of them lying under a ceiling fan in a simple Indian hotel room, staring up at the blades turning sluggishly in the dim light, quietly telling each other stories, her hand cool in his. She was wearing loose white cotton pants, and a loose white shirt, nothing underneath, her hair braided to keep her long white neck cool. The tumult of the Indian street reached them from below their balcony as in a muffled dream, a hawker selling tea, a cow lowing, the ringing of a rickshaw's bell . . .

The telephone was ringing and Piper jumped up with a start. He must have fallen asleep, for how long he didn't know. He lunged for the phone, for an instant unsure of where he was, and heard the clatter of a coin dropping into a pay phone, and then a Japanese lady's voice.

"Moshi moshi," the voice said. *"Moshi moshi."*

In Japan, the person answering the phone was supposed to speak first, and after a moment Piper recovered himself. *"Hai, moshi moshi, Advertiser desu kedo,"* he said. Literally, This is the *Advertiser* although. In Japanese you ended sentences with "but" or "although," and the rest was understood: although I'm probably not good enough to be talking to you, although I'm sorry in advance for any rudeness I may cause, although, although, but, excuse me, I'm sorry, forgive us.

"Shimizu de gozaimasu ga," the woman said. I am Shimizu but . . . *"Nichiyobi na no ni o-denwa shite sumimasen."* Please forgive my calling on Sunday. Her voice was hesitant, and she sounded frightened and out of breath.

"Ie, ie, tonde mo nai," Piper said. Not at all, not at all. He racked his brain to remember who Shimizu might be, or to remember a polite way to ask her, and meanwhile she pressed on.

"Ano, jitsu-wa . . ." So the thing is this, you know? Japanese couldn't carry on a conversation without the other side constantly chiming in with little supportive noises and phrases and this was especially true, Piper knew, on the telephone, with the visual clues missing. *"Hai,"* he said, noticing that he was bowing slightly into the phone like a true Japanese.

"Taisetsu na o-hanashi o shitai no desu ga, jikan ga arimasen," she said, speaking more rapidly now. This is important, but there's no time to talk. *"Yamada-san wa mada ikite irrashaimasu."* Yamada is still alive.

"Eh? Sumimasen?" Piper asked. What? He was wide awake now, and as the meaning of her last comment sank in, he said, *"Okusan desshyo?"* The wife, you must mean? Suddenly, he had a vision of an old woman fleeing into the murky corridor of the physics building, and he knew he was talking to the tea pourer.

"Ie," she said impatiently. No! In Japanese, which shunned directness and abhorred confrontation, that was equivalent to: No, dammit, wrong, listen to me. I'm talking about the husband, she said. And then, rushing now, and frightened again: I have to cut the line.

But before hanging up, she added mysteriously, *"Kore kara watakushi-wa Senso-ji ni itte, anata no tame ni oinari shimasu."* From here I will go to Senso-ji Temple to offer honorable prayers on your behalf. *"O-wakari ni natta kashira?"* I wonder if you've understood? There was a note of pleading in her voice.

No! he wanted to shout. He had the sense that she had delivered a coded message, an invitation of some kind, and he hadn't understood at all. *"Chotto matte, kudasai,"* Piper said. Please wait. He was frantic now, and his tongue and mind weren't working fast enough. *"Yamada-san wa, doko desu ka? Shimizu-san wa?"* Where is Yamada? And where the hell are you?

"Sumimasen, kore de shitsurei shimasu," she said, the words tumbling out. Literally, Sorry, but excuse me. *"Gambatte kudasai ne."* Don't give up, please. Carry on. Persevere.

And then Piper was listening to dial tone. The phone handle was slippery with his sweat. He hung up and grabbed a pen and paper to shakily scribble, as well as he could remember, what she had said. Then he stood again, and paced, from the window to the telex machine, and back to the window, and back again.

Finally, when his heart had stopped racing, he went back to the phone and dialed Kyoko's number. He had never called on a Sunday before. She answered after one ring and he said, "It's me."

There was a pause, and Kyoko said, *"Kyoo wa nichiyoo deshyoo?"* Today is Sunday, isn't it? She had never spoken Japanese to him before, and there was no "but" on the end of this sentence; in Japanese, that was as good as saying: It's a weekend, asshole. Though of course, he realized later when he reconstructed the day's events, she had no reason at the time to think he would understand.

"Yoku wakaru yo," he answered. I know that. *"Taisetsu koto desu."* This one matters.

There was a longer pause on the other end. Piper had long imagined how and where he would one day surprise Kyoko with his language skills, and now he allowed himself a moment to enjoy her silence. Finally, she said, in a tone he had never heard before, *"Doozo."* Please, go ahead.

In English he recounted as best he could his phone conversation with Shimizu. Then he realized she didn't know about Sato's discoveries, so he told her about that. Then she asked him to go over the morning conversation again, repeating several times the part about going to Senso-ji Temple in Asakusa "to offer prayers."

"What do you think it means?" he said.

"I don't know," she said. "Let's see if we can find out."

"Right. How?"

"Asakusa eki de aimashoo," she said. Let's meet at Asakusa Station. "And, John—I'm proud of you."

Piper looked at his watch and said, *"Sanji ni aimashyooka?"* Shall we meet at three?

"Eh, sanji de yoroshi wa." Three would be fine. She hung up, and Piper found himself, once again, clutching the phone with a slippery palm.

13

*T*he train was surprisingly crowded for a Sunday, but mostly with families heading for Ueno, with its zoo and science museum. Asakusa was the end of the line, two stops farther, in the heart of old Tokyo, and Piper thought, as he stepped off the orange train, that even the subway station looked different here, dingier, dimmer, somehow exhaling a scent of decades and decades of rough history. This was working-class Tokyo, plebeian Tokyo, a world away from the posh pasta bars and fashion houses of Shibuya. In the days of the samurai, this had been the neighborhood of raucous theater and wild festivals, hard-drinking tradesmen and hardworking women. Even now it remained Shitamachi, the low city, a gritty workaday world untouched by the investment banks and Brooks Brothers stores and fur-collared matrons of Japan's new wealth.

Piper climbed the stairs at the end of the platform and saw Kyoko waiting at the ticket gate, their usual meeting place. She gave him a long, hard look, as if searching for something different in him now that she knew he could understand her language. Or perhaps, he thought, she was simply wondering how she could have missed it, how this man she thought she knew could have hidden something from her for so long. Or maybe he was kidding himself. Maybe she was just wondering why he hadn't shaved and worn long pants, and wishing that he had.

They walked upstairs to the big intersection and away from the Sumida River toward the Asakusa temple. At first glance, this area was no more charming than any other part of Tokyo: graceless concrete buildings, cluttered neon, noisy traffic. A McDonald's faced the station, with a Luv Burger across the street. But occasional islands of old Tokyo poked above the ocean of tackiness, and the tackiness itself was endearingly unabashed, displayed without embarrassment or embellishment, with no false marble fronts or misspelled Italian menus. On a Sunday afternoon, with Japanese tourists and families from the countryside spilling along the main road toward the temple, the place throbbed to a different rhythm than upscale Tokyo to the south and west.

Kyoko and Piper turned with the throngs into Nakamise, a covered street of shops leading to the temple gates. On the left was an ice-cream store of the kind that had defined ice cream in Japan before Baskin-Robbins and Haagen-Dazs came to town, the kind with plastic models in the window of unspeakably green drinks and unspeakably gloppy parfaits. Farther along, the seedy mingled with the sublime. Centuries-old shops sold fans and oiled umbrellas and fine combs, handmade by grandchildren of grandchildren of those who had made them when Japan was closed to the West. Nearly crowding them out were booths of tacky souvenirs, of battery-operated dogs that yapped and strutted and flipped over, booths with a historical value of their own, calling to mind the postwar, pre-Walkman days when U.S. soldiers combed these shops for bargains, and when "Made in Japan" meant nothing but these shoddy mementos, these crude reproductions of old erotic woodprints alongside key rings that glowed in the dark and whistled when you clapped. And just before the temple gates was the traditional cookie store, where apprentices in white poured batter into antique molds, turned and re-turned them over a charcoal fire, sending out delicious smells which, Piper knew from bitter experience, were never matched in the tasting.

Finally, they walked through the imposing gate, past two glowering spirits that guarded the temple with monstrous red faces, gods of wind and thunder. Even here the atmosphere was that of a profane, exuberant bazaar, not a serene cathedral. Hundreds of Japanese tourists and pilgrims, and a few foreigners too, milled about the bustling stone-paved courtyard, feeding the thousands of flapping pigeons, photographing themselves in front of the famous paper lanterns donated by local geisha associations. Crouching fathers squinted up through their cameras in vain attempts to shoot their children and the tall concrete pagoda together. Temple workers sold charms and plaques and emblems of good fortune. Dozens of Japanese crowded around an incense-burning censer, waving supposedly curative smoke toward themselves and their babies.

Piper took in the scene and wondered what he should be looking for. With Kyoko he climbed the stairs of the main temple, under its sloped eaves. Worshipers approached the screened-off altar, threw coins into a wooden box and closed their eyes to pray, clapping twice to summon the gods' attention. Then they moved off and other worshipers took their place. The skittering of coins down the slanted sides of the wooden box mingled with the clapping, the bell-ringing, the shouting of children in the courtyard, the yapping of a battery dog that one boy had persuaded his parents to buy and then turned loose near the pagoda.

"Now what?" Piper said.

Kyoko shook her head. "I don't know," she said.

"You think she expects to meet us here?"

"No," Kyoko said. "Not from what you said. But she was trying to tell you something, I'm sure of that. 'Offering prayers on your behalf'—it's a strange way of talking, and she must have meant something by it."

"Unless I got it completely wrong," Piper said. Pregnant women, schoolboys approaching exams, young couples—everyone had something to pray for. This temple was known as a protector of newborns, and dozens of mothers came forward with infants, sometimes accompanied by grizzled grandfathers and careworn grandmothers from farm country. Plenty of elderly women in kimono shuffled up the steps in sandals and white socks divided at the toe, and Piper started at each one. Yet he felt somehow that Shimizu had already been and left, and wouldn't be coming back.

They had found seats on a bench to the side of the animated courtyard when Piper suddenly realized. He had been staring, without much thought, at a tree in one corner of the yard where pilgrims tied scraps of white paper, prayers which fluttered in the breeze and brought the gods' attention to troubles in love or work or school.

"One of those is a message to us from Shimizu," Piper said, pointing to the festooned branches. "I can't believe I didn't see it from the start."

"How do you know?" Kyoko said dubiously. Hundreds trembled in the hot summer breeze.

"What better way to hide a message than in the middle of hundreds of others?" he said. "And if she was being followed, no one would have thought it strange to see her tying a prayer to the tree."

"Okay, then, which one?"

"That I don't know," he said. "Let's go look."

Up close Piper began to lose confidence. There weren't hundreds of paper prayers, there were thousands. He fingered a few, inspecting their knots. Some looked newer than others, it was true, but plenty looked new enough to be part of today's crop. And even if they could untie each, one by one, Piper couldn't read Japanese well enough to distinguish a prayer from a curse from a secret message. Out of curiosity, he yanked one off the tree and unfolded it. He was turning to Kyoko when an older women accosted her, pointing at Piper and issuing a tongue-lashing that Piper was glad he couldn't follow. The lady clearly didn't approve of untying other people's prayers, and as Kyoko bowed and apologized for her boorish gaijin companion, unshaven and in shorts, Piper retreated behind the tree and leaned against a wall, trying to fade away. There, as the woman continued to berate Kyoko and Kyoko tried to inconspicuously back out of her path, bowing all the while, Piper noticed two things. He noticed a Japanese man standing in the shadow of the giant Thunder God Gate, in jeans and sunglasses and carrying a camera around his neck, who looked vaguely familiar. The man, like most of the people in the courtyard, it seemed, was staring at poor Kyoko and her tormentor. And then, while Piper was still trying to place the man's face, or slouch, or whatever had struck some chord, something closer swam into focus: a prayer of a different color. It seemed to be green on the side facing Piper, the side away from the crowds, and white on its public side, so that only somebody searching from Piper's vantage point might notice the distinction. Green, Piper thought. Maybe a joke, an allusion to the green tea she spent her life preparing and pouring.

Piper didn't move toward the prayer. He waited until Kyoko had finally appeased the old woman, and the old woman had wandered off, still grumbling, for what was, undoubtedly, her daily prayer, and the tourists had gone back to their picture-taking and the pilgrims to their incense-waving. And when Kyoko joined him against the wall, giving him one of her dirtier looks, he tried to show her the man with the camera, but he was gone, so Piper instead showed her the green prayer.

"If you're going to be tearing down more prayers, don't expect me to protect you this time," Kyoko said.

"I'm not, you are," Piper said. "I'll stand in front of you, no one will see." Piper positioned himself looking out toward the temple, another tired and bemused tourist, while Kyoko worked behind him. And after a minute he heard her exclaim in Japanese.

"What?"

"It's a map," Kyoko said. "A hand-drawn, detailed map. And at the bottom it just says, *'Gambatte kudasai!'* "

14

*W*ithout turning, Piper whispered excitedly, "Put it somewhere safe. We shouldn't look at it here."

Kyoko slid the paper into the front pocket of her jeans. "I know where we can go," she said. "Near here. A special place."

They exited through Thunder God Gate and turned right, leaving the crowded shopping alley behind. Soon they were walking down frayed, faded streets, once at the heart of Tokyo's entertainment district, now in a quiet backwater, as forgotten as the gleaming-haired geisha and acrobat-throated kabuki stars who once reigned here by night. Piper looked over his shoulder from time to time while Kyoko walked calmly, eyes straight ahead, until they arrived at an old wooden gate. "This way," she said.

Piper ducked his head and followed Kyoko through the gate—and, suddenly, into a separate world. Before them lay a classic Japanese strolling garden, its tiny hills and valleys rising and falling along the gently curved shores of a placid pond. On a rock in the middle, beneath a small gnarled pine growing from a small round island, a turtle closed its eyes in the sun. Kyoko and Piper followed a narrow path into dappled shade cast by miniature maples, around the pond, until they were facing a centuries-old tea pavilion and, rising behind it, the pagoda of the Asakusa temple. Nothing else of Tokyo could be seen. The pigeons, the tourists, the trashy souvenirs—Piper and Kyoko had left them all behind.

"Where are we?" Piper said reverently.

"Dembo-in, the abbot's residence," Kyoko said. "You're supposed to get permission to enter, but usually you can just walk in. I come here sometimes just to think, to be alone." The turtle, hearing their voices, slithered into the pond with a plop. Rings of water pulsed outward to the edge of the pond, and then all was still again.

They settled on a wooden slab of a backless bench, and Kyoko pulled the map from her pocket. It had been drawn on the thinnest of rice paper, and then folded and folded again. Kyoko carefully opened it and smoothed it on the faded jeans of her thigh. The work was painstaking, in several colors, with tiny, beautiful calligraphy drawn with a fountain pen. The green had been no joking allusion, but a forest; a stream was blue; the path to be taken, brown; their destination, a red circle.

"The map starts at a town in Niigata prefecture," Kyoko said, speaking slowly as she deciphered the miniature handwriting. "It looks like you go by road partway into the mountains, and then by footpath, until you get to this—this little building, I guess."

"And what is it? What's the building, what's the destination?"

"I don't know, it doesn't say," Kyoko said. "Just this little house, with a red circle at the back. I don't know—I suppose, if Yamada really is alive—maybe this is a map to find Yamada." She held the map up, turned it on its side, and upside down, and righted it again. "This is a beautiful piece of work," she said.

Along the route, the old woman had drawn tiny clues or landmarks that Piper could barely decipher: a ring of some kind; the number 440, with the 4's written in old Japanese characters, like tiny windows with their curtains tied open; a policeman, a rice bowl, a dog, a gun. "I suppose she had planned to give us directions," Piper said, as he studied the map. "When she found she couldn't talk on the phone or come see us, she drew in these little symbols." He handed the map back to Kyoko. "I hope we can make sense of them."

"John, what is really going on?" Kyoko said with a shiver. "I'm beginning to find the whole thing a little scary."

"Me, too," Piper said. "But there has to be a rational explanation." He waited for Kyoko to challenge that western assertion, and continued when she didn't speak. "The records say Yamada died after the war, like the others, but we know he lived at least ten years longer, right? Then he died, according to his wife. But now his tea pourer, who we believe was once a beautiful young woman of some uncertain importance in his life, says that he didn't die then, either, that he's still alive. Fair so far?"

Kyoko nodded, smoothing the creases of the map over and over with her thumb. A carp splashed in the pond, and they could hear some workmen, back from their tea break, beyond the old pavilion.

"So," she said slowly, staring at the map as though she could read the answer there. "Shimizu-san was in love with Yamada a long time ago, before he was married. Now she's old and a little, how do you say, scrambled in the head, and she imagines her old lover is still alive, she imagines people are after her, she imagines many things."

"Maybe so," Piper said. "She certainly sounded frightened on the phone this afternoon, that was real enough, but I suppose she could be frightened of shadows, like she seemed the other day. Still, that wouldn't explain how Yamada came back to life the first time."

"Okay," Kyoko said. "I can tell you're bursting with one of your theories."

"Well, how about this?" Piper said excitedly. "These physicists were exposed to radioactivity in some terrible accident near the end of the war. The cause of death was covered up, and maybe not just because of the U.S. Occupation. Maybe, after Hiroshima and Nagasaki, the government thought that the Japanese people simply couldn't accept that their own country had been working on the same horrible weapon, and that some young men had even died in the research. And maybe they were right; it might have just been too much for the nation's psyche, right?

"But Yamada somehow survived this accident. He came home, without telling his wife what he'd been working on, and everything was fine until ten years later, when he started feeling weak. By now he had heard enough about the survivors of Hiroshima to know what was afflicting him. But of course no one else could know, so they took him away and told his wife he'd died in a hiking accident. Or maybe he wanted it that way—he didn't want his wife to suffer while he died a horrible death from radiation sickness."

"And how did he come back to life this time, after dying such a horrible death?" Kyoko smiled, enjoying his tale without ceding her right of skepticism.

"I don't know," Piper admitted. "Maybe Shimizu-san is crazy, like you say. Or maybe . . ."

"What?"

"Well, you probably won't go for this one," Piper said. Another carp plopped in the pond. In a far corner of the garden a man was slowly raking. The late-afternoon sun cast longer and longer shadows. "Let's say there was no accident."

"I like it so far," Kyoko said.

"Okay, but the government still had to cover up its nuclear project, for all the same reasons," Piper said. "A demoralized people, starving, nothing left to live for, couldn't believe in their emperor anymore—and then, after seeing Hiroshima, to think they'd been trying to do the same—it would have been too much, like we said."

"Like you said."

"Okay. But some of the younger workers on the bomb couldn't be trusted to keep their mouths shut. They were demoralized, too, and horrified by Hiroshima, and they wanted to unburden their souls, to warn their fellow citizens in this new democracy, to expose the old Imperial Army, to . . . whatever. For whatever reason, they wanted to talk. So the government had them disposed of."

"Disposed of? You mean killed?" Kyoko said. "Please. If that's your western rational thought, I'll stick to the mystical East. First of all, even in the darkest days of the war, our government didn't go around killing people. They put people in jail, maybe, Communists, and union organizers, and Christians who were against the war. But this wasn't Nazi Germany, even though Americans think of us as the same. And besides—if they were going to 'dispose of,' as you say, the project team, why let its leader, Nishina, get away? And how about Okamoto?"

"Good point," Piper said. "Good point. But maybe Nishina and Okamoto were in on it, maybe they could be trusted. And I didn't say the government killed these guys." Piper stood up from the bench, walked behind and put one foot where he had been sitting, then immediately took it off again as he remembered the Japanese revulsion to sharing space with dirty shoe bottoms. He walked back around and sat next to Kyoko again, stretching out his long legs. "Look, a lot of people were getting killed in those days. Maybe the government just arranged to put them in the line of fire. Maybe they were deployed to Okinawa. Maybe not the government, but right-wing, paramilitary hit squads took care of them. Maybe—"

"Oh, please," Kyoko said. "It's getting ridiculous. And how does Yamada fit in?"

"Okay, here's the part I think you'll go for," Piper said. "Yamada somehow got away. He went into hiding, and after some time, maybe a few years, when things had calmed down and law and order had returned, he came home," Piper said. "And everything was fine, until he started writing his memoirs. They let him write part one; they just made sure no one ever saw it. I'm sure they can do that here. You know the publishers and advertisers and newspapers are all in cahoots. But then, he started to write part two—remember Mrs. Yamada saying that? Well, what do you think that was, that Yamada himself said would be so much more explosive than part one? Part One already described Nishina and their Tokyo Project, you read that yourself, so there had to be more. And what was it? The story of how his colleagues were rubbed out, of course!" He turned toward Kyoko. "You have to admit it has some logic."

"Rubbed out?"

"You know," Piper said. "Knocked off. Erased. Disappeared."

"And Yamada's returning to life again?" Kyoko said. "How do you fit that into your grand conspiracy?"

"Well, again, maybe Shimizu is imagining it," Piper said. "But maybe not. Maybe, when he started to write part two, he sensed he was in danger, and he gave them the slip. He didn't tell his wife, because he didn't want to endanger her, he wanted her to get on with her life. But Shimizu—well, he still loved her, or he needed her, or she helped him in some way. And he's been hiding out in this red circle, whatever it may be"—Piper tapped the map on Kyoko's firm thigh—"ever since, and Shimizu has been supporting him, bringing him newspapers, physics journals, typewriter paper, who knows what?"

Kyoko laughed. "You sure he hasn't been living there with Hashimoto's widow?" she asked.

"Run that by me again?"

"Don't you remember?" Kyoko said teasingly. "Hashimoto's fat sister in the farmhouse telling us that the wife, her young sister-in-law, had taken off to Niigata as soon as the war was over, and had never been heard from again? Aren't you going to fit that in?"

Piper said nothing for a moment and then laughed, too. "Another good point," he said. "You're beginning to think like a reporter. But you have to learn not to jump to wild conclusions."

Suddenly, Kyoko was looking into his eyes, favoring him with a dazzling smile. "You know, I'm disappointed," she said. "I would have hoped that studying Japanese would have improved your mind and cured you of these wild Hollywood ways of thinking." She put her hand on his. "But you're as bad as ever."

He leaned forward and kissed her on the lips, knowing that it was too soon, that she would push him away, that he might ruin everything. But somehow in the excitement of their shared secret, the prospect of setting out along the mysterious brown line of their perfect little map, the otherworldliness and stillness of the garden—somehow it all combined to carry them both along, and suddenly she was kissing him back, and it was as if all of the past three years, all of his life, had been leading to this moment, on this hard wooden bench, alone with the turtle and the carp and the lone distant gardener raking—to this kiss, this soft, insistent tongue, this smooth cheek, the warmth of this body turning toward him. Her long fingers slipped around his neck, holding him gently to her, and his hand slid down the length of her back, across her flat stomach, brushing the cool firm underside of her breasts. He felt another shiver run through her, and he felt he could have stayed there forever, kissing, pressing, imagining the sweet weight of those breasts. Forever, and yet, suddenly, not for another instant. "Let's go somewhere," he whispered thickly, caressing with his other hand the downy nape of her neck. "Have you ever been to a love hotel?"

"Hm-hmm," she nodded, smiling in the midst of their kiss. "Many times."

"I've always wanted to," he said. "Take me now."

"Uh-uh," she shook her head, and turned away, toward the pond, tucking in her shirt. "I'm not ready for that, John. Not so fast, not so quickly."

She looked toward him again, and ran her hand over the back of his neck, playing softly with his curls, and he was suddenly filled with irrational, lustful anger at what felt like a consolation gesture, and shook off her hand. But she missed his shift in mood, and said softly,

"Why don't you come home with me for supper, and meet my mother?"

He rose abruptly from the bench. "I'm not ready for that," he said, knowing even as he spoke that he sounded like a petulant preteen. "Not so fast, not so quickly."

She looked completely taken aback, and then her face shut closed. "I understand," she said. "You will meet my mother as a favor to me, after I do a favor for you." She also rose from the bench. "I guess my mother can live without the pleasure."

Piper could feel the blood pounding through his head, desire mixing with shame at his stupidity and mourning over what already seemed like an irretrievable mistake. "Let's just get going," he muttered.

"You go ahead," she said, sitting back on the bench. "I think I'll stay a while longer."

"Suit yourself," he said, and resumed his circumnavigation of the pond. He strode around its northern end, past the gardener, who barely glanced up, to the tea pavilion by the gate. Looking back across the pond, he saw Kyoko, again running her thumb over the creases of the map. For a moment, he thought he would jump in and swim back to her, back past the turtle, which had reclaimed its rock, back into history five minutes and a lifetime. But then, turning away, he ducked out through the gate, and emerged once more, alone, into the modern world.

15

*K*anda-san, the janitor, always wore a neatly pressed dark suit, white shirt and tie for his commute. In his basement office each morning he would change into his khaki uniform, and at day's end he would put on his suit again for the commute home. At first, Piper assumed the old man was ashamed of his job, but he came to understand that Kanda's commuting clothes reflected instead a sense of pride. Kanda considered himself a professional, and so he dressed like one. In Japan anyone who did his job well, be he bureaucrat or baggage handler, was a professional. And almost everyone did his job well.

Piper thought about this Monday morning because he arrived so early. Usually, Kanda was hard at work by the time Piper rolled in, but on this day Piper arrived early enough to greet Kanda on the way in, with his briefcase and rolled-up newspaper. Piper was early enough to watch the Self-Defense boys doing their morning calisthenics in disciplined rows in the exercise yard, with a handful of young women in tea-pourer uniforms bringing up the rear. He was early enough to watch the crows still tearing at last night's garbage, and to collect the morning newspapers from the mailbox, since Kyoko wouldn't arrive for nearly another hour.

If she comes at all, Piper thought dourly.

Days before, he had agreed to attend a breakfast session with a Foreign Ministry bigwig, the director-general for North American affairs, Sato's boss and, Piper thought as he dumped the newspapers on the small round table at the center of their office, as slippery, as unctuous, as oleaginous a character as one might ever not wish to breakfast with. Saeki was his name, and he was a man with a future. He'll make vice-minister, everyone nodded knowingly; he'll be ambassador to Washington. Piper had no idea where these little tidbits of inside information originated, but he suspected Saeki himself played a part. The man spoke beautiful English, wore beautiful clothes, sported a beautiful wife with connections to the Bridgestone tire family. He had allies in the top echelons of the ruling party, the Cabinet, the world of industrial tycoons. His chief failing was his mind, generally agreed to be average at best, but as long as he had Sato backing him up, that didn't much matter. And although he didn't like Sato, which sentiment Sato returned in spades, he understood his deputy's value and deferred to him on matters of substance. Sato would no doubt attend this morning's breakfast, filling in, correcting, doing whatever was necessary to repair any damage Saeki might unintentionally inflict on U.S.-Japanese relations.

It wasn't how Piper liked to spend his mornings, descending on a top official with a pack of fellow scribes for a free breakfast and a heaping bowlful of mushy quotes. Of course, most Japanese officials considered working breakfasts a barbaric American import, and didn't like them any better than Piper, especially since they were expected to live by the Japanese press system, too, chatting off the record and serving whiskey to the pack of bedraggled Japanese reporters that routinely descended on their homes at 11 P.M. for a "night attack." Piper could appreciate, even on a dark day like this, not having to live the life of a Japanese journalist, who might follow one politician for years, shadowing him sixteen hours a day, seven days a week, getting to know him far better than the reporter would ever know his wife or children.

Still, Piper wasn't enthusiastic about his own life on this particular morning. He hadn't fallen asleep until the early hours of the morning, and then a dream had tormented his fitful slumber. He had dreamt that he was showering with Kyoko. They were both naked, of course, and he was feverishly kissing her body while she held the map up to the water, watching it gradually fade away. He too watched, helplessly, as the inks of the map swirled around and down the shower drain, the green and blue and red blurring into a muddy brown, but he couldn't do anything about it, he couldn't stop himself from making love to Kyoko while she ignored him utterly, until finally, holding what had been reduced to a blank white sheet of paper, she stepped out of the shower, laughing.

So he awoke with little appetite for a feeding with his colleagues. But after the Friday telex, which he hadn't read until Sunday, Piper dared not miss this breakfast meeting, where the latest round of trade talks, beginning today, would no doubt be discussed. He grabbed a tape recorder from his desk and the necktie from behind the door and wrote a note to Kyoko, a note he had phrased and rephrased in his mind all through the night. Then, after reading what he had written, he crumpled the paper and flung it toward the wastebasket.

They had already finished their melon ($15 per slice in the restaurant downstairs, Piper knew) and moved on to eggs by the time Piper entered the private dining room on the tenth floor of what many considered the world's most elegant hotel. "Ah, nice of you to join us, Mr. Piper," Saeki said. "We thought you must have more important matters to attend to." What the hell does that mean, Piper thought, as he found a place and a white-jacketed waiter hovering near the table hastened to pour his coffee. Could Sato have told his boss about Piper's story? No, no chance. It was just Saeki being obnoxious. Piper was perennially late, and in perennially punctual Japan, that got noticed.

The usual suspects were arrayed around the long, narrow table with its thick white cloth. Christopher, of course, and Steve Harding, from the *Post,* and the bureau chiefs of *Newsweek* and *Time* and *U.S. News,* and reporters from the Associated Press and Reuters wires, as well, and from a few regional papers like Piper's. The Foreign Ministry had invited the B-list to this breakfast, but no doubt if anything happened in the negotiations, the A-list would get a separate, more useful briefing. Marianne, sitting across the table, theatrically stifled a yawn when he caught her eye. Sato was at the end of the table, hunched over black coffee, looking as though he hadn't slept since their Saturday assignation but might doze off now, as Saeki spoke.

The future ambassador was explaining why Japan could never import U.S. rice. How the discussion had moved from telecommunications to rice, Piper couldn't guess, but it was a familiar topic. Piper had heard the arguments so many times he could recite them better than most rice farmers.

"Rice has a special importance in our culture," Saeki was saying. "We would hope, in the interest of not inflaming relations further between our peoples, that our American friends would not push this issue. After all, our market is now entirely open to almost every other product, as you all know so well."

"Cars have a special importance in our culture," Piper said, immediately regretting his chronic inability to stifle the wise-ass remarks that bubbled to the surface. "You think we should stop importing cars, in the interest of the alliance?"

"Yes, we are very sensitive to those concerns, Mr. Piper," Saeki said, smiling as at a kindergartener who has just presented a Play-Doh sculpture for inspection. "That is why our manufacturers increasingly are producing cars in the United States, instead of exporting from Japan. You may be interested to know that the biggest exporter of American-made cars to Japan is Honda."

"So I've heard," Piper muttered. A thousand times, if once, he thought.

"Indeed, that is why we find it so strange that our efforts to create jobs and bring technology to your country are now being rewarded with threats to steal from us our legally built and operated factories," Saeki went on with sudden iciness and something near to hatred. "I can assure you, Japan will not sit idly by if those threats become reality."

Piper caught Marianne's eye, and she returned his look of astonishment. They both had heard Japanese diplomats deplore the expropriation bill too many times, but never with such bluntness.

"What do you mean?" she asked. "What would Japan do about it?"

"Ah, well," Saeki smiled. He seemed to have himself in check again. "You know we never discuss hypotheticals."

The conversation drifted back to the telecommunications talks. As the reporters alternately crammed scrambled eggs into their mouths and scribbled his remarks, Saeki stressed how many concessions the Japanese already had made, and how unreasonable the Americans were being. The United States was insisting that its companies win a certain percentage of all business in Japan, he was saying, but if the Americans don't try harder, what can we do? This was a familiar refrain, too. The Japanese work harder, make better products, invest more; the Americans are lazy, what they do best is complain. Later the visiting U.S. delegation—staying at this same hotel, running up a bill that on its own would knock the trade deficit for a loop—would hold a press conference at the U.S. embassy across the street, to complain about Japanese intransigence, insist that Japan could unlock the market if it chose and warn that further stonewalling would inflame Congress and help ignite a trade war that would send both countries, but especially Japan, into depression.

Piper finished his melon and took another croissant from the waiter soundlessly passing a basket of baked goods.

After breakfast, he rode down in the elevator with Marianne.

"That was an unusually childish shot you took at Saeki today, even for you," she said.

"Thanks," Piper said. "Good to see you, too."

"You look glum," she said. "What's up?"

"I really blew it with Kyoko yesterday," Piper said.

"Yesterday?" Marianne perked up. "A Sunday? This is interesting. Tell me more. This sounds like a major development. What were you doing with Kyoko on a Sunday?"

"Blowing it, I told you," Piper said. In the hushed lobby businessmen from many countries whispered and waited for rendezvous beside a display of prize-winning irises.

"You've been doing that for three years," Marianne said. "What's the big deal?"

"This time was different," Piper said. "I finally had a chance."

"Come on, I'll buy you an eight-dollar cup of coffee," Marianne said. "Not many girls would."

Piper shook his head. "I'll call you later," he said, and headed for the revolving door.

At the office Kyoko was primly opening and sorting mail.

"Hey," he said.

"Good morning," she said, and then, noticing the necktie, "Where have you been?"

"Gleaning pearls of wisdom from Saeki the Beautiful," Piper said. "It turns out things would go better if the Americans didn't push Japan so hard."

He sat on the couch and watched her open mail for a few minutes. "Listen, Kyoko, about yesterday," he said. "I'm sorry. I was a real asshole. I'll never behave like that again."

"There's nothing to be sorry for," she said, still busying herself sorting press releases and stock market analyses. "It was my mistake, and it won't happen again."

"Don't say that!" Piper pleaded. "It was not your mistake, it was my mistake. But it wasn't what I'm really like, I promise. It was just—it was just our first fight. We got it out of the way, and now we can move on."

Kyoko came over and sat next to Piper on the couch. "John, I do like you. You are very smart, and funny, and fun to be with. You don't hate Japan nearly as much as you would like everyone to think. And it turns out you are pretty good at kissing." She stood and walked to the window and looked out as she continued. "But I've known other men who were smart and funny and attractive, and very much in love with me, until I showed interest in them. Then they changed. The way you talked yesterday, I could imagine you changing, too, and I don't want that to happen."

"So there's no second chance?"

She turned to face Piper again. "As long as we're working together, I think we should keep our relationship as it has been."

Piper rose, retrieved the latest telex from his desk drawer and handed it to Kyoko. "Well, if that's your concern, it may not be a problem much longer," he said. She read the message, looked at Piper, read the message again. "This one sounds serious, John," she said. When he offered no disagreement, she pulled the hand-drawn map from a desk drawer. All the colors were as bright as ever, Piper noted with relief.

"So what do we do about this?" she asked.

"What choice do we have?" Piper said. "We have to follow the map. At least, I have to."

"They'll never give permission, you know that," Kyoko said.

"We won't ask," Piper said.

"John, is this really worth losing your job over?" Kyoko said. "This woman may be crazy, you said that yourself. There may be nothing at the end of this path. Yamada probably died decades ago; maybe he's buried in this red circle. And even if you do find something, what good will it be if you're out of work? Where are you going to print it? And who's going to pay for this trip?"

"I'm not going to lose my job," Piper said. "Look, there is something going on here, something big. Shimizu was scared for a reason. And if we can figure it out, and send in the story, a big fat exclusive with all the loose ends tied up, even they will recognize it for what it is, and everything else will be forgotten."

"That sounds like what you said before the last trip, before this latest telex," Kyoko said.

"Okay, I'll go myself," Piper said.

"That's not what I mean, as you know," she answered. "I just don't want you doing something you'll regret."

"That I did yesterday," he said. She didn't reply, and after a moment he said, "Look, I'll make a deal with you. Who are the two people who we know for sure are alive who seem to know something about what went on in Nishina's day? Okamoto, of course, one. And the tea pourer, right? Well, we can't go back to Okamoto. But you could go back to Shimizu, and then we'd know. If she's crazy, fine. If she has hundreds of maps in her little kettle room, each drawn from fancy and leading to some other imaginary circle, fine. But if she's not crazy, and if you see she's not, you'll come with me to Niigata tomorrow."

"Why me? Why don't you go talk to her? You're the one she's praying for."

"I can't go back without attracting attention, and maybe running into Okamoto, and scaring her all over again," Piper said. "You can pass as just another student, nobody will look at you twice."

"Thank you," Kyoko said. "That's not how you seemed to feel yesterday."

"You know what I mean," Piper said, adding, "I'll go with you as far as the campus gate."

So, wordlessly they retraced their steps, back into the cocooned heat of the subway, along the narrow alleys of Hongo-sanchome, past window exhibits of floppy disks and books on CDs. As they again approached the great red gate, Piper squinted at the stores across the street and said, "I'll wait for you in that coffee shop there—the Bali." Kyoko nodded, and strode through the gate.

Less than thirty minutes later Piper was flipping through his reporter's notebook, surprised at how few notes he had taken at breakfast, and wondering if he could nonetheless salvage some day story to feed the wolves back home, when the front door opened and the proprietess called out her standard "Welcome!" Piper had seen fear in many people, and he knew the expression "wide-eyed with fear" was wrong. It was more often narrowed eyes and clenched jaws, tightness and whiteness, and Kyoko showed all the signs now as she slid into the booth across the table from him.

"She wasn't there," Kyoko whispered. "And when I asked the young girl who worked there about her, she looked terrified. John, I think something must have happened to her."

A waitress approached with a cool washcloth and a glass of ice water and waited for Kyoko's order. "She'll have iced coffee," Piper said in Japanese after Kyoko herself said nothing.

When the waitress had left, Kyoko said shakily, "Don't you think maybe it's time to call the police?"

"And say what?" Piper said. "There was an old tea pourer, and now she's gone, and we don't really know her name, but we think she left us this treasure map, and a long time ago she may have been the lover of a physicist who your government may have killed in 1945, or else in 1955, or else he's still alive, and what are you going to do about it? Your stolid men in gray would love that."

The coffee arrived. Piper ordered another for himself, and they were silent for a moment. Kyoko emptied the tiny glass pitcher of liquid sweetener into her glass, stirred, and took a long drink. Piper asked her if she'd seen Okamoto, or anyone else. She shook her head.

"I went straight to the little room where they brew the tea," Kyoko said.

"And there were no signs of her? No colored pens, no photos on the wall?"

Kyoko shook her head. "But there was an extra apron, which I asked the girl about."

"And?"

"She just looked terrified again, and said she had to go serve some people upstairs. And she ran out, and I thought I'd better leave, too," Kyoko said. "John, what do you think has happened?"

"I don't know," Piper said. "But I know that on the phone yesterday she felt she didn't have much time."

Piper watched Kyoko's mouth as she drank the last of her coffee through a straw, and remembered the press of her kiss, and thought again of that hotel room in Madras, her cool, dry hand, her smooth brown leg. That's what we need, he thought—to get out of this drab, constricted little island to someplace warm and sensual and full of color.

Kyoko leaned back in her chair and pressed the washcloth to her face. "So what do we do now?" she said through the cloth.

"I don't know about you," Piper said. "I'm leaving for Niigata tomorrow."

"And what about the desk?"

"We'll just have to take a chance that nothing big happens in the next couple of days," Piper said. "Maybe I can get Marianne to cover for me."

"Okay," Kyoko said. "I'll meet you at the usual spot in Ueno Station at eight."

"Bring a sleeping bag," Piper said. "If we're going to end up paying our way, we might as well stay at youth hostels."

Kyoko smiled. "I'm sure Christopher does the same all the time," she said.

"Before we're done, he'll wish he'd camped out with us."

They slid out from the booth, and Piper took the check to the front of the coffee shop to pay. As they exited into the heat, Kyoko said, "By the way, what is an oriental honey, and who told Huddleston that I am one?"

"Don't take that the wrong way," Piper said. "Where I come from, 'oriental honey' is slang for a dogged, untiring investigative reporter."

"I see," Kyoko said. "You know, sometimes I feel I'll never get the hang of this language."

16

*T*hat evening Piper dutifully attended the U.S. embassy briefing on the telecommunications talks. It was due to start at seven; at eight the delegation had yet to arrive. Japanese reporters, all male, hung about the lobby smoking and chatting softly, watched over by a humorless U.S. Marine inside a bulletproof glass booth. Foreign reporters, who by and large did not smoke, waited in the auditorium. Piper slouched on a chair with his feet up on the chair in front, gossiping with Marianne. Her credentials hung on a chain around her neck, and she was chewing gum and absentmindedly popping a cassette in and out of her tape recorder. For Marianne, covering a press conference was akin to torture, and reporting in Japan, with its succession of tame breakfasts, receptions, speeches and factory tours, was one long Inquisition. She longed to be with guerrillas in the bush, with terrorists in the slums, with demonstrators choking on tear gas, and she was truly happy, Piper thought, only when the bullets began whining past. He was the opposite, as he had come to understand one steamy afternoon in Islamabad when an anti-American mob, repulsed from the U.S. embassy, had fastened on Piper and Marianne, both hunched over in a nearby ditch, as more accessible targets. Seeing no escape, Piper had mourned the waste and indignity of dying for his unappreciative newspaper, and was wondering whether the *Advertiser* would even put his obituary out front, when he looked over to see Marianne in ecstasy, eyes shining, lips parted, as he had certainly never seen her in their more private moments. She had grabbed his hand and pulled him out of the ditch, and somehow they had fled down an alley, rocks spattering the mud around them as they ran, until they reached their hotel, where Piper had repaired to the shower and Marianne to the telex room. The next morning she had telephoned his room, already bored with the story in Pakistan, to say that the war against the Tamil Tigers was heating up, hundreds of mutilated corpses had been found in a Sri Lankan village, and how about grabbing a flight to Colombo? Fortunately for Piper, the *Advertiser* was more miserly than the *Globe,* and he had begged off that day, as he often did when Marianne happily forsook placid Tokyo for the latest Asian hot spot.

So this press conference was just something she had to do while waiting for her next flight out. And, in truth, Piper thought as he watched Marianne restlessly playing with her tape machine, she resembled nothing so much as an airline passenger waiting impatiently in the terminal for a flight that has been delayed.

"You going to file tonight?" she asked.

"Assuming nothing's happened, you mean?" Piper said. "What would I say?" He assumed the voice of a radio announcer. " 'Nothing happened in the first day of a new round of U.S.-Japanese trade talks that are crucial to a number of industries which you have never heard of that make products which you cannot pronounce, senior officials reported tonight.' "

"Well, you know Christopher will be filing, and hyping for all it's worth," Marianne said, speaking in a quieter voice. The *Times* bureau chief, in a seersucker suit and pale blue tie, was holding forth to an embassy press aide, whose task was to keep the reporters in good humor during the delay. The embassy generally assigned one aide to the *Times* correspondent and one to the rest of the press corps. " 'U.S. and Japanese negotiators tonight teetered perilously close to a breakdown in trade talks that analysts said are crucial to one of America's key industries of the future, reliable sources disclosed tonight.' "

"That's very good," Piper said. "I had kind of guessed you must be ghostwriting his copy. Only you're wrong about one thing: he probably has already filed. Why wait for the press conference? The facts might spoil his story."

"Ooh, very catty," Marianne smiled. "But enough pleasant chitchat about our friends. Tell me what happened with Kyoko yesterday."

"It's too painful," Piper said.

"Listen, who do you think you're keeping secrets from?" Marianne said. "I know everything there is to know about you, in case you'd forgotten. You come too fast, you wear socks to bed. What more painful could there be?"

"Christ, Marianne, keep your voice down," Piper said. "I thought our time together was sacred to you."

"Right," she said. "Uh-oh. Here come our bulldog negotiators. I can hardly wait to hear the news."

The top-ranking American was a deputy secretary of something-or-other who until recently had served as chief fund-raiser for a Republican senator. He knew enough about telecommunications to dial a telephone, and was less of an expert on Japan. None of the American bargainers, in fact, could speak Japanese (every Japanese diplomat spoke English).

The deputy secretary raised Piper's hopes when he cheerfully opened his remarks by noting that he hadn't been in Japan since the 1950s, and that he was very impressed by the obvious industriousness of the Japanese people, their shiny new cars and tall buildings. This guy may be asinine enough to merit a story all his own, Piper thought; maybe he'll even talk about our little yellow friends. But the deputy secretary, after his first promising sally into unscripted territory, quickly retreated into safe and familiar diatribes prepared by his staff long before the talks began. Piper tuned out, his thoughts turning again to Shimizu and her map. If I file tonight, he reasoned, they'll expect something tomorrow, too; no point in spoiling them now.

After the briefing Piper and Marianne walked out together into the summer darkness, down the embassy's cement stairs and through its iron gate. A couple of blocks farther downhill squatted a cheap noodle joint where they often snacked, directly across the street from one of Tokyo's more elegant *ryotei*, a restaurant resembling an elegant private home, where politicians and bureaucrats and businessmen met in private rooms at night, sitting on tatami with their shoes and jackets off, their ties loosened and their cheeks reddening as they cut the real deals of running Japan, while pretty young women in kimono kneeled beside them pouring sake and beer. Each room looked out on its own exquisite garden, and the ladies in charge prided themselves on ensuring that customers in one room never saw the patrons in any other. Secrecy guaranteed, for a price that began, Piper knew, at about 35,000 yen per person—$300 or so, not including drinks or service. At their noodle place, on the other hand, you could get a bowl of udon for 400 yen, and the yakking television came at no extra cost, as did the scrabbling of rodents in the wall. Once Piper asked about the noises, hoping the chef might explain that the hot-water pipes tended to gurgle at night. Instead, the chef had laughed and given the wall a mighty kick, silencing the animals for at least twenty seconds. Piper liked to think of the creatures as mice, though he knew that wasn't likely.

While they waited at the counter, watching the chef and his wife labor over great vats of steaming water, Piper told Marianne an abridged version of his troubles with Kyoko. Marianne had always been dubious about what she called Piper's crush, partly out of some vestigial jealousy, he thought, partly because she didn't want him hurt, and partly due to her general suspicion of western men who chased after Asian women. It was true, Piper agreed, that some American males sought in Japanese females a pliability they could no longer find at home—a willingness to agree with every pronouncement, to laugh at every joke and to squeeze a husband's feet without back talk or complaint. Piper knew full well that in Kyoko's case he'd have to give as many back rubs as he got, it if ever came to that, but there was no point in explaining that to Marianne, nor in telling her that he'd be happy for the chance to rub Kyoko's back even if she never reciprocated.

So Piper tried to tell Marianne just enough to satisfy her curiosity without providing all the details, and then explained that he was in a bit of a jam, that his desk was fuming, that he had to leave town tomorrow on a story that his bosses wouldn't okay. He wondered whether she might help him out if something big broke in Tokyo, could he call, have her read him the wires, maybe give him a few quotes she wasn't using herself, so he could put something together from the boonies, slap on a Tokyo dateline, his desk would never know he was away? She was curious, as always, and Piper couldn't bring himself to tell her what the story was about—whether because it was so big, or because he feared it might crumble in the telling into no story at all, he wasn't sure. It wouldn't be fair, he told himself, to fill Marianne in and then expect her not to go after the story herself. But she didn't take kindly to being left in the dark.

"You've got a lot of gall, asking me to do your legwork so you and your girlfriend can gallivant off somewhere secret to scoop the rest of us," she said. "If you don't trust me enough to tell me about that, you better not trust me to get you any quotes."

"It's probably nothing at all," he said. "As soon as I understand what's going on, I'll tell you all about it, if there's anything to tell. And she's not my girlfriend."

"Whatever," Marianne said. "Anyway, I'm sure as hell not going to be your backup Kyoko. I guess you'll just have to struggle by on your own."

So Piper had packed his little laptop computer, which he could use to file from a pay phone, and his shortwave, so he could pick up the BBC and the Voice of America, and decided to hope for the best. With luck, he thought, they'd be back before the talks concluded. With luck, the emperor wouldn't get shot, the big earthquake wouldn't hit and Congress wouldn't pass the X-bill while they were out of town.

On Tuesday morning, at the ticket gates at Ueno, he met Kyoko, as always an eye of radiant calm in the storm of anxious commuters. She handed him a ticket, and they filed through. They were heading north again.

DISCOVERY

PART III

17

"*Y*ou have the map?" Piper asked.

Kyoko patted her front pocket. She was wearing jeans, a white polo shirt and black Reeboks and carrying a small backpack with her sleeping bag lashed to the bottom. Usually, looking at oriental women, Piper could tell in an instant if they were Japanese, or Korean, or from Hong Kong or California. Japanese themselves always claimed to be set apart from other Asians by some physical characteristic, although what that might be differed from telling to telling: higher cheekbones, more delicate bone structure, fairer skin. It was nonsense, Piper believed; stripped naked and fast asleep, there would be no distinctions. But certainly, awake, dressed, made-up, there were patterns. Korean women chewed gum so robustly they could never be mistaken for Japanese. Japanese women cut their bangs in a little-girl fashion that would be hooted out of Seoul. American women carried themselves with a confidence, a jauntiness, an obliviousness to their surroundings that made them seem clumsy and oversized by the standards of Japanese women, who were raised to approach life tentatively, eager to please and never offend. Japanese girls were even trained not to thrash about or take up much space while sleeping.

But Kyoko could pass as Japanese or American. Not only her voice and dress and hairstyle, but her carriage and personality seemed to undergo transformations. Today, as she led the way to the train platform, she might have been a university student from Berkeley here to brush up on her grandparents' native tongue.

They passed up the bullet train in favor of the cheaper express; they might well be spending their own money on this trip. Once aboard, Piper and Kyoko were able to find seats together. Kyoko tugged a sweater out of her pack to ward off the train's air-conditioning, stowed her pack overhead, sat down, kicked off her shoes, folded her legs under her and promptly closed her eyes. Piper stood leaning on the chair in front, gazing out the window at the controlled bustle on the platform.

It was then that Piper saw the man, and this time he was sure; at least, he was sure for an instant. For an instant he knew it was the man he'd seen at the Asakusa temple gate, and before that outside the little grocery in Kuji, talking to the taxi driver: a good-looking young man in a suit, short hair, square jaw, a muscular chest stretching his white shirt. Now he was checking the board listing the train's departure time and destination, now he was checking his watch; four more minutes, Piper noted, as he quickly checked his own. Now the man was turning away from the train, bending over the magazines at a kiosk on the platform. Now he was turning back, newspaper tucked under his arm, and seeming, chillingly, to look straight into Piper's eyes, though Piper knew the man could see nothing but his own reflection in the glass. Now he was checking his watch again and walking forward—Piper and Kyoko were in the rearmost car—until Piper, pressing forehead to the glass, could see him no longer. He might have boarded the train, he might not. For the first time ever in Japan, Piper felt fear.

He sat down, stood up, sat down again. He noticed he was sweating. He gently poked Kyoko, who opened her eyes alertly as though she hadn't been asleep.

"I think we're being followed," Piper said.

Kyoko glanced across the aisle, where a grandmother was tearing open a bag of dried squid for her husband, who sat near the window, staring at the train on the opposite track. She darted a look behind them, where a young businessman dozed with Walkman earphones on his head. Then she turned back to Piper. "What are you talking about?" she asked.

Her tone immediately made Piper doubt himself. Who was he kidding? This was Tokyo—civilized, peaceful Tokyo—not Moscow or East Berlin. And East Berlin wasn't East Berlin anymore, either. This kind of thing didn't happen except in books, and the books themselves were dated. In Beijing, Piper had been followed, but usually in an open, intimidating way; the security people there wanted foreign reporters to know they had company. But in Tokyo? This was a country where baseball games could end in a tie; what else did you need to know?

And yet, and yet. It wasn't as though all Japanese looked alike to Piper anymore. It was true, when he had first arrived in Tokyo, and met a hundred people in the first week, all of them with too many syllables in their names and not enough distinguishing features, he had had trouble. It didn't help that almost no one was fat, and that everyone tended to dress alike. But over time, his confusion had faded, and now he saw such variety among Japanese that sometimes he would eye a man on the subway and think, He must be Greek, or Italian, or is he Thai? And then he would realize that the man was Japanese, and that his mind still was not accepting the diversity that his eyes had learned to process.

And yet—the man in the temple had worn sunglasses. And the man in Kuji—well, Piper had to admit, he couldn't really remember his face. So how could he possibly be sure this man on the platform was the same? This man who may or may not have boarded the train.

"Maybe we're letting ourselves get carried away by all this," Kyoko was saying, politely speaking in the first person plural.

"You didn't seem so calm yesterday, when you came back from the physics building," Piper said.

The conductor was reciting the train's planned stops one last time over the public address system, politely urging riders to disembark if they had boarded the wrong train.

"That's true," Kyoko said. "But—well, last night, at home with my mother—"

"You didn't tell her about all this?" Piper said sharply.

"No, no, of course not," Kyoko said quickly. "I just mean, everything seemed so safe and normal, and it made me stop and think, this is Japan, after all. However much this place can get to you—well, it just doesn't seem like the kind of country where government agents go around—how did you say it?—rubbing out gray-haired old ladies."

"Yes, I know," Piper said. "It's the yakuza who go around bumping off gray-haired ladies, and then only if the gray-haired ladies won't move out of their little wooden houses so the yakuza's developer friends can build new parking garages."

"They don't bump off little old ladies, either," Kyoko said. "They just scare them, and maybe burn their houses down."

"Oh, well, then," Piper said. "If they can't take a joke, right?" But Japan could in fact be stultifyingly safe. Sometimes it seemed a policeman was always within sight, on foot or pedaling a clunky white bicycle or simply planted on a corner, impassively watching life go by. Only days after Piper had moved into his little flat, a stocky neighborhood cop had knocked on his door, politely seeking to register him.

The train began its glide out of the station. They were on schedule, of course, but the conductor nonetheless was back on the microphone, offering deep apologies for any inconvenience the railway company may have caused its customers in any way.

"Still," Piper said. "I think I'll walk forward and just see if that guy is on the train." He was starting to climb over Kyoko's legs when the door at the front of their car slid open. A young foreign woman wearing mountain-climbing boots and lugging a heavy pack, sweating as if she'd been stumbling through several cars looking for a seat, stepped in to survey the possibilities here. And right behind her, calmly waiting while she rested her pack on the floor and then hoisted it again, was the muscular man. Piper fell back into his seat and hissed, "There he is."

The man surveyed the car, eyes flitting over them as indifferently as the rest, and then, like any passenger having decided that better seats awaited elsewhere, he retreated. The door slid closed behind him.

"Well?" Piper said.

"I don't know," she said. "He doesn't look familiar to me."

"He doesn't look like that guy in Kuji? Don't you remember, how he slunk away when we came out of the store?"

"Oh, come on," Kyoko said. "I remember someone walking away, not slinking away."

"What about at the temple? You don't remember seeing him there? Wearing sunglasses, right when we were finding the map?"

"And a hat low over his eyes?" Kyoko smiled at Piper. "No, I don't. On the other hand, you may recall I had other things on my mind, like apologizing for a dumb gaijin who was desecrating our holy shrine."

"A job you handled admirably," Piper said. "Listen, I'm sure it's the same guy, Kyoko. Reasonably sure, anyway. At least, I really think he might be."

"That's convincing," Kyoko said. "You know, for a secret agent, he doesn't seem very discreet."

"That's true," Piper said. "Maybe they want us to know. Or maybe they figure all Japanese look alike to us, just like we all look alike to them."

"We?"

"Well, you're tainted by association, you know that," Piper said. "An honorary gaijin. Or dishonorary, as the case may be."

Piper watched out the window for a few minutes. They were following a different line than the train to Ichinoseki, this one through the northwestern suburbs instead of the northern. But they looked the same, as did, Piper knew, the western and southwestern suburbs, too. The train flashed past a narrow shopping street, and for some reason the scene stuck in Piper's mind: covered sidewalks festooned, like all such shopping streets, with plastic cherry blossoms in pastel greens and pinks, and the crossing bar, painted red and white, bouncing slightly as the train thundered past. A young woman on a bicycle waited to cross the tracks, a toe on the ground to balance herself as the red light flashed and the bells rang. Her cheeks were scrubbed red, she wore a white blouse and navy skirt and white ankle socks and sneakers, and onto a baby seat on her bicycle she had piled instead the morning groceries. Maybe the baby was home, taking its morning nap, while grandmother had her second cup of tea and leafed through the morning paper. Piper suddenly wished that he was off the train, with that woman, that he was that woman, or her husband, knowing how life would unfold from now until his death, a routine of small-town shopping and working and meals, evening television and weekend novels, strolls through the park with their baby girl, everything predictable, everything defined. Her husband worked in the local bank, he thought, from eight until six every day, checking ledgers and accounts that were never amiss, hoping someday to make branch manager, and what more could life offer than such security, a home, three meals a day, a laughing baby daughter with a rice-bowl haircut, grandparents nearby, a movie once a month. . . . He turned back to Kyoko. Why should she want to hitch her life to his, anyway? He would never feel at home here in such a life, but he would never feel at peace in the United States, either. What kind of life could he offer?

"In any case, I think we should find out for sure if he's following us, and lose him if he is," Piper said.

"How?"

Piper was looking at the foreign woman, who had settled into a seat a couple of rows ahead and was studying what looked to be a trail map.

"We'll do some mountain-climbing," Piper said. "Did you bring your map?"

"Yes, I already told you," she said.

"Not that one," Piper said. "Your regular map of Japan."

She stood and stretched to unzip a pocket of her pack on the rack above and pull out the well-worn map, her shirt lifting to reveal a narrow strip of flat brown stomach.

Together they studied the network of national parks they would be crossing as the train pierced the mountains that separated the Pacific Ocean coast from the Sea of Japan side of the narrow island. They decided to get off at Jomo-Kogen, about an hour out of Tokyo.

"We'll stand by the door in plenty of time, in case he's not very good at what he does," Piper said. "And then, one way or another, we'll know for sure."

"You're going to feel pretty silly when we're all alone on the platform," Kyoko said.

"Not at all," Piper said. "I've always wanted to see Jomo-Kogen."

18

*H*e followed them off the train. No, don't jump to conclusions, Piper thought. He disembarked at the same station. Maybe this is where he lives.

Nor was he the only one. There was the foreign woman struggling with her rucksack, and the usual farmers and salarimen and others who would transfer to local trains, and then there were the Japanese mountain climbers, dozens of them, each turned out as if to attack the Matterhorn. Ropes, pitons, equipment that Piper couldn't name. Some even wore lederhosen. Among them must be a few serious mountain climbers, while others would merely stroll a few miles and then pitch their tents, but all had to sport the ultimate in mountain gear, just as every ten-speed bicyclist in Tokyo wore stretch shorts in Day-Glo colors and little caps from the Tour de France. There was a right way and a wrong way to do everything, and there was no point in doing things wrong.

Piper and Kyoko joined the small crowd flowing toward the ticket taker, aware of the man about twenty feet behind them. Like Piper, he was tall, and easy to keep track of. He had no luggage that Piper could see, and no briefcase. He seemed relaxed, up to nothing in particular.

Piper struck up a conversation with the florid woman with the big orange rucksack, who turned out to be Australian. She was going hiking in a nearby national park, she said, and offered to show them the way, as best she could figure it from her hitchhikers' guide to Japan. They boarded a bus, idling, driverless, and hot. By now it was midmorning, and no breeze stirred the diesel fumes in the dusty plaza. The man was nowhere to be seen.

More and more hikers climbed aboard, including a group of

middle-aged women with carved Austrian walking sticks and scarves tied around their foreheads. The women sat behind Piper, while the Australian sat across the aisle, her pack resting on the seat beside her.

"I know you all like company when communing with nature," Piper said, "but doesn't this bus seem a bit crowded for a Tuesday, in the middle of nowhere? Even for Japan, I mean?" Kyoko eavesdropped on the ladies behind them, who were chattering and fanning their gleaming faces, and then turned to ask a question. The apparent leader of the group delivered a lengthy response.

"It seems the *nikko-kisuge* are at their peak," Kyoko said. "We're in luck." She was speaking to Piper and to the Australian, who said, "The what?"

"It's a kind of yellow lily," Kyoko said. "It blooms in July, and these highlands are famous for them. I'm sure we'll have plenty of company." That would be nothing new, Piper thought. He had once visited a park in Atami where the plum trees bloomed in February, when Tokyo, only an hour's train ride away, remained chilled and barren. He had imagined a lovely walk through the woods, alone, or joined perhaps by a few ladies in kimono being photographed with their parasols beneath delicate pale clouds of blossoms. Instead, after walking past one cement hot-spring hotel uglier than the last, he had reached the small park, only to find buses cramming the parking lot and garish stalls jostling for space along the narrow walkway, hawking sake or pressed rice cakes or plum-blossom souvenirs—plum wine, plum candy, plum dolls. The blossoms themselves could barely be seen, and as for what an American might call "experiencing" them—better to buy a postcard and study it at home. But the Japanese tourists seemed fulfilled. They had read the haiku ahead of time, they knew how blossoms look. Why be lonely now? And of course cherry-blossom time was even less lonely. All through March the evening news tracked the ripening buds, and when the trees were declared officially at their peak, all of Tokyo descended on the few city sites with enough remaining topsoil to support the cherished trees. Offices dragooned junior workers to seize choice spots twelve hours ahead of time, rain or shine, and the hapless young men stretched out on blankets, physically staking their claims until morning. By Peak Blossom Sunday, millions upon millions would be paying homage to the subtle delicacy of the flowers by guzzling beer and sake and whiskey, grilling fish on small hibachi, singing exuberantly into microphones rigged up to powerful loudspeakers and guzzling some more. One spring the trees might bloom in orange and blue polka dots, Piper thought, and no one would notice the change.

A driver finally boarded, closed the door and, with a great grinding of gears, set off. The muscular man hadn't bounded on to the bus at the last minute nor, craning his neck, did Piper catch sight of him in the square or in a trailing taxi.

"Think we lost him already?" Piper said.

"He probably lives around here, he's on his way home from a weekend in Tokyo, we've never seen him before and we'll never see him again."

"Maybe so," Piper said. "Anyway, haven't you always wanted to see the *nikko-kasugi*?"

"*Kisuge*," Kyoko corrected. "Sure. Why not go for a walk in the country when you're about to lose your job for not covering the telecommunications talks?"

"A low blow," Piper said. "But you can't frighten me. They won't come to an agreement until tomorrow at the earliest. We're safe camping out tonight." As usual, leaving Tokyo had picked up his mood.

"Camping out? You didn't tell me that part," Kyoko said, and then added, in a lower voice, "If someone really is after us, I'm not sure I'd want to spend the night in the middle of the woods."

"I'll protect you," Piper said.

"Great."

For a time, they chatted across the aisle with Audrey, the Australian. She had volunteered to teach English in a small-town high school in Kyushu, and her experience there, she recounted, had been educational, if challenging. The only other English teacher in her school could not speak or understand more than a few words of the language, especially in Audrey's unfamiliar accent, although he could teach the arcane points of grammar that students needed to pass their university entrance exams. When, on her first day, the teacher discovered that Audrey inexplicably could not explicate her use of predicates, nor even diagram the sentences she spoke, he refused to let her talk in his classroom. Learning to speak and understand would only distract his pupils from preparing for exams. The father of the house where she had been assigned to live, meanwhile, assumed that she must be a young woman of easy virtue—he assumed the same of all foreign women, especially those with large breasts—and he rarely lost an opportunity to barge accidentally into the tiny bathroom while she soaked, or to reach across her side of the car, to roll the window up, or down, or both, while driving her to school each morning, and to brush his arm against her chest each time he did so. One evening, after he had burst into the bathroom while she was soaking, and then taken his bath later, in the same water as was of course the custom of the house, she laughingly mentioned before turning in that he had so startled her she had been unable to keep herself from urinating in the tub. He turned green and from then on became distinctly less forgetful about knocking. And with time, she said, she had made friends with several teachers, and with the hardworking mother of her household as well. Now, after a brief vacation in Japan, she was hoping to get a job with Nikko Securities in Sidney.

"They own half the country already, you know," she said, speaking of the Japanese in Australia. "This is the future."

From time to time, Piper surveyed the road behind them, each time eliciting what he took to be a knowing smile from Kyoko. And indeed, he saw nothing suspicious. He dozed off, his head leaden and his mouth cottony from the heat. At their stop almost everyone piled off the bus.

Compared to the plum garden in Atami, this park proved almost deserted. At its entrance dozens of stalls offered fried noodles and octopus omelets, and there were huts where hikers could spend the night on fresh tatami, and bathe, and dine. Through the marsh itself, an elevated walkway ran for miles, giving the outing a theme-park air, and the walkway was well traveled today. Certainly, there was little danger of encountering deer or other wildlife. Yet the valley itself was glorious, hedged by mountains that each hid their peaks in little fleecy clouds, and bursting with flowers so yellow it made you happy just to look at them. Audrey and Piper and Kyoko and the band of Austrian-walking-stick women set off together, as if their public bus ride from the station had bonded them into an unlikely tour group.

Like all Japanese these days, the women wanted Piper to explain why America, his rich, powerful country, had turned on their poor island nation, which meant no harm and only wanted to get along in the world. Most of them were old enough to just barely remember the U.S. Occupation after the war, and they fondly recalled for Piper the awe they felt toward the GIs, those great, healthy, gum-chewing, wisecracking, galumphing specimens who tossed bizarre-tasting candy to children and strode across Tokyo in oversized boots. Now those specimens seemed to be turning into bullies, they said, kicking sand into the face of a loving, well-intentioned younger brother.

Piper listened absentmindedly, glancing over his shoulder from time to time, but he never saw the muscular man with short hair. It was midafternoon, and the sun was slipping behind the mountain range to the west, when their gangplank crossed a byway that seemed to wind into the mountains to the east, and Piper decided they should make a move. Promising to look for Audrey and the ladies' hiking auxiliary at a resting hut that night, he and Kyoko jumped off the elevated walkway.

The dirt path wound first through flat marsh and then headed up, into a band of woods. As they entered the trees, they stopped in the shadows and looked behind them: again, nobody.

"Still not satisfied?" Kyoko said.

"I know you think I'm crazy," Piper answered. "But we've come this far, we might as well make sure." The path climbed steeply, sometimes straight up into the woods, sometimes cut into the slope at sharp angles. The footing was soft and piney, but the path was narrow; some of the hairpin turns had all but crumbled away. After a few minutes Piper was sweating and Kyoko was breathing hard.

They came, after maybe ten minutes in the woods, to a large flat rock jutting out over the valley. From it, the elevated walkway was a jagged brown line through the yellow and green, with a steady parade of dots moving both ways along it. And then, as they rested, they both saw, at the same instant, one dot detach itself from the parade and set off in their direction. There could be no doubt: a solitary hiker was taking their path. *"Eh? Yappari,"* Kyoko said under her breath. What the hell? Could it be true?

"Come on, let's go," Piper said, scrambling to his feet and jumping down from the rock back onto the path.

"To where? For what?" Kyoko said. "I'd rather be with the others, down there, than alone with this guy at the top. What are we going to do when we get there?"

"I don't know," Piper said. "We'll figure something out when the time comes." Suddenly, he felt angry, not at the dot below, but at Saeki, and Okamoto, and all the other smooth hotshots with their veneer of civility and pacifism and goodwill to all men. It was all a show, and the foreigners who got the biggest dose of buttering-up, the Christophers and the rest, all fell for it, and why not? Wined and dined in exquisite Japanese restaurants, talking poetry and philosophy, watching Kurosawa movies, weekending at three-hundred-dollar-a-night ryokan where the maids bowed and scraped and flattered, always flattered: how deftly you wield your chopsticks, how clearly you speak Japanese, how piercingly you understand our unique and precious culture. All lies, of course, and the better you really did understand, the more nervous they became, and the less inclined to flatter. And all the while their goons were at work, and the establishment was plotting its takeover of the world—well, maybe not the world, but whatever choice, juicy parts of it Japan felt like biting off—and smiling, smiling, smiling, our precious friendship with the American people, the most important alliance in the world, we will always play second fiddle to you. Sure. Until you got at something they cared about, something they wanted to hide—for whatever reason; Piper still couldn't say why, he had to admit.

"Slow down!" Kyoko had fallen behind, and Piper realized he'd been nearly running up the mountain. Despite the lengthening shadows, he was covered in new sweat, and his pulse was racing. He stopped, waiting for Kyoko to catch up, and apologized.

"I guess he gave me a start," Piper said.

"I guess so," Kyoko said, looking at him oddly. "Are you sure this is a good idea? What are we really going to do?"

"We'll pull off somewhere, and let him pass us, and we'll go back down," Piper said. "That's all. He's wearing street shoes and a suit. By the time he gets back, we can be back on the train. I just don't want him following us to our red circle, whatever it may be."

The sun had dimmed to a bright glow behind the mountains facing them, which had taken on a grayish, purplish hue. The path grew steeper, and slippery. Little soil was here, and few things grew, and soon they entered a chilly fog. The valley, and then the woods, dropped from view, nor could they sense how far above lay the peak.

Suddenly, they heard a voice just ahead, and they both jumped, grabbed hold of each other and froze. The fog swirled around them; Piper thought he could feel each hair standing up on his arm. And then they heard it again, an eerie, detached, mechanical voice wailing, *"Irrasshaimase!"* Welcome!

"It sounds like a tape," Kyoko whispered. They crept forward, and a small shelter appeared out of the fog, with a matted roof, a bench—and a talking soda machine. Piper exhaled something that was meant as a laugh. Talking machines were among Japan's few technological innovations not to catch on in the United States, but they were fondly regarded here. Trucks called out, "Turning left," in incongruous female voices before they turned left. You couldn't get on an escalator in a Japanese department store without being reminded to grab the handrail and stand between the yellow lines, which were painted so close to the edges that it was impossible to stand anywhere else. Even at the mystical rock garden in Kyoto a never-ending tape advised visitors how to appreciate the scene, and reminded them not to linger. And why not? You could never have too much noise, nor too much companionship.

After resting on the bench for a few minutes, lost in the fog with their soda machine, Piper said, "Let's not go any farther."

They slipped and slid a few dozen yards downhill, found a niche from where they could see anyone coming up the path but not be seen from below or above, and sat down uncomfortably to wait, staring into the fog.

They waited, and waited, and waited. Piper would think he saw a man taking shape in the gloom, only to find that his eyes, and the swirling mists, were playing tricks. No one in the world knew where they were, he realized. Marianne knew he was out of town, no more. Audrey might remember that an American and his Japanese girl-friend had cut off the path, but she didn't even know his name. Kyoko's mother? She almost certainly knew only that Kyoko was gone for the week. He remembered Yamada, and his death in a supposed hiking accident. After fifteen minutes of waiting Piper had been afraid to make the smallest move. Now another fifteen minutes had passed, and his limbs were heavy logs beneath him. If the man came at them now, Piper couldn't hobble away, let alone run.

Ten minutes more. They might die from exposure before any assassin came along. Not wanting to risk even a whisper, he caught Kyoko's eye and shrugged. He would feel pretty silly hiking back down the mountain and passing the man, waiting calmly on the elevated boardwalk.

But then, suddenly, and much closer than Piper had expected, the man materialized, like a yacht suddenly slipping out of the fog into full view. Piper heard Kyoko catch her breath, but the man was oblivious; nor did he seem uncomfortable. He walked at a measured pace, his tie still knotted neatly at the throat, his shoes barely scuffed, his face calm and cheerful. He looked, Piper had to admit, more like a pleasant young bureacrat strolling through the Ginza than a killer stalking his prey. But then, Piper thought, he wasn't strolling through the Ginza. He was hiking a godforsaken mountain trail in pursuit of two negligible employees of a second-rate American newspaper. Why? What could be so important to him, and whomever he worked for?

The man passed their hiding place and, a few yards farther on, stopped, taking a deep breath into his wide chest. He seemed to study the ground for a moment, and Piper's heart clutched. But the path here was smooth rock; there couldn't be footprints. And after a moment he resumed his deliberate tread, disappearing quickly into the fog. Kyoko and Piper remained motionless until suddenly they heard, like a foghorn in the dusk, the distant call of the soda machine: *"Irrasshaimase!"* Piper smiled and gingerly, very gingerly, began to unfold his legs.

19

*T*he map proved to be remarkably accurate, and detailed in the oddest ways. Later, when Piper recalled their treasure hunt, he thought those details might just have reflected the way Shimizu looked at the world, or her haste in drawing the map, nothing more. But at the time, he and Kyoko felt they were deciphering a secret code.

They had given the man the slip—literally as well as figuratively, it seemed, as they skidded down the mountain. By the time they reached bottom, night had fallen, and more stars danced above the slumbering lilies than Piper had ever imagined might shine over these rainy, rocky islands. Almost giddy at their return to the civilized world, Piper had reached for Kyoko's hand, and to his relief she seemed happy for the contact. Her fingers were cool and dry and relaxed as they twined through his and he felt, for a few minutes, as if life might never again offer a moment so deliciously at peace.

In town they found a tempura shop still willing to cook, and even Kyoko ate ravenously, taking a third bowl of rice as they sat at the counter, watching the chef deep-fry, two by two, slices of eggplant and small filleted sardines and plump prawns. They took turns filling each other's glasses with beer, and Kyoko downed two before the oil in the chef's big vat was even bubbling.

"So tell me," she said after the second glass. "How pretty is your Japanese teacher?"

"What are you talking about?" Piper said. "He's over sixty, and not very pretty at all."

"Ah, I know you're lying," she said.

Piper laughed. "How can you be so sure?"

"Because you talk like a girl, like a well-brought-up young lady," Kyoko said. "And very well, too, by the way."

"I can't stand it," Piper said. "I kill myself to learn this language, turning my brain inside out, and now it turns out I was learning the wrong version of it. No wonder the lady at the bath always laughs at me."

"Don't worry, it's very endearing," Kyoko said. "So let's hear about your teacher."

By the time they paid the bill, ridiculously cheap by Tokyo standards, and left the shop, she did not shrug off his arm from around her shoulders. But their touching was comfortable, not electric; Piper knew the next move, if any, would have to come from Kyoko, and so he was only barely disappointed when their inn proved to be something like a tatami dormitory, where men and women were sent to separate rooms with futon and blankets to find floor space as best they could.

They rose early the next morning, scouted briefly and without success for Audrey and the ladies' hiking club and more carefully, but also without result, for the muscular pleasant-faced man. Then they boarded a bus, and a train, and another train, and a bus, until they reached the starting point on their secret map in the foothills of Niigata prefecture.

As they stepped off the bus, a scratchy children's tune floated toward them from loudspeakers in a tiny playground across the street. It was five o'clock, and all through Japan, loudspeakers at schools and parks were playing the same tune, or one like it, to warn children to head for home. As Kyoko and Piper watched a mother stoop to gather her son's toys from the sandbox, they debated whether to keep moving or to look for a place to sleep, and then set off the next day. Only a few hours of daylight remained, and they had no idea how long it would take to reach the red circle. And Piper, increasingly nervous about what news he might be missing, wanted to watch the seven o'clock NHK wrap-up. The government network's evening report was as dull and official as a Cuban newspaper account of last year's sugar crop, but it was reliable. If anything had broken Tuesday night, let alone during the day today, Piper wouldn't know anything about it, but wire copy would be flowing onto his editors' computer screens. And if something had happened, and his editor called and no one answered—Piper didn't want to dwell on the consequences.

On the other hand, they had finally reached the starting line, and neither of them wanted to hang around this sleepy town just waiting for another day. Piper felt sure that they had lost their shadow, but he was less sure the man would stay lost, even with sore feet. This was a country where conductors and bus drivers and even ordinary citizens made it their business to notice things and report what they noticed, and, in a remote town like this, a tall gaijin with a beautiful Japanese woman would be noticed, even in what Japanese liked to think of as their era of internationalization.

Besides, they had come this far; it was time, finally, to find out what the hell was going on.

At the corner an old-fashioned pay telephone stood on a rickety stand beneath a tobacconist's awning. It was the kind that didn't accept prepaid telephone cards, so Piper dropped in a copper ten-yen coin and asked the operator to call the *Globe* collect; he knew the number by heart. Marianne herself answered, drawling, *"Soo desshyo nee,"* as if deliberating whether to accept the call. She was joking, but Japanese telephone operators tended not to be big kidders, and this one promptly cut the connection. Piper retrieved his coin and tried again, and this time Marianne accepted the call with good grace.

"Pied Piper!" she said. She no longer sounded angry, he noted with relief. "Ready to reveal all?"

"I don't think you'd be interested," Piper said. "It's just a little feature on the young maiden selected by the Imperial Household Agency to deprive the crown prince of his virginity." Unlike in Great Britain, the sex life of the imperial family was never publicly discussed, which made it all the riper for private speculation.

"Big deal," Marianne said. "I found the catfish who deprived Prince Aya of his." Prince Aya, the younger brother of the crown prince, was a serious ichthyologist, like his grandfather Hirohito and his father the current emperor. "Seriously. Where are you?"

"In Niigata," Piper said. No reason not to be truthful, he thought, especially since Marianne would assume that he was in Niigata city, not the hinterlands of the prefecture. "What's going on in the big city?"

"Not much, don't worry," Marianne said. "Besides the prime

minister resigning, I mean, and Mitsubishi buying Chrysler. I don't think the *Advertiser* would be interested in either of those, would they?"

"Ho-ho," Piper said. "Are you telling me that after two days you have no decent gossip to report?" Not wanting Marianne to flare up again, Piper thought he'd act as though he just wanted to chat, and ask about the real news as a kind of afterthought.

"Well, since you ask," Marianne said slowly.

"This sounds delicious," Piper said.

"Word at the club is that Ribakoff and Fumiko are getting married," she said triumphantly.

"No!" Fumiko was a wealthy young assistant producer at CBS, almost as attractive as she thought she was, who floated teasingly between her two worlds of Japanese aristocracy and heartbroken foreign men. Piper had taken her to dinner once, but clearly hadn't ranked high enough on her social register to reach the heartbreak stage. Ribakoff was an NBC correspondent who definitely was not as attractive as he thought he was. He had arrived in Tokyo a year earlier, so the story went, leaving behind two ex-wives, two fiancées and promises to marry both of the latter within the year. "Do their networks know about this yet?"

"What are they going to do? Keep him off the air?" This was a joke, too, because Ribakoff, like all network correspondents in Tokyo, never got on the air anyway. The news in Japan, important as it may have been, was too visually dull; the producers in New York had seen file footage of Japanese cars being loaded onto cargo ships a few thousand times too often.

"And the girlfriends waiting at the altar?" Piper asked.

"No word yet," Marianne said. "I'm still reporting the story."

"Keep me informed," Piper said. "So what else?"

"One morsel per call, sorry," Marianne said. "Especially when you call collect."

"Fair enough," Piper said. "Anything in the news?"

" 'Anything in the news?' " she mimicked. "Very suave, very casual. I thought you called because you missed me, Piper-san."

"I do miss you," Piper said. "I just thought you might need some help with your lead."

"No, I've already filed on the breakdown in U.S.-Japanese relations and I'm finishing a sidebar on the possibility of war," she said. "Thanks anyhow."

"Come on, Marianne, give me a break," he said.

"Don't worry, they're still jawing," she said. "The Americans are profoundly disturbed at the lack of progress and seriously question whether the Japanese fully comprehend the degree of hostility now facing them in Washington. The Japanese are pleased at the progress so far, cautiously optimistic about arriving at a settlement but a bit disappointed by the strident and unrealistic American demands. Off the record they both say they don't think they'll settle until Friday, and they may need another round in Washington next month."

"Wouldn't that be fabulous," Piper said. "Then someone else would have to write the whole damn thing."

"Yeah," Marianne said, "but don't count on it. Otherwise the House passed the X-bill and sent it over to the Senate, raising the panic level here, as you might imagine. And the rainy season is officially over." The sun had been shining for days, but that bore no relevance to Japanese climatology. "So have you made it past first base yet?"

"Sensitivity is one of your finest qualities," Piper answered. Kyoko was standing next to him, half-listening while she leafed through a magazine on sale at the cigarette window. "No progress, but like Saeki-san, I remain cautiously optimistic."

"That's what makes you such a lovable sap," Marianne said. "She's with you now, I take it?"

"Right," Piper said.

"Well, tell her I don't blame her a bit for stiffing you," Marianne said.

"Thanks again," Piper said. "I'll call you tomorrow."

"Can't wait," Marianne said. "Good luck on your Pulitzer."

He hung up and Kyoko said, "What girlfriends at the altar? And what do you remain optimistic about?"

"Let's get going," Piper said. "I'll fill you in on all the juicy details on the way."

They had studied the map dozens of times, but Kyoko took it out of her pocket anyway and lovingly unfolded it. Shimizu had penciled in dotted lines where they should walk and smooth lines where they could ride. A dotted line seemed to carry them down the main street to an intersection with a kind of ring in one corner.

The street jigged and jogged instead of running straight; this must once have been a castle town, with streets built at angles to discourage enemy attacks. But the castle itself, like the local lord, was long gone. The town, too, seemed almost dead. The old commercial strip they were following was clearly losing out to bigger, flashier stores on the national highway nearby. They passed a dress shop with fashions that only Pyongyang might find fashionable, and in a dusty old pounded-rice-candy shop the owner sat behind the counter drinking tea and squinting over a cigarette. A little grocery store advertised Meiji ice cream; no Haagen-Dazs here; the store seemed proud just to have a freezer. At a corner, finally, was a shop that postdated the feudal era: Darling Donuts, part of a Japanese chain that had arisen to imitate, not very successfully, Dunkin and Mister. Inside, two high-school girls in braids and uniform were drinking cocoa and laughing. Piper started to cross the street, but Kyoko put a hand on his arm.

"This doughnut shop must be the ring on the map," she said. Sure enough, a hundred feet down the side road was a bus-stop bench and a chart showing what times the bus came through. The next was due in ten minutes; even here, Japan hewed to its schedule.

Piper and Kyoko sat on the bench to wait. The town was eerily quiet. Occasionally, an old man passed on a creaking bicycle, and once a teenage boy puttered by on a motorbike, his girlfriend seated behind him, arms around his waist.

The two high-school girls pushed open the doughnut-shop door, sounding an electric bell, and started toward them, still chatting and giggling, their white knee socks bright in the early evening light. When they saw Piper, they stopped short and fell silent, eyes averted. It was the kind of behavior that always made Piper want to expose himself, or shove a chocolate bar in his ear, or in some other way satisfy their most horrified expectations. But he controlled himself. The bus turned into their street.

The high-school girls scampered aboard, flashing their student passes, and Kyoko and Piper clambered after them, dragging their packs up the steps. As soon as they sat down, they understood the next clue on their map, the "440" in Japanese characters. At the front, as on the bus to Tataki village, a light jumped from fare to fare on a price board as the bus advanced. They would reach 440 yen in about ten stops.

"So far, there's method to her madness," Piper said.

"Yes," Kyoko said softly. "It would seem she comes here often, and not so long ago. I would guess the bus fare has changed a few times since the war."

"Even if the bus hasn't," Piper said, as the antique vehicle bumped into a pothole, sending them both bouncing into the air.

The bus wound into the foothills, through woods and past smaller and smaller plots of cultivated land. At a village at 360 yen, the two girls disembarked, casting one last furtive glance at the odd foreign couple. By the time the board neared 440, only a tall and pimply high-school boy at the very back and an old farmer remained. The farmer wore rubber boots that separated his big toe from the rest of his foot, in traditional Japanese style, and the back of his neck was red and lined with years of outdoor work. Piper wondered briefly if the authorities had replaced the muscular man with a more appropriate rural agent.

But when Kyoko and Piper began sidling forward, as 400 yen clicked to 440, the man made no move to follow. The driver growled something to Kyoko in a thick dialect, punctuating his comments with disapproving sighs and sucking-in of breath. Then he pulled onto a pebbled shoulder and let them off.

There Piper and Kyoko found themselves once again enveloped in exquisite silence. No wonder Shimizu had simply written a number; this was a place without a name, a ridge overlooking the town they had left behind and the plain extending to the Sea of Japan. Low in the sky before them, the sun cast a warm, almost palpable light. Behind them a bank of woods rose steeply. Leaning her pack against her legs, Kyoko once more unfolded the map.

"We follow this road," she said.

"Until we come to a policeman," Piper said, looking over her shoulder. "How in hell could she know there'll be a policeman? I can't imagine we'll come across a busy pedestrian crossing." With even the echo of the bus long faded, the road seemed entirely deserted, but they shouldered their packs and set off, Piper entertaining Kyoko with the gossip from Marianne.

"I feel sorry for Fumiko," Kyoko said.

"Why? It seems like she got exactly what she wanted," Piper said.

"She thinks she did, but she'll be disappointed," Kyoko said. "She comes from an aristocratic family, and to rebel against her father she decided to marry a foreigner. But she wants a foreigner with the same status in America as she has here, and she thinks Ribakoff has it because he went to Harvard and is a network correspondent and seems like a big shot in Tokyo. But she doesn't understand America. No matter what happens, no matter what job she has or her father has, her family will always have prestige. Her circle will remember that her great-grandfather was a marquis and her grandfather married the sister of a princess, and her family had a summer place in Karuizawa. But Ribakoff is only important as long as he has this job. He could lose it, or quit it, and he'd be nobody in Washington and New York, right?"

"I suppose," Piper said.

"And she'll feel tricked, but it will be too late," Kyoko said. "Even for a liberated Japanese woman, there are no second chances."

"So," Piper said. "What you're saying is, better to marry a struggling young journalist on his way up, right?" It was a lame attempt at a joke, but Kyoko answered gravely.

"No," she said quietly. "What I'm saying is, better to marry someone who knows there are more important things than status and prizes and which college you went to and which paper you work for."

Piper felt his ears burning. Kyoko, a few steps ahead, kept walking. After a few minutes, he said, "By the way, what did the bus driver say?"

"He warned me that this was a dangerous area to camp in," Kyoko said.

"Dangerous?"

"He said a long time ago the land here was poisoned, and local people don't go into these woods for mushrooms or anything else."

"Poisoned how?"

"He didn't say," Kyoko answered. "He said it's just an old story, and maybe not true, but anyway—*ki o tsukete.*" Literally, stick to your spirit: be careful. In the past Kyoko never would have used even the simplest phrase of Japanese, and Piper felt a small thrill of intimacy, a reprieve from the reproach he felt had been aimed at him a moment before. They walked on in comfortable silence. Piper was sure that Kyoko was thinking about the same kind of poison he was.

They almost missed the policeman. It was one of those cardboard figures common throughout rural Japan, holding up a hand to slow traffic. In Tokyo there were so many real policemen that cardboard ones weren't needed, although their city cousins—cutouts of construction workers bowing their heads in apology—stood by building sites, asking forgiveness for the inconvenience being caused. The cardboard policemen could be remarkably effective on drivers happening on them as they sped around curves, but this one had been knocked over and lay in the grass, face down. Piper actually was a few feet beyond it when his brain registered what it must be.

They turned back and hoisted the poor fellow back on his cardboard feet. A few weeds had grown around him. "I guess she hadn't been here all that recently," Piper said. Restored to his rightful place, the cartoon character was slowing cars with one hand while seeming to point toward a wooded path with his other.

"Now we walk until we hit a giant rice bowl, right?" Piper said.

"A rice paddy, I suppose," Kyoko said, and she was right. The path, more in shadow now than in evening sunlight, deadened at another road, more of a country lane, really, with a small triangular paddy directly in front of them. It was covered with stubble, instead of the lush green grass that should be growing now. The government was paying farmers to keep more and more land out of cultivation, and this must be one of the idled fields.

Aside from the ghosts of old rice paddies, there were no signs of human life. "What next?" Piper said.

"Right, past the dog and turn left," Kyoko said, without looking at the map.

"That'll be an even better trick than the policeman," he said. "I've never seen a cardboard dog, even in the countryside."

But after ten minutes they passed what looked like a small watchkeeper's cottage, and a classic Japanese dog, lithe and foxlike, bounded to the gate and began yapping. They strode past, listening to its barks echo into the hillside. For a time, there were no left turns, only a whitewashed wall following the lane. And then a break in the wall and a kind of driveway, with a chain pulled low across the entrance.

"Now all that's left is the gun, right?" Piper said.

"And the red circle." They stood uncertainly at the entrance. Late afternoon had definitely given way to dusk, and the dark woods were not inviting. Nor did they look forward to meeting up with the map's final clue, that odd-looking gun. Piper suggested they continue on. Kyoko disagreed.

"Everything on the map has made sense so far, and we've already passed the dog," she said. "I think we should go left."

"Okay," Piper sighed. "You speak the language. You lead the way."

Kyoko shot him one of her looks, and then stepped over the chain. Soon they were in deep woods, carpeted with ferns, roofed by tall pines and birches. The driveway, sloping consistently uphill, was little more than two tire tracks through the undergrowth. Kyoko walked in one, and Piper pulled even with her in the other. Around one last curve, they suddenly found themselves in an open field, startled by the clearing and by what they saw at the top of the field, shining in the glow of spotlights hidden in nearby trees.

It was an old farmhouse, a beautiful wooden farmhouse, and it was, without question, the farmhouse in the photograph Mrs. Yamada had given them not so many days before. But instead of six physicists posing in front, and a beautiful young woman stepping, startled, out the door, there was one man, white-haired, wearing a dark blue yukata and a hospitable smile, waiting on the porch expectantly, as though they had arrived slightly late for a dinner party.

"Yamada-san," Kyoko said softly.

"Is it a ghost, or is it real?" Piper whispered.

"He looks real," Kyoko said. "He looks very real."

20

*T*he man waited at his threshold in house slippers. As Kyoko and Piper approached, he said, in formal Japanese, "You are very welcome. Please come in. I am Yamada."

They bowed and introduced themselves and stopped to untie their hiking boots. Yamada bent low to proffer house slippers to his guests, then led them into the farmhouse's central room. Rough-hewn beams above them were tied together with old rope, and the earthen tones of tatami and wood and old ceramics all seemed to take on warmth from a central hearth with glowing embers. A black iron kettle hung above the charcoal, suspended by an iron pole from a carved wooden fish that was, in turn, dangling from the rafters. The fish alone would be worth hundreds of dollars in any Tokyo antique store, Piper knew.

"This is a beautiful house," Piper said, in English, and Kyoko translated demurely. Without prior discussion, they reverted, on instinct, to their normal working pattern. It was safer to give nothing away, not even the knowledge that Piper could understand Japanese.

"Thank you," Yamada said in Japanese. "You must know, I am not a real farmer, and I have ample time to care for my simple home." Indeed, the house was almost too perfect, Piper thought, like those old farmhouses that had been transported, beam by beam, to Tokyo to serve as restaurants or quaint antique shops.

They sat on blue-and-white cushions around the hearth, and Yamada began an elaborate brewing of green tea in an earth-colored pot. "I don't often have visitors," Yamada said through Kyoko. "This isn't an easy place to find. Someone must have given you excellent directions."

"Actually, someone gave us a map," Piper said, also through Kyoko.

"Oh?" Yamada looked up expectantly, but when Piper said nothing further, Yamada didn't pursue it. Instead, he said, "I understand you talked to my old colleague Professor Okamoto, and I gather he was not terribly complimentary to me." Yamada laughed. His face was strangely youthful, too smooth for his gray hair and veined hands, and his eyes were mirthless, even when he laughed. Now he lifted the teapot lid to inspect the progress of his brew and, apparently not satisfied, replaced it.

"I'm sure he would want me to say nothing. But I have nothing to be ashamed of. Or at least, I am too old now to waste time feeling shame for my mistakes," Yamada continued. "And—it was all so long ago—I can't imagine what harm there could be in the story now. Nor, I should add, what interest to readers of an American newspaper." Shrugging slightly in his gown, he poured steaming light green tea into three small ceramic cups.

Yamada took a sip and then set his cup gingerly on the hearth's wooden ledge. "So," he said. "How may I help you?"

Piper hardly knew where to begin. "Maybe you could start right at that cliff your wife told us about."

Kyoko nervously translated the question, and Yamada laughed mirthlessly again, a laugh that ended as suddenly as it began. Quietly, he asked, "How did she seem?"

"Very well," Piper said. "And very loyal to your memory."

"Yes," Yamada said. "Yes. She is a better wife, and a better widow, than I deserved." He was silent for a minute and then resumed more cheerfully. "Well, allow me to make a suggestion. Let me start the story now, and then we can continue over dinner, if you will do me the honor. You will spend the night here. I can offer only the simplest food and accommodation, but I'm afraid there is nothing else in the area, and you would be foolish to leave in darkness. Would that be too inconvenient?"

"You are very kind," Piper said, after glancing Kyoko's way. "We'd be delighted."

"Splendid," Yamada said. "Now I will begin making my excuses for being alive." He gave another little laugh, took another sip and began his story, stopping from time to time to allow Kyoko to interpret.

"During the war, as you know, I worked on a project with Professor Okamoto and others for the Imperial Army," Yamada began. "Like your scientists, we were investigating the potential of atomic energy."

"You were trying to build a bomb?" Piper interrupted.

"Of course," Yamada said. "Did Okamoto deny even that?"

"He said you told the army one thing and did another," Piper said. "He said you all knew that you had no hope of building a bomb, and the project was just a way to keep you all from being drafted."

"Well," Yamada paused to consider this. "It is true that we were working against great odds, and we all knew this. It is true that we failed. It is probably true that we would have failed even if your B-29 Superfortresses had not bombed our laboratory." He absentmindedly stirred the embers with an iron poker. "But it certainly would not be true to say that we were not trying our best. You see, we were patriots, like your scientists, but we were desperate patriots. We had more need of a secret weapon. We believed that your country would annihilate us and our emperor, and we were looking for a way to survive."

Piper had taken his notebook out of his back pocket and was taking notes as Kyoko translated. Yamada didn't seem to care.

"In any case, we did fail, Professor Okamoto is right about that," Yamada went on. "And as the war was ending, some powerful people in the army offered us a chance for a new life."

"What do you mean?" Piper asked.

"Well, this will sound strange to you today," Yamada said. "But many of our superiors, and many of my colleagues, assumed we would all be tried as war criminals. We assumed the Americans would be ashamed of having killed so many civilians in Hiroshima and Nagasaki, and that you would be eager to make examples of us, to show you were not the only ones pursuing this horrible weapon. Of course, as in so many matters, before and since, we read you completely wrong. You weren't ashamed of anything. But we didn't know that then.

"Anyway, I believe there was another factor as well, although the generals never said so," Yamada continued. "I think, after Hiroshima and Nagasaki, our own government was ashamed of us. They would have liked to say that they never would have committed such a crime against humanity, but for that to happen, we had to go away.

"I still remember it like yesterday," Yamada said. "It was a bright late-August morning. An army colonel made the offer, and said we could accept it or not, as we chose. But all five of us, the professor's closest assistants, had to go for it, or none, he said. He said the government would send us away, and give us new names, new identities. Our families would be told we were dead, and we could never contact them again, but they would receive a generous pension. In due course, we would be given jobs and allowed to pursue physics again—in a peaceful way, of course, and in remote places where our relatives would not run into us.

"Well, it sounds fantastic now, and it sounded fantastic then, believe me," Yamada continued. "But you have to remember, we all expected to be jailed, or even hung, and then where would our families be? Still without us, and publicly shamed, and certainly with no pension—the Americans would make sure of that. So we agreed. We didn't have much time to cover our tracks before the Americans arrived. So a couple of days later, with no fanfare and of course no good-byes, we came here, to this very house—all except Okamoto, who at the last minute backed out, even though it was supposed to be all or no one at all."

Yamada rose from his cushion, with remarkable grace for a man of his age, and apologized for speaking so long. "You must want to wash," he said. "Let me show you the way, and take care of a few things in the kitchen, and then we can continue, if I'm not boring you too much."

Yamada led them to what looked like his study. There was no tatami here, but an oriental rug, western-style chairs, a desk, a sofa and bookshelves filled to the ceiling.

"The washroom is through there," he said. There were actually two rooms, one with a toilet, the other a tiny closet with a small sink. Kyoko went first, while Piper examined the study. There was an old-fashioned fountain pen, but no papers on the desk. Most of the books were old, and in Japanese, but a few French and English titles were sprinkled among them: some Dickens, a volume of Shakespeare, Bertrand Russell, Orwell's memoirs of the Spanish Civil War. It was an oddly impersonal collection, as if left behind by a succession of summer houseguests.

When Yamada called them to dinner, they found he had set out three individual-sized tables, about one foot high, with a dinner tray on each. The trays and covered soup bowls and chopsticks were of lustrous black lacquer; the other foods were in pottery bowls of varying shapes and sizes. Yamada poured each of them a glass of beer and a cup of hot rice wine. On each tray also was a bowl of rice, a piece of broiled fish and a collection in broth of roots and ferns and other greenery that Piper recognized as what the Japanese call mountain vegetables.

"I collected those myself today," Yamada said, as Piper lifted the cover off his bowl, releasing a cloud of steam.

"Ah, so the woods aren't poisoned after all," Piper said, smiling.

"What?" Yamada said with what seemed like genuine alarm. "Where did you hear that?"

Kyoko told him about their bus driver, and Yamada shook his head. "Remarkable," he said. "You know, we used to come here sometimes during the war. It was a kind of retreat from the bombs, and the hunger, and the generals, too. Of course, the security people worried, because our work was top-secret, but they couldn't possibly station guards all around these woods. So we spread the word that the woods had been mysteriously poisoned, and that worked better than barbed wire. It's amazing that the story has been passed down through all these years. Please, eat."

Piper toasted Yamada's health with his sake and Yamada resumed his story.

"Well, as I said, we all came here, but right away I knew I'd made a mistake," he said. "For one thing, things were terrible in Tokyo, there was no food, and I just couldn't abandon my wife. Of course, one of my colleagues ended up sending for his, despite all their warnings, but it didn't occur to me then that I could break their rules. And anyway, I realized that I didn't want to run away from my life, or my name, or what we had done. I'd been lying about my work for years, and I'd been lying to my wife about the woman I was really in love with, and I was sick of it. I decided to go back to my wife, give up the other woman and stop lying.

"Well, they didn't like it, but they couldn't stop me," he continued. "Okamoto had promised to lie low for a while, and he ended up playing it very smart, coordinating everything and making himself indispensable without having to run away. But I wouldn't make any promises, I just went back. In the end, of course, it didn't matter. It turned out the Americans didn't give a damn about what we'd done, and when I tried to write a book about it, the Japanese didn't give a damn, either."

Yamada paused to eat a few bites, and Piper walked around the hearth to refill his host's sake cup, and then Kyoko's.

"You see, like a lot of Japanese after the war, I became quite angry, and quite socialist—more than socialist, actually," Yamada said. "People were desperately poor, and I blamed the emperor and the military and the industrialists who had gotten rich off the war, which had been such a disaster for everybody else. Okamoto, on the other hand, basically kept working for the same people we'd been working for all during the war, though of course their job titles were different now and so, in theory, was our mission: Build up science to build up industry! export! produce! The munitions ministry became the ministry of trade. We hadn't conquered the world with guns, so we'd do it with our factories. It didn't interest me. I left the lab to work on my book.

"But to tell you the truth, I still wasn't happy," their host went on, adjusting the tie on his yukata. "For one thing, Japan didn't want to hear what I had to say. At that stage, no one wanted to think about the war, or who had started it or why. Even today, not many people want to think about those things, but then! The whole country had swallowed the government's propaganda, just like before the war. Work sixty hours a week, and in ten years everyone will own a refrigerator!" He shook his head in disgust. "And there was something else, too." Yamada emptied his sake cup and poured himself another, relaxed enough to forget the protocol. Piper took it as a signal that he could stretch his legs out to the side of his tray.

"I was still in love with Shimizu-san," Yamada said. It was the first time anyone had mentioned her name, but he tossed it off as though they had been discussing her all night. "I know this isn't what interests you, but . . . Well, it's why I went and died again. You see, my wife and I met through *omiai*. It was a marriage our fathers wanted, but it didn't interest me. I was in love already. And you have to understand—Yukiko—Shimizu-san, that is—she was not always just a tea pourer. Her father was a great scientist, and she was almost part of our team during the war. In another time, maybe in another country, she would have been a great scientist herself. Her mind is much sharper than mine. But here . . ." Yamada shook his head again. "Anyway, she was not well off, her father died when she was young, and my father thought I could do better." Both Kyoko and Piper had stopped taking notes, and when Yamada paused, the room became deathly still. "I didn't have the courage to oppose him.

"So I married my wife, and I kept seeing Yukiko, all through the war. It was a golden time, strangely enough. We didn't have enough to eat, and our friends and classmates were dying, so it's a terrible thing to say, I know. But our work was exciting, and Yukiko and I were together, and it was as though normal rules didn't apply. Everyone's life was so disrupted, I didn't feel shame for what I was doing, and we couldn't imagine a time when husbands and wives would be together again, and I would have to face the consequences of my cowardice.

"After the war, that time came all too quickly. Everyone wanted to act as though the war had never happened. I went home to my wife, and tried to pretend that Yukiko had never happened." He stopped talking, took a drink and remained silent. Piper thought perhaps he was ending the story there, and began framing a question, but finally Yamada resumed. "Anyway, after about ten years at home, I couldn't take it anymore," he said. "So I went to Okamoto and asked if the old offer was still open." Yamada laughed his chilly laugh. "By then he would have liked to do away with me for real, I think, but this other—this was more complicated. Of course, the government didn't care about my personal problems, and they weren't worried about the Americans anymore. But to be honest, they worried about me. They were afraid of what else I might say or do, and I think they were happy for a chance to get me where I couldn't make trouble. So they agreed to arrange my death, and send a pension to my poor wife.

"Shimizu-san continued working for Okamoto," Yamada said. "That was part of the deal, you see." He smiled ruefully. "I think it was a way for them to make sure they could control us, that I wouldn't change my mind again. In fact, she was more of a rebel than I was by then. She thinks I've sold out, I suppose, but she is still loyal—which I guess is why she wanted you to hear my side of the story."

"Where is she now?" Kyoko said, speaking up in her own voice, as it were, for the first time all evening. She asked in Japanese and then translated into English for Piper. "Is she alright?"

Yamada looked puzzled. "Why wouldn't she be? Didn't she tell you how to get here?"

Piper didn't answer directly. "Monday she wasn't in her office," he said. "When did you last talk to her?"

"There's no telephone here," Yamada said. "I saw her two weeks ago, the Saturday after you visited Okamoto. I haven't seen her since, but I wouldn't expect to." He drank his beer. "I imagine she was just out buying the week's supplies when you went looking for her." He seemed unconcerned. "Let me make some more tea. I'll be right back."

When he returned from the kitchen and began fussing again with his fire and his tea, Piper said, "So what have you been doing ever since?"

Yamada turned up the corners of his lips in a half-smile. "I suppose you would consider it a wasted life," he said. "Okamoto and the others let me have this house, and I spent time fixing it. I tried farming, but neither I nor this land was suited to it. All my pension has gone to my wife, of course, and we've lived mostly on whatever they let Yukiko earn in the lab. You see, once I died the second time, I was under their control. Naturally, I stopped writing about the old days, but I grew more and more interested in poetry, and actually I've published a few things—not under my own name, of course." He laughed again. "These days I'm hardly sure what my own name is. Anyway, Shimizu-san comes when she can—more often since they built the bullet train to Niigata. And it's been a life, the life that was meant for me, I suppose. Maybe it's sad, that my best times came when I was trying to build an atomic bomb. But everything has flowed from those years."

They lapsed into silence, the scratching of Kyoko's pen, as always, lagging behind. A slight coolness drifted in from the meadow, and the piney outdoor smell mingled with the fragrance of fresh tatami and smoldering embers. Piper poured the last of his sake, now cold.

"What was it they were afraid you would write, in a second book?" he asked.

"That's the biggest joke of all, because what they were afraid of wasn't what I had in mind at all," Yamada answered. "I was going to expose the American nuclear arsenal, and how you were using Japan as a base for your imperialist conquest of Asia, as we thought of it then. Of course, nobody would have cared, any more than they cared about my first book. What they were afraid I would write was about how they had killed us off and hidden us around the country. It was recent enough in those days that it might have caused quite a scandal. But I never would have written about that—too many relatives would have been hurt."

"And now?"

"Well, now, I suppose it wouldn't create much of a stir," Yamada said. "It's a historical curiosity, and people might find it moderately interesting. But I wouldn't write about it, even now. Most of us must be dead, but there must still be some family members out there, like my wife, who would be very, very injured if they knew the truth. My wife—I imagine it would kill her, to think I'd abandoned her and been laughing at her all these years while she said prayers for me—that's how she would see it, I'm afraid."

Piper felt the pit of his stomach suddenly sink away. "So after all this, you're telling us not to write the story?" Piper brandished his notebook, now filled with the evening's scrawlings.

"No, no, I would never tell you what to write," Yamada said. "You found me, and you have your duty to perform, I understand that. I'm just saying, I hope you will think about people like my wife."

Piper felt nauseous. To have come all this way, to have finally nailed down a story, and then have the whole thing jeopardized by an appeal to his conscience—it was more than infuriating. Why should he worry about Yamada's wife? He wasn't the one who'd abandoned her. But he knew, even if he couldn't yet admit it to himself, that he wouldn't bring himself to publish the truth. If the government had instructed him not to, he would have written it in a second. But this way . . . Yamada had handled it perfectly, he thought, leading him along until the last minute—and then that final touch about it killing his wife . . .

With a touch of anger he asked, "Who else actually joined this witness protection program?" Kyoko translated without the sarcasm, and Yamada answered, "There may have been some I didn't know about, from other secret projects. I heard that one or two were sent to Russia to help their atomic program, in return for their releasing our POWs whom they held in Siberia for so long. I don't know, that was just a rumor. The ones who I know came out here at first were me, Inoki, Kawamura and Hashimoto. Hashimoto's the one who brought his wife. Of course, once I went back to Tokyo, I didn't see any of them anymore."

"And where are they now?"

Yamada shook his head. "As you may have guessed, Professor Okamoto isn't inclined to tell me his secrets." Yamada unexpectedly pulled a pocket watch from somewhere inside his yukata, and rose to a kneeling position.

"Could I ask one more question?" Kyoko said. "What good would it do to send all of you away, if Nishina and Okamoto stayed?"

"Well, not everyone went away, of course, you're right about that," Yamada said. "If you knew the Old Man, you'd know that he never would have hid or run away from anything he did. But he didn't boast about it, either. And I suppose the army just figured that even if the Americans questioned him, and Okamoto—well, there was no longer much of a lab, nor much of a team, and there were virtually no records, we made sure of that. So it would look as though there couldn't have been a crash program."

Yamada suddenly rose to his feet. "I'll show you what I mean." He padded into his study and returned with a well-thumbed copy of the American journal *Science*. "Here, read this," he said, handing the magazine to Kyoko. "It's about one of your eminent American scientists visiting the Riken after the war."

Kyoko read aloud, quoting the American's recollections of encountering a young scientist who had remained in the Tokyo lab. " 'He cooked and ate and worked in the same room in the laboratory, and was growing some potatoes in the yard,' " she read. " 'He was doing work that we had done in America with a whole panoply of people. So, as we looked around, we concluded this could not have been the site of a Japanese Manhattan Project.' "

"Yes, and now read this part," Yamada said, thumping the page with his finger.

"And as for whether Japan had been developing an atomic weapon," Kyoko read, quoting again, " 'they didn't talk about it and we didn't ask about it much.' "

"There, you see?" Yamada said triumphantly. "The plan paid off. But in a larger sense, of course, the whole thing didn't matter. The Americans didn't care, the Japanese didn't care, we all disrupted our lives for no reason at all." He laughed his chilly little laugh one last time and, switching to heavily-accented English, said, "As you would say, Mr. Piper, what will be, will be, isn't that right?"

"Right," Piper said. They all rose, and Yamada waved away Piper's offer to help with the dishes. After pulling a futon from a hidden closet, and spreading a blanket on the couch in the study, Yamada apologized again for the meager dinner, for the spartan accommodations and for the boring conversation. Then he bowed and withdrew.

In the morning, when Piper and Kyoko awoke, Yamada was gone.

21

S wirling motes of dust danced inside bands of light cutting down from two high, narrow windows. Outside, real birds, not crows, chirped and trilled. Inside, all was silent.

Piper had slept on the tatami, partly because his body was too long for the sofa, partly to confound Yamada's expectations, or what he imagined them to be, that the gaijin would take the couch while leaving the futon to his Japanese assistant. Now he propped himself up on one elbow. Beside the cold hearth, two meal trays had been set up. Piper had heard nothing. He checked under the thin mattress for the reporter's notebook he had slipped there before going to sleep. Then he rose and pulled on his jeans. It was just before seven.

In the study, Kyoko was up already, sleepily scratching her head as she surveyed the bookshelves, wearing a man-tailored white shirt and white socks. Piper tried not to look at the long stretch of tan legs in between, nor to think about whose shirt it might once have been.

"We seem to have been abandoned," Piper said.

"What do you mean?" Kyoko asked. The top three buttons of her shirt were undone, and she buttoned the lowest of the three as she turned toward Piper. He told her about the two breakfast trays and said, "I guess our interview is over."

"Why? Did you have anything more to ask?"

"No, not really." He sat down at the desk. "But I was thinking, why didn't we ask about the guy who followed us here?"

"Because we didn't trust him," Kyoko said.

"We didn't?"

"Well, did you?" Kyoko said. "Did you believe his story?"

"I guess I'd better not admit it," Piper said. "But why?"

Kyoko shrugged. "We probably shouldn't talk about it here." She poked her head out the door and scanned the central room, then resumed in a low voice. "But some of it just didn't make sense. Why would he leave his wife for another woman, and then live on the other side of Japan from her? Why not just leave his wife, stay alive, and stay in Tokyo? Divorce may have been rare in those days, but it wasn't unheard of."

"Because he's a weak man," Piper said, pushing with his long legs to turn the desk chair gently to and fro. "He as much as said so. He didn't have the courage to confront his wife or his father, just like he didn't have the courage not to marry her in the first place. So he just disappeared." He stopped twirling and looked at Kyoko. "Anyway, now who's being conspiratorial?"

"Maybe you're right," Kyoko said.

They washed as best they could in the tiny basin. While Kyoko was using the washroom, Piper looked through the desk drawers: a few pencils, paper clips, old magazines. If Yamada was still writing poetry, he didn't keep it here. Kyoko gave him a disapproving look as she emerged, towel and toothbrush in hand, and he closed the drawer and wandered back to the central room to let her dress. Each breakfast tray held two empty bowls, one for soup and one for rice, an uncooked egg, a small piece of broiled fish like the one they'd had for dinner, and a cellophane packet of seaweed in dark green strips. Containers of rice and soup with serving spoons and a pot of tea waited on the floor between the trays. At the front door, his and Kyoko's shoes had been turned around just so, facing out, for them to slip into as they left. Several other pairs were lined up in the foyer; there was no way to tell whether Yamada was home or not. Piper walked back toward the door he assumed opened into Yamada's quarters, and yelled good morning in Japanese. There was no response, and his shout seemed to rattle through the old farmhouse.

Piper thought about Kyoko's suspicions. He honestly hadn't doubted Yamada's story, although as he looked back now, he decided he hadn't felt completely at ease about it, either. He recalled Yamada's figure at the threshold, waiting for them to cross the darkening meadow. Had the whole evening been, in some sense, rehearsed? Certainly, Yamada had not been surprised to see them. That might be simply because the tea pourer, in high dudgeon after listening to Okamoto's arrogance and slanders two weeks earlier, had told Yamada her plan. But the tea pourer had telephoned Piper Sunday in desperation, not as someone fulfilling a plan carefully laid down during the previous two weeks. What made her hurry, and hide the map as she had? Why not just bring it over, or mail it? She was being followed, or thought she was. And yet Yamada last night had dismissed—no, hadn't even been curious about—their anxieties for his faithful mistress. Why? Maybe he was used to her paranoia, maybe she was forever imagining pursuers and hanging maps on temple trees. But maybe not; maybe Yamada already knew her fate before Piper and Kyoko arrived, and so wasn't curious and didn't want them dwelling on their curiosity, either. But how did he know? Could the tall, muscular man somehow have gotten word to Yamada, even though they'd lost him on the mountain? Yamada claimed there was no telephone here.

Piper walked to the front door, pried on his boots without tying them and stepped outdoors: no telephone wires. He lowered himself onto the front stoop. It was going to be a hot day, even up here in the mountains, but now a cool freshness sharpened the air. Birds were diving out of the woods, hopping about the underbrush of the meadow, and then flying back into the shadows of the tall pines.

Okay, there was no telephone. Did the muscular man beat them here? Not likely, but conceivable, Piper had to admit. Maybe they hadn't really lost him; maybe he had followed them back down the mountain from the talking soda machine and, guessing where they were headed, leapfrogged them during the night.

But even if he had gotten here first, what could be untrue about Yamada's basic story? Yamada hadn't stuck to Okamoto's lies about the atomic bomb program, if lies they were, and his tale would account for the mysterious red X's that Sato had found scrawled across the files. Maybe, Piper thought gloomily, their muscular shadow had merely offered Yamada a strategy: tell the truth, but appeal to the American's sense of sympathy for the poor bereft relatives, and he'll never write the story. Better than lying! Yamada had followed that script brilliantly, and now he was gone, so there'd be no chance to spoil the effect, to ask the questions they'd forgotten, to challenge him as Piper hadn't thought to do in the warm firelight of the evening. Like, why should I protect your wife from knowing what a selfish jerk you were?

"How about some breakfast?"

Kyoko stood on the edge of the tatami, still toweling her long, straight hair, barefoot in her jeans and a clean white polo shirt. She smiled down at him, and Piper allowed himself to imagine that this was their house, Kyoko was about to sit on the stoop behind him, sandwiching him between her thighs, wrapping her arms around his waist, resting her chin on his shoulder as they peacefully watched the birds and the squirrels before going inside to start another day together. . . . Piper let a moment pass, and when he hadn't felt Kyoko softly kissing the back of his neck, he reluctantly accepted that this wasn't their house and she hadn't just come from their warm double futon.

"Sure. I'll have a bagel with cream cheese, fresh o.j., and coffee," Piper said.

"Fine, if you don't mind tea instead of coffee," Kyoko said.

"No problem."

"And would rice be okay instead of that bagel? And we have some very fresh tofu, instead of cream cheese."

"Sounds perfect."

"Only I'm afraid we're out of orange juice," Kyoko said.

"Well, how can I complain, when you have everything else?"

Back inside, Kyoko folded herself onto a cushion and began ladling out rice and soup while Piper rolled up his bedding and shoved it into the hidden closet. Then he watched as she broke a raw egg over her rice, stirred it in, picked up a strip of seaweed with her chopsticks and expertly wrapped it around a bite-sized hunk of egg-rice mixture before sliding the little package into her mouth. Piper decided to do without the egg.

They sat quietly with their second cups of tea, and then carried the trays into the kitchen, which proved to be almost inconceivably authentic. Rough flagstones covered the floor unevenly, and a long stone trough served as a sink. "How can he cook anything in here?" Kyoko wondered.

"Well, I guess he's got enough free time to make do without a microwave," Piper said. "Have you noticed there doesn't seem to be a radio or television in the whole place? This may be the only house in Japan without at least one twenty-inch color set. That might be worth a story in itself." He badly wanted to hear the news, to find out whether they had missed a trade agreement. He glanced at his watch; Thursday's first edition had yet to close.

They took a last look around the beautiful central room, put on their shoes and packs and started down the meadow. The true blue of the sky and the crispness of the air did little to lift Piper's spirits. Here they were, after three weeks, and what did they have? Piper had been sure the government had covered up some terrible nuclear accident, so sure that he had written the lead a hundred times in his mind, seen the headline stripped across the top of the *Advertiser,* tasted the envy and admiration of his colleagues in the press club. Now it seemed there had been no catastrophe, and if he didn't use Yamada as a source, they had nothing more than what they'd taken away from Okamoto's office: a vaguely interesting historical tale about Japan's attempt to build an atomic bomb, disputed and denied by the only living veteran of the program, and Piper unable to explain why he had uncovered no other sources. It would just look like a bad job of reporting.

And if he did quote Yamada, he might destroy the lives of countless innocent relatives. He thought of the brother in the wheelchair and the mousy woman behind the grocery counter, of the fat woman in Tataki village, of poor loyal Mrs. Yamada in her tumbledown jalopy of a house—what a contrast to Yamada's perfect specimen of sturdy beams and fresh tatami! Truthfully, the idea of shocking the brother in the wheelchair didn't bother him much, and the hearty sister in Tataki probably could withstand anything. But Mrs. Yamada—he wouldn't want to be the one to break her heart or cause her suicide, as Yamada had hinted. Not that Christopher would blink twice at a chance like this, Piper thought. But that's why he's Christopher and I'm not. And who knew how many other deceived relatives like Mrs. Yamada there might be?

Of course, when you stopped to think about it, quoting Yamada might not be an option, even if Piper had the conscience of a Christopher. Let's say he wrote the story, basing it on quotes from someone supposedly dead for decades. Other reporters would swoop down on Okamoto and Mrs. Yamada, seeking confirmation, and both would act as though Piper were crazy, which Mrs. Yamada would genuinely believe. And what would Piper have to back up his story, if Yamada chose not to step forward? This house, which

Okamoto would make sure was empty, or even gone—why not, it wouldn't be so hard to arrange. No phone number, no photographs, no documents. A now-disappeared tea pourer, that was a joke. And Sato's evidence that something was amiss in the files. Well, that didn't mean much; bureaucratic mix-ups had happened before, and besides, he could never ask Sato to go on the record; he had climbed far enough out on a limb just checking the files. To be honest, he would have nothing.

They had solved the mystery, in other words, and the solution had left them empty-handed. And he had probably missed the only story his editors would care about all month, if the trade talks had been settled, and even more so if they had ended in rupture. Not to mention what was happening in Washington, or the Hiroshima anniversary, for which he also would have zip. Maybe he already had been fired. Maybe the paper already had selected his replacement—probably that handsome, conceited guy in editorial who spoke Japanese, who surely wouldn't make a mess of things like Piper had, who would cover this place the way they wanted, and would be given a decent cost-of-living allowance, and have lunch with Christopher, and work every day with Kyoko, and Kyoko would think, Now, this is a real reporter. This is a real man. This is . . .

At the bottom of the driveway, Kyoko had shrugged her way out of her pack and was thoughtfully eying the lane that ran alongside the property.

"I was just thinking, after all this, we don't have much of a story," Piper said tentatively, hoping to be contradicted. "Unless you think we should say to hell with Mrs. Yamada?"

Kyoko appeared not to hear him. She had pulled the secret map out of her front pocket and was examining it with a slight squint, as though she'd never seen it before. "Let's leave our packs and walk this way," she said, speaking slowly and pointing to the left.

Piper stared at her, trying again to figure what was on her mind. "You think we went to the wrong house, is that it?" he said, with more sarcasm than interest. "Maybe there's another Yamada down the road, right? It is a common name, after all. Or maybe he's going to die again and be reborn down there."

"No, it was the right house," Kyoko said soberly. "But I still think something's not right." As they set off down the lane, away from the little house and the yapping dog, Kyoko explained, "You know, everything on her map was there for a reason. The doughnut, the '440,' the rice bowl, the dog. But we never found the gun. Why not?"

Piper couldn't see that it mattered, but he didn't challenge her. It was pleasant, for a while, just to walk in the sunshine without his pack, with his shoulders still tingling from where his pack had been, and to leave the thinking to someone else. But after they'd been walking fifteen minutes or more, Kyoko's sphinx act began to irritate him. "What are we looking for?" he asked.

She shook her head slightly. "I don't know."

"Well, how long are we going to look for it? It's beautiful here, but I'm kind of curious about whether I've been fired yet or not."

She smiled and put an arm through his. "Don't worry," she said. "You haven't been fired. If this doesn't work out, maybe we'll find a romantic ryokan tonight, and next week you'll file a million boring business stories, and we'll do an anniversary piece from Nagasaki, if we're too late for Hiroshima, and they'll forget they were ever mad. Okay?" Piper's ears had stopped working after the part about the romantic ryokan. Did the "maybe" refer to whether they could find one, or whether it would be romantic, or what, exactly? Better not to ask. What was she feeling so good about, anyway? He just nodded and enjoyed the press of her arm and they kept walking.

And then, around the next curve, the road ended. Not petering out into the woods, or turning a corner, but dead-on blockaded by a high, forbidding jumble of barbed and electrified wire.

DO NOT ENTER, Kyoko read. PROPERTY OF THE AIR SELF-DEFENSE FORCE. One of the affectations of Japan's military, a bow to its "peace" constitution, was that the country no longer had an army, navy and air force: instead, there were the Ground Self-Defense Force, the Maritime Self-Defense Force and the Air Self-Defense Force. The Japanese, seeing the American War Department change into the Department of Defense, had taken euphemism one step further, and somehow the propaganda seemed to work. Foreigners and Japanese alike were always astonished to learn that Japan now had the third-highest military budget in the world. The numbers didn't square with the image of a scrawny, nonnuclear, peace-loving skeletal force, and in people's minds, the image usually won out.

"So this is the gun on the map!" Piper said.

"Mmm," Kyoko said dubiously. "I don't think so. If you were drawing the map, would you use a gun or a little jet plane to stand for an air force base?"

"I don't think my mind-set is relevant here," Piper said. "I wouldn't hang my map on a tree with a lot of little folded-up white paper prayers, either."

"And another thing," Kyoko said thoughtfully, again ignoring Piper. "The map shows the gun exactly where you take a left, not after it."

"Well, if this isn't the gun, what does it mean? If anything?"

"I don't know," Kyoko said once more. "But there's one other thing about the map. Here, look." She showed Piper that the dotted line carrying them up the driveway and through the meadow ended behind the house, not where they had found the front door last night.

"There has to be a reason for that, too," she said.

"Oh, come on, Kyoko," Piper said. "I know you have a thing for Shimizu, but what difference does it make which door we enter? Maybe she drew it that way because she always comes with groceries, and uses the back door. Or maybe Yamada spends most of his time in the garden, and she thought that's where we'd find him. She didn't expect us to arrive after dark."

"That's it!" Kyoko said.

"What's it?"

"It was nearly dark when we arrived, which is why we didn't see the gun," Kyoko said. "Come on, we obviously missed something on the way in."

"But so what if we did?" Piper was exasperated. "If you find a treasure, you don't worry afterward that you missed one of the clues on the treasure map."

"John," Kyoko said, "I know you think I'm being crazy, but I think we haven't found the treasure yet. Let's just look around one more time."

This time they walked in silence and without holding hands, and back at the driveway Piper sank heavily, and a bit grumpily, to the ground, leaning against his pack. Kyoko walked a few paces toward the house with the watchdog and turned back, as if she were approaching for the first time. Then she tried it from the other direction. Then she walked up the driveway, and into the woods, scanning the ground, the top of the wall, the bushes. She found no gun.

Finally, she sat next to Piper, defeated for the moment. "Let's look at your Japan map," he said. "I don't remember any air force base here." And while she unzipped her pack, he reclined wearily, looking up into the trees. There, at once, he saw it.

"Kyoko," he whispered excitedly, not really thinking about why he was whispering. "It's not a gun. It's a camera. Look!"

She followed his finger with her gaze and saw, five or six branches up in the pine tree above them, the underbelly of a video camera of some kind, pointed at the stretch of lane leading toward the watchdog. Now that they saw it, they both realized, without any doubt, that Shimizu had drawn that camera, and no gun at all.

"So that's how Yamada knew we were on our way," Piper said softly. "But why would he have a surveillance camera, when he doesn't even have a telephone?"

"We've been had, John, I'm sure of it. The whole house was strange," Kyoko said, whispering, too, as if the camera might have ears. "Where were the dirty dishes? the laundry? the garbage?"

"What are you saying?"

"I don't know, really, but we have to find what's behind the house, in the red circle," Kyoko said. "Let's let the camera watch us leaving, and then we can figure out what to do next."

They stood self-consciously, shouldered their packs and set off down the lane. Piper felt suddenly like an actor in a very bizarre film and he wondered who, and where, his audience might be.

22

*I*t should have been obvious, Piper realized afterward, that there would be more than one camera. It should have been obvious that Okamoto and whatever he was part of were playing for keeps. It should have been obvious, in fact, that Piper and Kyoko were not going to win this battle—that whatever forces lay backstage would be too powerful to be outwitted by a couple of amateurs from a midsized daily in the United States.

But as Piper retraced his steps along the country lane on that suddenly hot and humid early-August morning in northern Japan, nothing seemed obvious or clear. His heart pounded in his chest and his ears. The questions he should have been sorting through—about Yamada, and which pieces of his story might still be believed; about the barbed wire and the air force base and the surveillance camera; about the country house, the bent-over tea pourer, the secret map— all those questions muddled together in Piper's mind, which for some reason kept returning, unbidden, to one irrelevant image, of a handful of men on the other end of that camera, supercilious smiles curling beneath supercilious mustaches as they stared into their little scopes at a small black-and-white image of Piper and Kyoko inno- cently arm-in-arm just a few minutes before. And in imagining the watchers, Piper could see only the hard, flinty-eyed faces of Japanese soldiers in a World War 2 propaganda movie. Maybe we are all racists after all, he thought.

They aimed for nonchalance as they strolled along the wall and past the little guardhouse to a shady spot well beyond the Yamada estate. There they unslung their packs and sank to the mossy ground. Sitting beside Piper to form a common lap, her jaw clenched and her skin pale around her eyes, Kyoko pulled out the map of Japan.

There was not enough detail to help them much, but the map did show the outlines of what it called a former air force base, stretching from the foothills east of the Sea of Japan into the spine of the island.

"Maybe it's a secret prison now," Kyoko said. "Maybe that's where they've taken Shimizu."

"Let's figure out what's behind the farmhouse before we start worrying about secret prisons," Piper said.

"Easy for you," Kyoko said. "You have a U.S. passport. They're not going to put you in any secret prison." She spoke as if in jest, but Piper realized that for a Japanese, the idea of all-powerful authority could never be entirely a joke, at least not while confined on these islands.

"There is no secret prison," Piper said. "Japan is a liberal democracy with a free press, and people don't just disappear. Well, rarely. And the press is moderately free. And maybe the country is a quasi-democracy. Okay, so it's a one-party dictatorship, but it's a benign one. Usually benign, anyway. Or at least, seemingly benign. Or let me put it this way—"

"Enough!" Kyoko said, laughing a little. "You're not funny, or helpful. How are we going to get back in there?"

"You're sure you want to?" Piper asked.

Kyoko nodded. But the map of Japan was too broad-brush to suggest an alternative route, and their secret map showed only one dotted path to the farmhouse. Kyoko and Piper decided to set out cross-country, outflanking the camera in the tree.

In practice, the approach proved far less direct, as cross-country hikes often do. They crossed the dry, deserted paddy with no trouble, but plunging uphill through bramble and underbrush, they soon felt totally disoriented. Their packs felt heavier than before and Piper found himself wishing for a compass, and maybe some food. By now the sun was high, and his bowl of rice and seaweed had long since been depleted. He had just about concluded that they were irretrievably lost, and was wondering how his editors would react to his arrest for trespassing on a Japanese air base (FORMER ADVERTISER REPORTER NABBED), when he noticed the woods taking on a trimmer, more cultivated look. And then, suddenly, they were at the edge of the farmhouse meadow.

Everything looked as before. Birds flitted about, the house was still, no smoke curled above its thatched roof. Yamada was nowhere to be seen. Piper's heart was pounding as they circled through the woods to the back of the house, to Shimizu's red circle. When they pulled even with the backyard, Piper saw, with vague disappointment, that there was nothing much to see: a ragged piece of ground. Then he realized that he was looking with an American's eyes; for Japan, all that empty space itself was strange. There should have been a vegetable garden, fruit trees, a clothesline, futons airing, a tool shed, a pile of junk somewhere, maybe a compost heap. But there was nothing. Weeds, a few pines, a coil of old rope. The house itself seemed more weathered on this uphill side. At its base, almost flush with the ground, lay a pair of cellar doors, the kind that had to be pulled up and flung open, and their gray paint was peeling and cracked.

"Now what?" Piper whispered.

Kyoko took a deep breath and pointed to the doors. Of course. He'd been thinking like an American again. Japanese farmhouses might have crawl spaces for coolness, but nothing more. Certainly, nothing resembling the entrance to a suburban American bomb shelter of the 1950s.

"Shall we?" Kyoko whispered.

"Hold on," Piper whispered back. He asked for the map one more time, and once more traced the dotted path to the back of the house. Then he took some matches out of his back pocket. With a nod from Kyoko, and on the second try, he set fire to the map. Whether he did it to protect Shimizu, or somehow to invoke the prayer she had promised on his behalf, he wasn't sure. He held the paper by one corner as the flames devoured her beautiful work, and then let the breeze lift the black ribbon of ash toward the meadow. "Okay, let's go," he whispered.

The doors opened creakingly but with surprising ease. Kyoko pulled one, Piper the other, and they laid both gently on the ground. A cement stairway led under the house about five steps and then turned to the left, into shadow. Piper turned to Kyoko and smiled. Then they started down the steps, this time with Piper leading.

Around the corner, darkness quickly enveloped them. Piper reached for his matches again, lit one and saw, in the sudden flare, that the staircase dropped another forty steps or more before turning once more to the left, away from the farmhouse. He blew out the match and continued, counting stairs and keeping a hand on each wall. Almost no light reached the bottom, and when Kyoko joined him there, Piper struck another match. The flame revealed a heavy red metal door which must, Piper thought, be locked. And then what do we do? An anticlimactic end to the adventure.

But the door was not locked. It opened easily, in fact, and after stepping through a tiny foyer, they found themselves in a large well-lit underground room with walls of concrete block, studded with small holes in a stark design. A thick gray carpet covered the floor. The gray concrete simplicity and sharp cold angles seemed a world away from the warmth of rope-tied beams and rumpled pottery upstairs, and yet just as Japanese. A hard, polished table of smooth orange lacquer anchored the center, taking the place of the hearth. Cranes and pines and clouds and cherry blossoms floated on a background of dazzling gold on a six-panel screen that graced the wall facing them.

"If you are admiring the screen, you have very good taste, Mr. Piper," a familiar voice said in slightly accented English. "It is a sixteenth-century masterpiece by Hasegawa Tohaku. On loan from our National Museum, by the way."

Piper swiveled toward the voice. To the left, in an alcove of the large chamber, Professor Okamoto sat cross-legged on an orange cushion, a cup of tea in front of him on another low table, this one of gleaming black lacquer. Behind him, Saeki of the Foreign Ministry leaned elegantly against the wall, arms folded in a pose of bemused boredom.

"Please come in," Okamoto said. "You may leave your shoes at the entrance." He reached for a buzzer underneath the table. Piper stood at the threshhold, taking in the scene. Okamoto's thatch of white hair was as dramatic as ever, his hands and body as petite, his small round face as kindly and benign. But somehow, away from the piles of yellowing journals, he seemed more in command, less wizened. He had shucked his dowdy academic suit for something more businesslike, although he was practically undressed next to Saeki, dapper as always in a charcoal gray suit and red-silk tie. But there was something different about Saeki, too, Piper thought; and then he understood that Okamoto was the boss. Until now Piper had seen

Saeki only with subordinates and those he considered inferior, including, of course, Piper himself.

Piper found himself wondering why he was not more surprised. It was as if, eating fish and rice with Yamada last night, he had known Okamoto and Saeki were downstairs, listening to every word. As if from the beginning at Tokyo University that Friday afternoon, he had somehow known they would encounter Okamoto again.

But what he said was: "Where the hell are we?"

"You found *us,* Mr. Piper," Saeki said, with more than his usual lacing of contempt, Piper thought. "Why ask us?" Before this is over, Lord, Piper thought, if I come out alive, and if I don't win a Pulitzer, then at least let me punch Saeki once in the nose, okay?

But Okamoto spoke soothingly over Saeki's remark. "No, no, of course you are curious, Piper-san," the professor said. The Japanese honorific seemed to soften the atmosphere, unlike his earlier, almost sarcastic use of 'Mister.' "You are a very persistent reporter, as are you, Kimamura-san. You have not made our lives easier, I should tell you, but I think you have earned an explanation."

As he spoke, two concrete wall panels slid open noiselessly, and two slender young women in navy blue uniforms, each with long black hair, each carrying a tray, appeared one after the other at the opening. By turn they halted, bowed and entered. Okamoto spoke to them gruffly and they set their trays on the orange table, bowed again and retreated. The concrete panels slid closed. "Please sit down," Okamoto said, gesturing toward the trays.

Piper and Kyoko slid out of their packs, leaned them against the wall and stooped to unlace their hiking boots. Then they waited uncertainly. Scratched and sweaty from the cross-country hike, disheveled in his jeans and thick socks, Piper felt, not for the first time in this country, like a poor relation invited but unwanted in some stately home.

"Please," Okamoto repeated. Piper started toward the table, but stopped when Kyoko did not follow. Her voice, after Okamoto's reassuring tones, came as a sharp surprise, especially as she spoke in her throaty English. "Where is Shimizu?" she said.

Okamoto raised his eyebrows, and then chuckled. "You did not approve of our serving girls, Miss Kimamura?" he said. "Given your own, shall we say, professional experience, you must have very exacting standards, I suppose." The "Miss" again seemed more put-down than term of respect, and as to his reference to professional experience—Piper couldn't figure out what he meant, or why Kyoko seemed to stiffen at the remark.

Now Okamoto pushed a button recessed in the wall and, as the concrete panels slid open again, barked commands into the next room. Then he faced Kyoko, a kindly smile still on his face. A few minutes later the old tea pourer appeared. She waited expectantly, impassively, not glancing at Piper or Kyoko, looking exactly as she had in Okamoto's office two weeks before, bent over in a dark kimono, white socks, and slippers. Piper instantly found himself doubting that this wizened creature could have drawn the map that started them on this chase.

"Is there anything specifically you wanted?" Okamoto said, speaking to Kyoko, but still in English.

After a pause Kyoko shook her head. "No, no," she said, and then in Japanese, "I'm sorry to have disturbed you." Okamoto muttered to the bent-over lady, who retreated to a corner and shrank into the kneeling position of an over-the-hill geisha still eager to serve. Piper could not decide whether Okamoto kept her there as a rebuke to her, or to Kyoko, or both. The concrete panels slid shut again.

"Perhaps you imagined the worst of us, but as you can see, Miss Shimizu is quite healthy," Okamoto said. He gave a little bow toward Kyoko, who flushed and said nothing. "Now please take some refreshments, and then I will give you a tour."

To eat lunch somehow seemed an act of weakness, a concession to Okamoto that Piper did not want to make after Kyoko's embarrassment. But he was ravenous. As he attacked his thin sandwich of ham and white crustless bread, Okamoto continued in his calm, professorial way.

"Mr. Yamada would like you to know that he never wanted to deceive you," he said. "It was we"—he gestured briefly toward himself and Saeki—"who asked him to be your host last night, thinking we could spare you and ourselves some difficulties."

"So his whole story was a fabrication?" Piper asked.

"No, no, by no means," Okamoto said. "To be honest, I don't think Yamada-san would be capable of such wholesale deception. But he does certainly have, shall we say, a romantic side, so perhaps there were some exaggerations." Okamoto smiled, as if he and Piper were colleagues discussing a bright but wayward graduate student. There was none of the vitriol Okamoto had directed toward Yamada in his university office two weeks before.

"Where is he now?" Kyoko asked.

"You are the suspicious partner today, am I right?" Okamoto said with a smile. "Perhaps you are playing 'good cop, bad cop,' is that not the expression?" How does he know this stuff, Piper wondered. "I could summon him, too, to put your mind at ease, Kimamura-san, but Yamada is working. If you would, just this once, accept my word?"

"And that house upstairs?" Piper asked. "Was that just to put us on the wrong scent, too?"

Okamoto laughed and Saeki allowed himself a knowing smile. "We have been worried about your inquiries, I do not deny that," Okamoto said. "But please do not flatter yourselves too much. We were not worried enough to reconstruct an eighteenth-century farmhouse for your benefit. No, no. That house, as Yamada told you, was a kind of retreat for our team during the war. It has sentimental value for me, and for a few others who still remember those days. As our facilities here grew, we restored the farmhouse as a kind of memorial to our humble beginnings." Okamoto shrugged with a kind of self-deprecation. "Nowadays we use it for conferences, or for staff who may want to meditate in private."

"And as a front for visiting journalists," Piper said.

"That was a first, I can assure you," Okamoto replied.

"So the food doesn't really get cooked in that kitchen?" Piper said.

"Ah, you admired the kitchen!" Okamoto laughed. "No, the food is carried from our kitchens here, which are somewhat better equipped."

"And these facilities, as you call them—what are they?" Piper said.

"Why don't I show you," Okamoto said, "instead of sitting here and boring you."

"Yamada apologized for boring us, too," Piper said. "If one of you would try the truth, I'm sure we wouldn't be bored."

Okamoto laughed, as if delighted by Piper's joke. "I'm afraid you've left us little choice, Piper-san," Okamoto said. "By the way, you are the first foreigners ever to visit our lab. You should pat yourselves on your backs." Piper glanced at Kyoko to see whether she had noticed Okamoto's use of "foreigner" in the plural. Had Okamoto consigned her to the gaijin camp because she worked for an American, or as a subtle slur on her Korean heritage? Whichever, Kyoko showed no response.

They walked into a coatroom and Okamoto, explaining that they might pass through some clean rooms, handed each of them white coats, plastic gloves, hats, and slippers resembling showercaps. While the reporters outfitted themselves, Okamoto, looking even smaller standing than sitting, donned a white coat only, as did Saeki. "Our clothes have been disinfected," Okamoto explained apologetically. "They never leave the facility." For the same reason, he added, they would have to leave cameras behind.

To Shimizu, who was hanging back, Okamoto said, still in English, "Since Miss Kimamura worries about your health, why don't you join our tour?" He seemed determined to make Kyoko squirm. Shimizu looked uncertainly at Okamoto until he spoke briefly in Japanese, and then she too pulled a white lab coat over her kimono.

The next hour passed in a blur of centrifuges and cyclotrons, microchips and molecules, X-rays and lasers and isotopes and microscopes. Piper had satisfied his science requirement before dropping out of college by barely passing two courses designed to let the football team graduate: "Splash 101," as the students called it, consisting of field trips to aquariums and screenings of Jacques Cousteau films, and "Apes and Tapes," an exhaustive survey of primates who had—or had not, depending on whom you believed— learned to communicate with humans. Neither course had prepared him to cover Japan's increasing technological superiority over the United States. Fortunately for Piper and his readers, a kindhearted colleague at *Semiconductor News* never tired of explaining to Piper the difference between a D-RAM and a megabyte and the relative significance of each. But now, embarking on this tour without his friend from *Semi-News,* Piper's head began to swim.

His difficulties mounted as Okamoto set a brisk pace along endless gleaming corridors from one incomprehensible machine to another, nearly trotting on his short legs. They rode elevators up and down, crossed catwalks suspended high above cavernous halls of winking, whirring computers, donned protective earmuffs to enter metal-working shops manned entirely by robots dancing a slow and sexless ballet. Utterly lost, Piper loped alongside, trying to at least minimally comprehend while writing legibly with his plastic-wrapped hand. Days later, when he had a chance to look back through his notebook, he wasn't surprised to find that he could decipher almost nothing he had written on the tour.

Still, some impressions remained. If this was, in truth, a government facility, it was unlike any Piper had seen in Japan, as far from the shabby clutter of Tokyo's ministries as a gleaming Honda factory from the gloom of Detroit. It was huge, certainly, and mostly deep underground, though occasionally, when the hills outside dropped away to a valley, Piper guessed, they would come across an expanse of thick glass built into the concrete, from which they could survey the sun-dappled woods, silent and illusively cool. They saw a cafeteria, painted in bright reds and blues and greens, and a corridor of staff bedrooms, small and snug like ship's berths. Okamoto seemed happy to show them anything, balking only twice. Once, Piper started to enter a room that was, he could see through a small window in the door, full of cages. Okamoto held him back, explaining that laboratory mice and other animals were kept in an environment as free of outside bacteria as possible. And once, as he tried to open a locked and windowless door, he heard a white-jacketed worker shout something about *"toneru"*—tunnels. Okamoto explained that the plant was connected, through underground passageways, to old air-raid shelters on the air force base, in which the air was not filtered as in the facility itself.

All the while, as Piper tried to make sense of this miragelike complex beneath the simple farmhouse, Okamoto was talking, lecturing, explaining, recounting in his patient, sensible monotone a story so reasonable, so reassuring, and yet so tantalizing journalistically, that it hardly occurred to Piper to doubt it.

After the war, Okamoto recounted, some of Japan's brightest scientists had repaired here—not, as Yamada had said, to hide their past but, he explained, to protect Japan's future. In the last desperate days of war, many Japanese knew defeat was coming, rued Japan's attempt to live by the sword and understood that this desperately poor island nation, devoid of resources, shorn of empire, would have to find some other way. These people, Okamoto said, knew that Japan could survive only through hard work and sharp wits, through the industry and intelligence of its people.

But in those days there was also great fear of the conquering Americans. How much revenge would they exact? Would they reduce Japan, as some had proposed, to a feudal, agrarian state, never again to develop an industry that could feed a war machine? Perhaps the entire leadership class would be taken, perhaps any vestiges of science would be ground into the dust.

And so a few forward-looking people inside and outside the government, acting quietly, so as not to anger their own military nor alert the approaching Americans, decided to safeguard one of the country's few remaining assets, Okamoto said—its young minds. Files were doctored so that the occupiers would not become suspicious, and a few courageous volunteers agreed to leave their lives and families behind and devote themselves to Japan's future. Of course, Okamoto said, it was to be a future of peace and industry, not of war and nuclear horror. The young scientists would draw a road map for an experiment never before tried: achieving economic well-being without armed might.

At first, Okamoto said, they did little besides talk and write and draft plans that Okamoto forwarded to like-minded friends in the ministries. But gradually, over the next few years, their effort expanded. Beneath the house they had a small laboratory built, at first more to hone their skills than for any useful purpose. Those in Tokyo who knew of their efforts, directly or, more often, indirectly, found them useful, and the project attracted, discreetly, more funding. The team scoured scientific literature from the United States and advised the ministries where they might most profitably send young scientists, to which labs or companies in America, and for which specialties. When the Occupation ended, and the nearby air force base reverted to the Japanese, the facility expanded further. Graduate students returning from the United States—those whose discretion could be trusted—would stop here on their reentry and report. The lab would test what they reported, and send results and advice to friends in the ministries or the big industrial concerns. And some of those young scientists liked what they saw here, and chose to stay, and so gradually the team expanded, Okamoto said, until, he said, it became what you see here today.

An elevator chimed and they all stepped aboard. What a story, Piper thought: the secret command post of Japan's technological rape of the West. "But how can you possibly keep this place secret?" he asked. "There must be hundreds of people who know—construction workers, scientists, delivery people."

"Most delivery people stop at the base, and we bring goods in from there," Okamoto said. "The way you arrived, needless to say, is not the usual entrance." The elevator doors opened to a familiar-looking corridor. "The people who do know understand our mission," Okamoto continued. "They know that Japan is a poor island nation without natural resources, and they are patriotic, and so they are discreet." He smiled to Piper. "Until today, in any case, we have been fortunate."

Saeki spoke up for the first time on the tour. "We are a democracy," he said, "but a democracy with discipline. Unlike in your country, people do not feel obliged to reveal secrets simply to show they have been entrusted with them."

Kyoko, who also had been quiet throughout the tour, shot a skeptical glance at Piper. "But why keep it secret at all?" she asked. "This seems like something to be proud of."

"Very true, Miss Kimamura, very true," Okamoto said. Piper realized they had returned almost to their starting point. "But for two reasons, we have never chosen to advertise ourselves." He turned his small hands upward in a kind of gesture of humility. "One, as Yamada explained, is the harm we would cause the families of our pioneering scientists." Okamoto seemed not in the least embarrassed to show that he knew every detail of their previous evening's conversation. "The other is, well, a bit more delicate." They had reached the original cloakroom, and Okamoto was removing his white coat and hanging it on a hook. The others followed suit. "Of course, we view what we do here as perfectly proper and necessary, and beneficial, not only for our country, but for yours and the rest of the free world as well." He nodded toward Piper. "And yet, it could be misconstrued—in the hands of an irresponsible journalist, let us say." He smiled sadly, as if everyone in the group knew such loathsome creatures and how impossible they were to control.

They reentered the stark concrete room and took their former places, Shimizu again kneeling in a corner. The trays had been cleared. Piper, who had remained hungry even after finishing his paper-thin sandwich, noticed that he was famished again.

"Such a journalist, in fact, might describe this place as a center of industrial espionage," Okamoto continued, again smiling at the very ridiculousness of the idea. "He might say this was the secret brain center, the hidden headquarters, for Japan's raid on American science and technology, from where we sneaky Japanese plotted our return to world dominance and exploited the weakness of your generosity. Am I wrong? How would that be as a lead, as you might say, Mr. Piper?"

"A little wordy," Piper said. "But it might make the front page." Gleefully, he considered using Okamoto's phrases when it came time to write his piece.

"Yes," Okamoto said dryly, "I daresay it might. Which is why we have been fortunate to maintain ourselves here so discreetly."

"Until your luck ran out today," Piper said.

"No, no, Mr. Piper," Saeki said with a sneer. "I'm afraid it is you who have run out of luck."

"What my colleague means to say," Okamoto said, again breaking in quickly with a pleasant smile, "is that we are certain we can rely on Miss Kimamura's love of country. She knows how hard we have all worked for what we have achieved since our defeat. And I believe that you, too, Mr. Piper, will see the wisdom of silence, as difficult as that may be for a reporter of your vigor and inquisitiveness."

"Are you kidding me?" Piper laughed. "This is a great story. Why would I sit on it?"

"Well, I can think of three reasons, each of which I find persuasive," Okamoto said, still in his reasonable tone. "I hope and believe they will be persuasive to you as well."

Piper put his notebook down and exchanged looks with Kyoko. Suddenly, he didn't like the turn the conversation had taken, and he felt a chill in the pit of his stomach. Just as suddenly, he felt that

Kyoko might be right again, that they had yet to learn the whole truth.

"Okay, I'll bite," he said. "What reasons?"

"Let's have some tea," Okamoto said. "You must be weary from the tour." He pushed a buzzer and a moment later the two slender women in blue reappeared, bowing and murmuring apologies.

23

*T*he young women placed cups of tea on the table with small, satisfying clicks of china on lacquer. Piper thought he could hear a whirring sound from deep within the building, and the brushing of skirt on nylon as the women bent to serve. He thought, too, that in the stillness he could almost hear his blood rushing through his veins and arteries. Of course, there would be a catch; otherwise why would Okamoto show them the place, why not just lock the red door from the start? But what could Okamoto say to keep them from running the story? Surely he could not be so out of touch as to rely on Kyoko's sense of patriotism, yet Piper couldn't imagine what other arguments Okamoto might try.

The professor took several small sips of pale green tea, the cup large in his small veined hands. He had been talking for more than an hour, and his throat must be dry. After a moment he set the cup down, with another satisfying click.

"Well," he began, "I know, with most journalists, it would be foolish to talk about right and wrong. But since we first met almost two weeks ago, I have developed great respect for you and your colleague"—he nodded toward Kyoko—"and I have to think you are not immune from thinking of the greater good, even though you are a reporter."

"What greater good did you have in mind?" Piper asked.

"Well, the health of the U.S.-Japanese alliance, for one," Okamoto said. "Now I do not want to be melodramatic, but you know as well as I how close we are to rupture. At a time like this a story about our facility could go a long way toward provoking a mutually destructive conflict."

"You mean it could push the expropriation bill over the top in the Senate," Piper said. "That's not my problem, I'm afraid."

Okamoto continued as if Piper hadn't said a word. "And, on the other side of the balance, what would be served by some sensationalistic exposé?"

"What makes you think I'd write a sensationalistic exposé?" Piper broke in again. "You said yourself this place has been good for both countries. Well, I'm happy to quote you saying so, and give you all the space you need to make your case." The day the *Advertiser* gave anyone all the space they needed, Piper thought, was the day the paper fell under new ownership. But never mind. "As to what is served, how about the people's right to know? And not just my readers, but the Japanese people, too, who've been paying for this place all these years without knowing the first thing about it?"

"Ah, how noble," Saeki spoke up. "The great white reporter will give us a refresher course in western democracy and your precious First Amendment. The right to know!" He chuckled. "I don't suppose the right to keep your job and get on the front page and sell newspapers and win prizes has anything to do with it."

Okamoto looked pained, but this time he did not jump in to smooth over Saeki's comments. Piper took a sip of the acrid green tea so that his voice would not be shaking when he answered.

"You know," he said finally, "at one time you might have been right. Keeping my job and winning prizes might have been my goal. But I've reported on enough smug, slimy, fatuous, overdressed, empty-headed peacock officials who think they know what's best for everyone else to make me really believe in the people's right to know. And frankly, if your newspapers are too cowardly to tell the story, then, yes, I'm happy to do that service for the Japanese people." He saw Kyoko staring into her cup and wondered whether she was embarrassed by his outburst, persuaded by Okamoto's logic, or cheering him on.

Saeki smiled, as if he couldn't be bothered to respond to such a tirade. Okamoto, for the longest time, said nothing. Then he sighed. "Well, I'm disappointed in you, Mr. Piper," he said. "Disappointed, but not, I must admit, entirely surprised. Which is why we are fortunate that my first argument—which I find the most persuasive,

I have to say, but which apparently does not move you—is not the only argument we can make." He pressed the concealed button again. This time the concrete slabs slid open to reveal a young acolyte in glasses and a three-piece suit, who bowed, handed Okamoto an envelope and retreated. How do they know who he wants when he presses that buzzer, Piper wondered.

"With all of your mountain-climbing and—what is the expression—muckraking?"—Okamoto put an ironic stress on the "muck"—perhaps you have not seen the latest issue of this esteemed American magazine." He took a faxed sheet out of the envelope and, without a glance, handed it to Saeki, who passed it on to Piper.

Piper unfolded the paper and immediately recognized the typeface of the *Business Chronicle*, Zarsky's weekly magazine. The piece covered two columns under the headline HACKS ON THE TAKE, with a subhead asking, ALL THE NEWS THAT'S FIT TO BUY? Piper scanned the article until his own name jumped out at him. Then, ears burning, blood pounding behind his eyes, he returned to the top and read more slowly.

"When they bought Rockefeller Center," the piece began, "we adjusted. When they took control of our movie studios, we survived." Like all articles in the *Business Chronicle*, this one was unsigned, but the irritatingly breezy lead could only be Zarsky's work, Piper thought. "And when they started buying up our universities and laboratories, we said, well, that's the American way."

"But now *BC* has learned that the Japanese haven't stopped there. Under the table, behind our backs, they have been shoveling yen to American reporters, apparently in return for favorable coverage—or noncoverage—of their wheelings and dealings, their wheedlings and diddlings. Recently obtained documents prove that at least three correspondents—a travel writer, a computer expert and a Tokyo-based correspondent for a mediocre but sizable regional newspaper—are on the take." Documents? What documents could he possibly have?

The article discussed the first two cases first. The travel and technology freelancers had accepted free trips to and around Japan. They were quoted as admitting the gifts but denying that the money had influenced their writing. Editors who had used their pieces piously disclaimed any knowledge of the payments and insisted that no articles would have been printed had they known. "I'd like my money back, I'll tell you that," one editor said. Yeah, probably fifty dollars, Piper thought. Cheapskates, all of them.

Then Zarsky came to Piper: his big fish. "In a recent interview in Tokyo, John Piper, not surprisingly, didn't seem eager to discuss the little part he's been chosen to play in Japan's growing empire." Interview? Piper thought. That was an interview? "But documents obtained from well-placed Japanese sources show that Piper has received cash payments and reimbursements of travel expenses from the Foreign Ministry—that's the Foreign Ministry of Japan, of course. Why would an American foreign correspondent stoop so low? Hard to say, but Piper offered one hint during his brief and testy conversation with *BC*. 'God knows my paper isn't overpaying me,' he told us."

"I can't believe this," Piper exclaimed, and then continued reading silently: "And what has Japan gotten for its money? Again, it's hard to say, but one longtime correspondent with a reputation for hard-hitting coverage said of Piper, 'He's not exactly known for zinging it to the Japanese.' How many zingers have American readers missed thanks to Japanese generosity? A little digging by our press corps over there might tell us, but maybe none of our fine foreign correspondents feels motivated to dig. Hmmm. *BC* wonders why that might be. . . . In the meantime, read those Tokyo dispatches with your eyes wide open. And for now, over and out! Or, as Piper-san might say—*sayonara!*"

Piper looked up to see Saeki watching him, a slight smile curling on his face, while Okamoto calmly sipped his tea. Judging from the way Kyoko was staring at him, he must look stricken. He handed her the article and said, "This is a joke, right? You doctored the Xerox."

"Why, were you misquoted?" Saeki chuckled. "Or perhaps your remarks were taken out of context? How does it feel to be on the other side for a change?"

"No, I wasn't misquoted," Piper said. "But I never took any money from you, either, as you damn well know."

"We did not doctor the Xerox, I assure you," Okamoto said. "I'm sorry we cannot provide you with the actual magazine, but it should arrive within a few hours. Our colleagues in New York sent a fax of this page as soon as it was published, knowing of our interest."

He didn't seem to be bluffing. Well, Piper thought, they've won. My career is ruined, that goes without saying. And even if I still had a job tomorrow, anything I printed about this secret facility would look like a fantasy concocted to save my reputation. He could imagine how everyone in the press club must be savoring this little bombshell. Christopher would be saying he'd always had his suspicions, and that prick Engel from the London *Times* would point out that he'd always thought Piper was soft on the little Nips. Come to think of it, Engel was probably Zarsky's source "with a reputation for hard-hitting coverage"; they were comrades in racism and frequently helped each other out with witty blind quotes from "longtime Tokyo observers."

But who was Zarsky's initial source of disinformation? Zarsky wouldn't know a "well-placed Japanese source" if it stood up and bought him a beer, but he couldn't have invented the whole thing. "So how did you manage this?" Piper asked Okamoto. He noticed that Kyoko, having finished the article, was looking pale around the eyes again. "Is Zarsky on your payroll?"

"Oh, please," Okamoto said. "I don't want to sound boastful, but it's simple enough to manipulate a reporter without wasting money on him."

"So you just leaked him a few fake documents," Piper said.

"Well, something like that," Okamoto said. "Unfortunately, to enhance the credibility of our little operation, we had to sacrifice two other journalists who have been friendly to the cause of smooth U.S-Japanese relations. And this won't do our image any good, either; I hope you consider that before you start feeling sorry for yourself. But we had no choice; we needed an insurance policy, in case we couldn't dissuade you in other ways."

"Yes," Piper said. "But even if we had fallen for Yamada's little stunt and gone quietly home to Tokyo this morning, we would have discovered that you had already cashed your insurance policy, and I still would be finished as a reporter, isn't that right?"

Okamoto gave an apologetic little shrug. "The timing was delicate, yes," he said. "Next week's issue might have been too late. When you visited me in Tokyo, I tried to discourage you from wasting time on ancient history. I wish, for your sake, you had listened to my advice."

Kyoko, uncharacteristically, was staring at Okamoto. "I don't get it," she said, almost to herself. "I just don't get it." Okamoto looked at her oddly but did not reply. Piper pushed himself up from the floor and walked back to the golden screen on the concrete wall. It really was magnificent. Maybe he should have just written about the ethereal subtleties of Japanese culture, like some of his colleagues; about calligraphy and bonsai and haiku, about melancholy novels and Shinto priests in early-morning mists and aged potters designated as National Treasures. His newspaper would have been happy, the Japanese would have been happy, he could have lived happily ever after. Piper had disdained such reporting. Sometimes he had thought the whole kimono/tea ceremony/ivory-carving world was nothing but a front for the double-dealing Saekis of Japan. Sometimes he thought the Saekis were an aberration, that the real Japan wanted to live in peace with its haiku and bonsai and sumo, if only the Saekis would allow. Now, as he watched the three-hundred-year-old crane extending its neck in graceful flight against a sparkling gold sky, he realized that the two worlds were one. They could not be separated. Well, too late now, he thought; I've dispatched my last epiphany about Japan. They've won. And what a Japanese-style victory, at that: Let me in, let me see, let me nearly grasp the story of my career, and then, with no effort, snatch it all away. Like a seasoned sumo wrestler just stepping out of the way, turning his opponent's weight against him. An American would have locked the red door and posted armed guards there to boot, Piper thought.

"Why did you let us in this morning?" Piper asked, giving voice to his thought.

"If we hadn't, we had no guarantee you'd just give up and go home," Okamoto said, reasonable and comradely as always. "We didn't want you wandering the property, getting lost or hurt. And to eject you would only have made you suspicious. I hoped that, once you saw that all your dark imaginings"—he turned toward Kyoko—"were groundless, that you would see the wisdom of discretion in this case." He shrugged, and said with sudden iciness, "Fortunately, I did not rely entirely on that hope."

"And that man who followed us? Was he your boy?"

"Ah, yes, poor Masaki-san," Okamoto laughed. "His feet are

quite sore, thanks to you. But he stayed with you long enough to confirm your general direction. We were able to imagine the rest. We knew, after all, that you had visited Mrs. Yamada, and that she had given you a photograph of this house."

Piper started, and glanced involuntarily toward Shimizu, who remained kneeling in the corner, staring at the tatami. Maybe they still don't know about the map, he thought. For her sake, he moved quickly to another subject.

"Yamada said that some of your colleagues helped build Russia's bomb, in exchange for POWs. Is that true?"

"As I told you, Yamada has his romantic side," Okamoto said.

"Yeah, but was it true?" Piper said harshly. "You've gelded me, why worry now about what I know?"

But Okamoto's face was closed. "Please," he said with hard finality, "I think we've had enough questions and answers." He slowly pushed up from the table. Saeki and Shimizu, as if on cue, stood also. "I am sorry things have not worked out as you planned, Mr. Piper, but perhaps I can compensate in a small way. The telecommunications talks will end in about"—he checked his watch—"thirty minutes. Happily, they will end with an agreement. I have arranged for one of Mr. Saeki's colleagues in the Foreign Ministry to fax us the text, along with transcripts of the closing press conferences of both sides, as soon as they take place. Needless to say, we have whatever equipment you might need to send an article to your headquarters in America—to your desk, I believe you would say, is that not right?" He bowed modestly. "We would be happy to have you as a guest for this purpose."

Yeah, and probably you've already written the lead, too, Piper thought. "You're very optimistic to think I still have a job and a newspaper to file to, Professor," Piper said, pointing to the article that still lay on the table in front of Kyoko. But even as he spoke, he thought, Anything to keep me here longer. It was pointless, no doubt, but Piper could not so quickly erase habits of long standing.

"Well, just in case their copy of *BC* hasn't arrived yet, maybe I'll take you up on it," he said.

Okamoto bowed again and, as though already dwelling on his next appointment, headed for the door. As it slid open, Piper suddenly said, "By the way, Professor, what was the third reason?"

His back to the room, Okamoto stopped and tilted his small head, as if debating whether to throw strike three. Then he turned and said softly, "The third reason involves your able assistant, and her aging mother and unfortunate brother," Okamoto said. "As Miss Kimamura herself said, you have a U.S. passport. They're not going to put you in any secret prison." Suddenly, he broke from ice to laughter. "But enough of this foolishness. I think two reasons were more than enough." He walked through the opening alone, and the concrete panels slid shut behind him.

24

*W*ith Okamoto gone, Saeki bounced back to his old self, suave and in control. Snapping out a few words in Japanese, he sent Shimizu scuttling out and then turned back to Piper, still standing before the screen, and Kyoko, who had remained motionless at the table.

"We have arranged rooms so that you may spend the night, and transportation for the morning," he told them. You really have everything worked out, don't you, Piper thought. And aren't you pleased with yourself, too. "Separate rooms, of course," Saeki added, with a mocking little bow toward Kyoko. "Perhaps you would like to freshen up before you begin your work?"

A different young woman materialized at the doorway, bowed, and guided them to rest rooms behind the lab-coat closet. On the way, Piper leaned over to Kyoko and whispered, "I never knew you had a brother."

"You never asked," she said curtly. Then, more gently, she added, "That's why I needed my weekends."

In the men's room, Piper tried briefly to puzzle that out, images of Kyoko in her black leather skirt flashing through his mind to a soundtrack of Okamoto's sneering at her "unfortunate brother" and her "professional experience." None of it made sense, and none of his nonsensical imaginings were very pleasing. And why did Okamoto know more about her than Piper did? But then Okamoto seemed several stages ahead of both of them.

Piper finished first and was heading back when he overheard Saeki, in the main room, instructing the young man in the three-piece suit.

"*Cha ni yaku o ireroo,*" Saeki was saying. Put something in her tea.

"Onna dake o nokoru tame ni na." So the girl won't be leaving this place.

Piper froze and then, with great effort, forced himself to walk into the room, past the two bureaucrats and back to the screen. The clouds and cranes seemed to be swimming off the gold. I must have heard wrong, Piper told himself. I must have misinterpreted. Now the younger man was murmuring, *"Hai, hai,"* and something else that Piper couldn't catch, and was disappearing out the door. Now Saeki was approaching Piper with a smile.

"I am glad you have such an appreciation for our culture," he was saying, joining Piper as if on a Sunday afternoon stroll through an art gallery. "Have you seen Hasegawa's 'Maple and Cherry Tree' screen at the Chishaku-in Temple in Kyoto? No? A pity. You really must. One look at that will give you a better understanding of our country than a hundred trade negotiations." He really is a monster, Piper thought. Or maybe I misunderstood. I must have misunderstood.

Kyoko returned. "Well, shall we?" Saeki said. "I will show you the way, and then sadly I must leave you for Tokyo. But someone will be here to bring dinner and show you to your rooms whenever you are ready."

As Piper and Kyoko bent to retrieve their packs, Piper whispered, "Don't eat or drink anything." She froze, wide-eyed, and he quickly turned to face Saeki so she would not reply. She must be spooked enough already, as was he, by Okamoto parroting the comment she had made deep in the woods that morning. But she followed a few paces behind, saying nothing.

Saeki donned his lab coat and told them to do the same, allowing them to shove the hat and gloves and foot-coverings into their pockets; they wouldn't be entering any clean areas this time, he said. He led them to a gleaming communications center, where cursors blinked green on computer consoles and a printer hummed in one corner. The young man in the three-piece suit was waiting for them.

"Here's what we've received so far," the man said in flawless, British-accented English, pushing his glasses back up the bridge of his nose and producing a sheaf of papers. "They appear to have crafted a mutually advantageous agreement, by the way."

"Gee, that's great news," Piper said. He forced his eyes to focus on the shiny sheets of fax messages: the announcement of an agreement, a brief statement from the Japanese side, a longer statement from the Americans, a one-page glossary of technical terms.

"There are a few things that haven't been translated yet," the young man said, handing more paper to Kyoko. "Why don't you work at this station here, and I'll help you transmit when you're ready." He wheeled two desk chairs to a Fujitsu word processor.

"Well!" Saeki said cheerily. "I'm sure I'll be seeing you both in Tokyo. Good luck on your story!" He was out the door. The young man, after showing them a buzzer to press if they needed help, also withdrew, leaving Piper and Kyoko alone under the bright lights with the humming printer and blinking computers.

They sat. While Kyoko took pen to her Japanese documents, Piper made himself bang out a lead. He wanted them to think he was serious about writing this story, that he suspected nothing, and his leads always came out better if he wrote them before he knew too much. He could always revise if any of his facts proved wrong.

"TOKYO, August 2," Piper began. There was his first lie already, but he'd never explain a Niigata dateline, and he doubted his handlers here—or should he now say captors?—would allow one anyway. "At a time of spiraling tension, the United States and Japan today reached an agreement on trade in telecommunications goods and services that American officials said will crack open a lucrative market long closed to U.S. firms," Piper wrote.

"The agreement, announced late today, could dent Japan's massive trade surplus with the United States by as much as—" Here Piper stopped as Kyoko slid a page from the Japanese text onto his lap.

"Here, take a look," she said. He realized he hadn't heard her throaty voice in what seemed like hours, and it washed over his frayed nerves like a balm. "I've translated the first page."

Between the lines of dense Chinese characters, she had written in English, something she never did at home; usually, she just picked out quotes she thought he might use. As he read the first few lines of her translation, he realized what she was up to. "The Japanese government is delighted at the successful outcome of these difficult why can't i eat or drink negotiations and pledges its full resources to ensuring that American companies and how did he hear what i said this morning are able to take full advantage of it by competing openly and successfully in the growing Japanese market."

Piper looked around. He hadn't noticed any surveillance cameras, but you couldn't be sure. A small camera might be hiding inside any of the computer consoles, he supposed. As a rule, he assumed the Japanese could do anything they put their minds to, and he was rarely proven wrong. He kept the paper on his lap and picked up the English faxes. Pretending to scribble notes in the margins, he wrote, "Don't know but they're planning to spike your tea. We need to get you out of here."

Kyoko read his scribbles with sidelong glances and set to work on page 2 of her translation, handing it to him a few minutes later. "The government wishes to reiterate that the Japanese economy is now more open to imports than that of any other developed country john none of this makes sense i'm sure we're still missing something i'm going to poke around but pledges further efforts toward becoming even more of an import superpower."

Once again Piper was having trouble thinking clearly, but Kyoko's note forced him to face his own doubts. Okamoto's story had made perfect sense, and yet—was hiding this laboratory really worth all the trouble Okamoto had taken, having them followed, ruining Piper's career, threatening Kyoko? And what about the bus driver's warning? And how did Shimizu fit into all this? On his statement Piper just scribbled, "Be careful!!!"

Aloud, Kyoko said casually, "You need me for anything else?"

Piper flipped wearily through his faxes. "No, I think I'm okay," he said.

"Then I'm going to look for a more comfortable chair," she said. "I'll come back in time for dinner—wait for me." She must figure they won't harm her while I'm expecting to see her at dinner, Piper thought. He hoped she was as right as she was gutsy.

He went back to his screen, trying to plot their next move while he wrote. He could churn out these trade stories practically in his sleep, which was appropriate, he thought, given the effect they had on anyone who tried to read them. Still, it hurt to think that neither this article nor any other under his byline would ever appear again. He'd never again be able to work with Kyoko, or finish a story with

"Kyoko Kimamura also contributed to this article." And as for his dreams of winning a Pulitzer and moving up to the *New York Times*—here ended that joke. He'd be lucky to find work anywhere. Well, all that mattered now was to get Kyoko out. Then he could worry about the rest of his life. Presuming it didn't end in the next day or two, right here in Niigata prefecture.

"U.S. officials acknowledged that the agreement does not provide every assurance sought by U.S. industry, but they pledged that embassy officials here will monitor the pact closely to ensure that it is honored in spirit as well as—" As well as what, Piper thought. In letter? No, that didn't work. He rode the cursor backward, erasing the sentence fragment and thinking, How *did* they overhear our conversation this morning? They must have planted a bug last night, but where? In his pack, maybe, or even in some piece of clothing? He'd brought only one pair of jeans, it wouldn't have been hard to guess what he would wear. But was that possible? And over what distance? Again, he wasn't inclined to bet against their technical capabilities.

"U.S. officials, who have been criticized in the past for reaching agreements that had little effect on real trade, pledged tonight to monitor the pact closely to make sure that Japan abides by the spirit of the agreement," he wrote. No, that was no good either; he'd used the word "agreement" twice in the same sentence. Well, that's what copy editors are for, he thought. *Agreement, pact, accord, stipulation, settlement, understanding, concord, compact*—he'd used them all. Just once it would have been fun to use *breach, breakdown, rupture, rift, falling-out* or *split*. He'd have to bequeath that pleasure to his successor, Piper thought. Again he envisioned the handsome editorial writer sitting in the Tokyo office, Kyoko leaning over his shoulder, her hair brushing his cheek. . . . Piper shook the image out of his mind and glanced at his watch: nearly seven. Where was she? She should have been back by now. Outside, about an hour of light remained. This underground chamber was beginning to suffocate him. He decided to look for a bathroom before writing the last few inches.

The gray-carpeted corridor was deathly still, without even the slightest buzz from the fluorescent bulbs. He found and entered a men's room, but the lights were off, and as he groped for a switch, the door swung shut behind him, leaving Piper in total darkness.

Suddenly, there was a hand on his arm, and blindly, unthinkingly, unleashing all the frustrations and fears of the day, Piper swung out with his right arm, a mighty punch at what should have been chin level. His fist crashed into the bathroom wall and he cried out in pain.

"Shhh!" He felt a hand softly plucking his sleeve and leading him deeper into the bathroom. His eyes were watering, and with his left hand he could feel a trickle of warm blood on his right knuckles. It would have been a hell of a punch if anyone in this damn country was the right size, he thought. But he allowed himself to be tugged into what seemed to be a toilet stall. He heard the toilet flushing, and the hand was pulling him down, down, until his chin grazed what smelled like woman's hair. He jerked up involuntarily and then bent forward again, not quite as low. The hand moved up his chest, searching for his ear, and then he heard a whisper, so low he might almost have been imagining it amid the sound of roaring water.

"Mada anata no tame ni inotterun desu kedo," the soft voice said. I am still praying for you but. *"Mada wakatte irrashaimasen ne."* You still don't understand, do you? Piper started to speak, and the voice hushed him again. He heard the toilet being reflushed, and then the soft whisper was in his ear once more. *"Kawamura Bun-san ni kiite kudasai. Karenara minna shitte imasu."* Ask Bun Kawamura. He knows.

But I already tried that, Piper thought. His brother nearly ran me down in his wheelchair. Turning to where he hoped the woman's ear might be, Piper whispered, as quietly as he could, *"Moo shinda des-shyo?"* Isn't he dead already? After the woman's breathless whisper, his own sounded like an explosion. In the darkness he imagined he could feel the woman waving her hand vigorously in front of her face, in the classic Japanese impatient gesture for no. *"Mada desu."* Not yet. He heard the toilet flush again and then, still in Japanese, she told him to leave as soon as he could. Not by the way they had entered, she said. There was a motorcycle waiting at the front door. Level three, past the cafeteria. Take it, and the girl, and go. She is in danger. *"Ki o tsukete,"* she concluded. Be careful. Then she flushed the toilet once more, told him to wait two minutes and was gone. He heard the stall door swing open and closed, and then the bathroom door. He felt weightless in the total blackness. His hand was throbbing. As if exhausted, the toilet finally sighed to a stop.

Piper groped his way toward the door, found a light switch and flipped it on, blinking at the brightness. He used the toilet, ran cold water over his knuckles and went back outside. In the communications center, Kyoko was sitting in front of the computer, one leg over the other, her foot bouncing nervously. She smiled with relief when he walked in.

"Hi," he said. His voice boomed after the silence of the corridor and the whispers by the toilet. "Hungry? I'm almost done. I just need another quote or two from you." He sat next to her, and they took their faxes back on their laps.

Piper scribbled, "How'd you make out?" and then, pointing to his paper, said aloud, "See if you can find this quote in the Japanese version." She shrugged and jotted, "I grabbed some documents." He wrote, "Can you find the cafeteria?" She nodded. "How about driving a motorcycle?" She wrote on the Japanese statement, "It's been a while." He wrote, "You need to use the bathroom."

"I need to use the bathroom," she said aloud.

"I just came back from there," he said. "Let me show you where it is." Piper left the unfinished story glowing on the screen and his pack leaning against the wall, taking nothing but the papers on which they'd been scribbling. When they reached the bathrooms, Piper indicated with his head that Kyoko should lead on, and they padded down the silent corridor in stocking feet. Piper cursed himself for having left his shoes by the red door.

Avoiding the elevators, Kyoko led him three flights down a stairway, and then quickly along another corridor. Piper was just wondering why they had encountered no one during their tour with Okamoto or now, when they heard voices approaching. They ducked into a passageway and then further into a recessed doorway, holding their breath as two men and a woman, all in white coats, walked past, chatting and laughing. Probably on their way to dinner, Piper thought. We'll never get past the cafeteria this way. He waited for his heart to slow and the voices to recede. Then he donned his shower cap, gloves and plastic boots, and Kyoko followed suit. No doubt they would look strange in the plant's living quarters, but they'd have to take the chance. Piper would stand out even more without the hat.

This time they walked without stealth, still quickly, but down the middle of the corridor, hands shoved deep in their lab coats, as if on an important official errand with no time to change clothes. Kyoko led them right past the entrance to the dining hall and its hubbub of staff scientists at dinner. As two men in white coats approached, Piper stared at the carpet, and they passed without a second glance. Then, suddenly, he felt warmer air. They were at an entrance: double glass doors, giving on a circular driveway, with no guard in sight. The security must be farther out.

Piper waited for alarm bells or sirens as he pushed open the door: nothing. They were back in the woods. A few fingers of pink still laced across the darkening sky, but at ground level dusk was practically gone. A dusty old motorcycle had been pulled up to the side of the driveway. Kyoko checked the key in the ignition, straddled it and kicked it on. Piper mounted behind her and clasped his arms around her stomach. With a jolt, and a bump off the sidewalk, they were off. Trespassing, theft of government property; if they wanted Kyoko out of the way, they wouldn't have much trouble now, Piper thought, even without putting something in her tea. And him, too, for that matter. And he knew how Japanese justice worked, even in normal times: days or weeks at the mercy of the police, in jail, cut off from the world. Almost everyone confessed eventually. Maybe that voice in the bathroom hadn't been Shimizu. Maybe this was the final setup. And he had fallen for it, like every other trap along the way.

Around the circular driveway and out, the road led only one way. There were no streetlights, but Kyoko left the headlamp unlit, gaining speed as her eyes adjusted to the darkness and she gained confidence in the machine beneath her. Piper had never ridden one even as a passenger, he thought with some embarrassment. He wondered where Kyoko had learned. Piper was afraid he'd fall off if he looked over his shoulder, so he kept his wrists locked tight around Kyoko and his eyes straight ahead, and prayed that no one was giving chase.

After winding through woods for twenty minutes, they reached a straight road along a wide, treeless plain, cratered like the moon and stretching into velvety darkness under a sliver of real moon low in the sky. Kyoko roared down the straightaway. The unfinished story, their packs against the wall, their shoes near the red door—Piper hoped those signs would reassure their hosts and allow enough time to escape. Whatever security existed at the end of this road must be discreet; attention-getting electronic fences and guard platoons were the last thing Okamoto would want. On the other hand, Piper did not doubt that once the young man in the three-piece suit realized they were gone he could put out an alert that would shut Piper and Kyoko in like penned sheep.

The plain gave way to a small copse of woods, more like a screen of trees than a forest, and then to a flat, open expanse dotted with older, rickety buildings. A few streetlights and spotlights shone here and there in the darkness of what must, Piper thought, be part of the old base. At an intersection, Kyoko stopped, toes on the ground. As she strained to decipher an old sign facing them, Piper suddenly heard something behind a screen of trees to the right. He tapped Kyoko's shoulder, and she cut the engine and wheeled the bike off the road. Dismounting, they crept through bushes until, from behind two trees, they could make out the curious goings-on in a small parking lot before them.

In the dim orange glow of a single street light, a half-dozen workers in white jumpsuits were tending to as many white panel trucks, identical but for their markings. One van was inscribed with NEC logos, another bore those of the Fujitsu computer company. As Kyoko and Piper watched, two workers applied Hitachi decals to a third; the other trucks were still unmarked. Five workers, meanwhile, were gingerly maneuvering a large carton onto the NEC truck, while one supervised and softly called out directions.

Soon the haulers took a break, squatting on their haunches in the center of the lot, cupping matches to their cigarettes in the evening breeze. There was something eerily ordinary about their gestures in the night. The artists kept working, transforming a fourth truck into a Toshiba van. White moths fluttered near the orange light, and in the woods an owl hooted. Figuring that every minute heightened the risk, Piper caught Kyoko's eyes, and they retreated together through the bushes. Kyoko pushed the bike, its wheels whirring and clicking without the engine, back onto the road, the men's voices fading away behind them. Then she kicked the bike back on, Piper climbed on, and in a moment they were barreling down a straightaway and, suddenly, through a gate. Piper had a flash vision of a sleepy soldier jerking awake and saluting. And then the base was behind them.

Piper took a look at Kyoko: a shower cap on her head, no helmet, no shoes. With his curls poking out beneath his shower cap, he looked even more ludicrous, he was sure. If the guards from the facility didn't catch them, he thought, if the bug in his jeans didn't direct Saeki and his gang right to them, then some rural cop would probably haul them both in for psychiatric evaluation.

He leaned into Kyoko's ear and whispered, "Go north."

It was going to be a long night.

25

*K*yoko drove for nearly an hour, and gradually Piper relaxed, feeling the warm breeze of the night and the gentle rise and fall of her belly beneath his hands. Her long pale neck gleamed in the dark as the wind blew her hair toward him. He even dared look over his shoulder, and happily found the same emptiness behind them as in front.

She pulled over at last, into an abandoned gasoline station, and silenced the engine. Stiffly, they dismounted, stretched, shucked their white coats. As Kyoko began to speak, Piper hushed her, fishing a pen and notebook out of his back pocket and handing them to her.

"Even here?" Kyoko wrote.

Piper shrugged, to say they couldn't be sure, and so, in the beam of the cycle's headlight, they conversed through gesture and hurried notes. "Clothes bugged??" Piper wrote. "Need new, or laundromat."

Kyoko read that, and smiled despite herself. "Sure can find yr size jeans next village. Also shoes. Where to?"

"Back to Kuji," Piper wrote. Kyoko eyed him as though he were nuts, and thrust the notebook back, demanding an explanation.

"Great fish restaurant near station," he wrote. She rolled her eyes. "Also, Shimizu says 'we still don't understand anything.' She says 'Ask Bun Kawamura.' " Kyoko read that and then looked more confused, dragging her forefinger across her throat to indicate she thought Kawamura was dead. Piper nodded and shrugged, I've told you all I know. Then he wrote, "Brother also dead, Sato sd. 8 yrs ago." He shrugged again. Kyoko underlined Shimizu and scrawled three bold question marks. "Later," Piper wrote.

Kyoko reclaimed the pen. "Can't make Kuji one night," she wrote. "Daylight → arrest. No shoes, no helmets—not in Japan! Also, gov. plates." She pointed to the motorcycle fender. Then, responding to Piper's gesture, she pulled the map of Japan out of her pocket, and in the yellow beam, which they now shared with a collection of moths and smaller bugs, they examined possible routes. Piper pointed to Sendai, and to his watch; Kyoko gave a qualified nod. "From there by train A.M.," he wrote. "But first laundromat."

And shoes, she indicated by pointing to her feet. Piper slipped his notebook back in his pocket, and Kyoko folded the map. They rolled up their lab coats and stuffed them into the saddlebags, then ambled behind the old garage, to the edge of a dry rice paddy. Across the fields a stand of mountains rose before them, black against the near-black of the sky, hiding in its folds a few villages whose lights twinkled like tiring fireflies. Behind them, a truck rumbled along the highway with its cab windows open, allowing a snippet of baseball play-by-play to escape into the open air and float across the paddy. *"Boru-tsu!"* Piper thought he heard. Ball two! It was hard to believe that this Japan and Saeki's were the same country. It was hard to believe, in fact, what they had seen and heard that day. Yet the bulk of the Japan Alps rising darkly before him, the roughness of the pebbles beneath his stockinged feet, were real enough. Piper wrapped Kyoko's hand in his, and she turned toward him and they kissed. Standing on tiptoe, she drew him down to whisper in his ear, "I'm scared."

"Me, too," he mouthed, and they kissed again. Then they walked back to the motorcycle. On the road again he wanted to clasp his hands inside her jersey, against the warmth of her flesh. Don't think about it, he told himself. Think about Bun Kawamura, and Zarsky, and Okamoto. Think about what we still don't understand.

They rode east into some of Japan's most mountainous country. Kyoko slowed for the occasional village but whipped along the winding alpine roads. They saw few cars and fewer people; only a rare truck or bus told them that not all Japan was asleep. Once they passed a blue sewage truck, the kind that came to most Japanese homes once a week to suck dry their outhouses. Not so many decades ago, Piper knew, villagers and poor townsmen in these parts would have used or even sold their night soil. Now they still lacked flush toilets, but they had to pay someone to take the night soil away. That was prosperity.

By ten o'clock his legs ached, his empty stomach gurgled resentfully and he began to wonder how they could forage something to eat without making a spectacle of themselves. An interracial couple strolling in stockinged feet into a provincial store or restaurant was bound to excite some local conversation.

And Piper did not want to be noticed. Already, they were trusting to luck that their clothes were not bugged, or that they could wash any bugs away; that no one had outfitted their little Honda with a tracking device; that once the young man realized Piper and Kyoko had fled, he would assume they were heading back through the woods toward Tokyo; that no one would discover, at least until morning, that the cycle had disappeared. Piper had no idea how Shimizu had produced it, but he assumed it came from the base motor pool; they'd have to ditch it by daylight.

They entered the town of Nanyo. Kyoko slowed to a putter as she cruised the darkened streets, searching for something. After a few minutes, she pulled over, cut the engine and motioned Piper to wait. He watched her steal back half a block, vanish into what seemed like a private home and reappear a moment later with black pumps on her feet. Piper looked with astonishment; she just laughed. A few blocks farther on, she stopped again, half a block from a well-lit convenience store, and returned this time with a loaf of bread, some packaged cheese, four bananas, four cans of juice, a carton of milk for Piper, two cans of Georgia brand sweetened coffee and an apologetic shake of the head: slim pickings. Piper didn't care; he was ready to tear open with his teeth the plastic bag of bread, but Kyoko gestured for him to wait. They turned north again, straight up the island's mountainous spine toward Yamagata, and soon Kyoko pulled into a scenic overlook for their picnic. Against a gathering chill, they pulled their lab coats back on. A picnic table enjoyed what Piper assumed must be a spectacular view, but in the darkness each had to imagine the valley and mountains before them in his or her own way, chewing their white bread and processed cheese in silence, sitting atop the table with their feet on the wooden bench. What a sight we must be, Piper thought: two deranged hospital interns, on the lam.

In the early hours of the morning they reached the provincial capital of Yamagata and Kyoko again slowed to a quiet cruise, wheeling up one street and down the next until they found a laundromat, dark and closed. The glass door was locked, but halfheartedly so, as Piper had expected; he didn't imagine Yamagata experienced many laundromat B&E's. He had let himself into locked apartment doors often enough, and he had no trouble prying this one open with a credit card. Mentally tacking this on to his and Kyoko's lengthening rap sheets, he swung open the door and walked in.

It was cozy, as laundromats go: just four washing machines and four dryers, vending machines for soap powder and for juice and a couple of chairs at the back. A streetlight cast a silvery glow, and the day's washings had bequeathed a warm and soapy smell. There were no family quarters behind the public room, a lucky break. With further luck, Piper thought, no next-door neighbor will wonder at the nighttime noises. He fed three hundred-yen coins into a machine, yanked out a miniature package of Attack detergent and then, with an apologetic shrug to Kyoko, began stripping and tossing his clothes in a machine. His nakedness had never felt more ludicrous. Kyoko walked to the rear of the shop and turned away to undress. He saw her long back and taut bottom gleaming in the street light before he forced himself to look away. When she returned, she was clutching her pile of clothes in one hand and holding her lab coat closed over her nudity with the other. Piper shook his head: better not take a chance even with that. He made a show of turning away, staring fixedly at a tattered poster of Yamagata ski country on the far wall while she threw the white coat in the wash with the other clothes.

As water filled the machine, he was conscious, even as he tried to concentrate on the skiers at play, of Kyoko's approach. "I guess we can talk now, right?" she whispered. She put her arms around his waist, as if he were driving the motorcycle, and he could feel the warm, smooth length of her. "Do you really think they would have killed me?" she whispered.

He turned toward her, holding her against him, and felt her nipples graze his chest. "I don't know," he said. "It's hard to believe now, but it didn't seem so incredible when we were trapped in that overgrown bomb shelter." He told her of the Japanese words he had overheard, and of the conversation by the flushing toilet.

"Now they'll be after both of us," Kyoko said softly. "You should have left me and gotten yourself back to Tokyo to get the story out."

"You're right," Piper said with a smile. "I don't know what got into me."

He leaned down slowly and kissed her gently on the lips. Kyoko's mouth opened and he felt the flicker of her tongue, and suddenly they were kissing urgently, and pressing against each other. In his last semilucid moment, he thought about how this would cap off her rap sheet, and his too. Then he was thinking no more, and as she buried her mouth and nose into his neck, he lifted her onto the gently-swaying washing machine and kissed her hair, her shoulders, the soft outward slope of her hips, and before long he was sliding deep inside her, to the very heart of a lifetime of desire.

When they had finished, they remained still for what seemed like hours, her breath warm and reassuring on his neck, his hands still cupping her into him, his whole body utterly content, until with an abrupt clunk the machine shifted into its spin cycle, and she began to vibrate, and as she did so, to giggle, making him giggle, and soon they were both laughing, and then shushing each other and looking nervously out the window, which only sent them into greater paroxysms of silent, wheezing laughter, until he had slipped out of her and tears were rolling down their cheeks. He lifted her off the machine and hugged her until he couldn't hold her any longer, and then he carried her to the back of the room, where they collapsed onto a chair.

She sat on his lap, gently trailing her fingers through the hair on his chest. He noticed, with childish satisfaction, a few beads of perspiration on her upper lip. So she does sweat after all. Gently, he tickled the length of her back, teasing himself by reaching just to the swell of her buttocks, and then reversing course. How many times had he dreamed of this moment, and yet never imagined it right.

She broke the spell with a whisper. "What are they so afraid of, John?" she asked. "Why go to such lengths to protect an industrial lab? And what were they doing with those trucks?"

"It's not just any industrial lab," Piper answered, trying vainly to persuade himself that his own suspicions might be wrong. "It's the center of their rape of the west, and if it came out now, with the mood in Washington being what it is . . ." Even as he spoke, he doubted his own words. It couldn't be just that; their actions were too dramatic, too desperate. "What do your documents show?"

Kyoko picked them up and leafed through them slowly, frowning and shaking her head. "Maybe you're right," she said finally. "They look like simple commercial documents—shipping dates for computers, that kind of thing."

"This is from Okamoto's desk?"

Kyoko nodded. That made no sense, either, and neither of them spoke for a time. Then Piper said, "Listen, Kyoko. If we figure this out, and if we survive, you should write this story."

"No." She shook her head.

"Why not? You're untainted by Zarsky's article. It could be the start of a great career on your own," Piper said.

"For one thing, I'd be scared, and scared for my mother," she answered. She made no mention of a brother, and so Piper did not ask. "And for another, this is the story you've been waiting for all your life. I'm not going to take it away from you."

"It's already gone." He smiled and kissed each of her eyes. "Besides, you're the story I've been waiting for all my life."

"Yeah, I'll bet you say that to all the girls during the spin cycle," she said. "We'll see how you feel during the tumble-dry." The washing machine had in fact clicked off. Piper watched Kyoko's breasts sway as she lifted the wet clothes into the dryer and walked back toward him, smiling again. He thought he had never seen anything more beautiful.

"You know, now that we're not making love, I feel a little silly being naked in a laundromat," she said. "I don't know why."

"I guess that's just the kind of girl you are," Piper said, pulling her back down to him. "But if you're going to be uncomfortable, I guess we'd better do something about it." He kissed her again, probing gently for her tongue. "By the way," he said, between kisses, "whose shoes are those?"

"Mine, now," she murmured. "That was a *minshuku*"—a family-style inn—"and I figured there'd be many shoes at the doorstep. Nothing in your size, I'm afraid," she said, reaching down to illustrate her point.

He shuddered involuntarily at her touch. "You should be ashamed of yourself, stealing that way," he said.

"I am," she whispered in his ear. She trailed her fingers across his belly and inside his thighs, and soon she was standing and leaning against a machine, guiding him inside her from behind as he cradled her breasts and kissed her neck, and the rest of the world melted away once more.

26

*T*angled together, they dozed on the chairs. Sendai was only two hours distant, beyond the famous mountaintop monastery of Yamadera, and there was no point in reaching the big city too soon. Piper couldn't board a train without shoes, and he couldn't buy shoes until the stores opened. On the other hand, they wanted to junk the motorcycle by dawn, and they didn't feel entirely secure in the laundromat. So at about four in the morning, they decided to push off.

Again they stowed their lab coats in the saddlebag, not wanting to leave any traces, and Kyoko told Piper he would have to drive; she was too tired and, now, too sore. She would sit sidesaddle behind him.

"Impossible," he said. "It's bad enough driving a car in this country, with everyone on the wrong side of the road. But a motorcycle—I don't even know where the brakes are."

"Now's the time to learn," Kyoko said. On the deserted roadway she showed him how to accelerate, how to stop, how to shift gears. With trepidation, he kicked on the bike and wobbled perilously down the street. Even out on the main road, he hugged the curb, gripping the handlebars with whitened knuckles, his back rigid, legs tense, oblivious to Kyoko's arms encircling him. As they approached Yamadera, where they could only imagine the temple buildings clinging to rocky outcroppings in the darkness above them, Kyoko leaned forward to recite into his ear a haiku composed there by Basho: "How still it is! / Piercing into the rocks / The cicada's shrill."

"What is it with you people and cicadas?" Piper asked, turning sideways and yelling so the rushing air would carry his words back to Kyoko. "What's wrong with nightingales, or chickadees, or the mournful hoot of an owl?"

"That's the problem with you gaijin—if it's not pretty, you can't see the poetry in it," Kyoko yelled back. "I guess it takes a couple of thousand years of culture to acquire that kind of subtlety."

"Speaking of gaijin . . ." Piper said. He gingerly glided the bike to a stop at the side of the road before continuing. "This is a pretty big tourist attraction, right? So there ought to be some gaijin staying here, don't you think? And maybe one of them wears size twelve?"

Kyoko jumped off the motorcycle and bent over, arms and hair hanging low, to loosen her back, then straightened again. "We can try," she said. "I was here on my junior-high-school trip, I think I can find the place."

"No wonder you knew that poem," Piper said. "For a minute I was impressed."

They stopped a hundred feet beyond the hostel, and Kyoko darted back and returned, a minute later, with a pair of battered running shoes. "Eleven and a half," she said. "You'll have to make do." He shoved his feet into the undersized Nikes, leaving the laces untied.

Now that both were shod, they tried to plot their next moves; neither could face climbing back on the bike right away. Kyoko argued that they should travel separately from Sendai. Piper didn't like the idea, but he had to accept her logic: better not to fix themselves in the memory of anyone who might later be questioned about a tall foreigner traveling with a beautiful Japanese. They agreed to leave the motorcycle in Sendai and then take diverging routes to Kuji.

Just before daybreak they motored into the Sendai metropolis, bombed into the ground by the Americans, now prospering and vibrant and ugly. On the city outskirts they wheeled their motorcycle into a bike lot crammed with other Hondas and Kawasakis, and with a copper ten-yen coin Piper unscrewed the license plate and wrapped it inside his lab coat. Then he and Kyoko, under the lifting cover of darkness, stole one last kiss.

"See you at Dunkin' Donuts at six," she said.

"Or on the hour after that, if something happens," he said, repeating the plans she already knew. "You have enough money?"

She nodded. "Be careful." She smiled and, tossing her hair over her shoulder, started toward a municipal bus stop, where a few early risers already waited in a line. Almost despite himself, Piper suddenly called after her. She turned and waited as he caught up.

"Listen," he began hesitatingly, "you don't have to tell me if you don't want to. But—what was Okamoto talking about?"

She turned away, looking suddenly very tired. She watched a bus pull up, open its doors for the commuters to file aboard, and then roar off.

"My brother has never been . . . quite right," she said. "Where we live, for my mother, that is a shameful thing." She paused. "She believes no one would marry me if they knew. She believes neighbors shun us because they do know. Perhaps she is right. He is twenty-four, very sweet, and quite helpless, maybe thanks to us. He almost never leaves the house." She drew a long breath. "I worry about him—my mother is old—what if something happened to me? So I earn extra money on weekends, for his future. I work in a bar, a kind of bar. As a hostess. I earn a lot of money." She turned to Piper for the first time and said, "It's not what you're thinking." She stopped, then added, almost to herself, "though sometimes it's close."

"I'm not thinking anything," said Piper, whose mind was whirling. This is where she had headed every Friday night? He knew how hostesses earned their tips, pouring drinks, flattering their male customers, laughing at their jokes, being pawed over, sometimes more. Degrading work, and he couldn't imagine Kyoko doing it. Before he could say anything, she said, "Anyway, I've quit," and started running for another bus just then pulling in.

"Be careful," Piper called out again. Too late, too little; he couldn't be sure she even heard. As the bus pulled away, a cabin of fluorescent light in the morning gloom, he saw Kyoko fumbling for change with one hand and using the other to keep her balance. She didn't turn or wave.

Piper set off alone, on foot, toward the station, as they had planned. He walked parallel to Aoba-dori, the main drag, along a back alley of the now-quiet entertainment district. Piles of trash guarded the back doors of every eating and drinking establishment, guarded in turn by crows that seemed, Piper thought, a bit less fierce

than in Tokyo. Alone on the narrow street, Piper shoved the lab coat
and license plate into one of the larger mounds of garbage.

By the time he neared the station, a gray light was seeping through
the city. Piper glanced at his watch and, in a calculation that came
automatically, realized he could still make the first edition. He found
a telephone booth, gave a false credit card number to the operator
so police wouldn't trace him to Sendai, and reached the dictation
room at his paper. Caroline, his favorite from the old days of dialing
on deadline from the courthouse, seemed delighted to hear his voice.

"How are you, Piper? What time is it over there? How's the
sushi?" she bubbled. At her familiar voice, Piper instantly heard in
his mind all the other sounds of the newsroom on deadline: tele-
phones ringing, the clatter of plastic computer keyboards, Gravitz
the obit man growling at the unfortunate relative of yet another
deceased, Murphy yelling for copy. How could everything be so
normal there and so out of kilter here? For an instant Piper thought
he should just explain everything to his editor, lay out the story, ask
for advice. But he knew it would do no good; either he'd find he had
lost his job, or he'd lose it on the spot.

"Caroline, you haven't heard anything about my being fired?" he
asked. She laughed; same old Piper. It hadn't happened yet, or else
she hadn't heard. Of course, back in dictation they tended to be the
last to know.

Piper told Caroline that his computer was down and apologized
in advance for filing a story that couldn't match the excitement of his
murder yarns of old. "Your stories never bore me, Piper," she said
loyally. Wait till you hear this one, he thought. Off the top of his
head he dictated twenty inches on the telecommunications talks, still
with a Tokyo dateline and reading a few quotes from the faxed
statements he'd carried with him. Once Piper composed a story, as
he had the previous night, he could recall it almost word for word
for weeks, months, sometimes years. Now, as he slowly recited his
file, listening to Caroline's fingers thousands of miles away tapping
along, pausing, sometimes reversing to correct a mistake or retype
an unfamiliar name, he watched the city slowly come alive around
him. A miniature blue garbage truck, sparkling clean, moved slowly
past his telephone booth, its gaping rear being fed by two garbage-
men in equally spotless uniforms, hardhats and gloves. Men in suits

and schoolchildren in uniforms, heedlessly swinging their satchels, scurried toward the train station. Piper was suddenly gripped with a fierce, nostalgic love for everyone he saw, with an intensity he couldn't explain. Maybe it's the nostalgia of writing my last story, he thought.

He read one final quote from an American negotiator and asked Caroline to switch him to the foreign desk. He waited, again feeling sheepish at his reflex inability to pass up one last byline, but exhilarated, too, as always after filing on deadline, no matter how minor the story, no matter how many times he'd done it before. What the hell, he thought, maybe I won't be fired. And if I am, at least I will have kept on doing my job until—

"Piper? Vinnie here," a tinny voice broke in. "What the hell are you doing?"

"What do you mean? I'm filing on the telecommunications talks, what do you think?" Piper said.

There was a long pause. Piper listened to the distant roar of the Pacific Ocean on the phone line. And he understood. He had been fired, the instant his publisher saw that Zarsky piece. Of course. Piper should have known the *Advertiser* wouldn't have the guts to stand up to something like that, or even to wait long enough to hear Piper's side of the story. As if from outside the phone booth, Piper noticed that Vinnie was chattering away, more and more frantic as Piper didn't answer, about telexes, and hating to be the bearer of bad tidings, two-weeks' severance, tried to stick up for you, bush-league operation . . . Piper mumbled something and hung up. The job, his future, his reputation, none of that mattered; all Piper could think was, Now Kyoko and I are really on our own.

He entered a McDonald's—Makudonarudo to Japanese kids, who were always astonished to learn that you could find outlets of the same Japanese chain in America—and ordered a large coffee, large juice, large milk and two Egg McMuffins. "Ah, yes, a tall gaijin with curly hair," he could imagine the wide-eyed serving girl telling police in the same singsong falsetto with which she was now thanking him for his patronage. "He ate *two* Egg McMuffins! And milk *and* juice! I'd never seen such a thing before!" Foiled by gaijin gluttony, Piper thought. But the hell with it; he was starving, and too tired to worry.

At the station, functioning as if on automatic pilot, he bought a limited express ticket through to Aomori, though he would get off sooner, at Hachinohe, following the same route he and Kyoko had taken the previous week. This way the ticket seller might not remember a gaijin bound for Kuji. Kyoko would ride the same line part way, then cut over to Miyako and hop a train or bus up the Pacific coast, while Piper descended from the north. They had agreed that if by chance they found themselves on the same train for the first leg of the trip, they would act as strangers and ride in separate cars. But Piper still ached to find Kyoko on the platform, and his heart raced at every young woman with long hair who proved, from the front, not to be she. There was no sign of her, in fact, and Piper knew she must have departed at least half an hour before.

Still, he imagined he could sense her fragrance riding with him, and it kept him company all day as he dozed fitfully on the train, torturing himself as he had so many times before with images of her Friday nights away. Somehow, though, the torture was less painful now that he knew her secret. How could he have been so wrong in his imaginings? He woke to buy a boxed lunch of eel on rice and a plastic thermos of green tea, and then drifted off again. At Hachinohe, after buying his ticket to Kuji, he found he had thirty minutes to kill. He bought some rice crackers to present to Kawamura, dead or alive, and then, on a whim, called Marianne collect, hoping they hadn't tapped her phone.

"Pied Piper!" she said. "Where the hell are you?"

"Wandering in the wilderness," Piper said.

"And well you might," Marianne cackled. "How come you didn't share the payola with me?"

"So you've heard," Piper said. He could feel his face flushing all over again, just as when he'd first read Zarsky's slander.

"Heard?" Marianne fairly whooped. "It's all anyone here has talked about for the last two days. The whole club is in a dither over you!"

"I'll bet. What are they saying?"

"Well," Marianne hesitated. "There's the usual range of opinions. You can imagine, I'm sure. . . . So what is the story, anyway?"

"What do you mean, what is the story?" Piper replied hotly. "It's a lie, what do you think the story is?"

"Well, of course, no question, I never doubted that," Marianne said quickly. "But I mean, how did it happen? I mean, he claims to have documents, and the Foreign Ministry isn't denying it, they're just, you know, 'refusing to comment on unconfirmed press reports.' Everybody's trying to reach you, of course, and they're all calling me to ask where you are, as if I should know, and trying to figure out how it could have happened."

"I bet Christopher's enjoying it."

"You can say that again," Marianne said. "But you have to give him credit, he hasn't filed yet. He says he doesn't want to file without getting comment from you."

"He just doesn't like having to follow a Zarsky scoop," Piper said sourly.

"So how can he say he has documents, John? What's going on?"

"Well, he does have documents, I'm afraid," Piper said. "But they're phony. Though he may not realize they're phony, I'm not sure about that."

"But why? Why would anyone phony up documents to make you look bad?" Marianne said. "I don't get it."

"I'll explain everything when I get back to Tokyo in a couple of days," Piper said. "Now I have to catch a train. Are you going to be around? I may have something for you."

"Thanks, but I have to leave for Seoul in the morning," she said. "My desk wants me to cover the next round of north-south talks, yawn."

"Can't you do it by phone?" Piper said. "I think I'm really onto something big here."

"Yeah? What's it about?"

"I can't say yet," Piper said. "I'm not completely sure yet, to tell you the truth. But this time I know it's there."

"Yeah, and the check is in the mail," Marianne said.

"Okay, I don't blame you for being skeptical," Piper said. "But just remember, I gave you first dibs."

"On what?" Marianne suddenly sounded genuinely angry. "On hanging around Tokyo, pissing off my own bosses like you've pissed off yours, and you can't even tell me for what, or where you are? Come on, John, give me a break. What am I supposed to do with that?" He didn't answer; she was perfectly right. After a moment, in a softer tone, she said, "By the way, they settled the telecommunications talks."

"Yeah, I heard, thanks," Piper said. "Hey, Marianne?"

"What?"

"Did you file anything about me and the Zarsky story?"

There was a pause. "I had to," she finally said. "I got a query from the desk. Just a few inches, and they buried it deep inside."

"Sure, I understand," Piper said and, trying to lighten the tone, added, "Well, listen, don't fall for any of that North Korean propaganda, okay? And be careful on the DMZ."

"You mean Kim Il Sung isn't a great and all-seeing leader?" she answered, with the same false good cheer. "I'll try to remember. And John?"

"Hmm?"

"You going to be okay?"

"Sure, I'm fine," Piper said. He didn't feel ready to tell Marianne he'd lost his job, but he added, "There's plenty of jobs in the world besides journalism, you know."

"Yeah, I hear some of them even pay a living wage," Marianne said. "Well, take care of yourself."

"You, too," Piper said, and hung up. For some reason he felt like crying.

The train down the coast was as slow as last time, and as crowded. Piper found a seat beside a window and dozed off again. When he woke, they were riding beside a gray, white-capped ocean, a few minutes out of Kuji. Piper stood to retrieve his bag from the rack, then remembered that he had nothing but rice crackers. At Kuji, the last stop, he jumped off the train and loped along the platform, searching for familiar or suspicious faces and glancing over his shoulder to see if anyone was loping to keep up. There was no one, of course, and Piper told himself to be calm. They couldn't possibly have traced him this quickly.

It was not yet six, but he crossed the station plaza to the doughnut shop. In a booth at the rear, with her back to the wall, Kyoko was sipping a hot chocolate. Piper bought a chocolate honey dip and a glass of milk, slid into the same booth with his back to the door, took one look at Kyoko and silently swore not to part from her again until this whole thing was over. "I missed you," he said.

"Me, too.'

He didn't mention their last talk, and he didn't mention his talk with the desk. She hasn't lost her job, he told himself; why make her more anxious? They debated whether to risk taking a taxi to the store, and decided there was no risk. If the police or Okamoto's goons—Piper still wasn't sure whether those were one and the same—got as far as questioning people in Kuji, there wouldn't be much left to hide, anyway.

"And what do we do once we get there?" Kyoko asked.

Piper shook his head. "I guess we just sit on the guy's wheelchair until he tells us how to find his brother," he said. "Shimizu hasn't steered us wrong yet."

"As far as we know," Kyoko said. "And if that was Shimizu in the bathroom."

"It was Shimizu," Piper said. "Who else would say 'I'm still praying for you?' Besides, she's the only other woman I'd let take me into a dark toilet stall."

Kyoko smiled but didn't answer. "Why does she care so much, anyway?"

"I don't know," Piper said. "She sent us to Yamada, thinking he'd tell us the truth, or whatever it is she believes the truth to be. But he disappointed her, either because he got scared, or was threatened, or because her truth isn't how things are, either."

"Or because he still isn't the man she keeps hoping he'll be," Kyoko put in.

"Then she listened to Okamoto for the second time in two weeks, and just like last time she didn't like his version, either," Piper went on. "So she sent us to Kawamura, at considerable risk to herself, I would guess. Or else at no risk; maybe Kawamura is long dead, and Okamoto knows she's crazy but keeps her on out of the goodness of his heart, or to keep Yamada happy."

"Judging from what he's done to you, I wouldn't count on there being a lot of goodness in his heart," Kyoko answered.

"No," Piper said, draining his milk. "Not a whole lot. Anyway, shall we see what we can find out? With our luck, Bun Kawamura will turn out to be alive, but down in Kyushu somewhere."

"Or in Siberia."

They crossed back to the plaza. Kyoko tapped the window of a taxi at the front of the cab line, waking the driver, and he opened the automatic passenger door. Down the same narrow roads, across the same one-lane bridges, they drove to the fly-bitten neighborhoods of peeling paint and one-story cement houses on the other side of town, Piper recalling the hopes he'd felt the last time they made this trip. Kyoko had the driver stop and let them out by a gas station on the main highway, and they waited there until he had completed his U-turn and driven back out of sight. Down the hill, the bay looked dirtier than ever under an overcast sky. Seagulls wheeled and cawed in the winds of an approaching storm. A man on a motorcycle slowed as he passed, looking them over, and then roared off. They watched him go and then turned their backs on the main road, heading down the slope of the quiet side street.

Nothing had changed at the store. The same faded Coke sign rattled in the wind above the same uninviting bench and dusty windows. Kyoko slid open the door, setting off a brief atonal chime, and presently the same old woman in the same maroon kimono pushed through the curtained door. She took one look and popped back into the recesses of her living quarters before Kyoko could say a word. A few minutes later she reappeared, poking only her gray-haired head around the curtain.

"My husband isn't here," she said in Japanese.

"Machimashoo," Piper said. Let's wait. In English he muttered, "He can't have gone far." He was through pretending—pretending not to speak Japanese, pretending to be polite, pretending to know what the hell was going on. The woman disappeared again.

They waited in the dark, cramped aisles. They could hear a television from within the house, while outside the seagulls cried with greater desperation. Piper walked past the comic-book rack and peered into the little dimly lit refrigerator chest with its tofu, fish paste, miso and milk. He wondered whether anything had been sold since their last visit. He wondered how long they would wait. He was just about to suggest that one of them check the back door when the curtain opened again and the strong white-haired man with his great craggy head wheeled himself forward. He rolled until the curtain flapped shut behind him and then sat there, eyeing them and saying nothing.

"Shimizu-san sent us to find Bun Kawamura," Piper said, in

faltering Japanese. "She said he would tell us the truth. We would like to speak with him."

The man seemed to consider this for a moment and then began rolling himself backward, into the curtain which swung up to let him through, like the rubber fronds at an automatic car wash. Piper, exhausted, thought this was the end of the interview, and he wondered almost listlessly what would happen next. Would the man call the police if Kyoko and Piper just stayed put? What would the police do? Had the wide-eyed hero freed the bosomy naked woman from the long-tongued reptile? Fact mingled with fiction, and both seemed equally and utterly beyond Piper's control.

And then he realized that the man was not retreating, but holding the curtain open for them, waiting patiently, still not speaking. Hesitating for only a moment, Piper stepped through, with Kyoko right behind. The man let the curtain swing shut, and then pushed himself out of his wheelchair, gathering himself to a height almost as great as Piper's, and took a step forward and offered his hand.

"I am Bun Kawamura," he said in slow but clear English. "Please sit down."

27

*T*here were no windows in the room, only the curtained door to the shop and another that Piper presumed opened into a kitchen. A well-broken-in leather chair faced a television set in the corner, and a loveseat was pushed against the left-hand wall, next to the kitchen door. On the facing wall, invisible from the shop, bookshelves reached to the low ceiling, crammed with volumes in English as well as Japanese.

Piper and Kyoko sank onto the low couch while Kawamura folded the wheelchair with strong hands and leaned it against a wall. He shoved the leather chair to face them and sat down. Like a caged polar bear, he seemed too big for the room, with his strong veined hands and great intelligent head.

"*Oi!*" he called to his wife. Or was it his wife, Piper wondered. "Tea!" Then he turned toward Kyoko and Piper. "So," he said to them, in English again, "Shimizu-san says I should tell you the truth." He smiled. "Well, I would never disobey our Shimizu. And maybe she is right, maybe the time has come. But perhaps you would tell me your story first?"

"Of course, that's only fair," Piper said. "But maybe I could just ask—"

"About my sudden recovery?" Kawamura laughed. He had a quick, roaring laugh that was impossible to resist, and Piper found himself smiling, too. "That wheelchair belonged to my brother, as did this shop and"—he gestured toward the kitchen with evident distaste—"that woman. When he died eight years ago, I took the chance to escape my life and step into his. Of course, Okamoto and the others knew what I was doing. But as long as I made no fuss, and kept up appearances here so there would be no scandal, they raised no objection. I wasn't any good to them anymore, anyway; they were happy to be rid of me." He laughed. "It's not much of a life here, as you can imagine, but I've had enough excitement. Now I am happy simply not to be part of their world." His eyes crinkled in a brief smile. "Still, something tells me that you may be about to spoil my quiet little life by the sea." He stopped and leaned forward to help as the old woman entered with three cups of tea. When she had retreated, he said, "Now tell me why two great journalists would honor our humble city, not once, but twice."

There was something of the wise and patient professor in Kawamura that made you want to tell him about yourself and have him clap you on the back and say, Well done! So Piper recounted their tale, from Kyoko's initial story idea to their motorcycle escape from the underground lab. He described their first encounter with Shimizu in the gloomy stairwell, and their evening with the gracious widow Yamada, and how they had found the secret map and had been followed into the mountains. He described their dinner with Yamada—was it only two nights ago?—and their discovery of the security camera, and their subsequent return to the farmhouse. He told of Okamoto's affable, forbearing explanations, and of the disinformation leaked to Zarsky. He repeated the threat he thought he had heard from Saeki, and described his whispered conversation in the toilet. And he told Kawamura of the precautions they had taken to keep from being followed to Kuji. He left out only the help he had received from Sato.

When he had finished, Kawamura said nothing for a time. His chin had sunk into his chest, his hands were folded over his stomach. "Poor Shimizu-san," he finally said with a sigh. "She never lost faith in Yamada, and he did so little to deserve it." Then, waking from his reverie, he said, "So, Mr. Piper? What do you believe, now that you have heard all these stories?"

"I don't know what to believe," Piper admitted. "At first, I thought they must be covering up some kind of accident. Then, when I heard Yamada's story the other night, I have to admit I believed that, though I don't think Kyoko did." He glanced at her and continued. "And yesterday I believed Okamoto, too, at first. Then we realized there had to be more. But—that's why we came to you. We still don't know what we don't know."

"Yes," Kawamura said. He looked at Piper sadly, as though he were a student who had flubbed an easy oral exam. "Perhaps as a journalist you are trained to look for the most complicated explanation. As a scientist, I think the other way. I always try to find the simplest answer. And the simplest answer, in this case, is the right one."

"Meaning?"

"What were we doing in that lab with old Professor Nishina, Mr. Piper?"

"Trying to build an atomic bomb," Piper said.

"Right," Kawamura said. Piper felt as though the professor were giving his student one last chance. "So why do you suppose they moved us to the country after the war?"

Piper felt a chill go through his body. "To keep trying to build an atomic bomb," he said softly.

"Yes," Kawamura said. "To keep trying, and keep trying, and keep trying. Until we succeeded." He smiled weakly. "If you can call that a success." Kawamura pushed himself up from his armchair, murmuring, "Excuse me a moment," and disappeared into the kitchen area, leaving Piper and Kyoko silent on the couch.

Of course, Piper thought, it was so obvious. Why hadn't he seen? And yet, on second thought, maybe not so obvious. Japan with nuclear weapons? It seemed preposterous. And on third thought, not only preposterous, but impossible. He knew enough about nuclear weapons to know you had to test them, especially at first. How could Japan have tested weapons without the Americans knowing? We can monitor a jiggle in the earth in western China, Piper thought; how could we conceivably not know this?

Kawamura came back and said, "You will have dinner with us and spend the night here. It is not safe for you to go wandering the city." Then he sat down and said, "So. Now you know. And I have obeyed Shimizu's instructions." He laughed his sudden merry laugh.

"What are you saying?" Piper asked, this time too distracted to laugh along. "That Japan has its own atomic weapons? I can't believe it."

"Why is it so hard to believe?" Kawamura said, adding in a self-mocking tone, "Are we any less a great nation than Pakistan, or

Israel, or North Korea or, for that matter, America or Russia? Do we not also deserve the best?"

"But that's the point," Piper said. "We know about Israel and Pakistan, and every time Russia tests a bomb, needles go crazy in instruments all over the world, right? So how could you do it in secret?"

"Because we are Japanese," Kawamura said, still in a tone that might or might not be joking. "We are smarter than the rest." Then in a different voice he said, "But your questions are good ones, and I should not make light of them. Let me tell you the whole story, as Shimizu would want. By the way, I thought you reporters liked to take notes?"

Piper scrambled to pull his notebook out of his back pocket and flipped through frantically to find an empty page. He hadn't wanted to spook Kawamura by taking notes. Now, again, Kawamura had made him feel like a lagging pupil. Most of his book was covered with his own scrawling or Kyoko's notes from last night. "We left all our stuff behind," he explained apologetically as he riffled through the pages. The old man nodded and disappeared into the house again, returning with a cassette player. "A marvelous American invention," he said, holding the little Sony in his big hand.

"You don't mind?"

"Why should I mind?" he said. "Shimizu told me to tell the truth. Besides, this is a story that should have been told long ago."

The old woman called something from the kitchen. "Why don't we have dinner first," Kawamura said. "Then we can return to business." While he unfolded a card table, he asked Piper to lock the shop door, flip the sign to CLOSED and pull the shade. "Not that we're likely to get any business at this time of night," he said. "But you'll save me a trip in my wheelchair. You know, I never have gotten used to that thing. I wonder if anyone ever does." The woman brought out three trays of steaming rice and fried tofu and pickled spinach and miso soup, with beers on two of the trays and, Piper noticed with a smile, an orangeade for Kyoko. While they ate, Kawamura regaled them with stories about Kuji, its declining fishing industry, its comically convoluted politics. He asked about life in Tokyo, and about how things had changed in America, and what movies they had seen lately and whether they thought the quarter-ton American sumo wrestler Konishiki would ever join the ranks of the great champions.

And then, when the old woman had cleared away the trays and brought fresh tea, and Kawamura had folded the table and put it aside, he sank back into his leather chair.

"There isn't much to tell that you don't already know," he began, speaking slowly and staring at a spot somewhere above their heads. "Yamada and Okamoto each told you versions of the truth, but they each left some things out, too." He paused, as if putting his memories in order. "During the war we never got close to building the bomb, just as Okamoto told you, but it wasn't because we didn't understand the principles. We lacked time, and materials, and of course the space and money you Americans had. When our people saw what the bomb had done to Hiroshima and Nagasaki, some of them swore we would never do the same."

He sipped his tea. "But there were others who looked at Hiroshima and realized that no country would ever again be a great power without these weapons. And it was these people who arranged for our team to die, as it were, and be transferred into the countryside, to that lovely farmhouse you now know so well.

"Of course, at first we could do even less there than we'd been able to accomplish in Tokyo," he continued. "The government, or some element of what passed for a government in those days, was simply parking us there, to keep the Americans from getting their hands on us. Our team had been put into cold storage, you might say, and we felt honored to have been chosen. And gradually, as things settled down and the Americans gave up on really reshaping this country, as the right wing got back its grip on the bureaucracy and industry, our so-called friends were able to funnel things our way.

"Still, for a long time we were conducting science on a pretty small scale, and we could tell ourselves we were pure physicists, nothing more," Kawamura said. "Some of us won fellowships, under assumed names, in the U.S., to pick up on things we still didn't understand. Even without security clearance, it was amazing what we could learn when no one suspected us of being interested. Of course, nowadays, with the Americans begging for our help to build their Star Wars missile defense, we have an excuse to find out almost anything. How can you design a defense if you don't understand the offense, after all? But in those days, getting information was more of a challenge, and we attacked it with gusto.

"We didn't actually build our first bomb until more than ten years after the war, and we didn't test one until later still," he said. "The greatest challenge was building a small bomb, something you Americans are still working on. But as you know, we are masters at miniaturization." He smiled sadly. "The idea was that we would test the bomb deep underground, detonating it almost simultaneously with an earthquake, and so it would go undetected. As you know, we experience more than a thousand quakes a year on these islands. When we had a new design to test, we would set the device to go off automatically when our instruments registered a tremor near enough and strong enough. It was stressful, and labor-intensive, since we had to monitor the site around the clock, sometimes for weeks, never knowing when the test would take place. But it worked.

"Some of our work was really exceptionally good," he said. "We built neutron bombs before the Americans knew what they were, and we had testing equipment that I would guess the Americans would still love to have. Even with the Cold War ending."

"And you did all this with five guys from the Riken?"

"Oh, no, of course not, we weren't that clever," Kawamura laughed. "Okamoto was too restless, and too much of a manager, to be happy out in the farmhouse, and his job was to recruit new blood. As young physicists would return from fellowships in the U.S., he would pick out the ones he thought had the expertise and temperament and principles, or lack of them, to be part of a secret project like this. They would be sworn to secrecy, but they didn't have to give up their identities, like we did. We were the only ones who had died, officially, and that made us the permanent core of the group. Of course, there were plenty of other workers who knew something was going on, who helped build the tunnels and all, but they were told only as much as they needed to know. As Okamoto told you, they tended to be a patriotic lot. No one saw any reason to talk about what they knew, and no one saw what they didn't want to see. After all, how many pilots, even American ones, have flown over that field of craters and taken it to be some strange geological formation?"

"Or driven by it on a motorcycle," Piper said, almost to himself.

They were all silent for some time. Piper could hear water running in the kitchen as the old woman washed the supper dishes. Then Kyoko said, in a pained voice, "But why? Japan has done so well without nuclear weapons, why would anyone think we'd be better off with them?"

"I can hardly remember how I once would have answered that question," Kawamura said sadly. "At first, I think, it was just insurance, something we never expected to use or need. If the Americans someday abandoned us, if the Russians or Chinese or Koreans threatened us, we would not be naked to the world—simply that. But then, as these things always do, it took on a life of its own. There was a kind of secret society that knew about it, and those people felt privileged and superior to the people who didn't know about it, and that was reason enough to keep it going." He paused. "And also, there was a sense—and I shared this feeling, without any doubt— that we were redressing a national humiliation. Yes, we had lost the war. But did that make us any less virtuous than the Americans or the Russians or the French or the English? Why should they all have the bomb, and not we? Was only the white race advanced enough for this great honor? There was such a feeling.

"And now—now, I can only imagine how they are thinking," Kawamura said. "If the Cold War is ending, and America and Russia are going to disarm—well, who knows? It could turn out to be more than an insurance policy, don't you think? Someday, it could be a trump card."

Piper let that sink in, and then asked, "You're saying that even in the government not everyone knew about this?"

"No, definitely not," Kawamura answered. "I never completely understood how wide the network was. I think some prime ministers knew, and others didn't. The people with real power knew. In the Foreign Ministry, maybe the head of the North American division or the vice-minister, and the head of the so-called research divi- sion—what passes for our CIA—would be told. I know, because I sometimes gave the tour, the initiation rite, to bureaucrats assuming those posts."

"I just can't believe it," Kyoko said, seemingly too stunned to follow the details of their conversation. "I thought this was supposed to be a democracy. What would people say if this came out?"

"They wouldn't like it at all, I'm quite sure," Kawamura answered. "And what the Japanese people would say is nothing compared to how the rest of the world would react. It would be the greatest calamity for Japan since the war. Which is why Okamoto and his friends will go to great lengths to keep the whole thing secret." Kawamura suddenly rose. "Let's continue our chat outside," he said. "I haven't walked outside the walls of this weather-beaten little house since I was reborn a cripple eight years ago."

"Is it safe for you?" Piper asked.

"It's dark now," he said. "And anyway, I think the time has come."

Now that Kawamura had talked, and on tape, Piper found himself fretting about the risks the scientist might be taking, and the faith he might mistakenly be placing in Piper and Kyoko as shields. Maybe he didn't understand the concept of on and off the record, Piper thought, and assumed the story would never come out. Or maybe he assumed that the story would be published, and that the resulting publicity would put him beyond Okamoto's reach. Either way, Piper thought, he might be assuming too much.

"You know, you'd better not count on us for protection," Piper said. "We're damaged goods—I don't know whether I'll ever get this story out, or any other, for that matter."

Kawamura placed both hands on Piper's shoulders. It was an almost shocking gesture; Piper couldn't remember a Japanese man ever touching him before, discounting limp handshakes. Now Kawamura's fierce, sad eyes were locked on his.

"You must write this story," Kawamura said. "You must. These people—Okamoto and his friends—they have gotten crazier with the years, I believe, and more dangerous. They are frightening people. And they are powerful."

Piper suddenly remembered Kyoko's documents. "You know, before we go outside—there's one thing that still doesn't fit," he said. Kyoko handed the sheaf of papers across to Kawamura, who glanced at them casually and then with sudden intensity, his face blanching until it seemed whiter than his hair. After a minute he let the papers slip onto his lap, shut his eyes in a tight, clenched scowl and gripped his armchair with knuckles equally white. Then he rose, without a word, and walked into the darkened store, where they could hear him dialing a telephone. He spoke in muffled tones for a few seconds, waited, spoke again, and then listened for what seemed like ages, only grunting or asking a one-word question from time to time. Piper and Kyoko waited silently on the little couch, straining without success to make out a word or two through the curtain.

When he returned, Kawamura looked older and somehow smaller, shrunken, weaker than before. He sank back into his chair, closed his eyes again and said, "It's worse than I thought. I fear you are too late."

28

*F*or a long time Kawamura said nothing. He might have been asleep, a suddenly old man slumped in his chair, lips working soundlessly.

Finally, he rose and ducked into the inner rooms, and soon they heard a shriek from the old woman. She trailed him back into the living room, clutching his sleeve with one hand and clapping the other over her mouth in horror. "No, no, no, no, no, please," she cried in Japanese. "It's too dangerous. Let me push you. Please." She darted from Kawamura to the wheelchair and back, frantic and fumbling as she tried to unfold the chair without letting go of him.

"Enough!" he growled. He shook her off, walked through the shop, unlocked the door and stepped outside. Piper turned off the recorder and hurried after him with Kyoko, leaving the woman mournfully talking to herself.

"What is she so afraid of?" Piper asked when they were outside.

Kawamura shrugged. "These people you are unmasking will not fool around, and she knows that," he said. He looked up and down the steep street, which appeared deserted. "Besides, she has had enough shocks in her life. She was once my fiancée. When I went to Tokyo during the war, she married my brother instead. Then he went off to war, and came back in a wheelchair, and she cared for him for more than thirty-five years. I think she felt it was some kind of punishment for how she treated me. Anyway, when he died, I showed up. Back from the grave, as you would say. Or maybe from the urn, in our case. It was a shock to her system, and like me, she does not want any more excitement. But sometimes we must simply accept the life we were meant to lead."

"Yamada said something similar," Piper said.

"Did he," Kawamura said dryly. He breathed deeply, filling his big chest, and started at a fast clip down the hill, toward the harbor. The night was overcast and dark, and a stiff, warm breeze was blowing off the water. "We will have rain tonight," he said. They followed him to the piers, picking their way over the stone-strewn sidewalk, Piper looking over his shoulder every few steps.

"You know, they followed us last time," Piper said.

"Yes, I had a visit after you left," Kawamura said, adding with a small smile, "Thanks to you, I've had more company lately than in all the previous years."

"I'm sorry," Piper said. "We didn't realize until much later."

"It's not you who should apologize."

At the bottom of the hill Kawamura pushed open a chain-link gate and walked past a couple of motorboat fuel pumps, a few dinghies and some rusting fishing boats to the end of the pier. Waves slapped against the pilings, and the boats scraped and complained. Somewhere, a rope clanged against its flagpole. In the harbor they could just make out the dredges and retaining walls of the latest marine construction project.

"This was a beautiful harbor when I was a boy," Kawamura said. Piper and Kyoko strained to hear him above the wind and waves. "With a real beach, too. Now I wouldn't let a dog swim here."

He was quiet for a moment, and when he resumed, Piper at first thought he was still drifting on his old-man's memories. Only gradually, and with mounting horror, did Piper and Kyoko understand what Kawamura was finally telling them in his faraway voice.

"When I was still at the lab," he said, staring out at the waves and the rotating beam of a lighthouse across the bay, "we used to say that we could overcome any technical obstacle, except Japan's size. You see, even if we had as many missiles as you or Russia, in our tiny country there would be no place to disperse them. Any enemy could wipe them out with just a few missiles of his own, so why bother? And if we put them on ships or submarines, the whole world would know.

"One day I hit upon an answer," the old man said, still almost talking to himself. "A very smart answer, I am sorry to say. If our country was too small, I said, why not deploy our deterrent on the soil of our enemies? Then they could destroy our weapons only by destroying themselves. Most people at the lab thought I was joking, but not Okamoto. For me it was a fascinating theoretical problem; for him and the powers behind him it was real, very real. It was, at last, their chance for power, for vindication, for revenge. When I understood that, when I allowed myself finally to understand that, I left. But it was too late. And now—now he is making my theory real."

Kawamura stopped talking, as if he had made everything clear. Piper glanced at Kyoko and then, when the scientist did not resume, spoke up against the slapping of the waves, his voice reedy in the wind. "I'm sorry. I still don't get it."

Kawamura stared at Piper for a moment as if he did not recognize him. Then he seemed to snap back. "Okay," he said, speaking more quickly. "Every day we ship thousands of computers, televisions, cars, VCRs, all over the world, yes? In the past few months a few of those products—office computers, to begin with—have been equipped with miniaturized nuclear devices before shipment. Only Okamoto and his crew know which ones, and only they, through satellite communication, could detonate them. This is the list of the first shipments"—Kawamura held Kyoko's documents aloft—"destined, as you can see, for Washington, Detroit, Paris, Seoul, a dozen other cities, in computers made by Hitachi, Fujitsu, NEC and all the rest. This will be our deterrent, our sleeping deterrent. Japan will finally be safe, and the world will be at our mercy."

"It's not possible," Piper said.

"Oh, it's very possible," Kawamura said. "Even your country has been making nuclear mines, nuclear artillery shells and other small devices, for years now. And with our technology . . ." He left the sentence unfinished. "At first, they planned to send them only to the offices of Japanese trading companies around the world, who could be relied on not to tamper with them, to follow instructions. But now they have improved the technology enough so that is not necessary. We can sell them to our foreign customers. A bonus at no extra charge."

"And will they in fact be detonated?"

Kawamura shrugged. "In theory, I suppose not," he said. "We will just let it be known, in appropriate circles, that they exist, and then the world will stop pushing us around—that is the theory. But one of my few friends still on the inside"—he pointed back toward his shop, to indicate the telephone call he had made a few minutes before—"said your country's threat to nationalize Japanese property finally convinced these lunatics to act. You know, for years they have watched the Japan-bashing, the rising racism, the anti-Japan rhetoric, the collusion between Europe and America against the yellow people—a repeat of history, as they see it—and they have grown more and more paranoid, and the X-bill is the last straw, the final proof, as they see it, that, just as in the 1930s, the white world will never allow Japan to prosper. So if Congress goes ahead and the president signs the bill, a small device in a Michigan nuclear plant will be set off as a warning. The world will assume another Chernobyl has taken place, but the people at the top will get the message." He shrugged again. "I don't know whether it is true or not."

"How small are these small devices?" Kyoko asked.

"Oh, physically, they are very small," Kawamura said. "I told you we were very good at that, and no doubt they have improved further since I left. But they are powerful—certainly, one would be enough to destroy most of Detroit and your car factories."

Kawamura headed back toward shore, fairly loping, and when Piper and Kyoko caught up, Piper said, "I'm sorry, Professor, but it just doesn't make sense to me. Even if the blackmail worked for a time, surely we could find the devices eventually? And then wouldn't America just ban all Japanese products?"

Kawamura turned angrily on Piper, almost eye-to-eye in the darkness. "Of course it doesn't make sense," he said. "Any more than it makes sense for you and Russia to point enough nuclear weapons at each other to destroy the world a thousand times over." Then, in a softer tone, he continued: "These are angry people we are dealing with, angry about losing the war, angry about being pushed around by big brother ever since. Such anger doesn't make for logical thinking. But," he added, "that does not mean they are stupid, either. It would not be so easy to find these devices, hundreds of them, maybe—and dismantling them without the proper codes would be even more of a challenge."

"And if we just took out Japan, and all your codes and satellites and detonators?"

"Please, do not underestimate these people," Kawamura said

wearily, as if again disappointed in a laggard student. "Naturally, they will have taken precautions. Some of the devices are set to explode, at various intervals, unless they receive instructions to the contrary. Destroy us, destroy yourself."

They fell silent again. Piper noticed that he was shivering in the gathering breeze. Kawamura set out on a cement path that followed the bay, toward open ocean, striding with such vigor it seemed he would make up in one night for eight years of forced confinement. It was as if, now that the full truth had been revealed, they had not a minute to spare. Piper and Kyoko, on either side of him, half-ran to keep up.

Piper's thoughts turned to his past stories on Hiroshima, and how he had never come close to writing the truth, which was far too painful for what his editors liked to call a family newspaper. Each year he had repeated the numbing totals, the hundred thousand killed instantly and the hundred thousand horribly dead within five years. But he could not write of the blackened, hairless survivors, the "walking ghosts" in the flattened city, the skin of their hands peeled off and hanging down like gloves; nor of the children who helplessly watched their mothers, trapped alive beneath collapsed houses, screaming in pain and thirst, slowly dying; nor of the charred mothers who wandered wide-eyed through the hellish landscape, clasping dead infants to their burnt breasts. Maybe if he, and others, had done a better job telling that story from the start, Okamoto and the others never would have gone so far. But, no; he recalled Okamoto telling them that he himself had visited Hiroshima soon after the explosion. "Something I've lived with ever since," he had said. Some drew one lesson, some learned another.

As if reading his mind, Kawamura said, "You know, right after Hiroshima they came to us and asked us to redouble our efforts," he said. "Couldn't we build a bomb within six months, they asked. Japan was disintegrating around them, and still they couldn't see. They had children clawing uranium out of the mines." He paused. "Now, finally, their wish will come true."

"Is it true that one of you was sent to help the Russians?" Kyoko asked. She can't bear to hear any more about the present, Piper thought.

"Who told you that?" Kawamura asked, surprised.

"Yamada said he'd heard a rumor," she explained.

"That can't have been in his script," Kawamura said, almost to himself. "I wonder whether he slipped, or whether some little part of him still wanted to sabotage Okamoto." He shrugged. "In either case he is right. After the war the Soviets kept hundreds of thousands of our soldiers in Siberia, using them as slave labor. We sent one of our experts in exchange for some prisoners. You see, even then we were a great trading nation," he said with a brief laugh. "One of my colleagues, a poor unmarried fellow from Osaka, was chosen. He never came back, of course. In a way, though, he probably did more good for Japan with his sacrifice than all the rest of us put together."

"Inoki," Kyoko said softly.

"Yes, poor old Inoki," Kawamura said. "Who knows how much he helped the Russians? More than the Rosenbergs, I suppose. But they would have gotten where they are today without him, and without the Rosenbergs, too, for that matter. No single one of us was essential. At least, that is what I say to comfort myself now."

"And what about Yamada and Shimizu?" Kyoko asked. "What was their story?"

"Ah, in a way, the saddest of all," Kawamura said. Talking about the past seemed a kind of anticlimactic relief to him, too, and he slowed his pace toward the open sea. "Shimizu was the light of our team—smart, beautiful, engaged in every detail. Yamada loved her—well, we all loved her, I would say. But I had a fiancée, and Okamoto was already married, and anyway, for some reason, she chose Yamada.

"Near the end of the war, he suddenly made a match with a much wealthier woman," Kawamura continued. "It broke Shimizu's heart, but they remained lovers. She could not give him up—why that was so, I never understood. After the war, when Yamada went back to his wife, Shimizu stayed with us. She had nowhere else to go, really. She had no family and no money, and by the standards of that time she had been spoiled for marriage. And having worked only on our secret project, she never could have found another job, either—officially, she had no experience, no past.

"So she stayed with us. She's officially dead, too, you know, like the rest of us, and she has always had her pension sent to Mrs.

Yamada. But—well, it shames me to tell you what they—what we—did to her. You see, Shimizu became a kind of geisha for the project, and for our important visitors. There weren't any other women out there, you see, and she was very beautiful, as I said, and maybe we were punishing her for loving Yamada and not us. Anyway, Okamoto and the others never trusted Yamada; they worried he might suffer a sudden attack of conscience, and they thought they could use Shimizu as a kind of hostage to keep him in check. They didn't realize how useless it was to appeal to normal human emotion in his case."

It was so dark now, beyond the lights of the town, that Piper had to squint to make out his footing. The waves slammed angrily against the seawall. In the distance, they could see one last pier before the ocean.

"So Yamada went back and spent all his wife's money on drink and other women," Kawamura said. "Then he wrote his book. Shimizu believed he did it out of principle, that he had seen the light about the evils of our work. I think he was just looking for something to do, and maybe for fame, or money. When neither came his way, he blackmailed the project with this idea of a second book. He was ready to dump his wife by then, anyway. Once he was back, he forgot his socialist principles quickly enough and resumed his research, although, as Okamoto told you, he was never much of a scientist."

"And Shimizu?"

"Well, they kept her on, too," Kawamura said. "Partly out of charity, I suppose, partly because they didn't trust her either, although Okamoto has always underestimated her. He kept her in Tokyo, and let her see Yamada once in a while. She stayed on, loathing Okamoto and our work, because she loved Yamada. Still does, I suppose. She never stopped believing that someday he would do something brave, and somehow expose the lot of us."

They had reached the last pier. One naked light bulb burned atop a metal gate at its entrance, and the running lights of an old fishing boat at the end of the dock also shone in the dark.

"But now you're being the brave one instead," Kyoko said.

"No," Kawamura shook his head. He pushed open the gate and

started out along the pier. "You may recall I wasn't so talkative the first time you came calling. I'm only doing what Shimizu has shamed me into, and what I should have done years ago."

"What will become of her now?" Kyoko asked.

Kawamura shook his head. "If they find out what she's done, nothing good, I'm sure of that," he said. "As I told you, these are ruthless people. But maybe they won't find out. She's very clever, as I said, and good at seeming less clever than she is. Okamoto has the opposite talent, I'm afraid. Please wait."

At the end of the pier he knocked on the bow of the fishing boat and climbed aboard with one long step across the inky void. He disappeared into the hold, where another light flicked on. After a time, he reemerged and rejoined them.

"A childhood friend of mine and my brothers'," Kawamura explained. "He'll take you to Tokyo tomorrow. It will be safer than the train. Once they know how much you know . . ." Kawamura left the sentence unfinished.

Piper looked dubiously at this big man with his big head, his white hair shining even in the darkness, and thought, maybe this is the final trap after all. Maybe we'll both be dumped at sea. But he dismissed the idea, Kyoko offered a polite thanks, and they headed back toward town.

That night Piper lay on the floor of the living room next to Kawamura, who apparently hadn't claimed any lost conjugal rights when he returned from the dead. Kyoko slept in the other small room, next to the old woman. Piper doubted he would sleep, but in the middle of the night he suddenly felt Kawamura's big hand on his shoulder.

"You might as well get started before dawn," he said. "You will be safer that way, and there's no time to spare. Maybe you can see the rocks of Rikuchu Kaigan by sunrise."

One of Japan's Three Most Beautiful Views, Piper thought. No matter what, you can't avoid it.

"I have a going-away present for you," Kawamura continued, as Piper rubbed his eyes. When he left the project, he had secretly taken a sheaf of documents outlining the history of their work—seismic charts, work plans, weapon designs, results. "There are duplicates of these hidden somewhere in the research division in Tokyo, and more recent data would be there, too," he said. "Mine only go as far as eight years ago, of course. And here's your tape."

With some embarrassment, Piper presented Kawamura with his 1,200-yen box of rice crackers. At the door the scientist asked them to wait and reappeared a minute later with some food tied up in a cloth.

"You know," he said softly, leaning against the door to silence the automatic chime, "I hope you will not judge Japan by our work." It was hard to see whether he was looking at Piper or Kyoko. "I know Okamoto believes he is a patriot. Like our prewar leaders, he thinks the smartest have a duty to lead, and the rest, a duty to follow. I used to feel the same way," Kawamura said. "As I have aged, I have come to have more respect for our people, and less for myself."

He opened the door and stepped outside with them. "Well, enough speeches," he said, and with a solemn bow added, *"Gambatte kudasai.* Many lives may depend on you."

They thanked him and set off, but after a few steps Kyoko turned back and asked, "Why does Shimizu send her pension to Yamada's wife?"

Kawamura shrugged. "She feels ashamed, I suppose," he said. "For herself. For Yamada." He shrugged his big shoulders one last time. "For us all." Kawamura bowed once more and walked back into his shop.

29

*I*t had rained, just as Kawamura and the seagulls had predicted, but the rain had stopped, leaving the pavement slick under the street-lights and the air moist and warm. Every house was shuttered. Up on the highway a semi shifted gears in a lonely whine that echoed through the humid stillness. Down the hill a dark rat scurried across the street.

They picked their way back to the path along the bay. Piper folded the documents and slid them inside his pants, dropping the tape cassette into his shirt pocket. His toes ached inside his too-small shoes. "The captain's name is Arai," Kawamura had said. "He's expecting you." Piper looked over his shoulder: nobody. A few stars now brightened the sky, and Piper could make out seaweed and other storm-tossed flotsam slopping against the sea wall in the dark green water to their left. Kyoko just looked straight ahead, walking as fast as she could in her borrowed slippery pumps.

The naked bulb at the head of the dock still burned yellow in the night, but the boat at its end, the boat closest to open sea, was in total darkness. Piper felt his old doubts stirring. Waves sucked and smacked against the pilings beneath them as he leaned over to tap tentatively on the bow. The wind swallowed the sound of his knocking and he banged harder. Nothing; and then suddenly a short and tubby man crawled out on deck, stood and lifted his captain's hat in welcome, revealing a nearly bald round head.

"Friends of friends are friends indeed," he said gallantly, in Japanese. "I am Arai. Welcome aboard my yacht."

Piper stepped on to the small, swaying craft and then helped Kyoko across the void. Even in the dark, Piper could see how badly the boat needed a paint job. Once he and Kyoko were safely at the stern, Arai said, "We'll push off right away, without lights, if you don't mind. I will give you a full tour of my craft later." He spoke in a northern dialect almost incomprehensible to Piper. Kyoko, translating, said even she had trouble.

The little man started the boat's engine, then bounded forward again to untie the vessel. They putt-putted backward and then slowly turned out toward sea, a great swell lifting and slapping them down again as they reached open ocean. Piper turned to watch the lights of Kuji recede and disappear from view. He imagined Kawamura in his leather chair, holding an English novel in his big hands, one small lamp shining a pool of light around his great white head while his sister-in-law and erstwhile fiancée slept noisily in the next room. The smartest of the scientists they'd met, Piper thought, maybe the Oppenheimer of Japan, its Sakharov, the father of the Japanese bomb. And here he was in Kuji, strapped to a wheelchair, tuning in a short-wave radio to keep his English sharp, peddling tofu and milk and pornographic comics to underemployed fishermen and their wives.

Arai called them to the wheel. Stepping over piled nets and coiled lines, they joined him, peering into the rocking darkness. With Kyoko doing her best to interpret, he embarked on a jolly monologue.

"There's beer in the ice chest below—please help yourselves," he said. "I make it a point never to drink before five in the morning." He cackled. "You're lucky I happened to be here tonight. I'm only sleeping here until my wife takes me back. Of course, it's been sixteen years since she kicked me out." He cackled again and, wheezing, reached for a cigarette on the little dashboard in front of him. The noisy, hungry wind gulped down the flame on his lighter three times before he managed to light up, take a deep, rasping drag and continue. "I haven't made a trip this long in quite a while, you know. We used to take this boat out two weeks at a stretch, but the fish are all gone around here now. You have to go practically up to Sakhalin these days, and I'm too old for that. So is she, for that matter," he said, caressing the dashboard of the boat. "But I keep her in pretty good shape, you don't have to worry. Unless we run out of gas, of course." He cackled. "Can you row?" he said, turning abruptly to Piper. Then he cackled again. "Just kidding,—we'll make it alright. Should take about twenty-four hours, maybe a little more, depending on wind and weather. With luck you can buy me breakfast in Tsukiji tomorrow." He flipped on the marine radio. Tsukiji was Tokyo's raucous wholesale fish market, which sprang to life in the wee hours each day with auctions of giant salmons and spiny sea urchins and flounders still flapping against each other. "I used to know a lady who served the best noodles in Japan at a stall in Tsukiji. Wonder if she's still there. Fifty yen, in those days, and warm you right to your toes."

"So you live here, aboard this boat?" Piper cut in, looking about in disbelief.

"Here and there," the little man said vaguely. "Go below and make yourselves comfortable, grab some sleep. I'll wake you when we reach the cliffs."

The hold was tiny but neat, with a sink and ice chest on one side and a kind of sleeping bench on the other. There was just room for Kyoko and Piper to lie together, heads toward the bow, looking out through one small porthole at clouds sailing across the starry sky as the boat bucked and heaved over the Pacific Ocean. Piper pulled a light blanket over them both.

"You okay?" he asked.

"I guess." She hesitated. "I'm worried for my mother. And—"

"And what?" Piper's heart clutched, waiting to hear her regrets about their laundromat encounter.

"I don't know, I guess I'm feeling ashamed to be Japanese."

"I don't blame you—it's a terrible handicap," Piper said, flooded with relief. "But you handle it better than most."

"I'm serious," Kyoko said. "You know, I've always felt different from most Japanese—as though I would never fit in here, but would never belong in America, either," she said. "And there have always been things about us that make me crazy. Like Mrs. Kawamura giving you beer and me soda. Like how everybody has to dress the same, and act the same, and even think the same. Like how taxi drivers always find the lane with the most cars, instead of the fewest, because they figure everyone else must have a good reason. Like this great wall we build between us and anything foreign, traveling around the world in huge silly groups, throwing yen at anything that pleases us." She turned sideways and put her arms around Piper, so that she was speaking to his Adam's apple. "But there always seemed to be something good about us, too, you know? Despite all the narrow-mindedness. I really thought we wanted to live in peace with the world, if only we knew how. And we weren't going to tell everyone how to live, the way Americans always do.

"Now I feel I've been tricked, like just one more of the sheep they raise us all to be," she said. "It turns out there isn't anything better about us, and there's plenty that's worse."

"No," Piper said. "Like Kawamura said, you can't blame all Japanese. It's a bunch of renegades—arrogant, and powerful, maybe. But renegades."

"I wish I could believe that," Kyoko said. "I'm afraid they are the system, not the renegades. Think how many people must have known about this over the years, and said nothing to stop it. It's like Saeki said—'democracy with discipline.' That's no democracy at all."

"Maybe," Piper said. "But I think if people found out about this in time, they'd put a stop to it, and fast."

"Well, I guess we'll see whether you're right," Kyoko said sleepily.

"I hope we have a chance to," Piper answered softly.

Kyoko closed her eyes, her arm flung across his chest, her warm breath calm and even on his neck as the boat rose and fell. Piper turned toward her, put a hand on her cheek and whispered, "I love you." She was already asleep. Piper stared out the porthole, thinking about Shimizu and Kawamura and Yamada and the ties that had bound them through all these years. He thought about Okamoto's wondrous underground temple, such a long way from that postwar potato-growing scientist in the rubble. And he thought about stevedores in Baltimore and Oakland, Le Havre and Pusan, snapping gum and cracking jokes and grunting and sweating as they unloaded crates marked NEC or TOSHIBA or FUJITSU and sent them on their way, each dockworker an unwitting link in a chain of mass destruction. He thought about skin hanging off people's hands like gloves, and he wondered whether he and Kyoko would be in time to break the chain, or had Okamoto set everything in motion in a way that no one now could stop? What could the two of them do, after all? I fear you are too late, Kawamura had said. Kawamura, who had sired these nuclear Trojan horses and then put himself out to pasture . . .

Eventually, Piper, too, dropped off to sleep, and when he woke, his arm was dead weight beneath Kyoko. He tugged it free inch by tingling inch and sat up on the bunk. Through the little doorway he could see their captain's stubby legs, spread wide as Arai braced himself at the wheel. Ducking his head, Piper crept out of the hold and blinked and stretched in bright daylight.

"I didn't wake you for Rikuchu Kaigan," the captain said, as best as Piper could make out. "You looked so peaceful. Like honeymooners in the Inland Sea." He cackled. In Arai's day, Piper knew, before the Japanese had bought up most of Guam and Hawaii, newlyweds used to dream of three-day trips through the Inland Sea, or down to Miyazaki, at the southern tip of their own southernmost island. Now Hawaii was usually old hat by the time they married, and they honeymooned in less mundane spots, like Australia, or the Maldives, or Vienna.

The little man asked Piper to take the wheel and showed him how to maintain a steady course. They were heading southwest, parallel to the mainland, just close enough to keep its rocky cliffs a hazy line in the distance. Sunshine sparkled on the waves, and now and then the windshield of a distant fishing boat would glint brilliantly for an instant. Arai's boat, still shabby, seemed homier and more cheerful in the exuberant noon light, and the breeze carried aboard a salty smell of boyhood summers on the beach. Piper remembered the food Kawamura had packed, and the captain untied the bag and laid out lunch for both of them. He chattered cheerily, incessantly, and seemed not to care whether Piper understood. Kyoko, emerging an hour later, leaned into Piper and wrapped her arms around him as he steered.

They passed the afternoon in that way, taking turns at the wheel, snacking, resting, recovering from the past two sleepless nights, searching for dolphins through Arai's binoculars, fortifying themselves for whatever lay ahead. Sometimes Kyoko interpreted Arai's tales, sometimes not. As she and the captain chatted, Piper would find himself just watching her mouth, allowing her laugh and the Japanese words to wash over him like spray from the waves. The man asked no questions about them or what they might be running from. As far as Piper knew, Arai never learned their names.

It was almost dark when they heard the helicopter. Piper at first thought it must be a speedboat, and searched the waves with binoculars, finding nothing. When he lowered the glasses, the aircraft loomed startlingly close, its blades beating the air with noisy effort as it droned toward them. Even then it never occurred to him that there might be a connection to him, that he should hide his face, take cover in the hold, dive onto the deck. He simply stood at the stern and watched as the chopper approached and dipped low enough to beat a foam on the ocean surface. The aircraft circled once, tilted in a kind of ominous salute and then flew off toward land, tail wagging high in the air.

No one spoke. With the helicopter a silent speck on the horizon, they heard once again the noises they had stopped hearing hours before: the wind, the slapping of their bow on the waves, the feeble rumble of their own engine. Arai's laugh they never heard again.

"Tell him he'd better let us off somewhere outside the city," Piper finally said to Kyoko. "And before it gets light again tomorrow."

As dusk fell, they took turns steering and looking out toward shore, waiting for something to happen. Nothing did. Sometime after midnight the captain told them to go below again and get some sleep; they should be rested in the morning, he said.

"What about you?" Piper said. "You still have to get back."

"Don't worry about me," Arai said. "I'll have time enough to sleep."

So they crawled back into the hold and onto the bench. His mind racing in time with the black blades of the chopper, Piper was sure once again that he wouldn't sleep. But the next thing he felt was Arai shaking him awake. Kyoko sat up with a start and looked out the porthole. They all climbed out to the deck.

In the darkness the boat was scraping against a high seawall. Arai had thrown one looped line over a piling on shore. Out to sea Piper could make out the lights of dozens of tankers and cargo ships riding at anchor. He wondered whether any of them carried Okamoto's special crates.

"You're somewhere in Chiba, up Tokyo Bay from the city," Arai whispered. "Good luck."

"Someday we'll thank you properly," Piper said.

"Sure, sure, don't worry," the captain said. "Just go." Piper grabbed hold of a narrow metal ladder and pulled until the boat swung around and Kyoko could climb up. Then he clambered after her, patted his pants and pocket for the documents and tape and lifted the line over its piling and tossed it to Arai. They watched as the captain doffed his cap once more and nosed his boat back toward the bay. When they could see him no longer, they turned to take their bearings.

They seemed to be on a flat stretch of landfill, with several big buildings looming up in the darkness. Farther away they could see an elevated highway and, near it, a brightly lit rocky crag. In his sleepy haze Piper tried to remember where he had seen such an outcropping before.

Kyoko must have placed it at the same time he did, because they began to laugh in chorus. The rocky crag was Big Thunder Mountain. They had made landfall at Tokyo Disneyland.

FLIGHT

PART IV

30

A Japanese development company had built Tokyo Disneyland under license, promising to replicate the Anaheim original in every artful detail. Initially, there was to be nothing whatsoever to remind visitors they were in Japan. Anyone craving sushi had to eat their fish outside the gates. Eventually, management had relented a bit; elderly visitors to the theme park, arriving by the busload, sometimes couldn't get by on hamburgers, and a tasteful Japanese-style restaurant opened. Squid and baby-corn pizza became available. In the Mickey Mouse Revue, Mickey spoke and sang in remarkably fluent Japanese.

Still, to millions of visitors, the theme park was America—America at its best, without the druggies and muggers and welfare cheats who, many Japanese believed, had sent the real America into decline. Naysayers had predicted that Disneyland was too American to succeed in Japan, but they had failed to understand the spiritual kinship of Japanese and Disneyland philosophies. The emphasis on absolute, surreal spotlessness seemed only normal to Japanese visitors, as did expectations that all "cast members"—never to be referred to as employees—smile and love their work at all times. People lined up for hours to enter—not just kids, but newlyweds, teenagers on dates, housewives on outings. They marveled at the green lawn in front of Cinderella's castle; there were no lawns in Japan, where even baseball diamonds were dirt-covered. They exclaimed at the mechanical Indians in Westernland. On Main Street they posed, giggling, with Mickey and his friends.

All this Piper knew because he and Kyoko had visited Disneyland to write a feature on its fifth anniversary, one of Piper's few dispatches to wiggle its way onto the *Advertiser*'s front page. In general, in fact, the stories that had pleased his editors had been those depicting the utter weirdness of the Japanese, on the one hand, or their slavish devotion to Americana on the other. Mothers who sent their children off to kindergarten nearly naked through the winter to toughen them up, Zen monks who routinely beat their trainees, devotees of blowfish sushi, which, if not properly sliced and served, caused a slow and painful death by poison—these were the hardy perennials of the foreign news trade in Japan, all of them recycled by Piper and, more recently, in Zarsky's book. Just as appreciated were stories depicting Japan's attraction to popular American culture: to Disneyland, to James Dean and Madonna, to denim jackets with meaningless but evocative English phrases stenciled on their backs. Piper could only assume that both types of stories reassured his increasingly insecure readers about the coming Japanese juggernaut. Picturing the Japanese as lovably peculiar or fawningly admiring allowed Americans to ease back, if only momentarily, into their accustomed attitude of charitable, smug superiority, though Piper knew only too well how misguided such a sense was. The Japanese might be weird, but they weren't crazy.

Piper had done his part to perpetuate the myth of Japanese as openmouthed suckers. He recalled now how he had written with sly condescension about the luxury hotels that had shot up around Disneyland, their indoor pools and towering airy lobbies crowded with weekending Tokyoites. Piper and, he imagined, his readers had had a good laugh at these glamorous palm-studded retreats stuck between truck-clogged elevated highways and a tanker-filled dirty harbor.

But if Americans, spoiled by an excess of purple-mountain majesty, snickered at the idea of sipping piña coladas atop a sewage landfill, the Japanese saw no irony. What could be better than a weekend resort that allowed everyone to be home in time for his two-hour Monday morning commute? And long lines were just another selling point, since many Japanese couldn't have fun unless surrounded by thousands of other Japanese enjoying identical activities.

Certainly, it would be at its most frenetic today, Piper knew, a Sunday in August, when schoolchildren on holiday and their families would be cramming the sidewalks of Disneyland to watch the nightly Electric Parade. He shuddered at the thought, but then it occurred to him that they might turn the crowds to their advantage.

"So what do we do now?" Kyoko said. They were standing on a strip of grass between the bay and a service road that wound around the luxury hotels, past Disneyland to the train station. Piper swayed slightly as he tried to adjust to firm ground.

"I could use a shower," he said.

"That's true," Kyoko said. "You think we can get a room?"

"In August? No chance," Piper said. "Besides, I'd rather not be any more conspicuous than necessary." The helicopter had come as a nasty surprise; Piper knew that Okamoto and his gang would trace them, by finding the stolen motorcycle or in some other way, but he'd been counting on at least a twenty-four-hour head start. Now Okamoto had to know that Piper and Kyoko were heading for Tokyo, and his men would be on the lookout as soon as dawn broke over the bay. Their office and homes certainly wouldn't be safe, and probably their friends would be under surveillance, too. Coming ashore at Disneyland might give them a few extra hours, Piper figured; they'd have to make good use of them.

They crossed the service road to the nearest hotel and scaled an earthen wall that shielded its swimming pool from the road. A few underwater lights gave the pool and lagoon a tropical effect, but the deck area was dark, and they walked stealthily to the locker rooms. Kyoko started toward the women's side, but Piper whispered for her to join him.

"Forget it," she whispered back.

"I'll behave, I promise," Piper said. "I just don't want us separated again."

Kyoko leaned back in the darkness and studied Piper's face to see whether he was joking or not. When she realized he was serious, she followed him into the men's showers. He found a light switch, put the tape and documents where he could see them from a shower stall and undressed. But when he saw her undressing, his worries and his good intentions alike evaporated. Together they stood under the hot shower, steaming away the kinks from Arai's hard bunk, and he offered to wash her back, and her back led elsewhere, and before long he was holding her again, rocking back and forth as the water streamed around them.

Afterward, she said, "I'd hate to see you when you're not behaving." All towels were locked away, and they sat on a bench, dripping dry as he leaned against a locker and she leaned against him.

"So what now?" she asked quietly. "I can tell you've decided something."

"A condemned man's last wish: No tea, no rice, no raw egg and no damn fish bones for breakfast," Piper said. "Let's go upstairs and have some toast and bacon and hot black coffee. Then we'll make a couple of phone calls and spend a fun-filled day at Disneyland."

"Phone calls to whom?" Kyoko asked suspiciously. "John, how are you going to write this story?"

He tickled the back of her neck softly as he answered. "Kyoko, there's no way I can write this story any more," he said. He told her, finally, about his conversation with Vinnie. "So you don't work for me, anymore," he said. "On the boat, lying on the bunk with you, before the helicopter came, I fantasized that maybe we could do the story anyway, maybe the Zarsky thing wasn't such a big deal, maybe Okamoto and his friends really weren't so deadly. This is Japan, after all, right? You and I would write this story and someone, somewhere, would publish it, and we'd go to the Pulitzer award ceremony together, and the whole world would thank us for saving Detroit." He shook his head and continued. "But it can't happen that way. Nobody's going to believe anything I write, even if I had somewhere to send it, and our time is running out fast. We'd still have to do more reporting—we couldn't go with Kawamura as our only source, even though you and I know he's telling the truth—and we couldn't do the reporting we'd need while we're hiding out. No—this was the story of my life, I know that. But it's a story I'll never write." He smiled. "As Yoshitsune said, this is indeed a sorry world, where nothing happens as one hopes."

But Kyoko wasn't smiling. "So you're just going to give up? After what Kawamura said to us?"

"No, of course I'm not giving up, though to be honest I wouldn't bet on our chances right now, either," Piper said. "What matters now is that the story come out, and that it come out in a newspaper strong enough to stand up to whatever Okamoto and his friends can throw at it. The byline isn't important."

"Okay, so what is your plan?"

"I'll tell you at breakfast," he answered. He knew she wouldn't like it.

He was right. Seated upstairs in the still nearly empty coffee shop, at a window table overlooking the pool and, beyond that, the bay, she stared at him in disbelief. "Christopher? Why Christopher, of all people?" she said, after he had outlined his proposal. "At least, if we can't write it, why not give it to Marianne, or to Steve?" Steve was the *Washington Post* reporter, a mild-mannered, conscientious correspondent free of Christopher's arrogance.

"Marianne's in Korea, and I'm afraid Steve may be too ethical for what we need," Piper said. "We want someone to take this tape"—he patted his shirt pocket—"and write a story as if he had conducted the interview himself. Steve would insist on talking to Kawamura in person, verifying everything, and there's no time for that. Not for us, surely, and maybe not for Detroit, either."

"And Christopher? He's such a, you know, such a—I mean, how can you trust him to do this right?"

"For a story like this, Christopher will risk even his invitation to the prime minister's annual cherry-blossom party, I promise you," Piper said. "Of course, we have to get him a second source, and more up-to-date documents. We can't leave anything to him. Which is why we're also going to invite Sato-kun to Disneyland today."

"Oh, John," Kyoko shook her head. Piper followed her gaze out the window. The rising sun was a smudge of brightness in the smog. "Haven't you learned anything? Sato is Saeki's deputy, he's one of them. He's just better than Saeki at connecting with foreigners—including you. Before long he'll have Saeki's job and he'll be taking a tour of Okamoto's lab, if he hasn't already. I know you think of him as a friend, but . . . if you call him, you might as well throw the whole thing away. You might as well just call Okamoto."

"You're wrong," Piper said. "I know you're wrong." He picked up the check, considered signing somebody's room number to it when he saw the total, and then thought better of the idea. "Stick with me on this," he said to Kyoko. "Please. Have some faith. Besides," Piper added in a quieter voice, "how much choice do we have?" Piper thought of Saeki vowing that Japan wouldn't stand for America seizing its factories, and he remembered Sato sitting sleepily at the end of the breakfast table as Saeki made his threat. Was

Piper now trusting Sato because Sato was trustworthy, or because he didn't know where else to turn?

From a pay phone off the lobby, Piper's first call woke Christopher.

"Where the hell have you been?" Christopher said as he fumbled with the phone. "I've been trying to reach you for days."

"I know, I appreciate it," Piper said. "I'm ready to give you my comment. I'm also ready to give you the biggest story of your life." His heart skipped a few beats. "How quickly can you get out to Disneyland?"

"Always the funny man," Christopher said. "If I were you, I wouldn't be joking around right now."

"Believe me, I'm not," Piper said. "But I can't talk on the phone." He persuaded Christopher of his seriousness, and the *Times* reporter agreed, reluctantly, to come.

"I'm giving up brunch at the Dutch ambassador's for this," he said. "It better be damn good."

"I appreciate your sacrifice," Piper said, almost relieved by the familiarity of Christopher's condescension. He asked Kyoko where they could meet where there wouldn't be long lines. "Meet the World, near Star Tours in Tomorrowland," she answered without a pause. He looked at her in amazement, then passed that on to Christopher. "And Clive," Piper said, "try to wear something casual, okay? Someone may be following us, and if they pick up on you, too, we're finished."

"You're the last person in the world to be giving fashion advice, Piper," Christopher said grumpily. "I'll see you at noon."

"How do you remember the layout so well?" Piper asked Kyoko after hanging up.

She sheepishly admitted that their reporting trip had not been her only excursion to Disneyland. One of her boyfriends used to bring her out on Saturday afternoons. "He loved Michael Jackson in *Captain EO*," she said.

Sato was already awake when Piper called. "John, I've been worried about you, what's going on?" he said. "I think you've been set up, and I can't figure out why. The more questions I ask, the stranger it gets."

"I can explain," Piper said. "But you've got to meet me today."

Sato said he was scheduled to play golf that day with two American colonels out at the American base at Zama. "Saeki is making the foursome," Sato said.

Piper's heart sank, but he pushed aside his doubts again.

"You want me to cancel?" Sato asked.

"No!" Piper blurted. "No." He thought for a minute. "How soon could you get back to Disneyland?" They agreed to meet at six in front of It's A Small World. "And Tsuyoshi—don't tell anyone. Including Saeki."

Kyoko shook her head as Piper relayed Sato's comments. "He's playing golf with the guy, and you still can't see it," she said.

"Come on," he said. "I'm feeling jumpy just standing here."

At the hotel business center they copied Kawamura's documents and Kyoko's shipping records, nervously scanning the lobby all the while, and then each took a set in case only one of them made it through. They purchased the *Herald Tribune* at the newstand; the Senate had approved the X-bill and sent it to the president's desk, Piper read. Time was running out. The *Trib* also had run Christopher's story on the telecommunications talks, and when Piper saw how Christopher had hyped his lead—"a landmark achievement in U.S.-Japanese trade relations"—he felt tempted to call the meeting off. Instead, he just threw the newspaper away. Out front they waited for the Disneyland shuttle. In the distance, they could hear a helicopter rattling over the sea.

31

*T*o have called Disneyland "crowded" on that sunny Sunday morning would have been to stretch the word beyond its intended reach. Couples had to move in single file. Fathers jostled for position by the popcorn carts. Already, dozens of big-eared Mickey Mouse balloons had floated upward and lodged themselves in the rafters of the crystal arcade roof high above the walkway, leaving as many small children wailing on the ground. A six-foot-tall Minnie in red-and-white polka dots, apparently wrenched apart from her husband by the throngs, was mobbed as she made her way slowly along the pavement, her face frozen in its plastic grin. A young security guard, his English bobby's hat ludicrously accentuating his stick-out ears, looked on helplessly. As thousands of fun-seekers clamored for autographs and photographs, called to lagging children, argued their routes for the day, demanded ice cream or Magic Kingdom wands, the resulting cacophony hurtled and bounced around the World Bazaar arcade, rendering normal communication all but impossible.

After a wait of two hours Kyoko and Piper pushed through the turnstiles, picked their way to the head of Main Street and broke free into the open-air plaza facing Cinderella's Castle. Here, too, were crowds, especially at Fuji Film–designated scenic photo spots, where teenagers flashed the peace sign as their friends' cameras clicked. But here, at least, Piper felt he could breathe. He and Kyoko slowed to a stroll, wending their way to Big Thunder Mountain where, after another long wait, they traded one of their E tickets for a roller-coaster ride. Then they resumed their tour, checking behind them from time to time. Piper saw nothing suspicious, but any tail who couldn't stay hidden in this crowd had chosen the wrong line of work.

Shortly before noon they repaired to the Matsushita Meet the World pavilion. As Kyoko had predicted, it wasn't a major draw, tainted as it was by a vaguely educational aura. Even in Japan, kids didn't come to Disneyland to study. Kyoko and Piper waited in the cool of the lobby, watching the multitudes stream toward Star Tours and Space Mountain and the other more glamorous lures of Tomorrowland. A few dozen parents with small children in rented Disneyland strollers kept them company inside, happy for any refuge from the heat and lines.

Christopher showed up a few minutes late in white linen pants and a lime-green Polo shirt.

"You look lovely," Piper said. "Cool, crisp, casual. The perfect Disneyland attire."

"You look like you've been tumble-dried, no iron," Christopher said. It was true, Piper knew, he had taken on a certain manginess in the last few days, despite their morning shower. He hadn't shaved since the morning after their climb in the mountains, and in the humidity his uncombed hair had coiled into hundreds of uneven curls.

The carousel theater doors swung open and, welcomed in classic falsetto by a pretty uniformed hostess, the three reporters sidled along a back row, sinking into comfortable seats stage right. On a wide, curving screen, a magic fairy in the form of an animated white crane presented the wonders of Japanese history.

The three journalists paid scant attention, for as the crane enthralled two wide-eyed Japanese children, Piper whispered his tale to an equally wide-eyed Christopher. Piper himself found the story hard to believe as he talked. Again, he noticed he was shivering. Calm down, he told himself, speak slowly, speak confidently. Everything would depend on Christopher now; Piper had to make him understand.

The crane covered his two millennia before Piper completed their recent two weeks, so the threesome exited into the heat, walked around to the entrance and sat through the film again, and then for a third time, too.

Finally, at the end of his story, he handed Christopher the tape. "Recorded night before last, and all on the record," he said. "And here are the documents. If all goes well, you should get more soon."

"From whom?"

"I can't tell you, but you'll know him and trust him when the time comes," Piper said. "If you haven't heard anything by Wednesday, you're on your own. Report the story however you want, talk to whoever you want, write it or not as you see fit. It'll mean my source didn't come through, and we'll probably be finished, too." He paused, and could see the enormity of it all finally registering on Christopher. "Until then, don't say a word to anyone. Agreed?"

Christopher nodded. "What will you do?"

"I hope we'll stay a step ahead of the guys who are chasing us until your story appears. I want them to keep thinking we're the targets, not you. But I doubt we can last more than a couple of days, so the quicker the better, okay?"

"Okay," Christopher said. He stared at the documents for a time, seeming not to really see them. "You know, don't take this the wrong way, but . . . this is all a little hard to believe. I mean, hidden labs, hidden bombs—and not even a hint leaking out for all these years?"

"You mean, how come no one alerted the *New York Times?*" Piper said, and then thought, Easy does it, control yourself, don't alienate him now. "Look, it was hard for us to believe, too. All I can say is, when you meet my source, and read the documents, you'll believe it. Just hold on, it'll be a wild ride."

"Okay," Christopher said again. The wide-eyed children once again were mouthing their final platitudes about the beauty of Japanese tradition. "One more thing, though, Piper," he said. "Why me? I never had the feeling I was one of your favorites."

Piper thought for a minute. "Well, you waited on the Zarsky story, I appreciated that," he said. "Your paper has clout. And given the, uh, fairness you've shown the Japanese in the past, you'll have more credibility with this than some other people might."

"Meaning you think I've been a patsy?" Christopher said. "I know. I just don't happen to think it's our place to stand in judgment of another culture."

"Well, whatever," Piper said. "This isn't the time to debate. Just don't screw this one up, okay? All that's riding on you is the fate of the world, and of me and Kyoko, more to the point." They shook hands, and Christopher left the theater.

"You've certainly put a lot on Sato's shoulders now," Kyoko said after the *Times* reporter had disappeared toward Main Street. Piper just nodded. She was right, and he wished he felt as sure as he pretended.

It scarcely seemed possible, but the crowds were only now cresting. Piper and Kyoko stuck by the Meet the World exit, daunted by the prospect of rejoining the flow. Describing their peril to Christopher had somehow made it more menacing to Piper, too. Now every detail seemed to stand out in sharp relief: the little girls in their pink dresses and straw sailor hats, the boys in cute denim shorts, the fathers with summer-weight sweaters tied casually around their necks. Storybook characters made their way through the crowd, shaking hands, patting children on the head, posing for photographs: Snow White and her dwarfs, Captain Hook, the Bear from *Jungle Book*. Costumes concealed most actors, but a few foreigners appeared without masks, dressed as Mary Poppins or Cinderella and seeming almost as popular as Mickey and Minnie.

Piper and Kyoko wandered through the heat and haze and noise. At each attraction thousands of people snaked back and forth along cordoned paths designed to mask the length of the wait: three hours at Star Tours, two and a half at Space Mountain, half an hour for the gondola ride to Fantasyland. Despite a ticket book full of possibilities, neither felt inclined to join the lines.

They were lounging at the Sunkist juice parlor, drinking lemonade and wondering how they could possibly last until six, when Piper saw the man in a suit, perched on a low wall across the patio. Piper paid no mind at first. Plenty of fathers were wearing neckties, after all; to many Japanese men, "relaxing" meant leaving the house with only two Cross pens in their white shirt pockets instead of three. This one's girlfriend was freshening her lipstick, or his wife was riding Dumbo the Flying Elephant with the kids. But five minutes passed, and then ten, and the man remained, not exactly looking at them, but never looking away, either.

"You're an expert," he whispered to Kyoko, trying not to let his voice shake. "Does that guy look like he came out for *Captain EO?*"

She glanced across the patio. "It's a hot day for a dark suit," she said quietly. "If you figure Sato said something to Saeki over golf, and Saeki put in a call from the clubhouse at lunch, the timing is just about right."

"I don't figure that at all," Piper said sourly. Her suspicions were contagious. "We'd better get moving."

They squeezed their empty cups into an overflowing trash barrel, strolled as casually as they could toward the curving road that circled Cinderella's Castle, and climbed aboard an old-fashioned double-decker bus with open sides and back. From their seats near the rear of the upper deck, they could scan the crowd behind them as the bus puttered at a walking pace, trumpeting its comical horn from time to time. Why doesn't this damn thing move faster, Piper thought.

Kyoko spotted the man first. He was striding across the central grassy plaza, bisecting the circle as the bus putt-putted around the long way. His walk was not fast, but it was purposeful, and he shouldered aside oncomers, training his eyes on the bus as he moved.

"Now what?" Piper hissed. "We have to lose this guy before we meet Sato." Obviously, he thought to himself. You're jabbering. He noticed his hands trembled.

Kyoko thought for a moment, watching the man as intently as he appeared to be watching them.

"Let's try the Jungle Cruise," she said. "If we can get one or two boats ahead of him in that line, it would give us time to shake him when we got off."

Taken aback, Piper looked at her admiringly. "Have you done this before?" he asked.

They waited until the bus had completed its circle, so that the door was facing away from the man, a ways behind them on the grass. Then they practically slid down the stairs and darted through the crowds to the Jungle Cruise line. A sign warned of an hour's wait. Between their line and an equally long queue for the Western River Railroad, dozens of identical strollers were parked in neat rows, each with a hand-lettered name tag fluttering in the breeze.

Piper and Kyoko squatted so that Piper's head wouldn't stick up above the crowd. People quickly fell into line behind them.

"I think about twenty-five people can fit on one of these boats," Kyoko said. "So we have to hope he's at least that far behind us in line."

"What if he just hangs around the exit, waiting for our boat to come sailing back to port?"

"I don't know. Let's hope he doesn't," Kyoko said.

For as long as Piper could stand the suspense, they kept low and didn't turn around. When he finally looked, the man was there, as impassive as ever in his dark suit. About twenty other would-be cruisers separated him from Piper and Kyoko. "It's going to be close," Piper whispered.

As they shuffled toward the artificial river, Piper realized with a start that they'd pass within inches of the man a half-dozen times as the line doubled back on itself again and again. What if he just pulls out a pistol and pops us, Piper thought. Or a knife—he could slide a knife between my ribs and melt into the crowd. No, no, ridiculous. In Tokyo? In front of all these people? As they approached head-on, Piper stationed himself between the man and Kyoko and stared straight ahead, keeping the man within his lateral field of vision. There didn't seem to be bulges in his jacket, Piper noted with relief, and they shuffled past each other. Piper could feel drops of sweat rolling down his sides.

To focus his mind, Piper tried to memorize the names of the riverboats loading and unloading their passengers—the *Orinoco,* the *Amazon,* the *Niger.* But he lost track each time they doubled back on the man in the suit.

Finally, a young Japanese cast member in jungle fatigues and pith helmet allowed them into a preboarding holding pen, counting out a boatload of passengers. Behind them, they heard a commotion as the man, suddenly seeing he'd been trumped, tried to push in front of an elderly woman and her grandson. She turned on him in a fury, upbraiding him and instructing him in proper behavior, and he slunk back, stymied, as the man in the pith helmet rehooked the chain just in front of him. A minute later he was staring, expressionless, as Piper and Kyoko stepped aboard the *Congo,* along with the grandmother still muttering her disgust at the discourtesy of the younger generation. The boat set off along its underwater track.

Their fellow passengers roared with delight as their "captain" cracked jokes about the dangers of the jungle, shot into the gaping jaws of mechanical alligators, nearly got doused by mechanical elephants squirting their trunks. Piper barely noticed. Occasionally, just before the boat rounded a curve, they would glimpse a blue suit at the bow of the boat behind them. They'd have two minutes head start at most, Piper guessed. As the boat shuddered into a dark tunnel for the climax of the ride, Piper thought about slithering into the water right there, amid the glowing skulls and skeletons, and lying low as the next boat floated past. But someone would surely alert the captain, setting off all kinds of alarms, Piper thought. Better to stick to Kyoko's plan. As the boat glided out of the tunnel and toward the platform, Kyoko and Piper climbed across their fellow passengers' laps, triggering another tirade from the outraged grandmother. They jumped off even before the gate had swung completely open.

Ten yards distant another man in a suit held a small wrist walkie-talkie to his ear.

"Oh, shit," Piper said. Whatever made us think there'd only be one? As they strolled away from the river, the man, this one in more appropriate seersucker, strolled along behind them, making no pretense of discretion but not interfering with Piper and Kyoko, either. So, thought Piper, they don't want a scene in Disneyland. They're just shadowing us—for now. Until we leave the park, or until nightfall. Maybe it's time to go to the real police, he thought. Right. And say what? These guys may be the police. And if they're not, chances are they've planted some story with the police about these two dangerous thieves, fired from their jobs and on the run. No, we have to ditch them before six. If we're still being followed, we can't risk a meeting with Sato. And if we miss this meeting with Sato, there won't be another chance.

"What about the embassy?" Kyoko interrupted his thoughts.

"And say what?" Piper asked. "They're not going to believe this."

"Look, your life is in danger," Kyoko said, as if hers wasn't. "They should do something for you."

Piper agreed to try McGee from a pay phone. But no one picked up at his apartment, and at the office Knight, McGee's boss, answered on the second ring. When Piper identified himself and asked for his friend, Knight-san answered coldly.

"He's on administrative leave," the diplomat said.

"What? Why?"

"Why doesn't really concern you," Knight answered. "He sent some cables without authorization. Can I help you with anything?"

Piper hesitated, and then said, "Jim, I'm in trouble, and I think a lot of other people may be in danger, too. I need some help."

"We know, John," Knight said. "We've heard all about it."

"What?" Piper said. "Heard about what?"

"Come on, now," Knight said. "The payments, your job, stealing government property—why don't you come on in and we can try to work something out?"

"Jim, I didn't take any payments, and I didn't destroy any property," Piper said. "They're lying to you. They're lying because I've stumbled into a conspiracy that could put the whole world in danger."

"I'm sure you have, John," Knight said. "But you've also been under a lot of stress, haven't you? Why don't you come on in—where are you, anyway?"

I knew they wouldn't believe me, Piper thought. He had a sudden vision of Saeki sitting on Knight's couch, listening in on another extension of the phone with that little smile on his face. "Do me a favor, Jim," Piper said. "Go fuck yourself." He slammed down the receiver and put his forehead on the phone. Stop shaking, get a grip, get a grip.

He turned toward Kyoko and tried to sound jaunty, and knew that he missed by a long shot. "We're on our own," he said. "This calls for more radical measures."

"Meaning?"

"Meaning congratulations," Piper said. "We're about to join the cast."

32

*K*yoko vaguely recalled that the Electric Parade began and ended somewhere behind Fantasyland, so they headed in that direction. At her suggestion, after she had dismissed and then reluctantly accepted Piper's plan, they fell into line at It's a Small World, and the man in the seersucker suit soon fell in behind them. Here as everywhere, the wait seemed hopeless, but they shuffled forward faster than at the Jungle Cruise. As before, they snaked back and forth, brushing past their latest pursuer each time.

"John," Kyoko whispered, after they had eased past him a third time. "Why didn't they just kill us on the boat?"

"In the middle of our jungle cruise?" Piper tried to joke her question away.

"You know what I mean," she said. "With Arai. From the helicopter."

"Oh, then," Piper said, and shook his head. He had wondered, too. Maybe there hadn't been time to prepare, or maybe Arai's boat would have been too public, too messy. Okamoto would try to dispose of them without involving the coast guard or police.

In front of the pavilion, another large crowd was watching a live It's a Small World pageant, with costumed Japanese performing broadly recognizable versions of a Mexican hat dance, a Cossack kick step, an Argentine tango. The music from that pageant floated above the unceasing "It's A Small World" ditty piped out in Japanese falsetto to those waiting, like Piper and Kyoko, for "the happiest cruise that ever sailed."

They finally reached the pavilion, tore off another E ticket and inched their way down a long corridor to a cavernous room with the smell of a heavily chlorinated indoor swimming pool. When their turn came, Piper and Kyoko stepped onto a boat and then, rather than sitting, bounded across the craft, onto the opposing platform and toward the exit. As they darted past the astonished cast members in charge of packing and unpacking passengers, Piper glimpsed the man in the suit, wedged into the slow-moving line behind them, unable to follow them forward or retreat back out the entrance.

Hoping to escape before he could alert his friends by walkie-talkie, Piper and Kyoko dashed hunched over through the crowd, around couples and through groups, nearly tripping over a baby stroller, holding hands to keep from being separated. Drawing near the employees' gate, they crouched in the shrubbery until a new crop of oversized dwarfs emerged for its shift. With luck, Sneezy and Dopey can't see much out of their big molded heads, Piper thought. He pulled Kyoko up and through the gate behind the dwarfs into a private driveway, which they followed for a few yards before ducking again into some bushes. Here they waited silently. All quiet; so far so good.

"Now just act as though you belong," Piper whispered. Kyoko would hate this part, he knew, and held little hope for its success. But there was no turning back now, nor had she seen a better way. They stood and edged up the driveway to a series of outbuildings, including a large garage housing parade floats. A path to the left led to a women's changing room, and to the right, a men's.

"Good luck," Piper said.

He opened a door onto a surprisingly chaotic scene. Scores of young men milled about in various states of undress and various stages of transformation into storybook characters. Their shouts and conversation mingled with snippets of Disney melodies and occasional classical phrases as musicians warmed up, adjusting reeds and tightening strings. Small lockers lined the walls, and at the back larger costumes, which wouldn't fit into the little cubbies, hung on hooks beside a wall mirror. Some of the costumes were complete with big plastic heads; on other hooks hung theatrical clothes for the Cossacks and monks and gauchos of the Small World pageant. Piper found a bench, pulled off his shoes and massaged his crumpled toes. After absorbing the layout and rhythms of the room, he slipped back into his Nikes and walked purposefully to the back wall, chose a Pluto—or was it Goofy?—and pulled its molded helmet over his head. Within seconds, he was sweltering, and could barely see. Whatever these people get paid, it's not enough, he thought.

He removed the dog's head and slipped his hands into Pluto's front paws, stepped into the booted feet—and was stymied. How were you supposed to button these things? Now he'd surely be found out.

A young, dark-haired American was approaching. "Excuse me," Piper said. "Could you do me a favor?"

"Sure," the stranger said. He looked college-age. "I'm Danny Wolfowitz," he said, extending a hand. "Don't think I've seen you around before."

"I'm new," Piper acknowledged. "A. J. Liebling. Pleased to meet you." He offered a paw. "What do you do here?"

"I'm Prince Charming," Wolfowitz said with pride. "And it's a great gig, believe me. I was here last summer, too, teaching English, and that was okay, you know, but you have no idea what these Japanese girls are all about until you come back as Prince Charming, you know what I mean?" Danny seemed starved for an English-speaking confidant. "I could get into something every night if I wanted. And some of these girls are—I mean, they're crazy, you know?" His voice dropped to a conspiratorial whisper. "A lot of them shave themselves all over. I mean everywhere, if you get my meaning." Then, with a touch of melancholy, he added, "The only problem is, none of them are on the pill, have you noticed that?"

"Yeah, they don't allow it in Japan," Piper said. "It's a real problem."

"You're telling me," Danny said as he buttoned the back of Piper's costume. "Listen, who are you supposed to be? I thought they liked to put all the gaijin faces out front."

"I'm just in training," Piper said. "If I do okay, they'll let me be Peter Pan."

"Oh?" Danny said, looking dubiously at Piper in the mirror. "Well, listen, A. J., I can usually pick up an extra lady or two, and some of them will do just about anything for a gaijin. So what do you say—how about a beer after the parades tonight?"

"Sure, sure, that sounds great," Piper answered. He put his head back on. "Catch you later."

He was impressed by what he saw in the mirror. As fine a Pluto, or Goofy, as ever was. And the gaijin had disappeared without a trace. Practicing the little galumphing skip he had seen his colleagues perform, Piper headed for the exit, leaving Prince Charming behind.

A few minutes later an overgrown mouse with buck teeth and a long tail pattered down the same path and stopped a few feet away.

Piper whispered tentatively. "Kyoko?"

"John?" the mouse said. He could barely make out the word. Now he understood why these characters never talked as they made their jolly rounds. How was he going to communicate with Sato, even if they did hook up?"

"Who are you supposed to be?" Piper asked.

"One of the mice who help Cinderella sew her ball gown," Kyoko answered in muffled tones. "Don't you know anything?" She didn't seem to be enjoying her role. "I'm boiling in here. And you look ridiculous."

"Thanks." He felt ridiculous. Maybe this whole thing was a mistake. They should have just made a run for it, saved their lives, forgotten about trying to meet Sato, forgotten about Detroit. They'd be sitting ducks inside these costumes, slow, deaf, nearly blind. What a way to go. Piper tried to check the time and realized he couldn't see his wrist. "Whatever happens, stay close," he said. "I can barely see six feet in any direction."

Moving clumsily down the driveway, Piper managed to open the gate and rejoin the festive throngs. Children's yells and merry-go-round melodies and, from farther away, the Small World theme song floated into his costume as in a nightmare, a nightmare spinning out of his control. They turned toward Westernland, and Piper almost immediately tripped over a toddler, sending her sprawling; bending to right the screaming little girl, he only terrified her further. As the sobbing child buried her face in her mother's crotch, Piper thought, Keep moving. Don't attract attention. Keep moving.

After a time, they began to catch on. Piper waved, wound his paw around teenage girls while their friends snapped pictures, patted the head of an occasional brave child. Kyoko did likewise. For one frightening moment, another two mice joined them, and Piper realized he had no idea which was Kyoko. But the two soon melted away; fraternizing between dog and mouse is probably frowned on, he thought.

Near the Enchanted Tiki Room, Piper spotted four men in suits calmly conferring: the two they'd seen before, an older man with a mustache and—could it be?—their muscular friend from the mountain hike. Covered in sweat, Piper nonetheless felt a chill of fear run through his body. The goons had obviously lost track of Piper and Kyoko for the moment, and they looked worried. But Piper felt far from triumphant; we can't hide inside these things forever, he thought. If I had any guts at all, Pluto would walk over and knock all their heads together right now. But I don't; and besides, who knows how many more may be lurking? He nudged Kyoko to look that way, and they moved on.

Near six o'clock they circled back to It's a Small World. The ditty called out, tireless as ever, and to his amazement Piper found snatches of the English words floating up from some deep pool within his memory. "Though the mountains be high and the oceans divide, it's a small world after all." Piper scanned the multitude as best he could, posing and rubbing noses all the while. His eyes froze on another man in a suit; no, it wasn't Sato; could it be one of them? Piper couldn't tell. He began to doubt that Sato would show. Kyoko was right. Sato was a dutiful son of Japan—why would he fight against this juggernaut?

But then Piper saw him. His eyes had skipped past him several times, so unaccustomed were they to seeing his friend in jeans and a pullover. The bureaucrat had brought his wife and daughter, too, like any family on an outing. Smart boy, Piper thought happily. In the open-air theater of the live pageant, Sato sat on the aisle next to his daughter, in her pink dress and straw boater, and looked as rumpled and put-upon and benign as always. Piper wanted to give him a big kiss.

"Wait here," Piper said to a mouse he hoped was Kyoko.

He walked over to the Satos, patted the little girl on the head and then leaned toward Sato's ear. "Tsuyoshi," he whispered, as best as Goofy could whisper. "How was the golf game?" If the ghost of Hirohito himself had commanded Sato to commit seppuku, the man couldn't have turned paler. But he seemed to recover shortly. "Follow me," Piper said, and was confident that Sato would. He led the way down a narrow alley behind the Small World pavilion and into a small clump of evergreens. No one was about, and the noises of the park seemed to recede, but the ditty played on in his mind. "There is just one moon and one golden sun, and a smile means friendship to everyone." Even that doesn't hold in Japan, Piper thought irrelevantly; movie heroes here always smiled at the most tragic moments.

Piper tugged off Goofy's head and felt he could breathe for the first time in hours. A moment later Sato appeared.

"John," he said. "What the hell is going on?"

Now Piper talked as fast as he could, explaining everything, protecting no one, not even Shimizu. There was no point in half-measures now, he thought: if he was wrong about Sato, they were all done for—Shimizu, Kawamura, no doubt Kyoko and Piper, too. Sato listened in his usual way, intent, frowning, staring at a point somewhere off to the side, hands thrust into his pockets. At the end of his story, when Piper told Sato to reach into his costume, Sato started as if from a reverie.

"I beg your pardon, John?" he said.

"Reach into my back pocket," Piper repeated. "I can't do it with these paws."

"Oh, yes, yes, sorry," Sato said. He pulled out the documents Piper had copied that morning and leafed through them, shaking his head as he did so. "What a tragedy," he said, almost to himself. "What a tragedy."

"You don't seem all that surprised," Piper said.

Sato looked at him for a minute, but as though he were seeing something else. "Well, yes and no," he said finally. "I've known for a long time that something strange was going on, John. I would make inquiries, and every time I got close to finding out something, it would slip away. They didn't trust me, I suppose. So I imagined many possibilities—but never, never this. I never imagined this." He shook his head again. "This is a terrible tragedy for Japan."

"Yeah, among others," Piper said. "Listen, we don't have much time." He told Sato about the men in suits, and the helicopter, and his promise to Christopher earlier that day. "I just don't know who knows about this and who doesn't, and no Japanese newspaper is going to run this story. The only hope is to get it published outside Japan."

After a moment Sato nodded. He looked as though the perpetual weight on his shoulders had just become too much to bear. "You are right," he said. "I will do my best. Let's hope they haven't cleaned out the files already. But, John." He put his hand on Piper's arm. "You must be careful. Those men out there are not police, but they may have close ties to the police. And they are dangerous, I am sure of that." Sato looked at Piper as if noticing the Goofy costume for the first time. "Where will you go?"

"I don't know," Piper said. In truth, he had no idea how they would escape the theme park. He assumed Okamoto's men, whoever they were, would be watching every exit, including the employees' gates.

"And Kyoko? Is she safe?"

"She's here, too," Piper said. "We'll make it out together, somehow." He wished he could feel so confident. There was no one left to turn to now: not the police, not the embassy, not his newspaper. "But Tsuyoshi, until the story comes out—I'm worried about her mother."

Sato nodded. "I'll try to watch out for her."

"You be careful, too," Piper said. "I'll call you in a couple of days, if we're still alive." He put Goofy's head back on, and startled Sato with a clumsy hug. Then they headed, in opposite directions, back around the pavilion. As he rejoined the crowd, Piper saw Sato settling back with his family. Loudspeakers were announcing the imminent Electric Parade. Lights had come on as the sky turned a deeper blue. On stage a woman in traditional *hanbok* was performing a Korean folk dance. And Kyoko's mouse was nowhere to be found.

Piper fought a desperate urge to tear off Goofy's head, forcing himself instead to move normally, waving and occasionally breaking into his Goofy jig as he scanned the crowd. Maybe she just had to keep circulating, Piper thought. Stay here, she'll be back, he thought. Stay calm, stay calm, stay calm—and then, oh God, there she was, trailing a man in a dark suit toward the employees' gate. Piper lost all control and tore off after her. He heard a child crying in his wake and didn't stop. As the mouse and the dark suit disappeared through the gate, Piper kept running, fumbled after them, turned a corner and suddenly was nearly blinded. The parade was about to begin, and a dozen brilliantly lit floats were rolling into position. Shading his eyes, he blinked, and caught sight of them again. Now the man in the suit seemed to be lecturing the mouse, wagging a finger, shaking his head. The mouse was apologizing, nodding its big, silly head—could Kyoko bow even inside that thing? Then it was climbing aboard a float, and Piper understood: the man is not one of our pursuers, he is our boss, reprimanding Kyoko for nearly missing the parade. Thank God.

Piper pulled even with the bulb-bedecked Cinderella float, hoping at least that Kyoko would see him and know he'd be waiting when the parade ended. One mouse seemed to wag its head, or was he imagining? He nodded back, just in case, and moved on. He didn't know whether Goofy was supposed to march, too, but he didn't want to find out. In the locker room he yanked off Goofy's head for the last time.

The room was nearly empty; almost everyone must be taking part in the parade. Piper had no idea how they would escape Disneyland, but before he could even think about that, he had to find a way out of his costume. He was bathed in sweat, his toes felt crippled and his bladder was about to burst. Well, there must be a way. He shuffled his clumsy shuffle into a toilet stall and, with great effort, pulled his arms out of the costume sleeves. Then he sat on the toilet, pulled off the legs and painstakingly tugged the costume around until he could unbutton it, step out and relieve himself. It was a moment of uncomplicated happiness. Then he sat back down to think.

Obviously, he couldn't leave Disneyland as Goofy. But if he tried to leave as himself, even in darkness, even as the park was closing late that night, they would easily spot his brown curls poking above the throngs. He had vowed not to part from Kyoko again, but for her sake maybe that was the best thing, the only fair thing: let her go out alone, blend into the crowd and disappear into her country. I can hide here for a night, maybe two, maybe even long enough for Christoper to write his story, Piper thought. The chances were bleak, he knew, but he could think of nothing better. He flushed, returned to the costume room—and saw the monk's outfit hanging on the wall. Instantly, he knew what to do.

Rummaging through the unlocked cubbies, Piper extracted a pair of scissors, some shaving cream and a razor. He started for the bathroom, stopped, returned for one more razor and then headed for the bathroom again.

By the time a blaring rendition of "The Bare Necessities" heralded the parade's return, Piper barely recognized himself. His bald head gleamed grayish-pink in the fluorescent lights, his cheeks were equally smooth and the sober black and brown monk's outfit fit nicely, its robes perhaps a trifle short. Only the Nikes seemed out of place; but Piper reasoned that a California boy come to the Orient to find himself in Zen might well wear his old Nikes under his monk's robes, and maybe even carry a skateboard, too, just for old times. In any case, the Nikes would have to do.

As dwarfs and bears and pirates trickled in from the parade, collapsing on chairs and benches to rest before their nine o'clock repeat performance, Piper decided to put his disguise to a test.

"Hey, Prince Charming," he called to the approaching American, whose makeup was now streaked with sweat. Wolfowitz eyed him blankly. "Danny!" Piper tried again. "How about that brewski now?"

Prince Charming stared at him, and stared some more, and finally said, "Holy shit! A. J.? Is that you? What the hell have you done to yourself?"

Piper grinned, looked at himself in the mirror, and had to admit it was a grin that would take some getting used to. "What's the matter?" he said. "You don't think the girls will go for this? I thought you said they were into full-body shaving."

The prince just kept staring. Finally, he shook his head. "A. J.," he said, "you are just about the ugliest thing I have ever seen. If you can score like that, you're more of a man than I am."

"Okay, it's a bet," Piper said, clapping his arm around Wolfowitz. "I'll let you know in the morning." And, adjusting the cloth over his shoulder, Piper headed for the door, buoyed by the success of his disguise.

The sky was dark, but the light from the returning floats made the driveway nearly as bright as day. If Prince Charming's back, Piper thought, so are Cinderella and her mice. Indeed, he saw a few of the oversized rodents heading toward the changing rooms, while one held back in the shadows. He approached the hesitant mouse.

"Hare Krishna," he said. "Hare hare. Krishna krishna." Then he waited for a response.

After what seemed like a long, long minute, the mouse took off her head. "John," a wide-eyed Kyoko said. "John? Oh my God. John!" Then she burst out laughing, a kind of hysterical half-giggle, half-sob expressing all the fears of the day. She reached up and ran her paw over the dome of his head.

"How does it feel?" he asked.

"Speaking as a mouse, strange," she said. "As a woman, I'm not sure I want to find out." Then, quickly she was serious again. "Listen, these guys in suits are everywhere. I felt like they were staring at me all through the parade."

"Well, you're a fine-looking mouse," Piper said. "Just the same—we'd better get out of here."

Suddenly, an explosion ripped through the air, and Piper lunged to cover Kyoko, then realized that Disneyland's spectacular summer fireworks were beginning. He looked up to see the last embers of a blue fireburst sailing down.

"If we manage to get out, we'll have to find someplace far from Tokyo, as out of the way as possible," he said after catching his breath. "They'll be watching our apartments, and our friends, and probably the airports, too."

Kyoko scrutinized him thoughtfully. "Wait here," she said. "I have just the spot for the new you." And she disappeared into the women's changing rooms.

With remarkable speed, she emerged transformed, her long hair replaced by a bowl cut that barely covered her ears. Piper saw her with a pang, relinquishing into the summer night his long-treasured fantasies of those tresses sliding down his stomach, caressing his thighs. . . . Ah, well, there was work to be done, and he had to admit that she looked a different person, stronger in some way, even more beautiful than before.

As they exited the driveway one last time, Piper's blood froze. They were face-to-face with another man in a suit, a thuggier older man with a walkie-talkie and a bulbous nose, only a few yards distant. But the man looked past them without interest or curiosity. It works, Piper exulted. They'll never recognize us.

The plaza in front of Cinderella's Castle was impassable with people staring up at the laser show and fireworks, so they hiked the long way around through Tomorrowland. Between a shallow moat and the Meiji ice-cream parlor, the crowd was so dense they had to stop. Well, sneaking out in mid-fireworks would look suspicious, anyway, Piper thought; better leave with everyone else. At the counter nearby, an elderly woman was buying cones for her grandsons and hot tea for herself.

"You think it's okay for a monk to eat ice cream?" Piper asked over the cracking of the explosions.

"Of course. In Japan a monk can do anything," Kyoko said.

"Even sex?"

"Hypothetically, yes," she said, eyeing his head uncertainly.

"You once told me I'd look very distinguished this way," Piper said.

"I was being polite," Kyoko said. "You know how we Japanese value politeness."

Piper, pushing toward the ice-cream counter, was conscious of the smile still pasted on his face when the muscular man from the mountain path loomed out of nowhere beside them. Piper felt his blood freeze and his intestines tighten into knots. The man, his tie still neatly knotted, stared at Piper's getup and then smiled pleasantly, as if in response to a greeting from Piper. The one suit who would recognize Piper even in disguise, and he had found them. As the pyrotechnics thundered above, the man slid an arm under one of Kyoko's and spoke into her ear. The crowd, surging and swelling for the evening finale, seemed to press the three of them closer together.

Kyoko yelled up to Piper, her voice trembling in the night. "He has a gun, he says. We should come with him, he says." The man patted his side as if in confirmation.

For a second, Piper hesitated, frozen at the certainty of what lay before them. Then, without plan or forethought, he reached for the old woman's tea and flung it into the muscular man's face. His pained scream seemed soundless, his mouth opening in concert with another fireburst, his hands flailing at his blinded eyes. After a stutter of hesitation, Kyoko rammed her knee up into the man's groin, and he doubled over, his head almost in Piper's stomach. Piper clasped his hands and crashed them down into the back of the exposed strong neck. To Piper's surprise, the man's entire body sagged slightly, as if someone had let out a bit of air, and then he crumpled to the ground. The merrymakers around them, faces to the sky, seemed to notice nothing. A few feet away a grassy embankment sloped down to the shallow moat and, as the triumphant final volleys followed one another in quick succession, Kyoko and Piper slid the man down the hill. He rolled facedown into the water.

Piper bent down as if to retrieve him but was brought back sharply by Kyoko. "What do you think you're doing?" she hissed.

"Kyoko—he'll die there," Piper said. Now he was shaking, and gulping air.

"And what do you think they were going to do with us?" Kyoko said. "And everyone who lives in Detroit?"

The hump of the man's dark jacket, soaked through, was almost invisible in the pond now—a rock, a turtle's shell. Piper still hesitated, and Kyoko started pulling him away, through the crowds, toward Main Street, talking urgently all the while above the din. "And if he wakes up and tells everyone else you're disguised as a monk, how long do you think we'll last?"

As the last embers floated lazily toward Tokyo Bay, Piper and Kyoko allowed themselves to be swept back down Main Street by a good-natured crowd of exuberant teenagers, sleepy children, tired parents hoisting dozing toddlers. More than ever, Piper felt he was being carried away by a nightmare. Kyoko, except for a clenched jaw, looked as though nothing had happened, but near the gate she suddenly panicked. "What if they all do know? What if he told them already, before he grabbed me?" she said, trying to brake against the tide flowing toward the gates. "We'll never get out of here."

Now Piper shook off the vision of the man's darkening slumped body in the moat and took hold of Kyoko's arm. "Just think about our romantic night on Arai's boat," he said.

"Romantic?" She giggled, again sounding near hysteria.

"Okay, how about our romantic moonlit night in Hiraizumi?" Piper said. Into his swirling brain floated a poem for that ruined capital: " 'A mound of summer grass; are warriors' heroic deeds only dreams that pass?' "

"Now you're quoting haiku?" Kyoko said. "I can't believe it."

"It was in my guidebook," Piper admitted with some embarrassment. But his smile seemed to calm and embolden Kyoko. She put her hand on his elbow, as if to help support this holy man from the West, and, heads up, eyes straight ahead, they strode boldly though a turnstile, past dozens of men in suits and into the night. They were in the clear again.

33

*P*iper had been searching for "the real Japan" for so long that he felt sad, when he finally seemed to find it in Koyasan, to no longer believe in such a thing. Sleeping in a spartan Buddhist monastery 3,000 feet above the sea, kneeling at dawn services with chants and incense wafting past, wandering through misty stands of towering moss-covered cedars in the ancient cemetery on this tabletop mesa in the clouds, Piper might have been willing to call this Japan, to call it a life, had not another world been lying in wait to intervene again.

They had spent the night on trains, and dozing on station benches: from Disneyland by subway to Tokyo Station, thence south by circuitous locals to Mount Koya, home to Japan's largest Buddhist sect.

By early morning their train was winding its way through narrow wooded valleys and clinging to the sides of steep green mountains, gliding past perfect Japanese farmhouses with tiled, curving roofs and sliding doors of wood and paper. They reached the top, finally, by cable car, scarier than any Disneyland ride as it pulled itself, groaning, nearly straight up through the forest.

At the top they found themselves in another land—a land of stone lanterns and wooden temples, of songbirds flitting from pagoda to pine, of white-clad pilgrims swinging strings of copper bells that tinkled tunelessly as believers marched in wooden clogs. Even the cicadas here droned with clearer voices, leaving Piper longing for something he could not name. As they strolled toward the monastery precincts through cool early-morning sunshine, he read aloud, from a brochure they had picked up at the cable-car terminus, of Kobo Daishi, Japan's greatest Buddhist teacher, who had founded Koyasan more than a thousand years before and then had not died but entered a state of permanent meditation in which he remained to this day, here, at Koya, waiting for rebirth. Faith in the Daishi could "turn war to peace, fear to joy, and death to life," Piper read to Kyoko. "If we keep our mind peaceful like Buddha, talk gently like Buddha, behave mercifully like Buddha, there will be no war on earth."

They walked in the shadow of endless whitewashed walls of numerous simple monasteries, finally choosing one at random and entering through a modest wood-roofed gate. Crunching across a peaceful courtyard of raked stones, they reached the central entrance of the U-shaped temple. A young monk offered a sullen greeting, eyeing Piper's Disneyland robes and Nikes and shaved head as if they were some kind of mocking reflection of his own. But he agreed to give them each a room, fulfilling his godly duty even to such outlandish wayfarers as these. He instructed them to remove their shoes and unsmilingly led them up a narrow, uneven stairway to a corridor of sliding paper-screen doors, each of which opened to a room floored in sweet-smelling tatami mats. The monk assigned Piper a room a few doors away from Kyoko and invited them— pointedly, Piper thought, but perhaps he was imagining—to bathe. They took turns in the temple's spacious rectangular tub of perfumed cedar, and then slept until early afternoon. The tintinnabulating chimes of pilgrims on the narrow lane outside their temple wall finally roused Piper; he opened his eyes to find Kyoko sitting cross-legged beside him.

Calmed by their peaceful surroundings, they felt safe enough to venture out to the ancient cemetery, where for centuries Japanese had had themselves, or pieces of themselves, buried so they could be on hand when the great Daishi stirred. Shoguns and warlords, samurai and teachers rested beneath stone towers and mausoleums, and beneath other monuments lay the fallen of World War 2, sailors and pilots, soldiers and suicide warriors. In the newer part of the cemetery, to connect their loyal employees to the Daishi, Japan's great postwar corporations had raised emblematic rocket ships and globes, ships and cameras, all sculpted out of granite and marble amid the graves and tombstones. One company had posted little black-and-white mug shots of dozens of its workers, million-dollar salesmen now staking out routes in the next world.

They found a sun-dappled bench beneath the cedars. Already in early August here, an autumn smell warmed the air, a smell of brown leaves and fallen needles baking in the sun.

"Today is the anniversary," Piper said. "We missed our deadline." Here among the peaceful dead of Koyasan, Piper thought again of the "walking ghosts" of Hiroshima and Nagasaki.

"I thought of that, too," Kyoko answered. "At eight-sixteen this morning." After a pause, she added, "What will you do when this is all over?"

"You mean if we all survive?" Piper said. "I don't know. What shall we do?"

She smiled and took his hand. "I guess it all depends on whether your friend Sato comes through," she said. After a moment, she added, "Did he ask you where we were headed?"

"No," Piper lied.

That night their cheerless young monk served them vegetarian temple food in small, simple pots: sesame-tofu and mountain potatoes and a pink salty tea Piper could not name; and then Kyoko said goodnight and repaired to her room. Piper was still lying awake at midnight, watching the moon through his narrow window, listening to a frog croaking far away, when he heard his door slide open and saw Kyoko slip inside. She lay beside him, and on the thick, soft covers, they made up for the haste and hard edges of the laundromat and shower, kissing and exploring each other's bodies for what seemed like hours until finally, as in his dreams, Kyoko was kneeling atop him, her thin cotton yukata falling open as she rose and fell, her hands pushing off his chest, her breasts full and white in the moonlight.

When the gongs began clanging at five, echoing from one temple to the next, summoning everyone atop the holy mountain to early prayers, they were still lying beside each other. Caressing the back of her neck, tender and vulnerable beneath her now-short hair, Piper asked tentatively, "Would it scare you away if I told you I loved you?"

"No," Kyoko said.

"I love you." He kissed the inside of her elbow.

"Would it scare you?" Kyoko asked.

"I don't know," Piper said. "Try me."

"I love you," she said. "How was that?"

"I can't tell," Piper said. "Try it again."

"I love you."

"I think it's okay, but I'm still not sure," he said. "One more time."

She slapped him playfully and stood, modestly tying her yukata around her, and they padded off together to morning prayers. And in that way they spent the next few nights and days, far removed from television and newspapers and any word from the outside world. They explored subtemples, held hands in monks' gardens, sat on their own temple steps and gazed at the pebbled design and the single meticulously pruned cherry tree in a corner of their courtyard. Every night at ten they parted, and every midnight, after the monks had gone to bed, Kyoko came to him and stayed until morning prayers.

Only once did Kyoko say, "Do you think we'd know if Detroit had been destroyed?"

Piper just shook his head. "Maybe the whole world has been destroyed, and this is what comes next," he said.

It was on Wednesday, or it may have been Thursday, that Piper reluctantly suggested they call Sato. He allowed Kyoko to dissuade him that day, and the next as well. Neither wanted ever to descend. But on Friday, or was it Saturday, as they strolled once more through the cemetery, they agreed they could postpone the call no longer. Kyoko trusted Sato no more than before, but she worried for her mother and knew they could not hide forever, forever postponing whatever was to come. They were strolling back toward their temple, glum in their joint resolve, when they spotted the official black limousine idling outside their white-washed wall, its driver lazily buffing its already perfect sheen with an old-fashioned duster of real feathers. They stopped cold.

"Kyoko," Piper whispered urgently after making out the license plate. "I'm sure that's Saeki's car."

They began walking and then nearly running away, but then, as if in concert, both stopped. If they had been found here, they could be tracked anywhere; there was nowhere left to hide. And if Okamoto's people had intended physical harm for either of them, Piper reasoned, he would not have sent Saeki in an official limousine. They turned around and once again approached their temple.

What they saw, as they walked through the temple's roofed wooden gate, was Sato, in his usual crushed navy suit, sitting on the wooden steps of the central hall, tossing pebbles and spoiling the carefully-raked design over which Piper had trod so carefully, in fear of their young monk, all week. When Sato saw the pair approaching, a smile lit up his face. He stayed seated as they drew near.

"I hope you two have had a nice vacation," he said.

"We were about to call you," Piper said.

"I'm sure you were," Sato said dryly.

"How did you find us?"

"They tracked you down," Sato said. "Some American in Disneyland remembered your disguise. Then it was just a matter of putting the word out to conductors and ticket takers. They were about to come after you, when everything broke open and fell apart for them. Your friend Christopher published just in time to save your lives, I would say."

Piper and Kyoko sat down in the warm sunshine next to Sato, who pulled a pile of faxes from his briefcase. The top sheet, Piper saw, was a reproduction of a *New York Times* front page, with a three-deck headline across the top: JAPAN CONDUCTED SECRET NUCLEAR PROGRAM; EXPLODED DOZENS OF A-BOMBS WITHOUT U.S. KNOWLEDGE; MOST JAPANESE ALSO UNAWARE FOR PAST 45 YEARS. Piper's face flushed as he read the byline: "By Clive Christopher, Special to the New York Times." Piper passed the paper over to Kyoko and looked at the next day's front page, also with a headline stretching across the top: JAPAN'S PRIME MINISTER PLEDGES INQUIRY, CLAIMS NO KNOWLEDGE OF SECRET NUCLEAR PROGRAM. And the next: JAPANESE PREMIER RESIGNS TO 'ACCEPT RESPONSIBILITY' FOR SECRET BOMB TESTS; DOZENS OF OTHERS FORCED OUT; NATION IN UPROAR OVER DISCLOSURES. Each with Christopher's byline, of course. Piper scanned the articles quickly. They attributed the disclosures to "a *New York Times* investigation." There was no mention of Piper or Kyoko or the *Advertiser*. Kawamura was prominently quoted.

He looked over the lead articles once more and then said, "I don't get it, Tsuyoshi."

"Here, they ran a little box about you inside," Sato said, handing them another fax. Christopher had written a small article describing how Piper had fallen victim to a disinformation campaign after being "on the trail of the same story as the *New York Times.*" No quote or response from Zarsky, Piper was disappointed to note.

To Sato he said, "That's not what I mean."

"What do you mean, then?" Sato asked.

"What do you think?" Piper said. "Where are the bombs hidden inside computers? Where's the retaliation for the X-bill? What happened to the bomb threatening Detroit?"

"Ah," Sato said. "That." He grabbed another handful of pebbles. "To be honest, John, I tried to gently steer your friend Christopher away from that aspect of the story."

"That aspect of the story? That was the story! How could you? How could he? Why?"

"Well, the threat there may have been exaggerated somewhat," Sato said vaguely. "We're still looking into it, of course. But more to the point—what was our goal here, after all, John? To stop this terrible conspiracy with as little damage as possible to friendly relations, isn't that right? If everything had come out, it could have caused undue panic. What would Americans have thought of Japan?" Sato punctuated each question with the toss of a pebble. "A lot of people, Americans and Japanese, would have been hurt, unnecessarily."

"What do you mean, the threat was exaggerated?" Piper asked. "Are there bombs out there or not?"

"We're in the process of recovering all the products in question," Sato said soothingly.

"How can you be sure?" Kyoko asked.

"Well, of course you can never be one hundred percent sure," Sato said. "But they were very thorough in their record-keeping. You can take my word for it—the government will do whatever we must."

For a long time Piper said nothing. He wasn't sure which hurt more, giving away the story of his career, or watching it be botched. So Christopher had been bamboozled again. As Piper thought back, he realized that their crucial conversation with Kawamura had taken place on the dock, untaped, and that Kyoko's purloined documents, by themselves, would prove nothing. Without conviction,

Piper said, "You know, we're not all Christophers. Somebody will get the story out."

"Anyone is welcome to try," Sato said. "But they may find it's not so easy to locate sources or documentation." Somehow Piper understood that Sato wasn't bluffing and he knew, too, that he wouldn't have the stomach to begin reporting all over again. The story was gone, gone forever. He stared at Sato's pleasant, impassive face and for a moment felt a familiar sinking in his stomach. Had all the bombs truly been recovered? Had he and Kyoko really, finally, penetrated to the truth? Or might the "sleeping deterrents" still be asleep around the world, waiting, like the Daishi, for another day? And then, as so many times before, Piper pushed aside his doubts. His trust in Sato had brought him this far, he told himself; he couldn't stop trusting now.

After an awkward silence Sato added, "In any case, you should both feel proud of yourselves. The world will never know what you accomplished."

"What Christopher accomplished, you mean," Piper said.

"We know who really did it," Sato said. "Do you really care who gets the credit?"

Piper shrugged and was silent for a minute. He took Kyoko's hand. "Sure, I care," he said. It corroded his insides to see Christopher's byline on these pieces, these half-true, prize-winning pieces. But to his surprise he found he didn't care as much as he once would have.

"So tell us," Piper said. "Who else besides the PM has resigned?"

"Well, Saeki, for one," Sato said. "I'm the new director-general, by the way."

"Ah, that explains the limousine," Piper said. "Congratulations."

"We're still trying to figure out who knew and who didn't. We may never know for sure. When the story came out, Okamoto locked himself in his office at Tokyo University and slit open his stomach. He left a note saying he had done everything for the good of our country, and he burned as many files as he could."

"A patriot to the end," Piper said. "And Kawamura?"

Sato took a deep breath. "Kawamura was killed on Sunday," he said softly. "The police said his wheelchair rolled off the pier. He was strapped in, and he drowned. They ruled it an accident, at least initially. Shimizu died at about the same time—almost at the same minute, if you can believe the coroner's report. They claimed she wandered into the radioactive tunnels and got locked in, and died of hunger or exhaustion. People at the facility are still being questioned about her death. And your friend Arai and his boat are missing at sea." He paused. "I'm truly sorry, both of you. I acted as quickly as I could. I found the documents Sunday, and delivered them to Christopher, and began trying to clean house, to find out who was part of this thing and who wasn't. But I had to move carefully until his first story was published. By then, of course, it was too late for your friends."

Kyoko cleared her throat, but before she could speak, Sato said, "Your mother and brother are fine, Kyoko. I brought them to my apartment Sunday night, and my wife's been looking after them. It wasn't easy to convince your mother to come, by the way."

"I'm sure," Kyoko said with a weak smile. "Thank you."

"And Yamada?"

"Is in Tokyo, cooperating with us," Sato said.

Piper snorted. "Wouldn't you know, he'd be the one to survive." He stood and walked toward the gnarled old cherry tree, his feet again crunching across the pebbles. Suddenly, holding onto a branch, he found he was crying, sobbing dry, uncontrollable sobs for Kawamura, for Shimizu, maybe for himself and his ambition, for Japan's damaged soul, for Kyoko's damaged faith in her country, even for their muscle-bound shadow with the pleasant face and neat tie. He thought of the old tea pourer in her gray kimono furtively tying her map to the tree of prayers, of Kawamura tying his strong body to that ungainly wheelchair for eight years, and then dying a terrifying death inside it, of little bald-headed Arai, still waiting for his wife to call him home after sixteen years. *"Anata no tame ni inotte imasu,"* he whispered. I'm praying for you.

He heard Kyoko's light footsteps on the pebbles and felt her arm around his waist. Without looking at her, he said, "I guess Kawamura was right the first time—he should have just sent us away."

"No," Kyoko said. "He knew what he was doing. Kawamura, Yamada, Shimizu—they were all playing out a story they began decades ago. They just needed us to help write their conclusion. Kawamura believed in you, and you believed in Sato, and both of you were right."

"Are you sure about that?" Piper said. Kyoko did not respond. "And what about our poor captain?"

Kyoko just rubbed his back for a few moments. "Maybe he'll still turn up unharmed," she said softly.

They turned and together walked back toward the steps, to Sato tossing pebbles.

"You think you'll be able to expose everyone who was involved?" Piper asked.

"I don't know," Sato said, shaking his head. "It was rooted deep in the power structure, I know that, and you know that democracy here is a fragile thing. Even now there are people whispering that I am the one who should be punished for revealing our secrets to outsiders." Sato shrugged. "For a time, we will have the upper hand, and then—who knows?" He smiled. "We will continue struggling."

Sato stood and brushed off his backside. "Which means I better get back to Tokyo," he said. "I should warn you—your apartments and office are in a bit of a mess. They were ransacked, I suppose while Okamoto and his friends were hunting you. I had them left just as they were, as a kind of memorial to your courageous reporting." Sato shook both their hands. "Oh—and one piece of good news you missed," he said. "Your president vetoed the expropriation bill. He said that he didn't want to attack Japan in a moment of such confusion, and that he expects our new government to be more open on matters of trade."

Piper laughed. "Suckered again," he said. "You really hit a home run this time, didn't you, Tsuyoshi?"

Sato looked wounded but didn't respond. "I left some clothes in your room, John," he said. "Burn that costume, please. And call me when you get back to town."

They watched him cross the rock garden, and listened to the thunk of his car door closing, and then the chauffeur's, and the rumble of the limousine driving away. In the void left behind, the roar of the cicadas seemed louder than ever.

"Well, Christopher scooped us again," Piper said after a few minutes.

"Yes, but it was a noble failure," Kyoko said. "The kind we Japanese love best." She gave him a long, deep kiss.

"Let's take one more bath together before we go," Piper said. They took off their shoes and padded up the narrow, uneven stairway to their rooms.

34

*F*or some reason the jumble and racket of Tokyo Station delighted Piper as he and Kyoko made their way from the bullet-train platform to the street. If Japan was "in an uproar," as Christopher had reported, there was no sign of it here; the same hordes of worried, good-natured citizens were following their usual hurried, purposeful choreography through the terminal. Outside, too, Tokyo seemed unchanged: a gray sky, a long but orderly line for taxis, a clattering construction project choking traffic in the busy Yaesu intersection. Piper breathed deeply: bus fumes and sesame oil. It was good to be home.

They went first to the *Advertiser* office and, despite Sato's warning, were stunned by the chaos. It was as if a typhoon had blown through. Piper's desk looked no worse than before, he had to admit, and maybe better, since the aging mountain of papers atop it had been swept onto the floor. But the contents of every file cabinet had been spilled out as well, and a week's accumulation of mail had been kicked about, so that newspapers, envelopes, maps, yellowed clippings, torn books, old press releases and wire copy blanketed the floor. Even Piper's necktie and jacket lay crumpled on the ground, and the cushions of the couch had been slit open, disgorging strips of hideous yellow foam. In a far corner the packs they had left behind in Niigata leaned against a wall; Sato's handiwork, no doubt.

Kyoko went downstairs to pick up the mail that had arrived since the ransacking, and returned with an armful.

"Might as well dump it on the floor," Piper said. "We can hose the whole place down before my replacement arrives," Piper said.

But Kyoko set it all carefully on the table, as always, and flipped quickly through the newspapers and press releases. Near the bottom of the pile she found a personal letter. "Look at this," she said excitedly. "It's from Kawamura."

It was addressed to both of them, written in English in a formal, old-fashioned hand.

"I believe I have read almost everything written by your physicists present at the creation of the bomb," Kawamura had penned. "I feel I know them well, although they never heard of me, nor of our work. I have envied them, for if our work was secret, so perforce has been our remorse, whereas they could anguish so publicly—Oppenheimer with his 'profound grief,' and Rabi regretting 'how easy it is to kill people when you put your mind to it.' Well, perhaps our private remorse has been more in keeping with our character.

"In any case, my turn for penance is at hand, I am quite certain, as you have not been my only visitors this weekend. Please do not mourn for me; I have had a long life and a rewarding one, in its way. I could see that you two are very much in love. Do not let that slip away, as I did."

He had signed with a simple "K," but then had added two postscripts. "Perhaps it was your mentioning of Hiraizumi that put in my mind Yoshitsune's epic defeat of the Taira clan in battle. '. . . those who flourish must surely fall. The proud of this world endure but for a moment like a spring night's dream. In the end the brave are brought low and scattered like dust before the wind.' "

Then, without further comment on the Tairas, Kawamura had penned a shorter, final note: "Please take care of Miss Shimizu if you can." The letter was dated Sunday but had been posted Tuesday. Kawamura's timid sister-in-law, whom he so despised, must have found the envelope after his death and mailed it in a final act of courageous loyalty.

Piper read the letter twice, and then sank onto the mutilated couch, sending more bilious foam spilling to the floor. "Who did he let slip away, do you think?" he asked. "His brother's wife?"

Kyoko shook her head. "No, no," she said. "Shimizu, of course."

Piper waded to the window and saw, through the trees, that a spirited volleyball game had resumed in the defense agency exercise yard. Traffic was bottled up on the street, but no one honked; honking was against the rules in Tokyo. A giant crow perched on the telephone wire, ponderously lifting and folding its wings.

Just then the telex machine rattled and hummed, clearing its throat for an impending message. Piper turned and met Kyoko's eyes. "Well, come find out who's your new boss," he said.

"Wrong," Kyoko said. "If you're gone, I'm leaving, too."

But it turned out Piper wasn't gone, not anymore.

SORRY FOR ANY MISUNDERSTANDING BUT DON'T WORRY ABOUT BC MAGAZINE PIECE, the telex from Huddleston began. THE MAN UPSTAIRS READ ITS DESCRIPTION OF ADVERTISER AS QUOTE MEDIOCRE UNQUOTE AND DISCOUNTED WHOLE THING. OF COURSE I ALWAYS STOOD UP FOR YOU. THE MAN UPSTAIRS SAYS WELL DONE ON FAVORABLE MENTION IN NYT. ALSO HE SAYS PACIFIC CENTURY IS ENDING. FUTURE BIG STORY IS EASTERN EUROPE AND RUSSIA. HOW WOULD YOU LIKE TO OPEN MOSCOW BUREAU AND COVER THAT SUPER BOWL. GREAT STORY AND YOU'RE THE ONE TO TELL IT. WE WANT THAT HUMAN INTEREST ANGLE WE DON'T GET IN NYT. BY THE WAY SORRY BUT AD REVENUES DOWN SO CAN'T PAY MOVING EXPENSES. CHEERS.

The machine shuddered to a stop. For a moment Piper was too dumbfounded to speak. Then he turned to Kyoko. "What do you think?" he said.

She wrapped her arms around him. "I've always wanted to ride the Trans-Siberian Railroad," Kyoko said.

Piper ripped the telex from the machine, crumpled it into a ball and tossed it toward the wastebasket in the corner. The yellow wad hit the rim and bounced in.

"Swish," Piper said. "Basket. Three points."

"Nice shot," Kyoko said. "It only took you three years."

"Japanese girls are supposed to show respect, not make wise-ass remarks," Piper said, taking Kyoko back into an embrace. "You know, it gets pretty cold in Moscow."

"I'll keep you warm," she murmured, pressing against him. "Besides, maybe we can find Inoki."

"That's right!" Piper said, excitedly breaking away from her nuzzling. "Christopher missed that angle, too! Damn, that could be the biggest story of all, you know that? It figures he would blow it! That could be next year's Pulitzer for foreign reporting, no doubt about it. In fact, that—"

"John," Kyoko said, pulling him down to the couch.

"Hm?"

"Shut up, okay?" The telephone rang, and they paid no attention. Outside, shouts from the volleyball game drifted upward. A bus loudly ground its gears to move forward a few yards in the traffic. Behind it, a white panel truck with NEC markings eased forward a few yards, too. The oversized crow cawed insolently.

On the couch, surrounded by yellowed clippings and yellower foam, Piper and Kyoko heard nothing but each other's heartbeats.

*T*he book Piper found in the club library was *The Making of the Atomic Bomb,* by Richard Rhodes (Simon & Schuster, 1986), which, in the course of its prize-winning history of the U.S. Manhattan Project, provides a brief account of Professor Nishina and Japan's wartime efforts to build a bomb. The article in *Science* to which Yamada draws Kyoko's attention is the excellent account "Nuclear Weapons History: Japan's Wartime Bomb Projects Revealed," by Deborah Shapley (*Science* 199: 152).

While Nishina and Japan's atomic bomb project were real, all other characters in this novel are fictional, and any resemblance to any person, living or dead, is purely coincidental.

For historical information about Yoshitsune, I relied heavily on Ivan Morris's wonderful book *The Nobility of Failure: Tragic Heroes in the History of Japan* (Noonday Press, 1975). I am also indebted to *A Haiku Journey: Basho's Narrow Road to a Far Province,* translated by Dorothy Britton (Kodansha, 1974).